Marianne and the
of the East

NOVELS BY
JULIETTE BENZONI

One Love is Enough
Catherine
Belle Catherine
Catherine and Arnaud
Catherine and a Time for Love
A Snare for Catherine
Marianne
Marianne and the Masked Prince
Marianne and the Privateer
Marianne and the Rebels
Marianne and the Lords of the East

Marianne and the Lords of the East

★　★　★

JULIETTE BENZONI

Translated by
ANNE CARTER

HEINEMANN : LONDON

William Heinemann Ltd
15 Queen Street, Mayfair, London W1X 8BE
LONDON MELBOURNE TORONTO
JOHANNESBURG AUCKLAND

First published in Great Britain 1975

First published as *Les Lauriers de Flammes* Vol 1

© Opera Mundi, Paris 1974

Translation © Opera Mundi, Paris 1975

SBN: 434 06609 5

Printed in Great Britain
by Cox and Wyman Ltd,
London, Fakenham and Reading

Contents

PRINCIPAL CHARACTERS

Marianne Elisabeth d'Asselnat, now Princess Sant'Anna. The daughter of a French marquis and his English wife, both of whom perished in the French Revolution. She was rescued as a baby by her godfather, Gauthier de Chazay, and taken to England to be brought up by her spinster aunt, Ellis Selton. In 1809 she married Francis Cranmere who, on her wedding night, gambled away both her fortune and her virginity to an American privateer, Jason Beaufort. Much later, after many adventures in France and Italy, first as Napoleon's mistress and now, after her unconsummated marriage to Corrado Sant'Anna, as the Emperor's secret ambassadress, Marianne has come to see that Jason is, after all, the man she really loves.

Adelaide d'Asselnat. A French cousin of Marianne's, an elderly spinster and devoted companion.

Jason Beaufort. The man to whom Francis Cranmere lost Marianne's fortune and virginity. He generously failed to claim the second but reappeared later in Paris to become first her friend and then her lover, although not until he himself was unhappily married to the cruel and vindictive Pilar. Still fate, and Napoleon, seem determined to come between them. After a brief reunion in Venice at the start of the ill-fated voyage to Constantinople, Jason has fallen victim, in mind and body, to the evil Dr Leighton whose attempts to take possession of the brig, *Sea Witch*, ended in her capture by the Turks. Leighton was last seen taking to a boat with the heavily-drugged Jason as a hostage.

Gauthier de Chazay, a French Abbé, later Cardinal San Lorenzo, Marianne's much-loved godfather, who rescued her as a baby and was responsible for arranging her marriage to Prince Sant'Anna.

Francis, Lord Cranmere. Marianne's dastardly first husband. She fought a duel with him and left him for dead in the blazing wreck of Selton Hall, but he reappeared in Paris as an English spy, tried to blackmail her, and later concocted the plot of which Jason was the victim. He failed, and Napoleon had Marianne brought to Vincennes, in order that she might witness the preparations for his execution by the guillotine.

Matteo Damiani.. Illegitimate son of Corrado's grandfather and steward of the Sant'Anna estates. A gross and sinister figure, given to the practice of black magic, he abducted Marianne and, boasting that he had murdered her husband, forced upon her the child she is now carrying.

Arcadius, Vicomte de Jolival. A French aristocrat and one of Marianne's staunchest friends. Formerly her theatrical manager, now her business agent.

Dona Lavinia. Housekeeper and devoted retainer of Prince Sant'Anna.

Craig O'Flaherty. An Irishman. Jason's friend and first officer aboard the *Sea Witch.*

Gracchus-Hannibal Pioche. A former Paris errand-boy and now Marianne's faithful coachman, factotum and self-appointed guardian.

Prince Corrado Sant'Anna. Marianne's second husband. Scion of a great Italian family which, although rich and powerful, is also strangely accursed, he is the victim of some unspecified condition which makes him live the life of a recluse. Marianne has never seen his face. He married her because she was pregnant by Napoleon and since accidentally losing the child she has avoided going near him, although he has demanded her return, both directly and by application to the Emperor who, characteristically, has compromised by sending her as special envoy, first to his sister Elisa in Florence and now to her own distant kinswoman in Constantinople, the French Sultana, Nakshidil, born Aimée Dubucq de Rivery. But before setting out, Marianne has learned from Matteo Damiani that the Prince is dead, murdered by the hand of his own steward.

Part I

THE CRÉOLE SULTANA

CHAPTER ONE

Audience by Night

Driven by the strong arms of its four and twenty rowers, the gilded caique was literally flying over the smooth waters of the Golden Horn. Other vessels scattered like frightened chickens before it for fear of impeding the royal barge.

Seated beneath the red silk canopy in the stern, the Princess Sant'Anna watched the dark walls of the Seraglio draw nearer through the slow dusk that was beginning to fall over Constantinople. In another moment, they, too, would be enveloped in the shadows which had already fallen on the narrow streets and close-packed houses of Stamboul.

The number of other boats around them dwindled as they advanced because the crossing of the Golden Horn was forbidden after the firing of the sunset gun. But this was a law which naturally did not apply to vessels from the palace.

Marianne was perspiring in the court dress of leaf green satin which she had donned more or less at random with a view to the audience before her. These first days of September retained all the heat and humidity of high summer. For a week past, the city had been steeped in an atmosphere like a Turkish bath which had wreathed the monuments in a yellow fog and made the wearing of even the lightest clothing a penance, much less untold yards of heavy Lyons silk with long kid gloves reaching well above the elbow and almost touching the short, puffed sleeves of the dress.

But in only a short while now, perhaps no more than a few minutes, she was going to find herself face to face at last with the royal lady she had come so far, and at such pains, to seek. At Napoleon's command, she had crossed the whole of Europe for this meeting. What would be the outcome of her mission? The burden of it seemed to press more heavily on her shoulders with every stroke of the oars. To ensure the continuance of the war which had been dragging on for years between Russia and the Sublime Porte for the possession of the Roumanian principalities and so keep a large section of the Russian army engaged on the Balkan front while the Emperor crossed the borders of the Tsarist Empire and marched on Moscow. Now that she was here, it seemed a

3

frighteningly impossible task, made worse by the fact, which had become all too clear since her arrival in Constantinople, that things were going very badly indeed for the Turkish army on the Danube. It seemed to Marianne that the audience ahead, however comfortingly disguised as a mere cousinly courtesy, was going to be a singularly tricky one.

How would the Sultana react to the discovery that this distant cousin travelling for pleasure in the Levant and so eager to make her acquaintance, was actually the bearer of credentials from the Emperor and had come to talk politics? Or had she known it all along? Too many people knew about this journey, for all its intended secrecy. First and foremost the English had found out, God alone knew how, all about Napoleon's unofficial ambassadress. But no one, thank heaven, could possibly know the real object of her mission!

For a fortnight, now, Marianne had waited for an audience which no one seemed in any great hurry to grant her. It was a fortnight since, escaping from the English frigate on board which she had been held pending return to the land of her childhood as a hostage of war, she had arrived at the French Embassy draped like a sack of flour, and quite unconscious, over the shoulder of a notorious Greek rebel. That rebel, who had snatched her out of English hands and literally saved her from despair, was now her firm friend.

Marianne had spent those two weeks incarcerated in the embassy buildings, prowling up and down like a caged beast in spite of all her friend Jolival's pleas for her to be patient. The ambassador, the Comte de Latour-Maubourg, had been reluctant to let her stir beyond that small patch of French territory, for his countrymen had become unpopular with the Ottoman since the unfortunate matter of Napoleon's divorce.

The Sultan Mahmoud and his mother, that Créole cousin of the Empress Joséphine who had been captured by Barbary pirates and carried by her beauty to the supreme height of Haseki Sultan, were now inclined to favour England, in which they were encouraged by the British envoy, the charming Mr Stratford Canning, who would stick at nothing to further his country's interests.

'Until you have been presented to the Sultan's mother,' Latour-Maubourg had insisted, 'you had better avoid any unnecessary risks. Canning will do anything to forestall an audience. He has already shown that he knows how much he has to fear you. Are you not her Highness's kinswoman?'

4

'A very distant one!'

'A kinswoman, none the less, and as such we hope to see you received. Take my advice and stay indoors until your audience is granted. This house is watched, I know, but Canning will not dare to try anything while you remain inside it. Whereas he is quite capable of having you abducted if you step outside.'

It was good advice, energetically supported by Jolival, who was too glad to have his adopted daughter restored to him to run the risk of losing her again almost at once, and Marianne yielded. Hour after hour, she paced her bedchamber or the embassy garden, waiting for the longed-for summons. The house itself was one of the oldest in Pera, having been built in the sixteenth century as a Franciscan convent, and it possessed a charming cloister which had been made into a garden. Latour-Maubourg, a diplomat of the old school with a rigorous Breton upbringing behind him, had not judged it proper to bring wife and children to that infidel land, yet, even without a woman's touch, the ambassador had given to his garden and to the old house itself, an elegance which was wholly French. Marianne recognized it and it lightened the burden of her enforced captivity.

As well as Arcadius de Jolival, she had found there her coachman, Gracchus-Hannibal Pioche, the one-time errand boy from the rue Montorgueil. At the sight of his mistress, safe and sound, when he had thought her at the bottom of the Mediterranean Sea, the poor fellow had burst into tears and, child of the atheistical Revolution though he was, had gone down on his knees and thanked Heaven as fervently as any Chouan. His subsequent celebrations, undertaken in the company of the ambassador's cook and various bottles of raki, had very nearly been the death of him.

One person Marianne had not found. Her maid, Agathe Pinsart was gone, but not very far away, nor was there anything at all tragic about her going. Against all expectation, the poor girl had not only survived the barbarous and inhuman treatment she had suffered at the hands of Leighton and his mutineers aboard the *Sea Witch* but had made a conquest of the Turkish captain, who had captured the brig and released the prisoners, with her caustic charms. And, since Agathe, on her side, had been greatly impressed by the young *reis*, with his dashing presence, his silken garments and his splendid moustaches, their voyage to Constantinople had assumed all the appearance of an amorous idyll, culminating in a proposal of marriage from Achmet to his new sweetheart. Agathe, convinced that she had seen the last of Marianne and strongly tempted by the luxurious life of a Turkish lady, had offered only a token resistance, designed merely to enhance the value of her consent, and not many days before her mistress's arrival she had embraced both Achmet and Islam with equal enthusiasm. She was now officially installed in her husband's handsome house at Eyub, not far from the great mosque recently rebuilt by Mahmoud II to shelter the footprint of the Prophet.

Marianne would have liked to visit her former abigail, partly to see her in her new status and partly to reassure the girl about her own fate, but this too was considered unwise. So she could only wait, interminably, even though the waiting became more of a torture with every day that passed. Yet the ordeal had an end at last.

The imperial summons had reached the embassy just as the ambassador and his guests were finishing dinner. They were about to go into the drawing-room when the royal envoys were announced. These consisted of the Agha of the Janissaries and one of the Black Eunuchs belonging to the Harem. Both were magnificently dressed. Despite the heat, the officer was clad in a sable-lined dolman, laced boots and a broad belt made of linked silver plates with a whip thrust into it. His tall felt hat was swathed in a sort of bubble of silver gauze, forming an extraordinary kind of turban. The Black Eunuch's dress consisted of a long white robe, lined with fox fur, and on his head was a snowy turban set with a golden clasp.

They both bowed ceremoniously and presented a letter bearing the *tughra*, the imperial seal. The audience which the Frankish princess had craved was granted and would take place within the hour. She was allowed only a few minutes to change her dress and prepare to go with the Sultana's messengers.

In fact, while Marianne hastened to her room, Latour-Maubourg knew a moment's hesitation, fearing the consequences of allowing the Emperor's personal friend to go, unattended and at night, into the Seraglio. He feared that the flowery terms of the invitation might conceal a trap. On the other hand, since Marianne's object was to enter the Harem, it was scarcely possible for the French ambassador to request the favour of accompanying her, nor did the presence of the Agha of the Janissaries leave much room for argument. In any case the command, on a second reading, was unequivocal: the Princess Sant'Anna was to go to the Seraglio alone. A closed litter was already waiting at the door. With a caique and another litter, it would carry the princess to the place of the Sultan Valideh's choice and bring her back again, by the same route, when the audience was concluded.

And so, when Marianne came down again some minutes later, dressed for her audience, the ambassador said merely that he trusted they would not keep her all night, since he and Jolival proposed to wait up for her, whiling the time away with a game of chess.

'And may God go with you!' he added softly, like a good Breton.

As the caique rounded the Seraglio point, Marianne was thinking to herself that divine inspiration was precisely what she needed most. During the days of waiting, she had gone over in her mind a hundred times the things she meant to say, and had tried to picture the questions she would be asked and the answers she must make. But now that the time had come her brain felt curiously empty and she could not remember any of the speeches she had prepared so carefully.

In the end, she gave up and concentrated instead on trying to calm her nerves by filling her lungs with the sea air, cooled by the evening freshness, and her eyes with the magical vision of the fabulous city before her. With the coming of night, the voices of the muezzins had fallen silent in the minarets of the great mosques but the evening shadows, through which there still gleamed here and there the gold of a cupola or the rich moulding of a palace, were pierced little by little by a multitude of tiny lights, from the oiled paper lanterns which every citizen was bound to carry with him when he went out. The effect of all these little gilded lamps was charming and gave to the Ottoman capital the fairylike appearance of a vast colony of glow-worms.

They were on the Bosphorus now and the vast bulk of the Seraglio's formidable walls loomed over the glittering waters. The black points of cypress trees showed where they enclosed a world of gardens, kiosks, palaces, stables, prisons, barracks, workshops and kitchens, providing occupation for some twenty thousand people. In a moment they would be landing at the old Byzantine jetty of worn marble that led by a flight of shallow steps up to the two medieval gates in the walls between the palace gardens and the shore. This was not the main entrance, for the Princess Sant'Anna, despite the ties of kinship which lay between her and the Queen Mother, was deemed to be on a private visit and so would not enter the Sublime Porte, in the usual way of ambassadors and other important persons.

This was a private visit and the lateness of the hour, like the mode of entry, stressed its unofficial nature.

But while the Black Eunuch involved himself in a host of explanations designed to convey this to the Frankish princess without undue offence to her pride, Marianne was thinking that really it did not matter to her in the least and that, in fact, she infinitely preferred it so. She had never wanted to be burdened with an official diplomatic mission, the Emperor himself had stressed the private character of the undertaking and she had no conceivable wish to tread on Latour-Maubourg's toes, being only too well aware of the difficulties he was up against.

The oars were shipped and the caique drifted up to the jetty. Marianne was ushered from her awning into a kind of flat-bottomed egg-shaped litter, hung with brocaded curtains and smelling strongly of sandalwood.

Borne on the shoulders of half a dozen black slaves, the litter passed through the guard of Janissaries, armed to the teeth, outside the gates and entered the scented, humid atmosphere of the gardens. Here were roses and jasmine in abundance. The salty sea smell was lost in that of thousands of flowers and the slap of the waves drowned in the music of the fountains and streams that cascaded over steps of porphyry and pink marble.

Marianne stared about her, abandoning herself to the rhythm of the bearers. Very soon, a fragile building appeared at the far end of an alley. It was surmounted by a translucent dome that shone like a huge, multicoloured lantern in the darkness. This was a kiosk, one of the delicate, precious little pavilions with which the sultans loved to dot their gardens, each bringing to them something of his own life and tastes. This one, standing at the highest point of the gardens, was silhouetted against the dark background of the Asian shore and seemed to tremble on the brink of the Bosphorus as if it feared to lean too far and fall to meet its reflection in the water. Around it was a little secret garden planted with tall cypresses and a carpet of pale blue hyacinths which the Bostanji Bashi, the Head Gardener whose dominion extended over all the gardens of the Empire, kept in flower all the year round because they were the Sultan-Mother's favourite flowers.

The delightful retreat, set apart from the somewhat forbidding mass of the Seraglio as a whole, had a private, festive air, with rose-coloured lanterns hung about it. Fragrant shrubs that looked as if they were covered with snow crowded up against its slender columns and the exotic, turbaned shadows of the eunuchs of the guard passed to and fro against the blue, green and violet tinted glass of the windows.

As the slaves set down the litter, a gigantic figure surged forward from between the pillars and bowed low to the visitor. She beheld a round, smiling face, as black and shiny as if it had been well-polished, under a tall, snow-white head-dress in which gleamed a brooch of blood red rubies. A magnificent robe, sable-lined and covered with silver embroideries, fell majestically to his feet, covering a royal stomach which did honour to the palace kitchens.

Speaking in a soft voice, in impeccable French, this imposing person introduced himself as the Khislar Agha, chief of the Black Eunuchs, at the visitor's service. Then he informed her with another bow that he had the honour to present the 'noble lady come from Frankish lands to Her Highness the Sultan Valideh, most revered Mother of the Omnipotent Padishah'.

Marianne thanked him briefly and, with a little kick, sent the long train of the green satin dress shimmering behind her like a changeable river of crystal and pearls. Instinctively, she lifted her head, suddenly conscious that she was at that moment the representative of the greatest empire in the world. Then, gripping the slender stick of her matching fan between nervous fingers to give herself confidence, she stepped forward on to the great blue silken carpet which flowed down into the gardens.

In another moment she had paused, holding her breath to listen to the strains of a guitar, light and melancholy, as they came to her, the strains of a guitar playing:

> Nous n'irons plus aux bois,
> Les lauriers sont coupés;
> La belle que voilà
> Ira les ramasser ...

Marianne felt the tears prick her eyelids, and there was something sticking in her throat, something that might have been pity. Here, in this Eastern palace, the simple song, sung by children at play in France, had the plaintive sound of a lament. And she wondered suddenly what kind of woman this was who lived here, guarded by an ageless ritual. What was she going to find within those translucent walls? A fat woman, stuffed with sweets and self-pity? A shrivelled crone cut off from the world? The Sultana was roughly of an age with her cousin Joséphine and so must be nearing

9

fifty, which seemed a great age to the nineteen-year-old Marianne. Or a creature of exaggeratedly girlish ways, a superannuated school girl? No one had been able to give her even the faintest picture of the Créole girl who had risen to such a fabulous position, because not one of the people who had described her to her had ever set eyes on her. A woman might have told her more, but no European woman, to her knowledge, had passed the threshold of the Seraglio since the death of Fanny Sebastiani. And all at once, Marianne was afraid of what she was going to find, dearly though she had longed for this moment.

The delicate notes of the song still floated on the air. The Khislar Agha had paused, realizing that he was not followed, and was waiting.

'Our mistress likes to listen to the songs of her own land,' he said pleasantly, 'but she does not like to be kept waiting.'

The spell was broken. Thus recalled, Marianne smiled apology.

'Forgive me. It was so unexpected, and so charming.'

'The songs of their native land are always charming to those who journey far from it. Do not apologize.'

They went forward again and the sound of the guitar grew stronger, together with the scent of flowers which surrounded Marianne as soon as she entered the carved cedarwood doorway, set with a multitude of tiny mirrors. Then, without warning, the vast form of the Khislar Agha which had blocked her view had stepped aside and she found herself on the threshold of a blue world . . .

Marianne felt as if she were stepping inside the heart of a great turquoise. Everything was blue, from the huge carpets on the floor to the flowered tiles on the walls, and including the fountain that played in the centre of the room and the countless gold and silver embroidered cushions strewn about it and the dresses of the women sitting looking at her.

Blue also, of a luminous intensity, were the eyes of the woman squatting in the oriental fashion with a guitar in her lap among the cushions of a broad golden throne raised up on two steps which, owing to the gilded rail that enclosed it, had about it something at once of the divan, the throne and the verandah. And Marianne thought that she had never seen a more beautiful woman.

The years seemed scarcely to have touched the woman who had once been the Créole girl, Aimée Dubucq de Rivery, from Martinique, educated in the Convent of the Ladies of the Visitation at

Nantes and who, as she was on her way home to her native isle had been seized in the Bay of Biscay by the pirates of Baba Mohammed ben Osman, the aged master of Algiers. Her grace and charm were as vivid as ever.

Dressed in a long azure gown cut low over her breast, she was so covered in pearls that she seemed like a very creature of the sea. The sequestered life of the harem had preserved the pearly transparency of her skin and her long silken hair, its silvery locks threaded with pearls, framed a youthful face that still dimpled when she smiled. A tiny pillbox hat, tipped saucily to one side, was perched on her head and set in this minuscule headgear was a single rose diamond of immense size cut to the shape of a heart and glittering with all the colours of the rainbow.

With Marianne's entrance a silence fell. The birdlike chatter of the women died away and the strains of the guitar were silenced by the swift pressure of their mistress's hand on the strings. Conscious that she was the focus of at least a dozen pairs of eyes and more impressed than she cared to admit, Marianne stepped across the threshold and sank at once into a deep curtsy. Rising, she advanced the statutary three paces and curtsied again; three more paces and she dropped into the third which brought her to the foot of the throne while the measured voice of the Khislar Agha was still declaiming her various names and titles in Turkish. This took some time but before he could finish Nakshidil was laughing.

'Very impressive,' she said,' and I knew, of course, that you were a very great lady, my dear, but to me, if you will, you are my cousin and as such I am pleased to receive you. Come and sit here by me.'

She put down the guitar and moved to one side, holding out a small hand, sparkling with diamonds, to draw her visitor on to the cushions at her side.

'Your Highness,' Marianne said, taken aback by this simple, unceremonious welcome, 'you are too kind. I hardly like —'

The delicate laugh trilled out again.

'You hardly like to obey? Come here, I say, so that I may see you better. My eyes, alas, are not what they were and since I refuse to wear those horrid spectacles you will have to come very close to me, so that I can see your face clearly. There, that's better!' she added, as Marianne nerved herself to sit down timidly, just inside the gilded balustrade. 'I want to have a good look at you. I can make out your figure well enough. When you came in, in that blue dress, I thought a wave of my beloved sea had remembered me and come

11

to visit me. Now I can see it again in your eyes. I was told that you were beautiful, my dear, but indeed the word does not do you justice.'

The warmth and gaiety of her smile were quickly putting Marianne at her ease. She smiled back, still with a touch of nervousness.

'It is your majesty who is – oh, infinitely beautiful! And I beg you will forgive me if I seem bewildered. It is not often one meets a legendary ruler. And then to find out how much the reality surpasses what one has imagined!'

'Well, well! The orient has nothing to teach you in the matter of courtesy, Princess! But we have much to say to one another. Let us begin by securing ourselves a little privacy.'

A word or two was enough to scatter the women who sat about the throne, devouring the visitor with their eyes. Without a word, they rose and bowing silently they hurried out in a flurry of blue veils, but their disappointment showed clearly in their faces.

The Khislar Agha brought up the rear, as grave as ever, shepherding them with his silver staff. At the same time, black slaves entered by another door, dressed in silvery robes and bearing gold trays set with diamonds on which was the traditional coffee and the no less traditional conserve of roses which they offered to the two women.

In spite of herself, Marianne could not help staring as she took the cup from the kneeling woman before her. Accustomed to the comfort of wealthy English homes, to the luxury of the French imperial court and the refinements practised by such men as Talleyrand, even she was not prepared for what confronted her now. Not merely the trays, but every single item of this fabulous service was made of solid gold, encrusted with such masses of brilliants that the metal itself was almost invisible. The little spoon alone, with which she stirred her coffee, was worth a fortune.

The two women drank in silence while, over the rims of their glittering cups, the green eyes and the blue met and studied one another, discreetly. Because behind the spontaneous friendliness of her welcome, Marianne was conscious of an alertness in her hostess. The coffee-drinking ritual allowed them both a precious moment's respite before an engagement whose outcome neither could predict.

Marianne politely swallowed a spoonful of rose jam. She was not particularly fond of this Turkish national delicacy, disliking its rather scented sweetness. It made her feel slightly sick and gave her the feeling that she was eating some of her friend Fortunée Hame-

12

lin's cosmetics, for the Créole had attar of roses put into everything that went on her skin. But she drank the coffee with enjoyment. It was scalding hot and fragrant, and not too sweet. It was certainly the best that she had ever tasted.

Nakshidil was regarding her with amused curiosity.

'You seem to like coffee?' she said.

'There's nothing I like better – especially when it is as good as this. It's both a luxury and the friendliest of comforts.'

'Perhaps you would not say as much about the rose jam?' the Sultana said mischievously. 'I don't think you care for it.'

Marianne reddened like a child caught out.

'Forgive me, your Highness, but – you are right. I do not like it very much.'

'And I hate it!' Nakshidil cried, laughing. 'I've never been able to get used to it. Give me a nice strawberry jam now, or rhubarb, as they used to make it in my convent at Nantes. But try some of this halva, with almonds and sesame seeds, or the baklava with nuts which is something of a national dish with us,' she added, pointing out these items on the dish of sweetmeats. The first looked like a rather solid kind of blancmange of a fine cherry red colour, while the second was a cake layered with nuts.

Marianne was not in the least hungry but she forced herself to taste the things her royal hostess offered. More cups of coffee were brought.

Setting down the precious cup, she saw that the other woman was looking at her intently and realized that the difficult moment had arrived. She knew that she must prove herself worthy of the high trust reposed in her and she was eager, now, to enter the lists. But protocol demanded that she wait to be questioned. The question was not long in coming.

The Sultana's slender fingers strayed to the mouthpiece of a blue enamelled nargileh and she took a few reflective puffs before remarking in a light, conversational tone: 'It would seem that your journey here was a great deal more eventful and considerably less pleasant than you might have wished. Everyone has been talking about the great lady from France on whose account the English sent a squadron out off Corfu and who vanished in the Greek islands.'

The voice was amused but Marianne's quick ear had detected a faint but disturbing shade of disdain. God alone knew what tales the English had put about to damage her reputation. However, she decided to go carefully.

'Your Highness seems to be remarkably well-informed in such small matters.'

'News travels fast in the Mediterranean. Nor do these matters seem to me so small. English ships are not generally sent out of their way for persons of no importance – such as a lady travelling for pleasure. But the thing becomes much less astonishing if the lady in question should be also – an envoy of the Emperor Napoleon?'

Instantly, with the mere mention of that name, the cosy intimacy of the blue salon was blown away like a whiff of perfume on the wind. It was as though the Corsican himself had swept into the room in his usual tempestuous fashion, with booted feet and flashing eyes and all the commanding strength of his powerful personality. Marianne felt that he was there, watching her and waiting . . .

Slowly, she drew from the pocket fashioned in the long skirts of her dress the letter given her by Sebastiani and presented it, bowing gracefully. Nakshidil eyed her questioningly.

'Is this a letter from the Emperor?'

'No, Your Highness. It is from an old friend, General Horace Sebastiani, who begs to be remembered to you. The English were quite wrong to put themselves out over my journey, for I have no official mission.'

'Yet if you carry no word from Napoleon, you know his mind, do you not?'

Marianne merely bowed, without answering, and then, while the Sultana was swiftly perusing the letter, she calmly finished her cup of coffee, cold by this time, and forced herself to swallow the last morsel of baklava in order not to offend her hostess who had recommended it. It did not go down easily.

'I see that you are much valued in high places, my dear. Sebastiani tells me you are a personal friend of the Emperor's and that you are also held in real affection by the former Empress, that unhappy Joséphine who will always be Rose to me. Very well, tell me what it is that the French Emperor wants of us.'

There was a brief silence while Marianne chose her words carefully. She was beginning to feel slightly sick and it was necessary to concentrate.

She began: 'I must beg your Highness to listen carefully to what I am about to say because it is very important and involves the revelation of the Emperor's most secret and cherished plans.'

'Let us hear them.'

Slowly and quietly, making herself as clear as she could, Marianne told her companion of the imminent invasion of Russia by the Grande Armée and of Napoleon's desire to defeat Alexander, whom he accused of the direst duplicity, on his own ground. She pointed out how helpful it would be to the invader if the military operations taking place on the Danube could be prolonged until at least the following summer, the date fixed for the French invasion of Russia, so as to keep General Kamenski and his troops and the Cossack regiments engaged well away from the Vistula and from the vicinity of Moscow. She hinted further that Napoleon could be relied upon to show his gratitude for this undeclared assistance as soon as the Russians had been beaten by granting to the Sublime Porte all the territory at present being lost and more besides.

'If your Highness's forces could hold out until next July or August,' she concluded, 'it would be enough.'

'But that is almost a year!' the Sultana exclaimed. 'It is a great deal for an exhausted army whose strength is melting like butter in the sun. And I don't think —' She broke off as she caught sight of the change in her visitor's face, which had turned as green as her dress.

'Are you unwell, Princess?' she asked. 'You look very pale all of a sudden —'

Marianne hardly dared to move. The sweetmeats had been very good in themselves, no doubt, but, added to the hearty dinner she had already eaten at the embassy, their sugary sweetness in her over-loaded stomach was making her feel very ill indeed, and giving her a somewhat brutal reminder that she was, after all, nearly four months pregnant. At that moment the wretched unofficial ambassa-dress would gladly have sunk through the cushioned throne.

When she made no answer, the Sultana, startled by her sudden pallor, asked again: 'Is there something wrong? Please do not feel obliged to conceal it if you feel unwell —'

Marianne cast her a helpless glance and tried to smile.

'Your Highness is right – I don't feel very – ooh —!' In one bound, Marianne was off the throne and through the salon like a flash of green lightning. She brushed past the eunuchs at the door and making for the convenient shadow of the nearest cypress, which was luckily quite close at hand, set about restoring the unwanted contents of her stomach to the earth which had yielded them. The time this took was brief enough but it seemed to her endless and while it was going on she was far too preoccupied to consider the

15

shock that her precipitate departure must have caused. When at last she straightened, holding tight to the friendly tree for support, she was still in a cold sweat but the nausea was passing. She managed to gulp down a deep breath of the scented night air, cooled by the fountains, and felt better. Her strength was beginning to come back.

Not until then did it dawn on her what she had done. She had turned her back on an empress and dashed from the room like a thief in the middle of a diplomatic talk. The scandal it would cause! Enough to make poor Latour-Maubourg faint with horror! She stood for a moment under the cypress tree, unable to move, considering the probable consequence of her sickness, convinced that when she went back to the kiosk she would find a whole troop of eunuchs with drawn swords waiting to arrest her.

She was still hesitating there when a soft voice reached her.

'Princess, where are you? I hope you are not still feeling ill?'

Marianne breathed again.

'No, your Highness. I am here.'

Stepping out of the shadow of the trees, she found Nakshidil standing in the doorway of the little kiosk. She must have sent everyone else away for she was quite alone and Marianne, feeling very much in the wrong and also something of a fool, was grateful to her.

After this unlikely start to a delicate negotiation she felt that some apology was called for and the Princess Sant'Anna was just sinking into her best curtsy when she was promptly interrupted.

'No, please! Are you sure you are quite better? Take my arm and let us go inside — unless you'd rather stroll a little in the garden? It is cooler now and we might go as far as the terrace there, overlooking the Bosphorus. It is a favourite place of mine.'

'With pleasure — but I do not like to ask your Highness to put yourself out for me.'

'Who, me? My dear girl, I like nothing better than to take exercise, whether walking or riding on horseback. Unfortunately it can be a little awkward here. In our palaces in Asia it is easier. Are you coming?'

Arm in arm, they made their way slowly towards the selected spot. Marianne was surprised to find that the Sultana was as tall as she was and her slim figure was quite faultless. For that to be so at her age it was clear that the fair-skinned Créole could not have resigned herself to the lazy, cloistered existence of most women in the harem. She could only have kept that lithe, girlish figure by an addiction to the athletic sports so dear to the English. Nakshidil's interest, on the other hand, was all for her companion and while they walked she was asking with a deceptive casualness: 'Do you suffer often from these turns? Yet you look to be in high bloom?'

'No, your Highness. Not very often. I believe the blame for this must go to the cook at the embassy. There is a certain heaviness about his dishes —'

'And what I offered you was not of the lightest! Oddly enough, though, your sickness put me strongly in mind of what I suffered myself when I was expecting my son. I used to drink pots and pots of coffee and I couldn't stand halva or baklava – much less gulrecheli, the rose jam. The name and the colour are very poetic, to be sure, but I could never abide it.'

Marianne felt her cheeks grow hot and blessed the darkness which hid her untimely blushes. Even so, she could not control the slight stiffening of her arm which told her companion all she needed to know. Nakshidil understood at once that she had touched on the truth and also that it was a point on which her guest was peculiarly sensitive.

When the two of them reached the little terrace built of white marble, she indicated a curving bench plentifully furnished with cushions and evidently a much favoured spot.

'Shall we sit here for a little while?' she said. 'We can talk much more comfortably than in my apartments because there is no one to overhear us. Inside the palace, there are listening ears behind every door and every curtain. Here, we need fear nothing of the kind. See – where we are is like a kind of balcony overhanging the battlements and the lower gardens.' She glanced at Marianne's bare shoulders. 'But you are quite sure you won't be cold?'

'No, indeed, your Highness. I feel perfectly well now.'

Nakshidil nodded and turned to look across the arm of the sea to where the clouds were piling up over the hills of Scutari.

'Summer is nearly over,' she observed with a touch of sadness. 'The weather is changing and we shall probably have rain tomorrow. It will be good for the crops because the land is parched but after that will be the winter. It can be bitterly cold here and I dread it . . . But we will forget all that now. Tell me about yourself.'

'Me? But there is nothing interesting about me, your Highness, except in so far as I am the mouthpiece of Napoleon —'

The Sultana put up her hand with a gesture of impatience.

17

'Let's leave your Emperor for the present. His turn will come, although I cannot see what is to be said about him. Whatever you may think, I find you much more interesting than the great Napoleon. And so I want to know all about you. Tell me of your life.'

'My – my life?'

'Yes, the whole of your life! As though I were your mother.'

'But, your Highness, it is a long story —'

'Never mind. We have the night before us. But I want to know – everything! There are so many stories about you already and I like to get at the truth. Besides, I am your cousin and would like to be your friend. Don't you need a friend who has some power?'

The Sultana's silky little hand was laid on Marianne's, but she was already responding impulsively: 'Oh, yes!' It was spoken with such feeling that her companion smiled and was confirmed in her initial conviction that this young and ravishingly lovely creature stood in desperate need of help. Accustomed by the perilous life she had been forced to lead in this palace before becoming the mistress of it to watch for the slightest change of expression in the faces of others with a closeness on which her very life might depend, Nakshidil had been struck, from Marianne's first appearance, by the drawn look on her lovely face and by the unconscious pathos of her great green eyes. Napoleon's envoy was very far from anything she had expected.

The rumours which had been going round the Mediterranean in the past weeks had created a fantastic picture of a bold courtesan, a kind of boudoir Messalina, decked out by the Emperor, her lover, in a princess's crown, hardened in every kind of trickery and cunning and ready to stop at nothing, however flagrant, to ensure the success of her mission. Face to face with reality, it had not taken the Sultana long to realize that this picture was a complete fantasy, a mere caricature concocted by the British Foreign Office which had nothing to do with reality.

It was a caricature, moreover, which had been causing her a good deal of secret annoyance. The Princess Sant'Anna was a kinswoman, if a distant one, and it was tiresome to have such things said about a member of her own family. Consequently, a wish to form her own opinion had played no small part in her decision to grant the accused an audience. Now she wanted to hear all about this strange, beautiful young woman who seemed to bear a burden too heavy for her, yet bore it with pride.

Marianne began, a little shyly and reticently, to give a brief, superficial sketch of her past life but yielded, little by little, to her companion's very evident sympathy and understanding. Strange as the events of her own life had been so far, Nakshidil's far outdid them, for it was a much longer road from a convent in Nantes to the harem of the Grand Signior and a position of absolute power than from Selton Hall to the Palazzo Sant'Anna, even by way of Napoleon's bed.

When she fell silent at last, she found that she had described it all down to the smallest detail and that it must be very late because the silence that lay all about the little terrace where the two women sat was much deeper than it had been. The rumour of the city had died away and from the sea there came only the gentle slap of the waves and the measured tread of the guards at the Seraglio gates.

The Sultana, for her part, had not moved. She sat so still, in fact, that Marianne had the sudden, unnerving thought that she had fallen asleep. But she was only lost in thought, for a moment later Marianne heard her sigh.

'You've done a great many more stupid things than I ever did, for I only went where my fate directed, but I can't see that anyone could possibly blame you. When I think about it, love is to blame. It is love that has brought you both great suffering and great exaltation, set you on the strange road which has brought you to me.'

'Your Highness!' Marianne said, stammering a little. 'I beg you will not judge me too harshly —'

Nakshidil sighed again, then suddenly she laughed.

'Judge you? My poor child! Say rather that I envy you.'

'Envy me?'

'Why, yes! You have beauty, nobility, a famous name, you have wits and courage and you have that most precious and fragile of all gifts: youth. And more than that, you have love. I know, you are going to tell me that love has brought you little joy and even that just at this moment you could well do without it, but even so, it is there, driving you on and filling your life, coursing with the youth in your veins. And then, you are free, you have the right to do what you will with your own life, even to destroy yourself, if you like, in pursuit of this love of yours. The whole world is open to you. Yes, I envy you. You can never know how much I envy you.'

'Your Highness!' Marianne said, startled by the depth of sadness and regret in the soft voice, schooled to years of whispers.

But Nakshidil did not hear her. The story told by her visitor had carved a breach in the wall in which her spirit was imprisoned and all her regrets, her aching desires came pouring through it like the pounding seas though a broken dyke.

'Do you know what it means,' she went on, more softly still, 'do you know what it means to be twenty years old and to learn about love in an old man's arms? To dream of wide open spaces, of sailing the seas and galloping with the morning breeze on your face, of nights under huge, free skies, listening to the singing of the blacks and breathing in the scents of the islands – only to wake and find yourself in a cage amongst scheming eunuchs and an army of stupid, vindictive women with the souls of slaves? Do you know what it is to be always longing for a young man's love, for a young man's arms about you, strong and eager, as you lie on your silken cushions in the lonely room whence they take you from time to time to the bed of a man too old to make the contrast anything but bitter. . . ? And all this year after mortal year – the years that might have been the richest and warmest of your life?'

'Do you – do you mean that you have never known – love?' Marianne murmured, at once stricken and incredulous.

The fair hair stirred and the movement, slight as it was, drew a flash from the huge rose diamond that adorned it.

'I have known the love of Selim. He was the son of my husband, old Abdul Hamid. He was young, certainly – and he loved me with such passion that he chose to die to save me, me and my son, when the usurper Mustapha and the Janissaries swept through the palace. There was much warmth in his love and I was very fond of him, but as for the burning passion I might have known with – with another who filled my dreams when I was fifteen, the fever of love, the need to give and to take, no – those are things I have never known. So, little girl, forget your sufferings, forget all that you have endured because you still have the chance and the right to fight for your happiness. I will help you.'

'Your Highness is very good but it is not right for me to think only of the man I love. You forget that I am to bear a child, a child who would raise an impassable barrier between us, even if I could ever find him again.'

'That is true. I was forgetting that terrible experience of yours and its consequences. We must find a cure for those as well. You don't want to keep the child, do you? If I understood you rightly —'

'I hate it, your Highness, just as I hated the man who fathered it.

20

It is like a monstrous, loathsome thing inside me, feeding on my flesh and blood.'

'I understand. But at this late stage abortion would be dangerous. Your best course would be to retire to one of my houses and live there in seclusion until the child is born. I will take charge of it after that and I promise you that you will never hear of it again. I will have it brought up by people of my own.'

But Marianne shook her head. She was not prepared to spend the next few months in waiting for an event which both frightened and disgusted her. As for the dangers the Sultana had mentioned, she was well aware of them but feared them much less than the thought of living for five months cut off from all possibility of finding Jason again.

'I will have them begin the search for this American privateer of yours first thing in the morning,' Nakshidil said after a moment, reading her young kinswoman's thoughts like an open book. 'It is bound to take some time in any case. Are you still set on risking your life?'

'Yes. I'm only sorry to have waited so long, simply because I did not know of anyone who could help me. But now I must take the risk. If this child lives, even if I never see it, even if the whole world lies between us, there will still be an invisible tie, a living witness of all that I suffered at the hands of that abominable creature.'

There was a note of strain and fierce denial in the younger woman's voice and her companion recognized it. Remembering how she herself had felt on learning that the seed of the aged Sultan was germinating in the mysterious depths of her own body and the kind of revulsion which not even the triumphant prospect before her could altogether extinguish, she could guess at Marianne's frantic urge to tear out of her womb the thing that had been planted there in a fashion so horrible that she could not even bear to think of it as a child but only as a kind of monstrous growth, a cancer devouring her life and all her hopes of happiness. Once again, she put out her hand and pressed Marianne's but without speaking and her silence added to the girl's unhappiness.

'I – I disgust you, don't I?' she murmured.

'Disgust me? My poor child! You don't know what you're saying. The truth is that I am afraid for you. In the passion of your love and your longing for your lover, you are prepared to embark on a perilous course – and I fear you have not properly estimated the dangers and difficulties of it. Abortion is rare here, because our

21

country can never have too many men. Only – forgive me, but I must speak plainly – only prostitutes regularly resort to it, and I will spare you the details of how they go about it. Why can't you bring yourself to accept my offer? I should never forgive myself if any harm should come to you. And you must see that it would be foolish to lose your life over this, for then you could never be with your lover again in this world. Is that what you want?'

'Of course not! I want to live but if, with God's help, I were ever to meet him again he would turn from me in disgust – indeed, he has already done so. He would not believe a word of what I tried to tell him. And so, rather than endure his scorn, I would face death, yes, a thousand times over! I feel as though, once I'm rid of it, I shall be somehow cleansed, as if I've recovered from an infectious illness. But if the child were living, anywhere in the world, I could not feel that. It must never be anything more than a disease, faceless and formless, of which I have been cured, and then I shall feel clean and whole again.'

'Or else you will be dead.' The Sultan Valideh sighed. 'Very well, since you are so set on it, there is nothing I can do except —'

'The thing I ask?'

'Yes. But there is only one person here capable of carrying out this – operation with less than a fifty per cent chance of killing you.'

'I'll take that chance. Fifty per cent is pretty good.'

'No. It's very bad, but there's no other way. Listen. There is a woman living in the district of Kassim Pasha, on the other side of the Golden Horn, between the old synagogue and the Nightingale river. She is a Jewess, called Rebecca, the daughter of a skilled physician, Judah ben Nathan. She plies the trade of midwife, and with some skill, by all accounts. No dockside whores or street harlots from the Arsenal are admitted to her house but I know that she has lent her services from time to time, at a price, to the adulterous wife of some man in high position, thereby saving her from certain death. She is known also to the rich Europeans of Pera and to the Phanariot Greek nobility, but her secret is well kept and Rebecca knows that silence is the key to her continued prosperity. She will not take you without a strong recommendation.'

Marianne's hopes faded once again.

'Money?' she faltered. 'Does she want very much? Everything I had was stolen from me on board Jason Beaufort's ship —'

'Don't worry about that. If I send you to Rebecca, then it is my affair. One of my women shall come to you tomorrow, after dark, with a closed carriage. She will take you to the Jewess who will already have received her payment and her instructions. My woman will remain there with you for as long as necessary and then carry you by water to a house belonging to me in the vicinity of the Eyub cemetery where you may rest for a few days. Your ambassador will know only that you have gone with me on a brief visit to my palace at Scutari where I shall be going the day after tomorrow.' As she spoke, the weight began to lift from Marianne's heart, to be replaced by a sense of profound gratitude. By the time the soft, lisping voice ceased, her eyes were full of tears. She slid to her knees and, lifting the hand that still rested on her own, she raised it to her lips.

'Your Highness,' she murmured, 'how can I thank you —'

'Why, by saying nothing. You will embarass me if you insist on thanking me so much. This is a very small thing I do for you – and it is long since I had to do with an affair of the heart. You can't think how much I am enjoying it. Now, come —' She rose and shook out her pale coloured draperies, as though in haste now to shake off the burden of her confidences.

'It grows cold,' she said, 'and must be shockingly late besides. Your Monsieur de Latour-Maubourg must be wondering what has become of you. Your Breton's capable of imagining anything! He probably thinks I've had you sewn into a sack and dropped into the Bosphorus with a stone tied round your neck. Or else that Mr Canning has somehow spirited you away —' She laughed, relieved, perhaps, to have dealt with an awkward situation and possibly also by the chance to unburden herself of some of the accumulated bitterness of years. She chattered like a schoolgirl as she settled her muslin veils about her with all the care of a woman whose habit it was never to appear looking less than her best.

Marianne rose automatically and followed her. They made their way quickly back to the kiosk where the file of eunuchs was still gravely waiting and Marianne, hearing her companion giving orders for her return to the embassy with a doubled escort on account of the lateness of the hour, was appalled to realize that she had spent the best part of the night at the palace and still the mission entrusted to her by Napoleon remained unfulfilled. With a graciousness that was not, perhaps, entirely disinterested, the Sultana had encouraged her to talk about herself, turning what had begun as a diplomatic audience into a purely family occasion, in which the Emperor and

23

his concerns were out of place, and putting under a strong obligation of gratitude one who, in the ordinary way, should have been thinking of nothing but the success of her mission.

When, therefore, Nakshidil led her guest back into the pavilion and proposed a final cup of coffee while they waited for the arrival of the litter, Marianne was quick to accept, even if one more dose of that comforting beverage meant that she would not get a wink of sleep that night, or what was left of it.

She spoke seriously, striving to banish a trace of compunction at bringing the Sultana back to what was evidently unwelcome ground.

'Your Highness has been so very kind to me tonight that you have made me forget the real reason for my coming here. I am ashamed to think that I have talked of almost nothing but myself, when there are so many more important matters at stake. May I know how your Highness is disposed to regard those things I have said in confidence and whether you will consider mentioning them to his Highness the Sultan?'

'Talk to him? Well, I might, but —' and here she sighed, 'I am afraid he will not listen to me. It is true that my son's love for me is complete and unchanging but my influence is no longer what it was, and neither is his admiration for your Emperor.'

'But why not? Is it the divorce?'

'No. Rather it is because of certain clauses in the Treaty of Tilsit, of which he was informed by Mr Canning who had them from what source I do not know. It seems there was a letter from Napoleon to the Tsar, dated 2 February 1808, in which the Emperor put forward a proposal for the partition of the Ottoman Empire. Russia was to have the Balkans and Turkey in Asia; Austria, Serbia and Bosnia; France, Egypt and Syria, which would be a magnificent base for Napoleon to attack the British power in the Indies. So you see, we have small cause to love the Emperor.'

Marianne felt as if the ground were shifting under her feet and mentally cursed Napoleon's epistolary indiscretions. What made him write such dangerous letters to a man he was not wholly sure of? Was he so delighted with Alexander as to forget even the most elementary rules of caution? What could she say now to rid the Turks of their very justifiable belief that the French Emperor was prepared to sell them to the highest bidder? Should she deny it? There was small chance that she would be believed and in any case it was becoming increasingly unlikely that she could persuade them

24

to go on getting themselves killed to facilitate Napoleon's invasion of Russia.

However she was determined to do her duty to the end and so she went in gallantly to attack the English position.

'Your Highness is quite sure that the letter is genuine? The Foreign Office has never baulked at forgery where its interests were concerned, nor do I see how secret clauses of the Treaty of Tilsit, how a letter addressed to the Tsar in person —' She broke off, realizing that she had lost her audience. The two women had remained standing in the centre of the room but now the Sultana was engaged in prowling slowly round and round her visitor. It was evident that she had quite lost interest in a political discussion to which she felt she had already given a sufficient answer and she was subjecting Marianne's dress to the detailed scrutiny which any woman, be she empress or no, reserves for matters of such vital importance.

Nakshidil extended a cautious finger and stroked one of the full green satin sleeves with its frosting of crystal beads. She sighed.

'That dress is truly ravishing. I have never liked these long sheaths that Rose has made so fashionable. I preferred the hoops and frills of my youth. But this is enchanting. I wonder what I should look like in such a dress . . .'

Marianne was aware of a moment's hesitation while she adjusted herself to the ease with which the Sultana passed from matters of state to feminine frivolities. Should she lend herself to the game? Was it simply an attempt to evade the subject, or had this woman, risen to such dizzy heights, still kept something of her incurable Créole frivolousness? It did not take her long to decide. Smiling as if no word of politics had ever passed her lips, she said: 'I hardly dare to ask if your Highness would care to try it on —'

Nakshidil's face was transformed instantly.

'Really? Would you let me?'

Even before Marianne could answer, a brief command had summoned the women whose duty it was to help their mistress to undress, another brought forth a tall, gold-framed mirror in which it was possible to see oneself from head to foot, and a third sealed the entrance to the pavilion.

A moment later Marianne found herself standing in her underpetticoat of fine lawn watching as Nakshidil stripped off sky blue muslins faster than her women could assist her without snagging them. But the discarded veils were cast aside as contemptuously as

25

if they had been a heap of old rags while one of the women proffered the dress which she had been helping Marianne to remove.

Divested of her clothes, the fair Créole stood up for a moment as naked as a fish and as coolly unconcerned about it as any woman long accustomed to the communal bathing and beauty care of the harem. And her young cousin saw to her amazement that her body was as smooth and faultless as that of a woman of thirty. There was no trace of slackness or of sagging flesh, not a discoloured vein to be seen and Marianne was reminded sadly of the lament she had heard so short a time before.

That form, with its voluptuous curves, recalled to her another daughter of those distant islands, Fortunée Hamelin. It was so obviously made for love, a perfect instrument designed to bend and vibrate to the fierce tempest of sensual passion, which it had never truly known. Nor had the single pregnancy left the slightest trace. This beauty had the pointless, lonely splendour of a museum piece.

A feeling of profound pity swept over Marianne as Nakshidil emerged, as excited as a small girl, from the shimmering folds of the sea-green dress and let its heavy folds drape themselves about her. The dress was too long, its rightful owner being somewhat the taller of the two, but apart from that it fitted perfectly, so perfectly, indeed, that the Sultana clapped her hands delightedly.

'Oh,' she cried, 'how I should love to own this dress!'

Marianne had a mental vision of herself returning to the embassy in her petticoat, since there was really nothing she could do but make a present of the dress. But, equal to anything that might help to save her mission and install her firmly in the Sultana's good graces, she did not hesitate, but spoke up cheerfully: 'If your Highness will lend me a cloak or something so that I may not shock people when I go back to the embassy, I shall be happy to present you with the dress, since you like it so much.'

The blue eyes sparkled and gazed eagerly at Marianne.

'You would give me your dress?' Nakshidil said. 'Even though we do not resume our former relations with Napoleon?'

Marianne controlled herself sufficiently to give no sign. Her smile lost none of its warmth or sweetness and she managed to sustain a dignity and unconcern which came none too easily when dressed only in one's petticoat.

'Friendship is one thing,' she said quietly, 'and politics are quite another, very different as it seems to me. This is a gift from the heart – and I am only conscious of how unworthy it is. I wish I had something more precious to offer to your Highness in token of my gratitude —'

The Sultana's laugh held real amusement.

'I begin to think your Emperor would be well advised to put you in Latour-Maubourg's place! You're a much better diplomat than he is —'

Then, picking up the skirts that were too long for her, she went to her visitor and hugged her with true Créole warmth.

Still with her arms round her, she went on with sudden seriousness: 'I can do nothing for your Emperor, my child. Believe me, it is not from ill-will. I don't even bear him any grudge over Rose's divorce, or that notorious letter. There are such things as political necessities, I know that, and, as you say, these have nothing to do with human feelings. Those who serve them must forget that they have hearts – and sometimes consciences also. But things are going very badly for us on the Danube. My son, the Sultan, yearns for a well-trained, modern army but he has to meet the Russians with an undisciplined horde which, though gallant, is eaten with corruption. Its fighting methods are medieval and it is dominated by the Janissaries with their out-dated ideas and vendettas. No wonder it suffers heavy losses. Our grand vizier is shut up in Rustchuk asking for assistance and calling for an armistice —'

'You would consider – making peace?' Marianne gasped with a sudden pang.

'Short of a miracle – and I don't believe in miracles when dealing with an Empire that would gladly rob us even of the Dardanelles – we shall have to make peace before the winter is out. Khaled, the grand vizier, makes no secret of his desire to treat with Kutuzov because he is under continual attack by Ataman Platov's cossacks and running short of men.'

'But you must hold out, your Highness!' Marianne implored her. 'The Emperor does not ask for your continued resistance without reason. Very soon now —'

'Nearly a year —'

'Sooner, perhaps. I can tell you that Marshal Davoust and your cousin, Prince Eugène are gathering an immense army in Germany. If you can only hold out, the Tsar will soon be forced to relieve you of Kutuzov. Your war is lost now but Napoleon can turn the tables for you and give you victory – and the Danube principalities.'

Nakshidil, who had continued to hold Marianne within the warm circle of her arms, let her go and shrugged. The sadness of her smile was tinged with irony.

'Don't try to make me believe, Princess, that Napoleon is about to attack Alexander purely for the sake of helping us. I've told you, we ceased to have any illusions regarding his intentions towards us a long time ago. If he wants us to go on holding out there is one thing he can do – send us troops. A few regiments out of that immense army of his. Then perhaps the grand vizier might hold out, with more than the fifteen thousand men he has at present! Otherwise, it's impossible.'

'Will Mr Canning bring you any better help?'

'Not in a military sense, no. But diplomatically, yes. When it comes to negotiating the peace, he is pledged to help us and to obtain the best possible terms from the Tsar.'

'Oh, your Highness,' Marianne said reproachfully, 'has the Sultan so far forgotten his mother's country? Have you yourself forgotten it?'

'I have forgotten nothing,' Nakshidil said with a sigh. 'Unfortunately, my son has been taught to look on his mother's country with some distrust. Do you think Mahmoud can forget that one of his greatest enemies is French?'

'French? Who is that?'

'The Governor of Odessa. For years now that man has been building up a powerful city on the shores of the Black Sea and, more important, a harbour for the ships that come out to attack us at the very mouth of the Bosphorus. I am speaking of the Duc de Richelieu, the Tsar's friend, and more Russian than the Russians. Napoleon had better reckon with that irreconcilable emigré because he has the Tartar hordes at his beck.'

'But as your Highness says, he is an emigré, one of the Emperor's own enemies!'

'A Frenchman none the less. And that, in my son's eyes, is all that matters. You cannot ask him to let his people die to help a selfish ruler who never thinks of us unless he needs us.'

There was a silence in which Marianne saw the success of her mission slowly foundering. She had too much honesty not to understand the Sultan's reasons and those of his mother, for they were sound and such as demanded respect. Moreover, she had learned long ago, to her cost, to measure the depths of Napoleon's egoism. As Nakshidil had said, short of a miracle the Turks would soon be seeking an armistice and this was something that Paris must know as soon as possible.

Aware that it would be clumsy, even ill-mannered to persist after the kindness already shown her, Marianne abandoned the argument, for that night at least. She would have to report to the accredited ambassador but just now she felt very tired.

'If I might ask your Highness's permission to retire,' she murmured.

'But of course! But not like that!'

All the Sultana's gaiety had returned and she was issuing a fresh stream of orders. In another moment, Marianne found herself transformed into an Ottoman princess by virtue of a gorgeous yellow robe, thickly embroidered with gold, to which the Sultana, with princely generosity, had added a girdle, necklace and ear-rings set with rubies and pearls, and sinking, not without difficulty, into her farewell curtsy, watched by the Khislar Agha and the court ladies who had miraculously reappeared.

'We shall meet again very soon,' Nakshidil assured her with an encouraging smile as she offered Marianne her hand to kiss. And don't forget, you will be expected tomorrow night at the place I told you of. For the rest – trust me. I do not think you will be dis-appointed.'

Without elaborating further on these last words, which Marianne could not help feeling were a trifle enigmatic, the Sultan Valideh vanished into the recesses of the pavilion with her ladies following in a cloud of blue and left her visitor to be escorted slowly back to her litter by the tall black eunuch.

As she was borne back through the gardens towards the sea shore at the easy, swinging pace of her bearers, Marianne tried to sort out her ideas and sum up the evening's events. She did not find it easy, for her mind was torn between such contradictory feelings as grati-tude, disappointment and uneasiness. On the political plan she had failed, undoubtedly, and failed so completely that she hardly dared to ask herself how Napoleon would take the news. But she experi-enced no sense of guilt or regret, knowing that she had done her duty to the utmost and that as things stood no one could have done any more. At the same time, she agreed with the Valideh that Napoleon might have given a thought to Turkey before her army was at its last gasp. The promise of an expeditionary force would undoubtedly have carried far more weight than the urgings of a mere inexperienced young woman.

She turned her thoughts resolutely away from the political situation and began to consider her own immediate prospects. In spite of the very real danger she would have to face during the coming night, Marianne was beginning to glimpse light at the end of the tunnel through which she had been struggling for so many weeks, and she could not help seeing it as a happy omen for the future. Once this nightmare was over . . .

She became aware that thinking was growing more and more difficult as the swaying motion of the litter combined with the emotional exhaustion brought on by her sleepless night.

Away to the east, beyond the Scutari hills, the sky was growing lighter, turning from black to grey. Day was not far off. Marianne shivered in the cool, damp air that rose from the gardens. It had been so hot when she came but now she was really quite cold and was thankful for the silken veils in which they had swathed her. Hugging them tightly round her, she snuggled down among the cushions and abandoned the struggle. Her eyes closed.

When she opened them, the litter was already passing through the gothic gateway of the embassy and she realized that she had slept the whole way home. But her brief nap had only made her long for more. As her escort of Janissaries wound its way downhill again to the Galata landing, she turned to enter the house under the disapproving eye of a butler who was visibly more shocked than impressed by the magnificence of her Turkish costume.

He informed her, somewhat distantly, that his Excellency and Monsieur the Vicomte had passed the night in the saloon awaiting her Highness's return and were there still.

Marianne, longing for her bed, was tempted to leave them there and postpone what she foresaw would be a lengthy interview but she told herself that, after all, they had been sitting up on her account. Not to go to them would be ungrateful. And so she sighed and made her way to the saloon.

But the sight that met her eyes as she opened the door made her smile. Jolival and the ambassador were seated in deep, cushioned armchairs on either side of a small table on which was set out a magnificent set of cut crystal chessmen. Both were blissfully asleep: the ambassador sunk deep in his chair with his chin buried in the folds of his cravat and his spectacles on the end of his nose, Jolival with his cheek resting on his hand and the ends of his moustache lifting gently with his breathing and both of them snoring lustily,

30

albeit in different keys. They seemed so dedicatedly asleep that Marianne had not the heart to disturb them.

She closed the door very gently and, with an injunction to the butler to let the gentlemen sleep on, she went away on tiptoe to her own room, promising herself a long rest before she had to face the ordeal of the coming night.

Yet before that she would have to repeat to the ambassador every single thing that the Sultana had said so that he could send a detailed report of it to Paris. If Napoleon was really set on winning Ottoman support, he might even decide to send the military aid which alone could combat the English influence. But Marianne had no faith in that and she was quite sure that Latour-Maubourg was under no more illusions than she.

Well, we shall see, she told herself, by way of consolation.

CHAPTER TWO

The Nightingale River

The vehicle which entered the French embassy courtyard as darkness fell was a small, brightly painted araba curtained in green velvet such as might have been owned by the wife of any wealthy Galata merchant. It was drawn by a sturdy mule with gay red pompoms on its harness and the driver was a crinkly-haired black boy whose dark face gleamed softly in the light of the lamp that was fastened to the front of the carriage.

The apparition that descended from this equipage looked more like a ghost than a woman. She was wrapped from head to foot in a long ferej of dark green cloth and her face was covered by the thick veil without which no Turkish lady would have dared to stir abroad.

Marianne was waiting in the hall, dressed in the same fashion except that her ferej was of a deep violet blue and she was not wearing the veil. With Jolival beside her, she walked down to the carriage where the other woman stood waiting for her. When she saw that there was a man, and a European, with the one she had come to seek, the woman did not speak but only bowed and held out a scroll of paper, tied and sealed with blue. Then she straightened and stood quietly waiting for the contents to be read.

'What's this?' the Vicomte said crossly, taking a lantern from the hands of an attendant. 'Does it need all these papers for what you are about to do?'

Jolival had been in the worst of tempers all day long. He loathed everything about this expedition of Marianne's but most of all it made him horribly afraid for her. The thought that the young friend who was almost a daughter to him was about to put her health and perhaps even her life in the hands of probably incompetent foreigners horrified him. He made no attempt to hide his dislike of the project or the alarm it caused him.

'What you are doing is madness,' he protested. 'I was ready to help you in Corfu, when this damned pregnancy was barely started, but now I'm wholly against it. Not as a matter of principle, which is beside the point, but simply because it is dangerous!'

Nothing could budge him from this position and Marianne had

wasted her time and her persuasions. Arcadius was almost ready to go to any lengths to stop her going to Rebecca. It had even crossed his mind to tell Latour-Maubourg the whole and have the embassy put into something like a state of siege, or else to lock Marianne up in her bedchamber with guards below the windows. But the ambassador would probably have thought that he was mad and in any case it would be cruel to break up the unfortunate diplomat's peace yet again.

Certainly the ambassador had not been particularly overjoyed to learn that the Porte was considering an armistice but the news had not really surprised him. He had, on the other hand, been sure that the spontaneous friendship which had sprung up between the Sultan Valideh and the Princess Sant'Anna augured most favourably for his own future relations with the court, especially since this friendship had shown itself in an invitation to spend several days with the Sultana at her villa at Scutari.

Compelled to abandon his violent projects, the poor Vicomte had next endeavoured to persuade Marianne to let him go with her and here again she had found it extremely difficult to convince him that it would not do. She had to tell him over and over again that one of the Valideh's most trusted confidantes was to accompany her and guard against any possible accident, while the presence of another European might lead Rebecca to refuse her services altogether and so ruin all. What was more, she said, the house of a midwife was no place for a man.

Defeated but not convinced, Jolival had muttered irritably all day, his temper growing noticeably worse with the approach of evening.

Marianne, meanwhile, had been scanning the thick parchment scroll. It was an official document, inscribed in arabic characters and sealed with the imperial *tughra* which she naturally did not understand. But attached to it was a smaller letter, written on a silky vellum in a delicate, flowing hand which spoke of the long hours spent at a convent desk acquiring it. The faint scent of hyacinths that came from it recalled to the reader the blue pavilion of the previous night.

Writing in a charmingly old-world style reminiscent of Versailles and powdered heads, Nakshidil disclosed to her 'dearly-beloved cousin' the contents of the larger document which was nothing more nor less than the title of ownership of the *Sea Witch*.

The Valideh had purchased the American brig from the *reis*

Achmet and she was now the sole property of the Princess Sant'Anna. More than that, she was to be transferred to the naval dockyard of Kassim Pasha where she would be thoroughly overhauled, under the personal supervision of the Ottoman admiral, the Kapodan Pasha, before being handed over to her new owner.

'Our own naval carpenters being unaccustomed to the way of your great western ships,' the Valideh had written, not without a touch of humour, 'we have begged Mr Canning to procure for us the services of some of the English carpenters employed on repairs to vessels putting in to our harbours to give our men the necessary instruction in order to restore this ship of ours to her former condition . . .'

This admirable example of officialdom at work succeeded in dissipating Jolival's ill humour. He began to laugh and Marianne found herself laughing with him.

'If there was ever any doubt that this imperial kinswoman of yours is still a Frenchwoman at heart, this would be enough to do away with it,' the Vicomte said at last. 'Only someone born of the same country as Voltaire and Surcouf could have thought of anything so ingenious as getting the English ambassador to refit an enemy vessel, and making him foot the bill. For Mr Canning can scarcely be so curmudgeonly as to send in his account. Really, it's too good! Long live the Sultan's royal mother! She's a credit to her family.'

Marianne said nothing. She was glad to see him looking happy again. She herself was deeply touched by Nakshidil's gesture, for with her wholly feminine instinct the Créole had put her finger unerringly on the very thing which meant most to her young cousin: Jason's ship, the thing he loved as much and maybe even more than the woman whose image she bore.

By making this gift, with such delicacy and such truly royal generosity, and at the very moment when Marianne was on the point of facing fresh dangers for the sake of her lover, the Valideh had made it a symbol of her sanction, a sign of encouragement and moral support. It was a wonderful way of telling her: 'you are going to suffer but in the midst of your suffering you will remember this ship because while you have her you will hold the key to the future and to all your hopes in the palm of your hand. Death cannot touch one so powerfully armed . . .'

Marianne closed her eyes, seeing herself already on board the restored *Sea Witch*, putting out from Constantinople with all sails

flying and scouring every port in the world in search of her one true
captain. Suddenly, the outlook was much wider and brighter. When
the sun rose tomorrow, there would be great plans for the future
crowding round her bed to help her back to health but already,
mistress of the American brig and strong in the backing of her
powerful kinswoman, Marianne was beginning to feel that the
world was hers.

She opened her eyes and bestowed on Jolival a smile so radiant
that he had not the heart to utter another word of protest.

'I must go,' she said. 'We've wasted too much time already. Keep
these precious papers for me. I know they will be safe with you and
I can't take them with me where I'm going. Kiss me goodbye
now —'

With a warm rush of affection, he put both arms round her and
kissed her on both cheeks. Suddenly, he was feeling happier. The
fear which had been gnawing at his stomach all day was fading.
Miraculously, the letter had set him thinking, like Marianne herself,
that nothing really dreadful could happen to a woman with such
forces to protect her.

'Take care of yourself,' he said simply. 'We'll see if God will still
listen to the prayers of an unbeliever that all may go well.'

A calm voice spoke suddenly from behind the white veil which
hid the Turkish woman's face.

'All will be well,' it said. 'The Jewess knows that she will be
beaten to death if there should be any accident, so do not worry.'

In another moment, Marianne was seated in the cushioned araba
and leaving the sometime Franciscan convent. The mule began
pulling strongly up the steep, roughly cobbled street. A chill wind
whistled down the narrow thoroughfare, parting the curtains of the
vehicle. Marianne's companion snatched up a white muslin veil and
hurriedly covered the girl's face with it.

'It's better so,' she said as the other put up a cautious hand to her
face. 'Our customs can be very useful when one wishes to escape
notice or recognition.'

'No one knows me here. I have little to fear —'

'Look – there is the night watchman beginning his rounds. He
has only to catch sight of an unveiled woman in an araba to set a
whole host of unlikely rumours afoot.'

A tall, thin man in a rough linen caftan with a broad belt and a
brimless red felt hat with a piece of dirty muslin tied round it had
just come round a corner. He had a lantern in one hand and with

35

the other he was tapping the pavement at regular intervals with a long metal-shod staff. As he passed, he glanced idly through the curtains, which were still blowing in the wind, at the occupants of the araba. Marianne needed no telling to hold the veil close across her face. She shivered.

'It's cold tonight, and yesterday it was stifling —'

The other woman shrugged indifferently.

'It is the meltemi, the cold wind off the Caucasian snows. When it blows, the whole city freezes but the weather here changes very swiftly. And now, let me introduce myself. My name is Bulut, which means Cloud.'

Marianne smiled, liking this cloud. The ferej could not disguise the fact that she was plump and comfortable and her bright eyes twinkled merrily above her white veil and did not avoid one's gaze.

'I know nothing of your country's manners. How ought I to address you?'

'I am called Bulut Hanum. Hanum signifies Madame and is used in conjunction with the first name. With your Highness's permission, I shall address you in the same way to avoid attracting attention. Rebecca must not know who it is that she has in her care tonight.'

'So I am to be Marianne Hanum?' Marianne said with a smile. 'It makes a pretty name.'

This small excursion into local customs had broken the ice. Madam Cloud began chattering like a magpie, visibly delighted with a task which made a striking change from the monotony of her usual existence. She could not have been as young as her eager, girlish voice suggested for she disclosed that she was an old friend of the Valideh whom she had known since her first arrival in the harem as a little fair-haired slave girl, terrified by her capture in mid-Atlantic, her stay in the pirate city of Algiers and her voyage to Constantinople aboard the Barbary xebec. At that time, Bulut herself had been a member of the harem and had attained the rank of Ikbal[1] having twice enjoyed the favours of the imperial bed. But after the death of the old sultan she had been one of those 'pensioned off' by the new master and bestowed as a convenient gift on various senior court officials. Bulut had been married off to one Halil Mustapha Pasha who held the onerous but enviable position of Defterdar, or Minister of Finance.

[1] The Ikbals aspired to the title of Kadine, which would be theirs once they had borne the Sultan a child.

This change in her situation had in no way displeased Bulut, now rejoicing in the title of Bulut Hanum, for she had never minded being included amongst the harem's expendable property. Her marriage had procured her a lofty social station and a mild, easy-going husband whom she ruled with the carefully-concealed firmness which any Turkish wife worthy of the name brought to the management of her husband. According to his wife, Mustapha Pasha was a perfect *kibilik*, the very model of a hen-pecked husband and one who had adopted as his private motto the Kurdish proverb which said that he who did not fear his wife was less than a man.

Alas, this model husband had been gathered to Allah in paradise some years since and Bulut Hanum, being left widow, had entered the household of the Queen Mother, with whom she had remained on the friendliest terms, as mistress of the robes. It was to this friendship that she owed her familiarity with the 'Frankish tongue' which she spoke easily – and with breathtaking rapidity.

While Bulut chattered on, the araba pursued its way through the steep streets of Pera, crowded with vines, Christian religious houses, European embassies and the houses of rich merchants, preceded by a man with a lantern who gave vent, from time to time, to a nasal shout of 'Dikka-a-at', like a muezzin with a bad cold. The tiny cafés, run by Venetians and Provençaux, which lined the main street were all shut by now, since, except during the nights of Ramadan, which had ended some three weeks earlier, few people stirred out of doors after sunset in the Ottoman capital. The districts of Pera and Galata, where the law was less severe, were something of an exception to this rule, but even here it was necessary to carry a lantern or pay the penalty. Thus it was that those few pedestrians who were about all carried the swinging lanterns made of pleated paper in a metal frame which gave to the threefold city its air of being permanently *en fête*.

The carriage made a sudden right turn along the side of a building whose immense walls were surmounted by cupolas and by a minaret that gleamed in the light of the rising moon. The talkative Bulut was silent for a moment, listening. The thin notes of a flute came trickling from the building, like a tiny mountain spring.

'What is it?' Marianne asked in a whisper. 'Where is the music coming from?'

'From within. It is the *tekke* – the home of the Mevlani Dervishes. It means that they are beginning their prayers and they will whirl and whirl all night, like planets around the sun.'

'How sad the music sounds. Like a lament.'

' "Listen to the reed flute", was the teaching of Mevlana the mystic, "for it says: from the time that I was first cut from the reeds of the marshes, men and women have bewailed in my voice . . . All things that have been severed from their roots look to the time when they shall be joined again." '

Madam Cloud's voice had grown remote and for a moment Marianne was carried away by the poetry of her words which found a strange echo in her own heart that was aptly underlined by the music of the flute. But then she noticed that the araba had stopped at a sign from her companion and that Bulut Hanum, who had taken several backward glances in the past few minutes, was turning round again to peep behind them through a gap in the curtains.

'Why have we stopped?'

'I want to make sure of something. I think we're being followed. When I gave the order to stop, I saw a figure slip behind one of the buttresses of the tekke wall. Someone who didn't want to be seen, because they were not carrying a lantern. Well, we'll see.'

She tapped the driver briefly on the shoulder as a signal to move on and the araba resumed its progress down the sloping street. At that precise moment, Marianne, who was also peering through the gap, distinctly saw a shadow detach itself from the deeper darkness of the wall and follow at a respectful distance.

'Who can it be?' Bulut muttered. 'It's a bold man who would dare to follow a lady of the court, and a bolder still to walk abroad without a light. I hope it's not an enemy.'

There was a quiver of alarm in her voice, but Marianne was not afraid. The darkness inside the carriage hid her smile. She was very nearly certain that she knew their mysterious follower. It must be either Jolival or Gracchus-Hannibal – if not both, for she had a strong impression that there were two shadows there.

'I can't think who could be interested in us,' she said, so calmly that an involuntary sigh of relief broke from her companion's ample bosom. 'Is it far now to where we are going?'

'Ten minutes or so. The Nightingale River runs along the bottom of this valley into which we are descending now, beyond that line of cypresses. Beyond that again you have the buildings of the Arsenal and the whole of the Golden Horn as far as the Sweet Waters of Europe.'

The view from below the tekke was certainly a magical one, taking in all the area of the harbour which shone like quicksilver in the moonlight, pricked out with the black needles which were the masts of ships. But the beauty of the scene had no power to captivate Marianne for she was in a hurry to reach her destination and get it over. Delay now made her vaguely uneasy. After all, she had no proof that the shadowy forms were Jolival and Gracchus . . . Latour-Maubourg had not concealed the fact that the embassy was watched and the British ambassador might still be hoping to lay hands on Napoleon's envoy. His spies were so well-organized that he could not fail to be aware of the length of the previous night's audience. So it was with a trace of nervousness that she asked: 'When we reach this woman's house – shall we be safe there?'

'Absolutely. The guard of Janissaries responsible for the protection of the Arsenal and the naval dockyards is within easy reach of the synagogue and can watch that also. The slightest disturbance in the neighbourhood will bring them in a moment. We shall be as easy in Rebecca's house as inside the walls of the Seraglio. But the main thing is to get there . . . Hurry, driver! Faster!'

She repeated the order in Turkish and the mule went like the wind. Fortunately, the way, which had been steep at first, had levelled out a good deal and the uneven cobblestones had given way to beaten earth. In a short while they were travelling along a narrow lane that ran along the valley bottom, beside the stream.

Seen at close hand, this was infinitely less poetic than from the heights of Pera and gave no hint of deserving its romantic name. It was full of rubbish and gave off a nasty smell compounded mainly of ooze and rotting fish. Indeed the whole district, huddled up against the walls of the Arsenal which lay between it and the sea, reeked of poverty. The wooden houses, their walls eaten by the salt winds, crowded about an ancient, half-ruined synagogue, their flat roofs and gutters etched against the slate-blue of the sky. Many of them had their ground floors given over to shops, shuttered at this hour, and here and there was the low door of a warehouse or the heavily barred window of a moneylender with the star of David displayed above the lintel.

But although the houses were old and decaying, the strange thing was that the doors were all stout enough and the locks shone with care. Banks and warehouses were guarded by massive locks and iron bars that showed no trace of rust.

'This,' said Bulut Hanum, 'is Kassim Pasha and Rebecca's house lies over there.'

She pointed to a garden which made a kind of bulge adjoining

39

the synagogue. The black spires of three cypress trees showed above it and the summit of the grey wall itself was softened by snowy drifts of jasmine.

'Is this the ghetto of Constantinople?' Marianne asked, struck by the cheerless desolation of the houses.

'There are no ghettos in the Ottoman Empire,' Bulut answered gently. 'On the contrary, when the Jews were driven out of Spain by the Inquisition they found a welcome here where they could be free and even respected, for racial prejudice is a thing unknown to us, as it has always been. Black, yellow or brown, Arab or Jew, it is all one to us as long as they contribute to the prosperity of our empire. The Jews live where they will and gather of their own free will about their synagogues, of which there are now some forty in the city. The greatest number are to be found in the adjoining district, but this community is not to be despised.'

'But even if they are not forced to live here, surely they must be very poor, if not actually in want?'

Bulut laughed. 'Don't be taken in by the impoverished look of the houses hereabouts. They are very different inside, as you will see for yourself. The children of Israel are a prudent race, for although they get on well enough with us Turks they are like cat and dog with the rich Greeks of Phanar who hate them because of their all too often successful rivalry in trade. For this reason, they prefer to keep their wealth hidden away from prying eyes and not to provoke their enemies by the splendour of their homes.'

Yet in spite of her companion's reassurances Marianne could not help a feeling of inexplicable discomfort and uneasiness. It might have been due to the two shadowy forms who had now, whether they were there or not, become discreetly invisible, or to the valley itself which might have been charming, in spite of its tumbledown hovels, if it had not been built up against the forbidding walls of the Arsenal, scarcely more cheerful than a prison, with the warlike figures of the Janissaries mounting guard on the battlements, the lighted matches for their muskets in their hands. But there the arsenal was, solid and menacing, like a dyke built to stand between this wretched district and the sea. Even the little river vanished beneath its walls, as though it, too, were flowing into captivity through the low arched opening guarded with thick iron bars.

But when she tried to explain this gloomy impression of hers, remarking that it was sad to see the Nightingale River ending in a cage, her companion only laughed again.

'We aren't mad!' she exclaimed. 'Of course we've sealed the valley off from the Golden Horn! None of our sultans wants to see another invader repeating Mehmet the Great's exploit.'

And she described, with pride, how, in the spring of 1453, the Sultan Mehmet II, in his determination to reduce the city of Byzantium by sea as well as by land, had had his fleet carried over the hill of Pera with the aid of a slipway made of planks of wood greased with mutton fat and lard. Having been hauled up to the head of the valley by a system of rollers and pulleys, the ships had gone swooping down through Kassim Pasha and into the Golden Horn, to the terror of the besieged.

'We have been careful to take precautions,' Bulut finished. 'It never does to give one's enemies ideas.'

In the meanwhile, the araba had come to a halt before a carved cedarwood door let into the garden wall. Underneath a thick coat of dust could be seen a lot of rather primitive designs of flowers and leaves, above which hung a small bronze doorknocker which Bulut Hanum was already working with an impatient hand. The door was opened almost at once.

A servant girl in a saffron robe stood there, bowing deeply. The many scents of the garden leaped to meet them, filling their nostrils as though they had each been handed a bouquet of flowers. The sharp tang of the cypress trees mingled with the sweetness of the jasmine and the fragrance of fruiting orange trees with that of dying roses and clove pinks, and there were other, less easily identifiable scents.

It was a garden full of contrasts. The rampant, jungle growth of the roses contrasted with the neat, well-ordered beds, marked out with box, which were the domain of the medicinal plants. Herbs both beneficent and deadly grew there thickly, around a semi-circular pool into which a trickle of water splashed endlessly from between the worn jaws of an antique stone lion.

The maidservant, still bowing obsequiously, trotted before them towards the house which, although somewhat less dilapidated than its neighbours, forfeited all this slight advantage by an architecture so improbable that Marianne could not restrain a grimace of distaste. The thought of spending as much as twenty-four hours in this nightmare of wood and stone depressed her unutterably. It was made up of a weird juxtaposition of brick and carved wood, interspersed with panels of Brusa tiles decorated with fabulous monsters, the whole surmounted by an astonishing assortment of turrets,

41

balconies and onion domes. Bulut Hanum, however, was evidently well-accustomed to the oddness of it for without abating one jot of the dignity due to a friend of the Valideh she directed her well-rounded person to a brassbound door beneath a flattened arch and passed inside.

Marianne followed her through a tiny entrance hall and found herself on the threshold of a large room, dimly lighted by a bronze lantern hung on long chains from the ceiling, from which came a number of little, flickering flames. Below it stood a tall woman who bowed as they entered but did not speak. Nor was there the smallest hint of obsequiousness in her bow. She bowed and that was all. Marianne stared at her in amazement.

Without quite knowing why, she had been expecting a short, fat, oily creature, not unlike the second-hand clothes dealers who were to be seen about the Temple in Paris. The woman who stood calmly and silently observing her could not have been more different.

Rebecca's face, framed in the gold-embroidered head-dress worn by Jewish women, was the colour of ivory and set in it were a pair of large, black and singularly penetrating eyes. A hooked nose and a mouth rather too heavy could not rob her of a degree of beauty which was derived chiefly from the very real intelligence of her expression.

Marianne's uneasiness increased as she took her seat, automatically, on the low divan that Rebecca waved her to. She felt a fluttering inside her that presaged the onset of an inexplicable sense of panic. She felt that she was threatened by some danger against which there was no possible defence and she forced herself to fight it while Bulut Hanum made the first move in the conversation, for it was surely ridiculous. What had she to fear from this quiet and, all in all, rather distinguished-looking woman, when she had come here prepared to submit to the dubious practices of some dirty, evil-smelling crone? Where was her courage and her will to be done with the intolerable burden within her?

But the more she tried to reason herself out of it, the more insistent grew her fear. There was a buzzing in her ears, preventing her from hearing what Bulut was saying, and a mist before her eyes, blurring the outlines of the shelves of books and of pots and bottles of every size and shape which alternated with the panels of stamped leather on the walls. She gripped her icy hands together as hard as she could to fight off the nausea that was creeping over her and at the same time, paradoxically, a wild urge to run away . . .

A firm, warm hand slipped something between her cold fingers and she sensed that it was a glass.

'You are sick,' said a voice, and the deep, musical tone of it surprised her, 'but more than that, you are afraid. Drink and you will feel better. It is sage wine . . .'

Marianne put the cordial to her lips. It was sweet, strong and mild at once. She took a few cautious sips and then emptied the glass and handed it back with a grateful smile. Her surroundings had become clear again but so too, unfortunately, had Bulut's voice as she chattered on incessantly with expressions of sympathy and compassion for the French princess's obviously exhausted nerves.

Rebecca stood beside her, studying Marianne. Suddenly, she smiled.

'The noble lady is right. You had better rest for a while before I make my first examination. Lie back on those cushions and relax. We will go into the next room for a moment while we decide what is to be done. Meanwhile, try and tell yourself that no one here wishes you harm, quite the reverse. You have only friends here — more friends than you know. Trust us, and rest.'

Rebecca's voice had a strangely persuasive power and Marianne, soothed as by a miracle, did not even try to resist. She stretched herself out, meekly, on the silken cushions, from which came a scent of ambergris, and let comfort steal over her. Her body no longer felt heavy and her fears of a moment ago had fled so far away that she could hardly believe they had been real. She watched Bulut Hanum's green ferej and the Jewess's gleaming head-dress melt into the shadows at the far end of the room and spared the Sultana a grateful thought for sending her to Rebecca . . .

Before going out, Rebecca had opened the three small windows which lighted the big room during the day – no doubt just as feebly as the bronze lamp was doing now. But they let in the scents of the garden and Marianne breathed them in with deep delight. They spoke to her of the earth, of life and all the quiet happiness that she had been seeking for and never found. Could it be that this frightful house was after all the harbour and refuge where all her troubles would melt away and the chains fall from her at last? When she left it again she would be free, freer than she had ever been, relieved of all her fears and the threats hanging over her.

In place of the hanging lamp, extinguished by Rebecca so that her patient could rest more easily, a small oil lamp had been set on a low table at the foot of the divan. Marianne found herself fascinated by its tiny flame and the night-flying insects that were already being attracted to it. She looked kindly at the brave little flame, fighting gallantly against the surrounding darkness and driving it back.

The scents of the garden, the darkness and the slim, bright flame moving above the brass bowl of the lamp came together in Marianne's mind to form a symbolic portrait of her own life. But the flame, especially, seemed to her the embodiment of her own tenacious love and it held her eyes while the rest of her body melted formlessly into the insidious softness of the cushions. It was a long time, months even, since she had felt as comfortable.

Then, little by little, the wonderful feeling of well-being became a great languor. The eyes that watched the lamp closed very slowly – and then, just as she was on the point of sinking into sleep, Marianne saw a white shadow detach itself gradually from the darkness filling the greater part of the room.

It was like a ghost, draped in snowy white, or veiled in smoke, which grew and grew until it filled all her vision – something huge and terrifying.

Marianne tried to cry out. Her mouth opened but no sound came. It was as though she were already in the grip of a nightmare. She fought desperately to keep her eyelids open against the weight that was on them. And still the phantom went on growing. It was bending over her . . . She made a frantic effort to escape from the power of the drug that paralyzed her and to tear herself from her couch, but the deep cushions held her as if she had been welded to them. Then, softly, the shadow began to speak.

'Don't be afraid,' it said. 'I mean you no harm. Far from it. I am your friend and you have nothing to fear from me.'

The voice was low and toneless and infinitely sad yet, even through the mists that enveloped her, Marianne seemed to remember, through some tenacious thread of memory in her brain, another voice, very like it, heard once from behind a tarnished mirror, the voice of a man without a face, a shadow like this. Could it be the same? Could the ghost of the husband who had died in his tragic loneliness have followed her here, to the very edge of Asia?

Then the power of thought, like that of movement, deserted her. Marianne's eyes closed and she sank into a curious, almost trance-like sleep which left her not wholly unconscious of her surroundings. Voices were speaking hurriedly nearby in some foreign tongue and she thought she recognized Bulut Hanum's high-pitched tones, sounding very much alarmed, and the Jewess's lower ones, alternating with the deep voice of the phantom. Then she felt arms round her, lifting her strongly and surely, without even a jolt. There was a pleasant smell in her nostrils, of the Turkish tobacco called lattakia mingled, unexpectedly, with the fresher smell of lavender, and her cheek was pressed against some fine, soft, woollen material. Half-consciously, Marianne understood that she was being carried away . . . Once again, there was the fragrance of the garden, the cool night about her, and then a slight dipping motion as the arms which held her set her down on some kind of mattress. By the sort of violent effort of will that a sleeper will make in an unconscious effort to escape from the grip of a nightmare, she managed to open the dragging curtain of her eyelids and saw a man holding a long pole that might have been an oar silhouetted against a starry sky. But then the dark mouth of a tunnel loomed up ahead, with the points of a raised grille hanging down like monstrous teeth, and the smell of the willow trees gave way to a stench of mud and refuse. A bird trilled briefly from a tree nearby but the faint, mocking sound was lost at once, smothered by the sheer weight of the walls that now imprisoned the Nightingale River on whose bosom Marianne was being borne away, a captive like itself. The stream was no longer free to run beneath the open sky, since men had decreed it so, the stream . . .

In the thick blackness enveloping her on all sides, Marianne gave up the struggle at last and let herself slide down into the abyss of sleep.

She awoke from it as suddenly as a cork popping out of a bottle to find herself in a strange room filled with sunshine. It was a magnificent bedchamber done out in flowered silks in tones of blue and mauve and but for the flood of sunlight, which took away any suggestion of the mysterious, might easily have been mistaken for a chapel, from the collection of gold and silver icons covering the whole of one wall.

Candles, a petrified forest of them, were burning before the holy images, their flames swamped by the brightness of the room, and standing in their midst, engaged in replacing the burned-out stumps with fresh, was a figure dressed in black.

Marianne took it for a priest at first but then she saw by the long hair coiled beautifully under a lace veil that the figure was a woman, and a remarkably impressive one.

This was due less to her height, although she was tall and slim and very upright, despite the years that showed in her grey hair and lined face, than to the erectness of her carriage and the strong, autocratic features which, for all the determined chin, were entirely hellenic in form.

When the last candle had been renewed and the old stumps put away in a leather bag, the unknown woman took up the gold-headed cane which had been propped against one of the candlesticks, crossed herself rapidly in the orthodox fashion, from left to right, and then, turning her back on the shining icons, came towards the bed, her gait making light of what was evidently a pronounced limp. A yard or two away from it, she stopped and, leaning both hands on her cane, studied Marianne gravely.

'In what language would you like to converse?' she asked in a lilting but otherwise faultless Italian.

'This one will suit me very well,' Marianne replied, in her best Tuscan, 'that is unless you would prefer to speak in French, English, German or Spanish?'

If she had been hoping to impress the other woman with her accomplishments she was quickly set down. The stranger only chuckled.

'Not bad,' she conceded, in French this time. 'I speak all those, and six or seven others also, including Russian, Walachian, Serbo-Croat, Chinese and Turanian.'

'I congratulate you,' Marianne retorted. Not for anything in the world would she have shown that she was impressed. 'But now that is settled, would you think me very stupid, Madame, if I asked you who you are and where I am?'

The old lady came closer so that Marianne could smell the scents of incense and ambergris, and gave another of her sardonic chuckles.

'You are in my house,' she said. 'In my house in Phanar.[1] And I am Princess Morousi, widow of the late Hospodar[2] of Walachia. I am happy to welcome you as my guest.'

'Thank you. It is very kind of you to make me welcome, Princess, but I should like to know how I come to be here at all. Last night, I went with a Turkish lady, a friend of the Sultan Valideh, to —'

'I know,' the Princess interrupted her. 'But I know also that there are places to which no woman has the right to go without her

---

[1] The Greek quarter of Constantinople.
[2] Governor.

husband's permission. You are here, therefore, because he brought you here.'

'My husband? But there must be some mistake! My husband is dead. I am a widow!'

The old Princess gave a compassionate sigh and struck the ground with her stick to give emphasis to her words.

'I think, my dear, that the mistake is yours. Unless you are not the Princess Sant'Anna, wife of Prince Corrado?'

'That is who I am, but —'

'Then we are not at cross purposes and I tell you again that it was Corrado Sant'Anna himself brought you here, to this house, last night.'

'But that's impossible!' Marianne cried, on the verge of tears. 'Unless —'

A dreadful thought had crossed her mind, but so fantastically improbable had been the whole course of her life since the burning down of Selton Hall that not even this could surprise her very much. If she had really come to this strange place in her dead husband's company, then it must be that she herself had died and this unaccustomed room and this woman with her ability to speak every known language must both exist in the next world. The Jewess, Rebecca, had simply poisoned her and she had gone to sleep on earth never to wake again except in this rather luxurious kind of purgatory, watched over by a distinctly unconventional angel. But then how could anyone know what the life after death was going to be like?

In her bewilderment, she was half expecting the door to open and admit a patriarch or some other long-dead person, or perhaps even her own father or mother, when her companion went over to the icons and fetched a candle which she brought to Marianne.

'Feel the flame,' she told her. 'When it burns you, you will know that you are just as much alive as I am. Nor, unless I'm much mistaken, are you in the least ill. I trust that you slept well?'

'Yes, thank you,' Marianne acknowledged, putting her finger unhesitatingly into the flame and withdrawing it at once. 'Indeed, I feel better than I have for a long time. But I still can't understand what you mean by saying my husband is alive — and here, in this house. Does that mean that you know him — that you have *seen* him?'

'When he has never permitted you to do so?' the Princess agreed tranquilly. 'That is quite true.' She drew a chair, a curious, X-shaped

47

thing with a goatskin seat, up to the bed and continued: 'My child –
my age allows me to call you so, for you are not really very old, you
know. It is natural for you to be full of questions regarding your
peculiar situation. I think I may be able to answer some of them, but
not all. I have known the Sant'Anna family for a long time, you
see. Don Sebastiano, your husband's grandfather, was a frequent
guest of my parents when I was a child. He was a great friend of
ours and that friendship has been passed on to his descendants.
After the tragedy which struck his family, young Corrado spent
much time away from Italy, where he could not live a normal life,
and naturally found his way back to us, sure of finding a welcome
and understanding in his dreadful plight.'

Curiosity, abruptly reawakened, drove out every other feeling in
Marianne, including all the fears she had experienced since waking.
Surely this woman held the key to the mystery surrounding her
invisible husband, and at the least she wanted to possess that key
herself. Unable to control herself any longer, Marianne broke in on
her hostess.

'So you know?'

'What do I know?'

'The reason why my husband shuts himself away like a hermit in
his ancestral home? The reason why I know him only as a voice in a
mirror, a hand in a white glove parting a black curtain, a horseman
in a white mask glimpsed from afar? The reason why he married
me, a stranger, already pregnant by another man, because that other
was the Emperor, instead of getting an heir of his own body?'

Princess Morousi inclined her head gravely.

'All these I know. In each case, the reason is the same.'

'Then, tell me! I want to know. I have a right to know.'

'That is so. But it is not for me to tell you, for you have asked me
the one question to which my conscience will not allow me to give
you an answer. All I can tell you is that, in spite of what that devil
Damiani told you, Corrado is not dead. I think that at the last
moment something stronger than himself stayed the wretch's hand.
He missed his stroke and Corrado was only wounded. Then he
dared not strike again but chained him in a dungeon, deep under
the old Soranzo Palace in Venice, expecting him to die there. But
the prince did not die. He recovered from his wound and
escaped —'

Suddenly, Marianne saw again the wide hall of the Venetian
palazzo in which she, too, had been imprisoned. She saw the black

servants lying dead and Damiani's huge body sprawled across the marble staircase, still clad in its golden robe, with the blood oozing slowly and a pair of iron fetters and a length of chain upon its breast. she had pushed all these mysteries to the back of her mind, because of the hideous memories with which they were bound up, but now they rushed out again in a new light.

'So it was he —' she said slowly, as though still trying to grasp what she was saying. 'So it was he who killed Damiani and his slaves that terrible night in Venice?'

'It was he. But it was not done for revenge, but simply out of the most elementary justice. He held Damiani's life forfeit for all the crimes that he had planned and executed. It was both his right and his duty.'

'I am not the one to deny it. But then, why did he run away? Why not come to me and tell me the whole? I, too, was a prisoner in that palace. He must have told you that?'

'He did,' the Princess agreed.

'Instead of which he opened my prison door and then vanished without waiting to wake me even! Yet he was in his own house and no one could touch him. We could have got rid of the bodies and waited for the officers together – oh, I don't know . . . He set me free and then by his very flight put me in danger. I could have been arrested.'

'No, because you, too, were in your own house. As for him, he was obliged to remain in hiding since he could no more show his face in Venice than in Lucca. Had he done so, no one would have believed him. The military governor's men would have taken him for an impostor and he would have been taken up and put to death for sure. Believe me, he could not have stayed.'

Here again was the same tiresome riddle that Marianne came up against every time. She wondered if she would ever meet anyone who would be prepared to treat her as a grown-up person, a woman in her own right, and reveal to her a secret which was already shared by a good many other people. True that most of those were dead . . .

Still trying instinctively to penetrate the heart of the mystery, Marianne said casually: 'How is it, then, that he cannot appear in public as the Prince Sant'Anna in Italy and yet is able to do so here?'

'What makes you think he uses his real name here? Matters are scarcely less difficult here than they are in Tuscany. Only I and my younger brother John Karaja, who is Dragoman[1] to the Porte, know the real identity of him who calls himself Turhan Bey.'

'Turhan Bey?' Marianne said, stunned. 'Do you mean to say that the Prince Sant'Anna has turned *Muslim*!'

At that the old lady laughed heartily. Her laughter was frank and full-throated and its character so very individual that Marianne might have imagined herself in a dovecot full of cooing doves.

'By no means!' the Princess cried at last, her laughter subsiding into a fit of cavernous coughing. 'If that were so your marriage would be invalid and I cannot see a prince of the Church lending himself to such a cruel jest. It was your godfather who arranged your marriage, was it not?'

'Yes,' Marianne said, grasping at a new hope. 'Do you know him as well?'

'No, but I know of him. To return to Turhan Bey: he owes his position here to the gratitude of Sultan Mahmoud for having saved his royal life from the attack of a pair of snakes while hunting in Cappadocia. His Highness honours with his friendship a man whose real name he does not know, whom he believes to be a rich foreign merchant attracted by the beauty of his imperial city and the life that men lead here.'

Marianne bit back a sigh of disappointment. Obviously, it was impossible to persuade the old lady to divulge what she evidently regarded as another person's secret. And yet the more that she discovered about the strange man she had married, the more she wanted to know.

'Madame,' she said at last, 'I must beg you to say no more – or else to tell me everything. I can't bear to be obsessed by so many questions which no one will ever answer for me.'

Princess Morousi placed both hands on the knob of her stick and got to her feet with a visible effort. At the same time she favoured the younger woman with an utterly unexpected smile: unexpected because it was so wholly young and mischievous.

'No one? Not a bit of it! Someone is coming in a moment who will answer all your questions. And I mean all – every single one!'

'Someone? But who?'

'Why, your husband! What happened last night has forced him out of his silence at last. Besides, he wants to enlighten you a little and do away with some of the misapprehensions under which you have been labouring.'

[1] Court Interpreter.

Marianne felt as if she had received an electric shock. She sat bolt upright in her unfamiliar bed and made as if to throw back the covers, which were, in any case, very much too hot.

'He is here?' she asked, lowering her voice instinctively.

'No. But he will be coming very soon, in an hour I expect. You will have time to prepare yourself to meet him. I will send a woman to you.'

The old princess turned towards the door, walking with a step that was slow, almost pathetic, so earnestly did she strive to overcome her lameness. She grasped the long bell pull of lilac silk which hung there and rang twice. She was already in the doorway when she swung round suddenly and Marianne, who was already half out of bed, stopped short, startled by the pain and grief imprinted on that face which, lined as it was, had not lost all its beauty.

'There is one more thing I should like to say.' The old woman spoke in a hesitant tone which clearly did not come easily to her.

'Of course. What is it?'

'When you meet Corrado face to face, it will be something of a shock. You may feel some horror or revulsion. Oh, don't be afraid,' she added quickly, seeing her involuntary guest's green eyes widen. 'He is not a monster. But I do not know you well enough, indeed, I do not know you at all, and so I cannot tell how you may react to the sight of his face. I would beg you only to remember that he is first and foremost a victim, who has suffered long and deeply – and that you have the dangerous power to hurt him much more in the space of a few minutes than life, with its cruel ironies, has done already. Remember also that the outward form which you will see, although unusual for an Italian prince, conceals a heart which is noble and deeply generous and as free from all meanness as it is from malice. Remember, finally, that he gave you his name at a time when others might have scorned to do so.'

'Madame!' protested Marianne, stung by this last reminder and the tone in which it was uttered. 'Do you think it is wise to insult me when you seem to be anxious, above all, that I should do nothing to upset the prince?'

'I am not insulting you. The truth is never an insult and there are times when it should be spoken in full, even though it may not be pleasant to hear. Don't you agree? I should be disappointed if you did not.'

'Yes, I do,' Marianne said, unpleasantly conscious of having lost once more. 'But, please, won't you answer one more question, only one, and which concerns no one but yourself?'

'What is it?'

'You love the Prince Sant'Anna very much, don't you?'

The old woman stiffened and her free hand went to the great golden cross which she wore on her breast, as though to bear witness to the truth of her words.

'Yes,' she said. 'I love him very much. I love him — as I might have loved the son I never had. That is why I do not want you to hurt him.'

She went out quickly, shutting the door sharply behind her.

CHAPTER THREE

Turhan Bey

An hour later, Marianne was pacing up and down a vast room on the ground floor with a roof like a cathedral and big, arched windows opening on to a garden planted with cypress trees and huge banks of roses whose dying flowers made a brave pretence of spring.

Dominating this austere apartment and the stiff, throne-like ebony chairs with which it was furnished, was a huge portrait of a splendidly moustachioed gentleman in a frogged hussar's jacket and a shako with an enormous plume like a firework display, with a jewelled dagger stuck in his silken sash. This was the late Hospodar Morousi, the Princess's husband. But Marianne, entering, barely glanced at him. The room seemed much too large for a private interview and she felt nervous and ill at ease.

The prospect of this meeting, coming so suddenly and unexpectedly after she had looked forward to it for so long and then put it out of her mind as a thing impossible, had left her thoughts in a turmoil.

From the day of their marriage, she had regarded Corrado Sant'Anna as an enigma, half-irritating, half to be pitied. It had wounded her that he would not trust her enough to show her his face. At the same time, she had longed with all her generous heart to help him, to bring some comfort into what she guessed was a cruel lot, endured by a man of outstanding nobility and generosity of spirit, one who gave so much and asked so little.

She had been genuinely distressed to learn, as she thought, of his tragic death at the hands of a murderer in whom he had trusted too much. She had wanted to see the guilty man punished and when Matteo Damiani had boasted of his crime before her face she had felt herself Princess Sant'Anna indeed and as much his wife as if they had lived together for many years.

And now, suddenly, here she was faced with one fantastic piece of news after another: the mysterious prince was not dead, he was coming to her here, and she was going to see, perhaps even to touch him, here, within the four walls of this very room which, suddenly, for all its size, seemed to her too small for such an event. The phantom horseman, the rider of Ilderim the Magnificent, the man who went out only at night and in a mask of white leather was coming here . . . It was almost unbelievable.

Would he still be wearing the mask that she had glimpsed on one eventful night? Marianne wished that she had thought to ask her hostess. But it was too late now. Princess Morousi had vanished.

A little while before, when Marianne had dressed herself with the help of a skilful abigail, a servant with a flowing beard had come to her with a request that she would go downstairs. She had expected to see her hostess again but the manservant had shown her into the drawing room and then retired, closing the door behind him. Marianne had realized that she must face what might well prove to be the most momentous encounter of her life alone.

The sleep which had begun in the house of Rebecca the Jewess must have lasted for a long time because the sun, which she had taken for morning when she woke, was setting now behind the long, black spindles of the cypress trees. Its light reddened the stone walls of the ancient building whose foundations must have gone back to the ill-judged crusade of the blind Doge, Henrico Dandolo, and set the tiny motes of dust dancing before the gloved hands of the late Hospodar.

The sounds from the garden were growing muted, while those of the great city scarcely penetrated the walls of this ancient palace. In a little while they would cease altogether, as the voices of the muezzins called the faithful to their evening prayers.

Marianne gripped her hands together and gnawed her lip. Her nerves were at full stretch. Her visitor, more feared than longed-for, was late. She had paused in front of the portrait and was regarding it with unconscious severity and then, before she could resume her fevered pacing, the door opened again to admit the bearded servant who stood aside, bowing deeply, as a tall, white figure appeared in the doorway. Marianne's heart missed a beat.

Her eyes widened and her lips parted soundlessly as the newcomer stepped into the sunlight and bowed in his turn, without speaking. But even while she was stunned into silence, Marianne knew that she was not dreaming. She was looking, between the pale caftan and white muslin turban, straight into the dark face and bright blue eyes of Caleb!

Time seemed to stand still. The silence stretched out between these two united by the bonds of matrimony and yet divided by so much else. Conscious of the rudeness of her stare, Marianne pulled herself together, with an odd sense of relief overwhelming her.

Despite everything her godfather and Dona Lavinia had said to her, she had been expecting the worst. Prepared for a being so hideously deformed that she could scarcely bear to look at him, she found that the reality, however strange, was anything but frightening. Recalling her first meeting with Caleb, on the deck of the *Sea Witch*, Marianne was again struck almost with pleasure at the sight of that strong and splendid face. By whatever name, this man was beyond doubt the handsomest she had ever set eyes on.

On the other hand, the fact of his being who he was raised a whole new set of problems just as difficult as the last and chief of them; what was Prince Sant'Anna, not to mention Turhan Bey, doing in the forecastle of Jason's ship, masquerading as an Ethiopian slave? Moreover, now that she saw him again, she realized that she had always wondered a little about that claim to be Ethiopian, for although the man called Caleb was certainly dark-skinned, he was nothing like as dark as the deep black common to the inhabitants of that country.

Seeing that she was too busy gazing at him to speak first, Corrado Sant'Anna nerved himself to break the silence. He did it very gently, speaking as softly as though he feared to shatter something precious, for the look on the young woman's face was not the one he had feared to see there. No, the great green eyes regarding him held neither fear nor revulsion but only an infinite astonishment.

'Do you understand now?' he asked.

Without taking her eyes from his, Marianne shook her head.

'No. Less than ever, I think. There is nothing repulsive about you – far from it. I'd say, even, that you – you are very handsome. But you must surely know that. So, why the mask? Why the seclusion? Why all this mystery?'

The bronze lips smiled bleakly, showing a flash of white teeth.

'I thought a woman of your quality would have understood the reasons. I carry the burden of a sin not my own, nor my mother's, either, although it cost her her life. You know, do you not, that my father strangled my mother at my birth, never dreaming for an instant that he and he alone had passed on the black blood which darkened my skin.'

'How can that be?'

'Do you know anything about the laws of heredity? I thought not. I made a study of them, when I was old enough to understand.

A learned Cantonese physician explained to me one day how it is that the offspring of a black person and a white may exhibit no negroid characteristics at all and yet may, in his turn, produce a black child. But how was my father to guess that his mother, the she-devil who brought disgrace to our family, had conceived him of her black slave, Hassan, and not by her husband, Prince Sebastiano? Obsessed by Lucinda and her satanic legend, he believed that my poor mother, too, was sunk in dishonour – and he killed her.'

'I know that dreadful story,' Marianne said quickly. 'Leonora Franchi – Mrs Crawfurd, I mean – told it to me. How cruel, and how stupid!'

The Prince shrugged. 'Any man might have done the same. Your own father, perhaps, if such a thing had happened to him. I have no right to blame mine – especially since he spared my life. Not that it has been much of a blessing to me. I'd rather he had let my mother live and done away with me – the blot on his escutcheon.'

There was so much bitterness in the deep, serious voice of the last of the Sant'Annas that Marianne felt strangely stirred. It occurred to her suddenly that there was something ridiculous in the two of them confronting one another like that, in the middle of the vast, empty room, and she pointed to a pair of cushioned stone seats set in one of the window embrasures, at the same time managing to smile.

'Wouldn't you rather sit down, Prince? We could talk more easily – and we have so much to say. It might take a long time.'

'You think so? I do not mean to inflict my presence on you for longer than necessary. Believe me when I say that if matters had stood otherwise I should never have dreamed of revealing myself to you. You thought me dead and it was probably better so, for you have suffered much through me, although I never willed it. God knows that when I married you I hoped with all my heart that you would find, if not happiness, at least tranquillity and peace of mind.'

This time, Marianne's smile was without constraint and as the Prince had not moved she took a step towards him.

'I know that,' she said quietly. 'But do, please, come and sit down! As you have just said – we are married.'

'Barely!'

'Do you believe that? God, who joined us together, counts for something. We might be friends, at least. Didn't you save my life, that night by the little ruined temple, when Matteo Damiani was going to kill me? Didn't you kill him in Venice and set me free?'

'Didn't you repay me by saving me from being flogged to death by John Leighton?' he retorted. But he abandoned his resistance and let her lead him to the window bay, which was still flooded with evening sunshine.

Now that she was closer to him, Marianne recognized the smell of lavender and lattakia that she remembered from the previous night and it was enough to recall the strange events of that night, pushed to the back of her mind by the surprise she had just had. Before she could stop herself, she had asked the question which sprang to her lips.

'It was you, wasn't it, who carried me off from Rebecca's house last night? Princess Morousi told me —'

'It's no secret. Yes, it was I.'

'Why?'

'That is one of the matters I was alluding to a moment ago, but for which you might have continued to believe me dead. In a word – the child.'

'The child!'

He smiled again, the same bleak smile that lent such charm to his almost too perfect features. Now that she was able to see him close to, and in full sunlight, Marianne was surprised to feel again exactly the same jolt of spontaneous admiration that she had felt seeing him on board the *Sea Witch*. A bronze god, she had thought then, a splendid animal. But the god had feet of clay and the wild animal was wounded.

'Have you forgotten the reason for our marriage? When my old friend Gauthier de Chazay spoke to me of his god-daughter, she was with child by Napoleon. In making her my wife I was gaining an heir worthy to continue our ancient line, the child I had ceased to hope for and had always refused to beget for fear of handing on the curse that lay on us. That child you lost, as a result of the fire at the Austrian Embassy, a little over a year ago. But now you are carrying another.'

Marianne's face flushed and she sprang up as if she had been stung. She saw it all now, she saw a great deal too much, things it frightened her to see.

'You don't mean that you want —'

'Yes. I want you to keep this child. I have had a watch kept on the Jewess's house from the moment I arrived here. There is no one

57

else you could have gone to for a service of that kind without grave risk to your life. And I was not going to have it. You see, as soon as I realized that you were going to have a child again, I saw fresh hope —'

Marianne stiffened angrily. 'Hope? You can call it that? But surely you know – when you seem to know so much – who fathered it?'

Prince Sant'Anna merely bowed his head in answer but showed no other hint of emotion. In the face of that impassive countenance, Marianne's anger blazed up uncontrollably.

'You know!' she cried. 'You know that that – that lackey Damiani raped me, that he forced himself on me – on me, your wife – again and again, week after week until I thought I should go mad, and you dare to tell me that my ordeal gave you hope? Don't you see that it's the outside of enough?'

'No,' came the cold retort. 'I don't. Damiani has paid for what he did to you. For what he did to you, I killed him and I killed his three witches also —'

'For what he did to me or for what he did to *you*? Was it my shame you were avenging, or the death of poor Dona Lavinia?'

'For you and you alone, and that you may believe since, for my part, I am still very much alive and so, for that matter, is dear old Lavinia. She had the good sense to feign death when Damiani attacked her and he thought, in good faith, that he had killed her. But she is still alive and so far as I know is at this moment governing our house at Lucca. But to return to Matteo. It is still a fact that, criminal wretch though he was, he comes of the same blood as I myself. A bastard, maybe, but far more of a Sant'Anna than Napoleon's son could ever have been.'

Marianne's anger had given way for a moment at the good news that Dona Lavinia was still alive but it flared up again at the injury contained in this last remark.

'Well I loathe even the memory of the man!' she cried. 'And it sickens me, this thing inside me that I will not even call a child! I do not want it, do you hear? I won't have it! Not for anything in the world!'

'Be sensible! Whether you like it or not, this *thing*, as you call it, is still a human being, already there, at this moment, and it is your own flesh and blood that is going to the making of him. He is part of you, made of the same substance —'

'No! No!' Marianne was protesting like a child arguing in the

58

face of all the evidence. 'It's not possible! It can't be! I won't have it —'

'Come now. You know that isn't true. You wouldn't be fighting it so desperately if your heart were not engaged, if – if Jason Beaufort had never entered your life. It's because of him, and him alone, that you want to be rid of this child.'

It was not said as a reproach, simply as a quiet statement of fact, but in the eyes that were fixed on hers Marianne could read such sadness and resignation that, on the point of proclaiming aloud the power of her love and her right to live it, she remembered just in time that Jason had once condemned this man, whose name she bore, to die under the lash. A little ashamed, she let her eyes fall.

'How did you know?'

He made a vague movement with one hand and shrugged again.

'I know a great many things about you. From your godfather, firstly, for whom I have a great love for he is kindness and understanding itself. And surely it was natural for me to feel some interest in your life? No,' he added quickly, seeing her movement of protest, 'I have not had you spied on – or not directly, at all events. To have done so would have been to demean us both. But someone else did, against my orders and, indeed, without telling me the whole. But most of my information comes from the Emperor himself.'

'The Emperor!'

'Why, yes. Considering the circumstances of our marriage, it was common courtesy for me to inform him of it personally and to give him certain assurances concerning you, since I was to give my name to his son. I wrote to him and he wrote back – more than once.'

There was a pause while Marianne thought over what she had just heard. It was not hard to guess who it was who had set spies on her. Matteo Damiani, of course. But that there had been correspondence between Napoleon and the Prince came as something of a surprise to her, although when the Emperor had told her, after François Vidocq had brought her back from Normandy, that he wished her to return to her husband, he had mentioned a letter from Sant'Anna. She was not sure whether to interpret this as a sign of affection or of distrust and decided it was best to probe no further for the moment. There were too many other points on which she desired enlightenment.

Corrado, respecting her silence, had been looking out at the gathering darkness of the garden. The sun had sunk behind the

59

trees, outlining them dramatically against long streaks of purple and gold. A faint chill was creeping into the room and the air was vibrant with the muezzins' high-pitched calls.

Marianne hitched up the green silk shawl which had slipped from her shoulders.

'And was it the Emperor who told you that Jason Beaufort would be in Venice?' she asked at last, with a little hesitation.

'No. By that time I was in no position to discover anything at all. I learned of the trap which had been laid for you – and of what followed, from Matteo himself. In the end, I think, his ambition had driven him mad. I was chained and helpless and he had great satisfaction in describing it all to me. Thinking about it later, it seemed to me that it was for the pleasure of that he kept me alive.'

'Then how did you come to be aboard the *Sea Witch*?'

Again, that faint, bleak smile.

'That was pure luck. When first I managed to escape my one idea was to see justice done and set you free without your seeing me. Damiani had told me that you thought I was dead and at that time I saw no reason why you should ever learn otherwise.'

'But he had told you he wanted me to give him the Sant'Anna heir he needed?'

'Yes, but I could see that he was sick, drugged, practically insane. I did not think that he could do it. So I struck and fled, to escape any awkward questions on the part of the authorities. I wanted to get to Lucca, the only place where I could show myself with any safety. I'd found money in Matteo's room – enough to pay a boatman to take me to Chiogga. And it was there that luck took a hand. I caught sight of the American brig – and the figure on the prow. I'd known for long enough whose ship she was but your face on that figurehead told me I was not mistaken and I wanted to find out if she had come for you. I think you know the rest . . . And I want to ask your pardon.'

'My pardon? What have I to forgive?'

'For yielding to the impulse which took me aboard that vessel. I had sworn that I would never stand in your way but that day I could not help myself. I had to see this Beaufort, know what kind of man he was. It was something stronger than myself . . .'

For the first time since he had come into the room, Marianne really smiled. The surge of indignation which had taken possession of her a moment ago was still quivering inside, but she could not help feeling a sudden liking for this strange, unhappy man.

'Don't be sorry. But for you, I don't know what would have become of us on that hellish voyage – and by now my old friend Jolival would be a slave or worse! As for Captain Beaufort – it was not within your power to save him from – from disaster!' Her voice broke and she said no more, knowing that she could not trust herself not to break down. The mere mention of Jason's name was enough to overset her, even though she knew that it was out of place here and that, for all the unusual nature of the contract between them, it could not be pleasant for Prince Sant'Anna to be obliged to discuss his wife's lover.

In fact he had risen with some abruptness and was pacing the room with his back to her. As before, on the deck of the *Sea Witch*, Marianne was struck by his lithe, easy bearing and by the impression of controlled strength about him, but she was discovering that even with his face uncovered, even without the leather mask whose whiteness, now, was self-explanatory, this man remained an enigma, not easily to be understood.

She was too much a woman not to wonder how he felt towards her. The shattering announcement he had just made, the fact that he could say in so many words that he wanted her to have the child conceived under such appalling circumstances, was almost insulting. It suggested that the Prince cared nothing for her feelings and that, to use a favourite expression of Napoleon's, she was in his eyes nothing more nor less than a *womb*!

And yet, when he could have gone quietly back to his Tuscan estates after killing Damiani, he had deliberately chosen a perilous adventure in order to go after a wife who, when all was said and done, had not been much good to him. What was it he had said? 'I could not help myself . . . It was stronger than I was . . .' Or was his real interest in Jason? Curiosity, after all, was not an exclusively female prerogative. Perhaps it was only natural that he should want to meet the man his wife loved. But it was a very great risk to take for such a meagre satisfaction because, in going aboard the *Witch*, Corrado Sant'Anna had been cutting himself off from all his usual roots. All he would have found at the end of the voyage as originally planned was the vast, unknown American continent, lying on the other side of the ocean – and the lifetime of slavery to which he would almost certainly have been condemned by the colour of his skin.

Unable to find an answer to any of these questions, Marianne gazed helplessly at the tall, white figure. Their conversation had reached such an extremely difficult stage that she was at a loss how to go on. But it was the Prince who broke the silence.

Standing before the portrait of the Hospodar which he was studying with remarkable concentration, he said, without turning round : 'Man has a very great need to perpetuate himself. That one up there tried all his life to do it but without success. I am an aberration in my family tree which will pass and be forgotten, but only if there is an heir – one who is normal and free from the taint I bear – to come after me. You are my one chance of that. Will you give me my heir?'

Marianne knew that the moment she dreaded had arrived and she screwed up her courage for the battle ahead. When she spoke, her voice was gentle but firm.

'No,' she said. 'I can't. Nor have you any right to ask it of me, knowing my horror of this child.'

Still, he did not look at her but he said : 'That evening, in the chapel of our house, you swore to honour – and obey.'

There was no mistaking his meaning and Marianne shuddered, overcome by a bitter sense of shame because this unexpected husband of hers, whom she had thought to keep quite apart from her private life, had known, better than anyone, in what light she had regarded her marriage vows. What had seemed to her then a mere formality had become all too serious now.

'It is in your power to compel me,' she said in a low voice. 'You have already done so, indeed, by bringing me here. But you will never obtain my consent willingly.'

He came towards her slowly and Marianne stepped back instinctively. There was no trace of sadness, now, in that dark, handsome face, nor yet of gentleness. The blue eyes were chips of ice and where she had expected to see disappointment she read only cold contempt.

'Then you will be taken back to the house of the Jewess tonight,' he said, 'and by this time tomorrow nothing will remain of the thing that so disgusts you. For myself, it only remains for me to bid you goodbye, Madame.'

'Goodbye! When we have only just met?'

He bowed curtly. 'This is where we part. You had better forget that you have ever seen my face. I can trust you to keep my secret, I hope. You may inform me of what you have decided through Princess Morousi when you see fit to do so.'

'But I haven't decided anything! This is all so sudden, so —'

'You cannot live openly with another man and yet continue to bear my name. These new laws of Napoleon's will make it possible for you to obtain a divorce as you could not have done before. Make use of them. My men of business will see to it that you have no cause for complaint. After that, you will be able to carry out your original intention, before your plans were so rudely interrupted at Venice, and follow Beaufort to America. I will take it upon myself to inform the Emperor, and your godfather when I see him.'

Stung by his contemptuous tone, Marianne gave a little shrug.

'Follow Jason?' she said bitterly. 'You may well say that, when you know it is impossible! We don't know where he is, or even if he is still alive . . .'

It was these words which finally succeeded in shattering the Prince's iron control. Abruptly, his anger exploded.

'And that's the only thing you care for in the whole wide world, isn't it?' he snarled. 'That slave trader behaved to you like a swine, he's treated you like a wench out of the gutter — Have you forgotten that he would have given you to the lowest man on board his ship? To the runaway slave he picked up off the dock at Chioggia, whom his friend Leighton thought to sell at a good profit at the first opportunity? And still you want to lick his boots and crawl after him on your belly like a bitch in heat! Well, you will find him, never fear, and then you may go on destroying yourself for his pleasure.'

'How do you know?'

'I'm telling you he's alive! The fishermen of Monemvasia who found him, wounded and unconscious, when his precious Leighton cast him off, like unwanted baggage, when he could get no more use of him, have cared for him, and are doing so still. Moreover, gold has been given them, and their orders are clear. When the American is quite recovered, he will be handed a letter telling him that you are in Constantinople, and so, too, is his ship. For after all,' he added with a scornful laugh, 'we cannot be sure that your presence alone would be enough to bring him here! So you have only to wait and your hero will come to you. Farewell, Madame!'

He bowed briefly and before Marianne, stunned by his outburst, could make a single move, he was gone.

Marianne stood for a moment in the middle of the darkening room, as though turned to stone, listening to the angry footsteps dying away along the stone floor of the wide hall. She was a prey to the strangest feeling of loneliness and desolation. The brief meeting, a first encounter which looked very much as if it would also be the last, had left her oddly drained. She felt unhappy and miserably conscious of having in some way, by her own doing, stepped down from a pedestal.

Now that she knew what her extraordinary husband was really like, things had begun to assume very different proportions and she could no longer afford the same detachment and mental freedom in relation to everything concerning him which had been hers hitherto. Things were very different now and if the Prince's anger – of which she was very well aware – sprang largely from disappointment, that, in turn, might be less for the child denied him than for the woman who denied it.

At that moment, Marianne was so overwhelmed with shame and remorse that even the joy of knowing that Jason was still alive could not bring more than a glimmer of light.

By guarding the life of the man who had used him so cruelly, by having him tended and cared for and providing him with the means to be reunited with all that he loved best in the world, the pretended Caleb had given both of them, Marianne and Jason alike, a lesson in magnanimity it would have been hard to equal.

Feeling rather ashamed of the not very admirable part she had elected to play, in the belief that it was her right, Marianne wanted to run after the Prince and stop him but by the time she had managed to pull herself together the front door had slammed behind him. To chase him then would have done no good and only made her look ridiculous, so she went out into the garden instead, drawn by the coolness and the quiet. Hugging the shawl round her shoulders, she stepped out through the stone bay and began to stroll along a little blue mosaic path that wound its way between the rose trees and the beds of glowing dahlias which blossomed like colourful set pieces on either hand.

To go into the garden had always been a natural reaction with her, whenever she wanted time to think or to recover her temper. As a little girl at Selton, she would run and hide herself in the farthest corner of the park, where the shade of the great trees was densest, whenever she was suffering from one of the childish tragedies that seem so trivial to grown-up persons. In Paris, too, the little walled garden in the rue de Lille had often been the scene of solitary, anxious meditations as Marianne sought there, if not comfort or counsel, at least a brief respite from her troubles.

She plunged into this unfamiliar garden as though into a soothing bath but its solitude, as she very soon discovered, was by no means absolute, for she was approaching a seat, half-hidden in an arbour of clematis, when she saw the figure of a man rise to its feet. This time, the man wore European dress and she had no difficulty in recognizing her old friend Arcadius de Jolival. She came upon him so suddenly that she had no time to be alarmed, while her capacity for astonishment had been somewhat blunted by the revelations of the past two hours.

Consequently, she said nothing more than: 'Oh, are you here? How did you get here?'

'As fast as I could,' Jolival said crossly. 'We were at our wits' end at the embassy, having had no word of you since last evening. So when a message came to say that you were at the house of Princess Morousi and I was cordially invited to join you there, I lost no time about it, I can tell you, but packed a bag and came. As for our friend Latour-Maubourg, while he hasn't the smallest idea how you come to be staying in Phanar with the widow of the Hospodar of Wallachia when you set out to go to Scutari with the Sultana, he's so delighted to find you moving in circles so close to the Ottoman throne that he's lighting candles to every saint in the calendar remotely connected with diplomacy. He's going to be very disappointed to see you back again. He won't understand it in the least.'

'See me back again?'

'Good God! If you're going back to that angel-maker of yours tonight, you'll hardly be coming here afterwards to convalesce, will you?'

Marianne looked hard at her old friend, but he sustained her regard unflinchingly.

'You heard what passed – in there?' she demanded, indicating the room behind her. Jolival bowed.

'Every word. And don't ask me what miracle brought that about, because I'll only repeat that I heard. You see, I'm like your cousin Adelaide. I've never managed to believe that it's a cardinal sin to listen at keyholes. It seems to me a useful talent, first because it's easier than you'd think, and secondly because it helps to avoid a great many mistakes, as well as saving lengthy explanations which are always tiresome and often embarrassing. So you need not tell me what passed between you and Prince Sant'Anna, because I know.'

'So that you also know who he is?'

'As a matter of fact, I knew that before you did because it was the Prince himself who came to the embassy. I may say that he did so under the name of Turhan Bey but, in return for my word of honour, he consented to raise that white mask of his.'

'What did you think when you learned the truth? You must have been surprised at least to find that the slave Caleb was really Prince Sant'Anna?'

The Vicomte de Jolival twirled the thin, black moustache which, in conjunction with his large ears, gave him such a startling resemblance to a mouse, then shook his head and sighed.

'Well, not altogether,' he confessed. 'In fact, I don't think I was surprised at all really. There was too much about Caleb that did not fit, so many peculiarities to suggest that the character of the runaway slave was a cover for someone a great deal more distinguished than we guessed. I believe I even said something of the sort to you at the time. Of course, it never occurred to me to identify him with the mystery man you had been married to, but the fact explained a good deal. So much so, that when I met him face to face it was like finding a satisfying answer to an irritating riddle.' He gave her a little smile. 'And now,' he added, 'I'd like to hear your own impressions. What were your feelings, Marianne, when you saw your dark-skinned husband?'

'Honestly, Arcadius, I don't know. It was a surprise, of course, but, all in all, not such a horrid surprise as I'd feared. Indeed, I confess that I don't really understand his behaviour, all this mystery he surrounds himself with —'

'I know, I said so to him. You don't understand because you are a woman, and because, in spite of the colour of his skin, or maybe even because of it, he is an exceptionally handsome fellow. His Negro blood has brought a new vitality, I might almost say a new virility, into a line which, if not actually decadent, had undoubtedly reached such a stage of inbreeding as to be verging on it. But you may believe me when I tell you there is not a gentleman in the world, not a man at all, indeed, who could fail to understand him, or to understand the terrible way his father reacted on being presented with a black baby. I suggest you try asking our friend Beaufort the same question —'

'Jason comes from a country where they treat black people as slaves and use them as beasts of burden —'

'Not everywhere. You must not generalize. Nor, as far as I

66

know, have the Beauforts ever been known as slave drivers. But I'll agree that his upbringing might prejudice his answer. But ask any man you meet – ask me, even.'

'You, Arcadius?'

'Yes, me! I've never liked my wife, but supposing I had taken it into my head to give her a child and she had made me a present of a coal black bundle – for I dare say the Prince was a few shades darker on arrival than he is now – why, upon my honour, I do believe I might have throttled Septimanie myself. And taken good care to hide the babe away.'

'A man may have a dark skin and still be a person of consequence. Othello was a Moor and he became a great man in Venice.'

That made Jolival laugh. He inserted two fingers in the pocket of his brocaded waistcoat and helped himself delicately to a pinch of snuff.

'The trouble with you, Marianne,' he said, 'is that you read too much Shakespeare, and too many novels, as a child. Othello, supposing that there ever was such a person, was a warrior of genius, and your truly great men can get away with almost anything. But do you think that if Napoleon had been born with a skin the colour of bronze, like that handsome husband of yours, that he would be on the throne of France today? Not a bit of it. And where the Prince is concerned, I think that the secluded life he chose, his hermit-like existence, was also a kind of tribute to his mother. It was for her and for her reputation that he imposed that penance on himself and cut himself off from love . . . I have the greatest respect for the man, Marianne, and for his most moving desire to see the continuation of his family, at the expense of his own justifiable aspirations, and even of his own normal emotional and physical needs.'

During the course of this speech, the Vicomte's voice had taken on a depth of seriousness which went straight to Marianne's heart.

'You think I'm wrong, don't you? You think I ought to have agreed to have this child?'

'It is not for me to think one way or the other, my dear. Nor have I the right to judge you. You are entirely your own mistress, as regards both your future and your person. You have bought that right dearly enough.'

She gazed at him intently but was unable to discover the least hint of blame or disappointment in that friendly face, and yet she sensed that, had he loved her less, her old friend might perhaps have judged her more severely.

67

'I can admit it to you, Jolival. I am ashamed of myself. He has never been anything but good to me. He risked everything for my sake, to protect me – and his care has even extended to Jason, whom he has no cause to love. I am sure it gives him no pleasure to know that that vile Damiani was the father of this child, and yet he longs for it as the greatest blessing heaven has to offer. That, too, I find hard to understand.'

'Hasn't it occurred to you that he could simply have wiped Damiani out of his mind and be thinking of this child simply as yours, Marianne?'

Marianne gave a tiny shrug.

'That would suggest he feels a great deal more strongly than I can believe possible. No, Jolival, the Prince sees this child simply as a Sant'Anna. On the wrong side of the blanket, maybe, but a Sant'Anna for all that.'

'What does it matter to you what Prince Corrado's feelings are, seeing that you will not do it. Because your answer is still the same ... isn't it, Marianne?'

Marianne did not answer. She moved a few steps away, as though trying to lose herself in the shadows of the darkened garden. She wanted to shut out every influence but those of her own, inner voices. The inward struggle was almost won, but she needed time to acknowledge it. She knew already that she was beaten but the thought brought no bitterness. It was almost a relief and mingled with it was a kind of joyful pride, for the thing that she was about to give was something that no one else could. Moreover, the joy it would give to that self-condemned recluse would be bound up with and somehow magnified by the revulsion she had overcome and by the physical ordeal that she was facing for him. It might even have some power to influence fate and constitute the first step to a happiness which was for ever out of reach as long as it was founded on another's pain.

A seabird's cry came from somewhere close by. A gull, surely, like the many that had swooped and dived so often in the *Sea Witch*'s wake. It brought with it the call of the open sea, of the wide open spaces beyond which the sun set on Europe and rose again on other lands unknown. She had to make herself worthy of all that ...

Marianne turned suddenly. By the stone seat, Jolival's black figure had not moved but was standing quite still, as though waiting

for something. She walked back slowly and, when she was close
beside him, she spoke, very softly.

'Jolival? I suppose you know where Prince Sant'Anna lives?'

He nodded and she saw his eyes gleam in the darkness.

'Will you send word to him that I agree? I will give him the
child he wants . . .'

69

Part II

SEBASTIANO

CHAPTER FOUR

Pitt's Niece

Towed by four caiques, each with its full complement of rowers whose colourful rags added a cheerful note to the cold, almost wintry morning, the *Sea Witch* moved out of the graving docks of Kassim Pasha, rounded the towers of the Arsenal and, crossing the Golden Horn, bore down majestically on the moorings reserved for her on the waterfront of Phanar.

The Turkish shipwrights, working under the direction of a dour Scots foreman, had done a good job and the vessel, with her gleaming brasswork and satin-smooth mahogany and her brand new sails neatly furled, shone like a new toy in the hazy brightness of the sun which floated like a flat, white disc behind light, swirling veils of mist. And Marianne, standing on the quay with Jolival beside her, watched with joy and pride the approach of Jason's ship made new.

The oarsmen knew their work and in a few more minutes would have covered the mile or so from Kassim Pasha to Phanar. The American brig, flying, by the Valideh's command, not her own colours but the arms of Sant'Anna, so as to forestall any possible international complications, would come to rest among the forest of spars along the quayside, slipping in between a pair of squat, round-bellied Greek polaccas whose nearness served to emphasize her slim, rakish lines, to wait there quietly until her rightful master should come discreetly to claim her.

Discretion was necessary since relations between England and the youthful States of America were worsening rapidly. The conflict which was to go down in history as the Second War of Independence was already in the air and Nakshidil, knowing the vigilance and energy of the British ambassador, Mr Canning, had no wish to see the vessel she had presented to her kinswoman made the subject of an embargo that could not well be denied.

The rather tricky piece of manoeuvring needed to bring the brig's side up against the quay was accomplished to a chorus of encouraging shouts. Marianne and her companion were surrounded by a small crowd of people drawn by the unusual spectacle of a western ship amongst the Greek and Turkish vessels for whom the Stamboul

73

waterfront was generally reserved, European shipping being confined to the moorings of Galata opposite.

It was a noisy, colourful crowd, made up of seamen and all the various street traders who daily thronged the waterside in the Greek quarter of the city: sellers of fruit and of little cakes dripping with honey, sellers of fried foods with their black cauldrons, sellers of raki and rosolio, the rose liqueur so popular with the natives, open-air sweet vendors and itinerant cooked meat vendors, mingling with the weirdly assorted population which haunted the harbour taverns by day and night. A fine smell of roast mutton and caramel floated on the morning air and once again Marianne was conscious that she was hungry.

It was almost two months since she had agreed to perform what she had come to think of as her duty to her husband. And ever since that day, as though heaven had only wanted that sign of goodwill from her to grant her that respite, the painful sickness which had troubled her from the start of her pregnancy had completely disappeared. Instead, she had begun to eat with an appetite which was causing her some alarm about the size of her waistline once the child was born.

'I can't get into any of my dresses,' she would wail practically every morning after she was dressed, and generally added in a tragic tone: 'I'm going to look like la Visconti!' For Marshal Berthier's stout mistress was famous for the peculiar collection of corsetry with which she endeavoured to contain the ebullience of her person.

Whereupon Jolival would assure her that she had never looked so well, that the cossetted life she led had given her a bloom like a camellia, which was true, and that, in any case, any man worthy of the name much preferred a cosy armful of plump flesh to the collection of bones which fashion all too often demanded.

'Besides,' he added, 'if we do set sail for America at last, you'll have several weeks of ship's diet to make you as thin as a starved cat if that's what you want.'

So Marianne smiled and sighed and, abandoning Monsieur Leroy's elegant creations, fell back on the local style of dress which was a great deal fuller and more comfortable for a mother-to-be.

At that moment, that cultivated nobleman the Vicomte was attentively following through his quizzing glass the evolutions of the ship under the command of Achmet Reis, Agathe's husband, from whom the Valideh had purchased her and who had consented to bring her round from the dockyard to her new moorings.

74

'The Turks are fine sailors,' he remarked. 'It's a pity they can't bring themselves out of the middle ages and start building modern ships which don't look as though they might have fought at Lepanto. God forgive me if that isn't a galley I see over there!'

'Don't be so critical, Jolival. It's not a hundred years since the French put their last galley out of commission. Besides, it's only a matter of time. The Sultan Mahmoud, if Allah preserves him, is determined to introduce reforms and to open his empire to progress. But he can do nothing until he has succeeded in mastering the Janissaries and silencing their wretched kettles once and for all. Both his Highness and his mother are waiting their chance and cultivating the virtue of patience meanwhile, but it is their first care —'

Since becoming a guest of the Princess Morousi, Marianne had paid several visits to her imperial kinswoman and a friendship was developing between the two women, as also with the exuberant and talkative Bulut Hanum, who was still mystified by the events at Rebecca's house but, as a devoted subject, had bowed to it unquestioningly since her mistress approved. All this meant useful information for Marianne which she passed on generously to the unfortunate Latour-Maubourg who was losing ground more and more, for naturally, and just as Marianne had expected, no reply had been forthcoming from the Emperor on the subject of his attitude to the continuance of the Russo-Turkish war.

The *Sea Witch* had come alongside and her wooden walls loomed over the quayside, like a sea hawk among chickens beside her dumpy neighbours. She was so clean and bright that Marianne's eyes filled with tears and she forgot her irritation.

It was a morning for hopeful thoughts. When Jason came back he would be so glad to find his beloved ship made new again that the clouds which had gathered between him and Marianne would melt away of their own accord. A few quiet explanations and everything would be all right again, the bad dream would fade away . . . The Prince would have the heir he longed for and she who had been for a brief while his wife, become once again, thanks to the Emperor's lawyers, Marianne d'Asselnat, would be free to make her life with the man she still loved as much as ever . . .

Of course there was still, somewhere in the world, someone who was legally Mrs Beaufort, but Marianne refused to think of her, or even to remember. Pilar had chosen Spain, the country of her ancestors, whose dark violence and stern piety she had inherited, and had probably buried herself and her ruthless passions in a convent somewhere. She was no longer a threat. But when would Jason come?

A few days earlier, when Turhan Bey had paid one of his courtesy visits to Princess Morousi, Marianne had summoned up courage to mention his coming, expressing a timid surprise that it should be so long delayed. Her heart had beat a little faster as she did so, for she was afraid of hurting the Prince, but he had not seemed unduly troubled by the question. He had looked at her with the inscrutable expression of his dark, invariably calm blue eyes which always made her feel slightly uneasy, and had answered gravely: 'It's not so surprising. He was gravely ill, for Leighton had left him for dead in the drifting boat where he was found. More-over, ever since Corfu he had kept him under the influence of a dangerous drug – we think it was ergot – which did not help. Even so, the personal physician of the Pasha of the Morea, who attended him, has assured me that he will live but hinted at a protracted convalescence. But you may be sure that he is well cared for.'

'The Pasha of the Morea's physician?' Marianne had asked. 'Then how is it that he is being cared for by fishermen?'

'Because it is infinitely better for him. Hassani Maji is a man of God and my friend, and as such he has been tending Captain Beaufort secretly. The American would not get out of Veli Pasha's hands without a substantial ransom. Remember that Veli and his father, the Pasha of Janina, and also of Egypt, Mehmet Ali, have been for some time asserting their independence of the Porte and behaving like independent rulers. Though the time may come when they may well be sorry for it. But, to return to Jason Beaufort, I don't expect his convalescence to be less than six months.'

Six months! Marianne had been doing rapid mental calculations. Supposing that Jason had been picked up at some time early in August, that meant he would not be in Constantinople before mid-winter, or even until the spring, according to how long it took him to reach the Bosphorus. That meant a long wait still, because it was not yet the end of October. On the other hand, a small voice whispered to Marianne that that might be all the better since the child was due at the end of February.

That would allow her to meet him looking her normal self, and she had not been looking forward to facing him with her present plump cheeks and unattractive barrel-shaped figure.

'Marianne, you really are taking a shocking risk, you know.' Marianne started to hear a voice scolding her. 'It's cold and damp here on the waterfront and you have been waiting here for three-quarters of an hour or more, standing in the middle of a jostling crowd. And I told you to take care of yourself.'

She roused herself from her thoughts to find that Jolival had left her side and was talking to Achmet on the deck of the *Sea Witch*. His place had been taken by a fair-haired man of middle height who sported curling sidewhiskers and an air of elegance which was wholly English. He was regarding her with strong disapproval. She smiled and held out her hand.

'Were you really watching me all that time, doctor? Then you were very patient to wait for three-quarters of an hour before coming to scold me.'

'I wasn't watching you, Princess, but Lady Hester and I have been all that time over there in consultation with a host of Greek sea captains, each one a more talkative rogue than the last. I kept hoping that we had done and could go home but these fellows can out-talk a whole tribe of Indians! As for Lady Hester, she's the queen of them all! I lost patience at last, but she is still at it. Look at her, standing on that gangway in that outlandish dress of hers, with that huge devil in the red cap and the unforgiveable dirt! Upon my word, I'll swear that she enjoys these arguments. If her friends in London could see her now . . .'

Marianne laughed heartily. It was not the least odd part of her situation that her doctor now should be an Englishman, Charles Meryon, and that he should also have become her friend. Within twenty-four hours of her installation in the house in Phanar, she had become involved, quite naturally, in her hostess's social life, which she had discovered to be altogether cosmopolitan.

Princess Morousi had, in fact, no interest at all in politics and it seemed to her quite natural to open her house to guests who, in any other place, would not even have spoken. She had no more racial prejudices than she had opinions on the justice of this or that war or private quarrel. Her friends were drawn impartially from Greeks, Turks, Albanians, Russians, Wallachians, French or English. All she asked was that she should like them and, above all, never be bored by them. In return for which she dispensed lavish hospitality and a friendship not to be bought at any price but which, if disappointed, never forgave.

And so Marianne, the friend and secret ambassadress of

Napoleon, had found herself, thanks to the Princess, thrown into the very arms of the niece of the great Pitt, the mortal enemy of France and of Napoleon in particular, and between her and the Lady Hester Stanhope there had sprung up an immediate and spontaneous affinity which she had not even tried to suppress.

Lady Hester was surely one of the strangest and most remarkable people England had ever produced. The death of her uncle, whose support, helper and hostess she had been for several years, followed by that of her betrothed, General Sir John Moore, killed fighting at Corunna, would in the ordinary way have relegated her to a discreet retirement. But after queening it as a social and political hostess, Lady Hester, at thirty-four, was in no mind to resign herself to the narrow, stifling existence of an old maid in some English country house.

She had chosen instead a life of adventure and, eighteen months before, on the eighteenth of February 1810 to be precise, she had shaken the dust of her native land from her feet. She had taken ship at Portsmouth for the eastern lands which had always exercised a powerful fascination over her eager, imaginative mind, with no great idea of ever returning. But she did not set out alone. With her on the frigate *Jason*, that old acquaintance of Marianne's, had gone such a suite as might have accompanied a queen in exile.

After a voyage of several months, they had arrived at last at Constantinople where the traveller had been settled for a year now, delighted by the charm of the city and receiving and received by the best society, including the Sultan himself, and living in considerable splendour on the remittances which her *cher ami*, Michael Bruce, received from his father, for Lady Hester for all her expensive tastes, had little in the way of fortune. She was also planting a large thorn in the flesh of the British ambassador.

Canning, in fact, was soon of the opinion that Lady Hester was the eleventh plague of Egypt, while for her part, the illustrious traveller did not trouble to conceal from the handsome diplomat that she classed him among the irretrievable spoil-sports.

On the other hand, she had done her utmost, ever since her arrival, to obtain an introduction to the French ambassador. She had a strong desire to travel in France after completing her oriental tour – a desire made all the stronger by the fact that this was something not allowed to English people at that time – and to see for herself the effects of imperial government on a country just emerging from a revolution the principal object of which had been the suppression of the monarchy. Considering that the French ambassador would be the best person to open to her the doors of this peculiar country, Lady Hester had been scheming for months to meet Latour-Maubourg, who had ended by shutting himself up at home in an effort to avoid her. He had gone to earth in his one-time convent and went out no more than he could help.

His situation was quite difficult and complicated enough without making things even more difficult for himself and risking trouble with Napoleon by requesting a passport for the niece of the late Lord Chatham. It made his hair stand on end even to think of the imperial frown at such an untimely request.

At that moment, the thorn in the ambassador's flesh was collecting a crowd almost as large as that gathered round the American brig, to which, in point of fact, she bore no small resemblance. She was very tall, even for an Englishwoman, and was dressed in a peculiar, half-masculine, half-feminine attire, consisting of a black ferej lavishly trimmed with gold and swathing a figure which would have done credit to a Roman matron. But instead of enveloping herself completely in this garment, she wore it with the hood flung carelessly back over her shoulders, revealing a proud head with a finely chiselled profile, a haughty nose and sensuous red lips and swathed in a voluminous white turban.

In this array, which borrowed those aspects of both male and female dress which suited her best, she was confronting a Greek sailor considerably smaller and more excitable than herself. From time to time she let fall on his hairy head a few cool words which seemed, nevertheless, to have the power to send the little man into a frenzy.

Marianne and Doctor Meryon, watching the scene in some amusement, saw the Greek cross himself frantically three or four times, calling heaven to be his witness with rolling eyes and waving arms, then tear off his cap and hurl it to the ground and jump on it, then pick it up again and put it back on his head, liberally coated with dust. At last, quite suddenly, he seemed to calm down and something that was undoubtedly a gold coin gleamed in his grimy, outstretched hand.

'God help us!' Meryon groaned. 'She's closed with that pirate —'

'Closed? What bargain is she striking? Why has she given him that gold piece?'

'Because we are leaving here, my lady, and for the ends of the earth, I think. Lady Hester has given up her idea of travelling in

France but she is determined not to spend a second winter in Constantinople. She was too cold last year, she says, and so she means
to go to Egypt. And she's not too nice about the means, as you can
see. Finding no honest Christian vessel that would take her, she has
turned to these God-forsaken pirates —'

'Oh, come, Doctor, surely not! The Greeks are as good Christians
as you and me. Different, perhaps, but that is all.'

'I don't care if they are. The fact is that I'm fated to die a
thousand deaths on board the hideous discomfort of a polacca in
mid-winter. I'd prefer a Turkish xebec, even.'

'Then you'd certainly be on a heathen ship, my dear doctor,'
Marianne observed, hiding her amusement at his tragic tone in the
high fur collar of her wide moss-green cloak. But in another
moment she was crying: 'But, my dear friend, are you going away
and leaving me all alone? What will become of me without you to
take care of me?'

'That is exactly what I have been trying to impress on Lady
Hester! I have a great many friends and patients here who are going
to miss me very much, for my own sake as well as for my pro-
fessional services. I've a duty to remain until after your confinement. And I don't know what the noble Turkish dames will say to
my sudden departure. I am thinking particularly of the Kapodan
Pasha's lady —'

Marianne had been thinking of her also, and again she had to
hide a smile, for rumour had it that Mr Meryon's services to the
Ottoman admiral's wife were somewhat more than purely medical.
There were other Turkish ladies, too, who placed great confidence
in the young English physician and he made no secret of his pleasure
in the company of these silken, twittering, bird-like creatures.

'And what did Lady Hester say?'

Meryon shrugged.

'Nothing – or as good as. She won't listen because she wants to
go to Egypt and nothing will do for her but to go at once.'

'What? But I thought she was so anxious to meet Monsieur de
Latour-Maubourg? Has she given up? I'd never have thought it of
her.'

The doctor coughed and glanced discreetly about him. 'That's
just it,' he murmured. 'She has seen him —'

'She has! Well, here's a piece of news! But where? When? Tell
me quickly! The suspense is killing me!'

'Last week, at Bebek, on the shore of the Bosphorus not far from

80

where we were staying in a friend's *yali*.[1] Your ambassador agreed to a private meeting because Lady Hester had been threatening to call at the embassy openly, in broad daylight, and ring the bell until he let her in – Hush! Here she comes!'

Lady Hester was approaching them with the long, mannish stride which had prompted Lady Plymouth to remark that it was a pity women were not eligible for the Grenadier Guards. In another moment she had joined them and was sketching a slight, humorous bow, touching her fingers to her forehead, lips and breast.

'*Salaam aleikum*,' she said. 'Something tells me, Marianne dear, that my poor Charles has been pouring the tale of his wrongs into your sympathetic ears. You must pity him, I know.'

'My pity is for myself, Hester, not for him. He tells me you mean to deprive me of my doctor and of my friend. I've a good mind to add my complaints to his.'

Lady Hester laughed. 'The French are past masters at the art of flattery disguised as something else – and vice versa, too! But I hope you weren't taken in by his piteous account of all the poor creatures who'll be languishing at death's door on account of his leaving them? The truth is that all his patients enjoy the best of health but he is going to miss the lovely ladies Water Lily, Tulip and Morning Star – not to mention your beautiful self, my dear —'

She paused and, dropping her light, bantering tone, continued seriously: 'The truth is, also, that I must go.' She lowered her voice a little. 'Has Meryon told you that I saw Latour-Maubourg?'

'He was just saying so —'

'When my arrival interrupted him. Our encounter was agreeable, but unproductive. The ambassador made it quite clear that there is no possibility of my being able to visit France. Indeed, I knew it already, long before, only it amused me to put the fear of God into that poor man —' She broke off and glanced round, frowning to see a pair of *kavas*[2] hovering so close that they were practically hanging on her words. She took Marianne's arm. 'Surely there is somewhere else where we can talk? I want a private word in your ear.'

'Would you like to come back to the Morousi Palace? The Princess is at her house at Arnavut Koy, so we can be quite comfortable.'

'I'm never comfortable in Greek houses. There are always people listening at every keyhole.'

[1] Palace.
[2] Turkish law officers.

'Then I can think of only one other place. Come with me.'

'Where?'

'Here,' Marianne said, leading the way to the *Sea Witch*. 'No one will disturb us on board.' And after all, she told herself privately, what could be more natural than for her to go aboard her own ship?

Her pleasure in the use of that pronoun was immense. Yet in coming down to the quayside that morning, she had not meant to go aboard. It had seemed to her that Jason's ship should remain inviolate until her master's return, waiting, as it were, to be brought to life again by the ring of his boots on her decks. But now she told herself that this was foolish and that the *Sea Witch*, built with Selton money and purchased anew by Nakshidil, was as much hers as Jason's. And suddenly she wanted very much to stand once more on the deck where, for good or ill, so much had happened to her.

Leaving Dr Meryon to stroll gloomily up and down the quayside, the two ladies crossed the gangway and, with a wave of the hand to Jolival who was chatting with Achmet on the poop, they made their way to Marianne's old cabin, now tastefully restored.

'There,' Marianne said with a little sigh, making her friend sit beside her on the bunk. 'We couldn't have a better place. No one will overhear us here. You may say what you like.'

Lady Hester, however, seemed in no hurry to speak. She was looking about her, frankly curious.

'Does this ship belong to you?' she asked at last. 'I saw that she was flying your family's crest. I was not aware that you were ship-owners —'

Marianne laughed. 'My family is somewhat limited, my dear Hester, and no one goes in for shipping – least of all myself. No, the *Sea Witch* belongs to a friend of mine, a very dear friend. The ship was captured by the Turks and her Highness, the Valideh Sultan, who is, as you know, a distant cousin of mine, purchased her and made me a present of her. The flag is a pretty gesture but I can't really think of her as mine – only as in my care for a while.'

'Who is her master?'

'Do not ask me that,' Marianne said quickly. 'I cannot tell you.' Then, to soften the abruptness of her words, she smiled and added: 'Call it a kind of superstition. I'd rather not mention his name until he comes —'

'And when will that be?'

'I don't know. Tomorrow, perhaps, or not for another six months. He has been very ill and is recovering slowly, a long way from here. But that's enough of that. Tell me about yourself.'

But once again it seemed that Hester Stanhope had lost interest in the important communication which had demanded such secrecy to impart. Ever since first setting her high-arched, aristocratic foot on board the *Sea Witch*, her grey eyes had brightened and her nostrils flared 'like a hound on the scent', Marianne thought, watching her. So that it came as no great surprise when Lady Hester took a deep breath and, regarding her companion with a mock severity, said: 'Do you mean to say that this ship, which ought to be riding the high seas, is going to stay cooped up in harbour, empty and unused, with her sails stowed, until the problematical arrival of a captain who might be anywhere?'

'Yes, that is precisely what I mean.'

'Then let me tell you it's absurd. And dangerous. You'd do much better to engage a trustworthy captain on the spot, let him get together the best crew he can find and then give orders to set sail.'

'Set sail? But I don't want to. And wherever to?'

'Egypt. With me. I have to go as soon as possible and I need a ship. In the absence of anything better, I was resigning myself to a wretched polacca, but this brig is a godsend!'

Marianne frowned. She had always known of the English passion for the sea but this time she thought that her friend was going too far.

'I'm sorry, Hester. I don't like to disappoint you but it's out of the question. Quite apart from my condition, which makes it most inadvisable for me to put to sea, the ship does not really belong to me, as I have said, and she does not sail without her master.'

She had spoken almost curtly, expecting argument, but nothing of the kind was forthcoming. Hester's voice held no trace of annoyance as she answered smoothly: 'I said that I must leave, my dear – but you, too, would be well advised to quit Constantinople, or run the risk of serious trouble.'

Marianne blinked and stared at her friend as if she had taken leave of her senses. Yet there was no indication of insanity on that arrogant, handsome face, only determination and a slight anxiety.

'What did you say?' Marianne demanded. '*I* should do well to leave? And why, may I ask?'

'I'll tell you. Charles has told you, I suppose, about my interview with your ambassador?'

83

'Yes, but I can't see —'

'You will.' Passing swiftly over the details of a meeting which, as it had ended in failure, no longer held any interest for her, Hester went on to describe the sequel to her romantic excursion to the remote *yali*. On the following day she had received a summons to present herself at the British Embassy. Mr Canning wished to see her.

Somewhat disconcerted by this sudden desire for her company, she had gone at once and Canning had not been slow in coming to the point.

'Lady Hester,' he had demanded, almost before she was well into the room, 'where were you yesterday?'

But Hester Stanhope was not a woman to allow herself to be browbeaten without hitting back and for sheer rudeness her reply was equal to the question.

'Why? Have your spies not told you?'

After this beginning, the interview had soon developed into a battle royal. The ambassador informed his intractable country-woman that he was tired of her continued intimacy with members of the French ambassador's suite, that he considered the previous day's clandestine meeting as the last straw and that she might thank her position as Pitt's niece that she was not called upon to endure the consequences of her irresponsible behaviour – as she surely would be if she did not break off her outrageous friendship with 'one of Bonaparte's mistresses, and a notorious spy into the bargain'.

'So I told young Mr Canning that I was quite old enough to choose my own friends and requested him to mind his own business. He did not like that at all, you may be sure, and still less when I reminded him that you were a kinswoman of the Sultana's and deserved to be spoken of with more respect. I thought he would have had a fit!'

' "Lady Hester," he said to me, "either you give me your word to break with these people, and with that woman in particular, alto-gether, or I will have you expelled from this city and put aboard the first boat for England. As to that pinchbeck princess of yours" – I'm sorry my dear, but those were his words – "I'll soon persuade the Sultan to send her back where she came from and then, once her ship has left the Bosphorus, we shall be able to get our hands on her and see to it that she causes no more trouble." '

Marianne gasped and could not speak for a moment. She was

both angry and indignant but she kept her temper and even managed a contemptuous smile.

'Surely Mr Canning is deceiving himself a little about his influence with the Porte? Have the Sultana's cousin dismissed like a housemaid! Unthinkable!'

'Less than you might think. Canning means to make you the subject of a secret clause in the treaty he will be concluding with Mahmoud, a condition, as it were. And, for once, Mahmoud will not be asking his mother's advice about it. You will be expelled with the utmost discretion, and put quietly on board ship, so that by the time the Sultana asks for you, you will be far away and she will have no choice but to forget all about you.'

'But what is this treaty? Do you know?' Marianne asked, feeling the colour drain from her face.

'Not precisely, but I have an idea. The rumour is that a Russian fleet is approaching the Bosphorus and the Turks are powerless to prevent it sailing right through and bombarding Constantinople if it has a mind to. Canning has asked the Admiralty for assistance and an English fleet under Admiral Maxwell is on its way here at this minute. Do you imagine the Sultan will hesitate between the lovely Princess Sant'Anna and half a dozen ships of the line?'

'I thought England and Russia were allies? Or is that only when it comes to fighting Napoleon?'

'Something of that, perhaps. But then there will be no question of the two fleets engaging one another. The mere presence of the English ships should be enough to deter the Russians from going too far against a country under British protection, especially since that country is already prepared to make peace. And so your only chance is to leave with me, you see?'

Marianne rose, without answering, and went to the brass-rimmed portholes that lit the cabin, where she had stood so many times in the past. But she was not looking at the scene they framed. She had no eyes for the busy harbour and the exotic crowds. She had the curious feeling of being trapped inside a block of ice and her only feeling was a kind of sick and weary disgust.

So the man's world of politics was still harrying her, even after she had abandoned all desire to play the smallest part in it. She was discovering that it was not enough to give up and live as quietly as she had done for the past two months, carrying the child which was her pledge for the future. Even then they would not leave her in peace.

Canning, who from the moment of her arrival in Constantinople had dreamed of sending her back to England as a prisoner, to moulder her life away in captivity, had not been softened by her condition or the discreet retirement of her days spent in her friend's house. He probably saw it only as a screen for further intrigues, a convenient base for threatening his own standing with the Porte. Marianne Sant'Anna, secret agent, had disguised herself as a pregnant woman in order to spin her sombre web more busily than ever . . .

And he was actually going so far as to make her removal a secret condition of an important diplomatic agreement! It would have been extremely flattering, if it had not been so absurd. But it was worrying as well because to achieve his ends the twenty-eight-year-old ambassador was prepared to make light of the protection of a queen.

Marianne's position was all the more dangerous because it would not be hard for a small group of determined men to enter the Morousi Palace secretly at night, carry her off and smuggle her on board ship. For all its medieval battlements, the palace was utterly unguarded. Its doors were ever-open and servants almost without exception as old as their mistress. Moreover its main entrance gave directly on to the Phanar waterfront. The captive could be carried from her bed to a boat while she was still half-asleep.

Marianne felt the ship move gently under her feet, tugging at her moorings with a small creaking sound that was like an unobtrusive call, or perhaps an answer. It seemed to be begging her to set sail. After all, why not? Why should she not put to sea in her ship, with her friends? Not for Egypt, no. There was nothing for her there. But for Morea . . . Why not go to meet Jason and save him from the necessity to come to this city he had hated instinctively and did not want to see?

'Well? Have you decided? Shall we go?'

Hester spoke a little anxiously, reminding Marianne abruptly of her presence. She gave a little shiver and glanced round quickly, shaking her head.

'No. I can't. Whatever the danger, I must stay here.'

'You're mad!'

'Possibly, but there it is. Don't be cross with me, Hester, and please don't think I don't appreciate what you have done for me. I am truly grateful to you for the warning —'

'But you don't believe a word of it! You're very much mistaken if you think Canning threatens idly. I know him too well to doubt that he will do precisely as he says – to both of us.'

'I do not doubt it for a moment. I have learned to know him also. Indeed, I may have to go, but not to Egypt. There is no reason why I should, you must see that. The best, the most sensible thing would be for me to go to France or to Tuscany —'

Almost before the words were out of her mouth she was regretting them, for a gleam had come into Lady Hester's eyes. Surely that passionate traveller was not going to offer to go with her, perhaps disguised as a man if need be and carrying a forged passport? Much as she liked the tall Englishwoman, Marianne found the prospect less than alluring, foreseeing it as an endless source of trouble of all kinds. But the light in the grey eyes vanished as swiftly as it had come, like a lamp snuffed out.

Hester rose in her turn, unfolding her long limbs and bringing her turban within an inch of the ceiling.

'If that Latour-Maubourg of yours had not pointed out all the innumerable diplomatic complications that could result from my being in France,' she said with a sigh, 'I would have made you take me with you and revelled in it. But it would be asking for trouble. Only think it over again, my sweet, and ask your friends' advice. In any event, I shall not be going for another three days yet. You still have time to change your mind and decide to spend the winter in the Egyptian sunshine. And now we had better go and find poor Meryon before his patience runs out. The poor boy can't bear to let me out of his sight for a moment.'

But when they reached the quayside Dr Meryon had disappeared and Marianne, who had some reason for not sharing Lady Hester's belief in her all-powerful charm over the young physician, could not suppress the thought that he had made the best of his opportunity to escape. Perhaps he had gone to pay a farewell visit to the Kapodan Pasha's adorable wife?

One hour later, having left her friend to carry her disappointment back in solitude to her house at Bebek, Marianne was closeted with Jolival in the Morousi drawing-room, pouring out the tale of all that she had just learned.

Arcadius heard her out in silence, nibbling his moustache as was his habit when he was thinking deeply but not seeming otherwise much perturbed.

'So there we are!' Marianne concluded. 'At this moment, Canning's plan is to have me expelled from the country officially and, unofficially, bundled away like an unwanted parcel.'

'I'd worry more about the unofficial side,' Jolival said thoughtfully. 'However cool his relations with Napoleon, the Sultan is going to think twice before expelling a dear friend of his. I'm inclined to think that, if you had his words correctly, Canning has been overestimating himself a little there.'

'What do you mean "if I had his words correctly"? Are you trying to say that Hester might have invented it?'

'Not everything, no – but some. What I find so surprising in the whole story is that she didn't coming running here to warn you a week ago, when this escapade of hers had only just taken place. That would have been the action of a friend. But instead she simply waited until she happened to meet you on the waterfront and then made haste to put you on your guard as soon as she saw that you were the possessor of a much larger and more comfortable vessel than any she could hope to find here to carry her to this eastern dream of hers. Once agree to take her to Egypt and she'll have you going right round the world.'

'There's no question of my going round the world, or even to Egypt.' Then, struck by his reasoning she added: 'Do you really think she could have made it up?'

'That,' Jolival said, 'is what we have to find out! But whatever happens, we had better speak to Prince Corrado before we decide anything at all. He is the prime cause of your being stuck here, as well as being your lawful husband, so it is for him to settle what is to be done. I'll send word to him at once and after that I'm going in search of a friend of mine who has the *entrée* to the British Embassy. He may be able to tell me how much truth there is in what Lady Hester told you.'

'Jolival, have you really English friends? You, of all people?' Marianne asked in surprise, knowing he had little love for the country where his wife had chosen to make her home.

'I have friends wherever necessary. But don't worry, This one is not English but Russian. He started life as a page to Catherine the Great and he has more friends in diplomatic circles than anyone I know.'

Her friend's quiet good sense had done much to calm Marianne. She smiled at him over the piece of embroidery she had begun to occupy herself during the long hours she spent resting on a sofa on the orders of Dr Meryon while he stood at the table and scribbled a few hurried lines.

'I see how it is. If your friend is as familiar with the insides of embassies as of gaming houses, he must be a mine of information.'

Jolival shrugged, adjusted the set of his well-cut pearl grey coat, picked up his hat and stick from a chair and, bending, dropped a light kiss on the top of Marianne's head.

'The trouble with you women,' he said mildly, 'is that you never appreciate how much we do for you. Now, just you stay here quietly until I come back and, above all, don't be at home to anyone. I shan't be long.'

In fact he was back again in a remarkably short time but the happy confidence he had displayed on setting out had given way to a tension that was revealed in the heavy crease between his brows and the frequency with which he sought his snuff box. His mysterious and well-informed acquaintance had confirmed the acrimonious nature of that final interview between Lady Hester Stanhope and the British ambassador and also the fact of an imminent agreement between Canning and the Sultan but he knew nothing of British intentions towards the Princess Sant'Anna or whether her expulsion from Turkey was to form part of that agreement.

'There's no reason why it should not be true,' Marianne cried. 'If Canning is prepared to send packing a woman of Lady Hester's quality, and a niece of the late Lord Chatham also, why should he hesitate to deal with his country's enemy?'

'For one thing, he never threatened to send Lady Hester packing. According to Count Karazine, he merely told her she would do better to leave the city and not persist in making friends with "those damned French". Nothing more than that. And I'm inclined to believe he's right. Canning is too much the gentleman to talk of expulsion in connection with a lady.'

'That only goes to prove that I am no lady in his eyes. Do you know, Jolival, he called me a pinchbeck princess!'

'I can imagine that rankled with a daughter of the Marquis d'Asselnat but, as I said before, you mustn't over-dramatize. As far as our friend is concerned, I'm quite sure of one thing. She'd rather leave the city of her own accord than wait for the results of the letter she wrote to Lord Wellesley in the first flush of her anger after her quarrel with Canning, making cruel fun of the ambassador. Read it for yourself.'

Like a conjuror, Jolival suddenly produced a sheet of writing paper and held it out to Marianne. She took it automatically but with unconcealed amazement.

'But how do you come to have the letter?'

'Count Karazine again. He really is a most efficient fellow. This is only a copy, of course, and none too difficult to come by. Lady Hester was so angry that she could not resist the pleasure of reading her vindictive epistle to a few friends. Karazine was one of them and since he possesses an amazing memory . . . I must say, it's a remarkable document.'

Marianne began to read the letter. The very first words made her smile.

'Mr Canning,' Hester had written, 'is young and inexperienced, very zealous, but full of prejudice . . .' There followed a lively account of their differences and the masterly epistle ended: 'In conclusion, I would entreat your lordship not to receive Mr Canning with a mere, stiff bow and a forbidding countenance, or to permit the ladies to make fun of him. The best reward for all the services he has rendered would be to appoint him to be commander-in-chief and ambassador extraordinary to those peoples having the greatest need of the suppression of vice and the cultivation of patriotism: this last consisting in tying oneself in more knots than dervishes at the mere mention of the name of Bonaparte . . .'

Marianne laughed aloud.

'You shouldn't have shown me this letter, Arcadius. It's done me so much good that for a little more I'd take Hester to Alexandria after all! If Canning ever gets to hear of this —'

'But he knows already and lies awake at nights thinking about it, you may be sure. He must be haunted by hideous visions of the red dispatch box going the rounds of the Foreign Office to the general delight.'

'Well, the ambassador's sleepless nights won't help me, Jolival. Far from it,' Marianne said, suddenly serious again. 'If he holds me responsible for Hester's freaks, it will only make him hate me more than ever. So, the question remains. What am I to do?'

'Nothing for the present, I'm afraid. Wait and let your husband decide for you because I honestly don't know what to advise.'

The answer came that very evening in the person of Prince Corrado who arrived a little before sunset, while Marianne was taking a gentle stroll in the garden on Jolival's arm. The blue mosaic paths were covered now with fallen leaves that rustled with a dry, papery sound as the hem of her dress brushed over them.

Corrado bowed to Marianne with his habitual, frigid politeness and then clasped Jolival's hand.

'I was at home when your letter was brought to me,' he said, 'and I came at once. What has happened?'

In a few words the Vicomte outlined to him the gist of what had passed between Marianne and Lady Hester Stanhope and of his own subsequent investigations. Corrado listened attentively and it was soon clear to Marianne that he was not taking the matter lightly. By the time Jolival had finished, the crease between his brows was mirrored on the Prince's face.

'Lady Hester may have been exaggerating a good deal,' the Vicomte said at the end, 'but then again, she may not. We have no means of finding out and we don't know what to do for the best.'

Corrado thought for a moment.

'Exaggerating or not, the threat remains,' he said at last. 'We are obliged to take it seriously because with a man like Canning there is never any smoke without a fire. There must be a fair amount of truth in what you have been told.' He turned to Marianne. 'What do you want to do?'

'I don't want to do anything, Prince, except keep out of trouble. I think it is for you to decide for me, for are you not – are you not my husband?'

It was the first time she had used that word to him and it seemed to her that the shadow of some emotion disturbed the calm of the fine, dark-skinned face. But it was only for an instant, like a fleeting ripple on the smooth surface of a pool. Corrado bowed.

'I am obliged to you for remembering it at such a time. I should like to think of it as a mark of confidence —'

'And so it is, believe me.'

'You will agree to abide by my decision?'

'I am asking you to take the decision, because I don't know what I should do. I wondered,' she went on, a little timidly, 'whether I ought not to leave Constantinople perhaps – and sail to the Morea – or to France.'

'No purpose would be served by that,' the Prince returned evenly. 'It would be dangerous as well because you would run the risk of meeting the English fleet and this time you would not find it easy to escape. What is more, Captain Beaufort may well have left Monemvasia by now, and you might easily pass one another at sea and not know it.'

All of which was depressingly true. Marianne bent her head so that the Prince should not see the disappointment written all too clearly on her face. All afternoon, she had been hugging the thought of a voyage to Greece that would serve to reunite her with Jason all the sooner.

Jolival guessed at her feelings and it was he who asked the next question.

'What, then?'

'Remain in Constantinople, only not in this house, of course. An abduction from Phanar would be too easy.'

'Then where shall we go?'

'To my house – at –Bebek.'

He turned back to Marianne and, without giving her time to utter a word, continued, very quickly: 'I'm sorry to force this on you. You cannot wish it and I had hoped to spare you the need to share my roof, but it is the only way. You might ask Princess Morousi to shelter you on her estate at Arnavut Köy, it is true. Indeed, it is quite close to Bebek. But that would not avert the danger. It is the first place they would look for you and, if Canning really has obtained the Sultan's help in this, the English could turn for help to the garrison of Rumeli Hissar, which is nearby.'

'But it's even nearer to Bebek,' Jolival objected.

The Prince gave him a slow smile and his white teeth gleamed. 'Yes – but who would think of looking for the Princess Sant'Anna in the house of Turhan Bey, the rich African merchant who is honoured with the Sultan's friendship?'

The irony of his words was not without a hint of bitterness but Marianne was beginning to think that where the Prince was concerned it was better to keep her imagination under control. It was impossible to guess what were his real thoughts or feelings. Dressed in the eastern clothes which surely became him more than European garments would have done, he was still the same as he had been on Jason's ship – a marvellous figure of stone, with a control that would not break even under the lash. He was one of those who would die without uttering a sound. What he was saying at that moment, however, was not without interest.

'If you accept my offer, a Turkish woman will come here to-morrow, at some time during the morning, ostensibly with a message for your hostess. She will have a boatman with her. You will change clothes with her and, disguised in the veil and ferej, you will leave here. The perama which brought her will carry you to my house. You need not be alarmed. The house is a very large one –

I owe it to the generosity of the Sultan – and my presence there will not intrude on you at all. There will also be someone there to care for you whom I hope you will be glad to see. My own dear Lavinia.'

'Dona Lavinia? Here?' Marianne cried, filled with a sudden happiness at the thought of the old housekeeper who had been such a comfort and support to her at the time of her strange marriage and whose advice had helped her so much during those trying days at the villa dei Cavalli.

The shadow of a smile passed over the Prince's face.

'I sent for her when you agreed to keep the child for it is she, and no one else, who will naturally have charge of him. She has just arrived and I was going to bring her to you. She is very eager to see you again. I – I believe that she is very fond of you.'

'I love her too and ——'

But Corrado was not to be drawn into such dangerously emotional terrain. Turning to the Vicomte, he went on: 'I hope that you, Monsieur de Jolival, will also honour me by accepting my hospitality?'

Arcadius's bow was the epitome of politeness.

'I shall be very happy to do so. For you must know, Prince, that I rarely leave the Princess, who is pleased to consider me as something between a mentor and a favourite uncle.'

'The part suits you to perfection, never fear. Unfortunately, you will be obliged to live as quietly as the Princess herself because if Canning guesses that she would never have flown without you he is bound to have you followed as soon as you show your nose in the city. Happily, I can offer you the use of an excellent library, some very good cigars and a cellar I am sure will meet with your approval, to say nothing of a beautiful garden, well-hidden from prying eyes.'

'That will suit me very well,' Jolival assured him. 'I have always dreamed of retiring to a monastery. Yours sounds just right.'

'Good. Then you will begin your retreat tomorrow evening. Your best way to Bebek will be to go to the French Embassy while it is still daylight, as you sometimes do for a game of chess with M. de Latour-Maubourg. You are in the habit of staying the night there, because no boats are allowed to cross the Golden Horn after sunset except those belonging to the Sultan.'

'That's true.'

'This time you will leave again after dark. I'll come for you myself at midnight. I'll be waiting in the street. You only have to make up some excuse. Say that you are spending the night with friends in Pera or something of the sort. The main thing is to have you out of Stamboul before curfew.'

'One more detail – if I may call Princess Morousi a detail,' Jolival said.

'Once you are both gone, she will make the biggest fuss she can – which is saying a good deal – lamenting your ingratitude in quitting her house in such cavalier fashion, without taking the trouble even to inform her where you are going. No, don't worry, she will know all about it. In fact she will be the only person besides myself and you to do so. I know that I can trust her absolutely.'

'I'm quite sure of it,' Marianne said. 'But do you think Canning will be taken in by her outcry?'

'It doesn't matter whether he is or not. What does matter is that he does not know where you are. After a few days, he is bound to think that you have taken fright and run away and will stop looking for you.'

'I expect you are right. But there is still one thing to be thought of. What about the ship?'

'The *Sea Witch*? She will stay where she is, until further developments. It was a mistake for the Sultana to have our crest flown from the masthead. Very kind and thoughtful, certainly, but a mistake all the same. From tonight, that flag must disappear. I'll replace it with the one flown by all my own ships.'

'The one flown by your ships? Have you ships?'

'I told you I was known here as a rich merchant. In fact that is precisely what I am. My ships fly a red pennant bearing a lion with a T-shaped torch in its paw. If you are willing for the brig to fly that flag, it will be thought in high places that you have sold her to me in order to obtain the money for your flight. And it will not stand in the way of Mr Beaufort's recovering his property.'

Marianne found herself at a loss for an answer. She was finding out that there was still a great deal she did not know about this amazing man whose name she bore. She had noticed a good many ships, xebecs and polaccas, flying that curious flag with the flaming T on it in the harbour of Stamboul but it had never occurred to her that they could belong to her husband. She began to think that it would be interesting to live for a time with such a man, quite apart from the promise of security it offered and the joy of finding Dona Lavinia again.

As they talked, the three of them had completed the circuit of the garden and found themselves back on the vine-covered terrace outside the drawing-room. Autumn had turned it to a wine-red canopy which glowed redder still in the light of the lamps that were now being lit all over the house. But a pervasive odour of roast meat and frying onions emanating from the kitchens robbed the moment of its poetical effect and brought it down to earth. It was dinner time and Marianne was hungry, as always.

An ancient serving man with long white hair came into the drawing-room, bent under the weight of a lighted candelabrum almost taller than himself. The Prince bowed, touching his forehead, lips and breast in the eastern fashion.

'I'll bid you goodnight,' he said, as though concluding an ordinary call, 'and shall hope to see you very soon.'

Marianne swept him a little curtsy.

'Very soon indeed, Turhan Bey, if I have my way. Goodnight to you also.'

The aged retainer made haste to open the door and the Prince followed him quickly but turned in the doorway to deliver one parting counsel.

'If I may be allowed one piece of advice – on no account have any further communication with the lady in question. She is a great deal too intelligent and she has everything to gain from frightening you. Such people make perilous friends.'

The following evening, enveloped in a black ferej and veil of the same colour, Marianne left the Morousi palace. Behind her, like a shadow, went a tall Albanian with a dagger like a small cutlass stuck in his belt. His drooping black moustache gave him a strong resemblance to Attila the Hun and he glared round him with a fierce, black eye that defied anyone to cross him. But there were plenty more Albanians like him on the waterfronts of Stamboul and his gaudy clothes were in harmony with the multicoloured crowds that swarmed there from dawn to dusk. He also possessed the added advantage that he was dumb.

With him to protect her, Marianne reached the unremarkable little perama waiting, among a hundred others like it, at the jetty of Aykapani. In another moment she was gliding over the grey waters of the harbour, under a fine, persistent rain which, although unpleasant, was almost as impenetrable as a fog, towards her new home.

CHAPTER FIVE

Arcadius is Angry

Rain! It had begun just after Christmas, which had been unusually mild, and since then it had not stopped, a thin, persistent drizzle soaking everything in sight. The fishing village of Kandilli, across the Bosphorus on the Asian side, showed only as a vague blur with the inevitable minaret standing up like a quill pen. The bright colours of the boats and the houses painted pink, blue, green and yellow, dissolved in the watery mist to form a kind of grisaille in which even the spires of the cypress trees merged into the general grey. The Bosphorus was cheerless, a broad salt river heaving sullenly day after day with sea birds shrieking overhead.

These days were mostly spent by Marianne in the *tandour* whose windows, covered with gilded grilles, overhung the grey waters. This was a small, circular apartment, furnished with a number of divans, their feet converging in the centre on a large tiled stove covered with a brilliantly embroidered woollen blanket the edges of which could be lifted by the occupants of the divans to cover their feet and help to ward off the cold and damp.

The palace of Humayunabad, built by Ibrahim Pasha in the previous century and now, by favour of Mahmoud II, the property of Turhan Bey, possessed a number of such comfortable chambers but Marianne had chosen this one on account of its oriel windows overlooking the Bosphorus, from which she could watch the shipping passing back and forth each day.

The view was much livelier than looking at the dripping gardens which, for all their splendour, were enclosed by high, defensive walls that made them almost as depressing as the fortress of Rumeli Hissar whose battlemented walls and three round towers rose out of the water, guarding the narrows with their guns. So huge and lofty were its walls that they remained visible even through the chill sea mists that rolled in from the Black Sea beyond and smothered the place where two worlds met.

Except for an occasional short stroll in the gardens, whenever the rain stopped for long enough to allow it, Marianne would spend hours and hours in this room, resisting all attempts on the part of Jolival and the Persian physicians whom the Prince had procured for her in place of Dr Meryon to persuade her to take more exercise. She was nearing her time now and she felt heavy and sluggish. She could hardly bear to look in the mirror and see her figure, now swollen beyond all possibility of concealment, and her sunken face, entirely dominated by a pair of great green eyes.

The sight of the sea, though, had become like a drug to her and it was almost more than she could do to drag herself away from it. The nights, when she was forced to leave her divan to go to bed, seemed endless, in spite of the soothing draughts administered by her doctor, who was becoming alarmed at her increasing tension.

With her hands lying idle on the embroidery that she would probably never finish or on a book she did not read, she would lie there from the morning gun that marked the beginning of the day until the evening one that ended it, enclosed in her glassed-in bird-cage, like the after-cabin of a ship, watching the vessels slipping past the palace and the little landing stage with the marble steps going down into the leaden water, always looking for one who never came.

The year 1811 had gone out silently and already the first month of the new year had passed away. Yet still Jason had not come. And every new day ate a little more cruelly into Marianne's hopes, until she had almost come to despair of ever seeing him again. If it had not been for the *Sea Witch*, she could even have believed that he had abandoned her for ever and his love for her was dead. The brig, still riding at her moorings in Phanar under Turhan Bey's colours, was her one hope and she clung to it with all her strength. He could not ignore the ship he loved, even if the woman whose face she bore on her prow was nothing to him any more.

Weak and ill, with a weight of misery in her heart, Marianne blamed herself for what she privately thought of as her cowardice. The old Marianne of Selton, who had put a sword through her husband on her wedding night to avenge her honour, would have turned her back on any man who treated her as he had. But that had been two hundred years ago and the frail, unhappy woman who lay huddled like a sick cat among her cushions had strength only for the one thought that still kept her going: the longing to see him again.

One of Turhan Bey's merchantmen, on a regular run from Monemvasia with a cargo of Malvoisie wine, had brought news that the American had left the Morea for Athens early in December but no one seemed to know what had become of him after that. Once arrived in the ancient capital of learning, he appeared to have vanished into thin air.

A hundred times over, Marianne had made Jolival repeat to her what the fishermen had told the messenger sent by Turhan Bey with instructions to bring Jason back with him if he so wished. The stranger had read the letter which had been given to him, according to instructions, together with a sum of money, as soon as he was fully recovered. Then he had simply put it in his pocket and begun making inquiries about a boat for Athens. After warmly thanking those who had nursed him with such kindness, he had pressed on them half the money he had been given and, early one morning, had embarked on a small vessel trading along the coast as far as Piraeus. By the time Turhan Bey's man arrived, he had been gone for a fortnight.

What had he been seeking in Athens? The tracks of the man who had deceived him, broken him, robbed him and abandoned him to the cruel sea, stripped of everything he cared for in the world: his love, his ship and his illusions? — Or the means to reach Constantinople? Or had he done with Europe and its people and simply sought a ship to carry him to Gibraltar and the vast Atlantic?

Alas, as time went on, Marianne leaned more and more towards the latter theory. She was never going to see Jason again in this world but perhaps God would have mercy on her and take her life in exchange for that of the child about to be born.

Every evening at the same hour, just as the first lights were shining from the Asian shore, Prince Corrado would come to see how she did. He would appear in the doorway of the pavilion which had been set aside for her use and which was divided from his own by the whole width of the garden. For the palace of Humayunabad, in the rambling way of eighteenth-century Turkish buildings, was an amazing collection of pointed roofs, grottoes, swags and mouldings, extravagantly decorated kiosks jutting out over the water or the gardens, like huge, gilded cages, with pools and pavilions for every conceivable purpose, from baths to every other aspect of everyday life, and all adorned with the same painted columns.

The ritual was always the same. As though making clear his determination to avoid the smallest intimacy with his unlikely wife, the Prince would arrive in company with Arcadius, having collected him from the library where the Vicomte spent most of his days, surrounded by a thick cloud of smoke, dividing his time between his favourite Greek authors and the study of Persian. The door of the pavilion would be opened to them by Gracchus who conducted them, with all the dignity of a real butler, to the salon where Dona Lavinia watched unobtrusively over the mother-to-be. There, he handed them over to the housekeeper and returned to his post in the vestibule where he had nothing to do but yawn and play cup and ball with himself and keep the door.

Marianne's youthful coachman had left the French Embassy on the same night as Jolival and with the same extravagant precautions. Jolival had explained to him as concisely as possible how the Ethiopian Caleb had become transformed into Turhan Bey and Gracchus had refrained, with amazing self-control, from asking any questions or showing the smallest astonishment. Nor, bored though he might have been since his arrival at the palace at Bebek, would he have quitted the door he had been told to guard against the machinations of Mr Canning for anything in the world.

Gracchus had never cared much for the English. As a good child of the Revolution, he hated anything to do with the dreaded 'Pitt and Coburg' of his boyhood. He had never approved of his mistress's acquaintance with that same Pitt's niece, but Mr Canning he had regarded as a creature of the devil and his servants as so many demons. The news that they had dared to threaten his dear Princess had sent him nearly frantic. As a result he was guarding the graceful doors of painted cedarwood entrusted to him like a Janissary defending the Sultan's treasury. It was all he could do to refrain from subjecting the Prince and Jolival to a thorough search every evening, such was his fear that *Canningue* might have disguised himself as one or other of them the better to reach his victim.

Dona Lavinia, in turn, would lead the two men to the *tandour* and then she, too, would withdraw to resume her needlework and her vigil, ready to answer her young mistress's call. Her presence, indeed, was among the very few that Marianne could endure, even in her tormented state, and she would often beg her to sit with her. For the silent Lavinia knew better than anyone how to be quiet.

The reunion between the two women had taken place without an unnecessary word. They had embraced, like mother and daughter after a long absence, and then Dona Lavinia had resumed her services to the younger woman as though she had never left off. Since then, she had surrounded her with every care called for by her condition but she had never made the slightest allusion to the expected child, nor had she shown any of the ill-timed jubilation that anyone else could not have failed to betray. She knew too well what the longed-for heir was costing the young Princess Sant'Anna.

And so she was the only person Marianne would have near her. She bathed her and helped her to dress, did her hair and brought her meals and slept at night in an adjoining chamber, with the door left open, ready to answer the least call.

Sunk in her mental apathy, Marianne was aware of this unspoken solicitude. She allowed herself to be nursed like a child but, as her time drew nearer, she would call for Lavinia more and more often, as though she felt the need to reassure herself that when the time came she would be there to help her through her ordeal.

As for the Prince, his visits invariably followed the same pattern. He would come in, inquire after her health and try gently to rouse her from her melancholy with news of the outside world and the day's gossip from the Ottoman capital. From time to time, he brought her a present of a new book, a few flowers, a jewel or some unusual or amusing trinket. The one thing he never brought was scent for which, from the sixth month, Marianne had developed an aversion. Even Jolival would change his clothes completely on emerging from his bouts of smoking in the library so as not to offend her with the smell of Turkish tobacco on his person.

At the end of a quarter of an hour, Corrado would rise and bow and bid her goodnight, leaving Jolival to keep her company. Dona Lavinia would hold back the velvet curtains and his tall, graceful figure would vanish through them to be heard of no more until the following night.

'He reminds me of Aladdin's geni,' Marianne confided to Jolival one day when she was feeling a little more cheerful than usual. 'I always feel that I have only to rub one of the lamps and he will appear before me in a pillar of smoke.'

'I shouldn't be surprised. The Prince is undoubtedly a most remarkable man,' was all the Vicomte said. 'And I don't mean in his appearance only. He's a person of very high intelligence and a most cultivated, even artistic turn of mind . . .' But his panegyric had ended there, for Marianne had turned her head away and relapsed again into her depression. And the good Jolival could not help privately wishing Jason Beaufort at the devil. Just then he would have given a lot to be able to root him out of the girl's sick mind.

Her longing for the handsome privateer was killing her slowly and Jolival, helpless in the face of that speechless misery, could do nothing to comfort her. Where were those happy days when Marianne, superficially in love with Napoleon, had committed every kind of folly but without ever, as now, tearing herself to pieces on the thorns in her path?

He dared not question her about her feelings for Corrado. For himself, the deeper he penetrated, not without difficulty, into the Prince's strange, secret, self-contained personality, so well protected as to be almost impenetrable, the more Jolival liked him. He found himself deeply sorry for the malign trick of fate which had laid on an innocent and altogether exceptional being an antisocial mask which made him an outcast among his own kind.

If the truth were told, Marianne could not have explained her own feelings towards the man whose name she bore. He fascinated and irritated her at the same time, like a too-perfect work of art, while the instinctive liking she had felt for the slave Caleb had undergone some modification when applied to the Prince Sant'Anna.

Not that she had ceased to pity him as the victim of an unjust fate, but her compassion had been somewhat superseded by her pity for herself. She might even have taken a real pleasure in the company of a man of his quality if he had not been the one who was making her go through her present ordeal. But as the days went by, she began to blame him for her sickness, her lassitude and the temporary eclipse of her beauty.

'I look like a starving cat that's swallowed a balloon,' she wailed, catching sight of herself in the mirror. 'I'm ugly – ugly enough to put off any man, however besotted!'

On this particular evening, she was looking even worse than usual. The high cheekbones stood out starkly in her face, betraying her listless wretchedness all too clearly. Her long hands were hardly less pale than the full gown of white wool which enveloped her from neck to ankle, so that Jolival found himself wondering how she would survive her approaching ordeal.

Dona Lavinia said that she was eating almost nothing now, and that little out of duty more than actual hunger. Her hearty appetite was a thing of the past and for three months now Marianne had no need to worry about her figure once the child was born. She would be downright thin. Always supposing she came safely through the confinement itself.

The ritual quarter of an hour reached its end and the Prince rose to take his leave. He was bowing ceremoniously over Marianne's

101

hand, as he did every night, when Dona Lavinia hurried in and murmured something in his ear. He stiffened and frowned.

'Where are they?' he asked.

'At the main entrance.'

'I will go at once.'

The Prince's habitual calm had gone. Contrary to his usual custom, he hurried from the room with barely a word of excuse. Jolival watched him go with an uneasy expression and even Marianne was roused to curiosity by such unaccustomed behaviour.

'Is it some bad news?' she asked.

Lavinia hesitated. She might have said that the news had been for Corrado's ear alone but she was incapable of resisting her young mistress's soft voice and melancholy look. So she merely replied as evasively as she could: 'Yes and no. There has been an attempt to steal one of the ships in the harbour, but the thief has been caught and brought here.'

'To steal one of the ships?' Marianne repeated vaguely. 'Do you know which one?'

Before Dona Lavinia could answer, the heavy velvet curtain covering the entrance to the *tandour* was put aside by the Prince's own hand. His blue eyes scanned each of the faces raised to his in turn and came to rest on Marianne. He was evidently under the stress of some strong emotion.

'Madam,' he said, using very nearly the same words as Dona Lavinia a moment earlier, 'there has been an attempt to steal your ship. My people seized the thief and have brought him here, with three or four men he had employed to assist him. Do you want to see him?'

'To see him? Why should I? Why don't you see him yourself?' she said, in sudden alarm.

'I have no wish to see him. I merely caught a glimpse of him in the hands of my men. And I still think it is for you and no one else to interview him. My presence would only complicate matters and I would rather leave you. He will be here at any moment.'

Then Marianne knew why it was that her heart had beat faster and why she was suddenly nervous. She knew now who was the thief. And she felt magically alive again. The will to live revived in her wasted body. She was herself again and no longer simply the receptacle for an alien existence which was consuming her.

And yet there was a flaw in the happiness that flooded her being. The man she was about to see had been taken in the act of trying to take possession of the brig. What if he had succeeded? He was unlikely to have left her anchored secretly in some quiet bay while he returned to Constantinople in search of the woman waiting for him there. It was not easy to hide a vessel of that size. He would undoubtedly have taken to the open sea to escape pursuit and Marianne was afraid of finding out that, to a seaman, his ship could mean more than the woman he loved. It was this fear which made her strive to stifle the small voice within that threatened to spoil her wonderful moment.

She stretched out both her hands to Jolival in an instinctive gesture, seeking his support, and he came to her where she lay on the divan and gripped them in his own. They were icy cold and she was trembling in every limb, but the eyes she lifted to Corrado were full of stars.

'Thank you,' she said softly. 'Thank you . . . from the bottom of my heart.'

She put out her hand to him but he seemed not to see it. His face as he bowed and left her was closed and set. But Marianne was too happy to consider what he might be thinking at that moment. With the unconscious selfishness of all people in love, she was thinking only of the one who was coming.

She turned to Jolival with a look of alarm.

'I want a mirror,' she said. 'I must look dreadful – shockingly ugly!'

'Ugly, no. You could never be that – but shocking, certainly. I dare say you're sorry now that you didn't listen to your Uncle Arcadius and try to eat a little more. All the same, it's no bad thing that you should look a trifle peaky. But you must try to be calm. Do you want me to go?'

'No, no! Don't go! Only remember how we parted. Who knows if his long illness has made him think differently about me? I might need you. So don't leave me, my friend, I implore you – besides, it is too late.'

Quick footsteps rang out in the next room. A voice spoke sharply, and the sound of it made Marianne's senses swim. It was answered by Dona Lavinia's infinitely gentler tones. Then the curtain was lifted once more. The housekeeper in her black dress appeared and curtsied deeply.

'If it please your Serene Highness, Mr Jason Beaufort.'

As he strode through the door, the small room seemed to shrink. He was so tall that Marianne thought he must surely have grown since she had seen him last. But otherwise he was unchanged. There was still the same masterful face, the same tanned complexion and dark blue eyes, the same unruly black hair. Neither time nor illness, it seemed, had any power over Jason Beaufort. He returned from the edge of the grave as much himself as if nothing had happened.

Marianne gazed at him wonderingly, forgetting in an instant all that he had made her suffer, as Mary Magdalen must have looked at the risen Christ, with eyes bright with tears and light.

Unhappily, the object of her gaze was not endowed with the same divine serenity. He stopped dead in the doorway, the anger which had driven him into the room cut off short. He had been told that he was going to meet the 'owner' of his beloved brig and had been prepared to tell the thief exactly what he thought of him. But the sight of the two faces before him left him wholly thunderstruck. And since Marianne's voice had suddenly deserted her, it was left to Jolival to break the silence. Releasing the girl's hands, which were quieter now and not so cold, he rose and went to meet the privateer.

'Come in, Beaufort. I'm not sure that you are welcome, but you have certainly been expected.'

The Vicomte's voice was noticeably lacking in warmth. Jolival was the last man on earth to bear a grudge but it was clear that he had not forgotten the time that he had spent in irons aboard the *Sea Witch*, along with poor Gracchus, or the sufferings endured by Marianne. It was these that Jolival could not forgive. If he had not known how deeply his young friend loved this man, if he had not seen her pining for him all these weeks, it would have given him a very real pleasure to have thrown him out of the door, and the more so because, although he had said nothing, he, too, had been shocked by the attempted theft. His state of mind was reflected in his greeting. Consciously or unconsciously, he was spoiling for a fight.

But Jason's anger had fallen from him as swiftly as the curtain fell into place behind him. He had been staring at Marianne as though at a ghost but now his eyes left her and swung to Jolival, losing none of their astonishment as they took in the diminutive figure drawn up to its full height before him.

'Monsieur de Jolival,' he said at last. 'What are you doing here? I thought you were dead.'

'Very kind of you, I'm sure,' snapped the Vicomte. 'I don't know who put that idea into your head. That you should picture me work-

ing a treadmill for some fat slave-owner, that I could understand –
but from there to burying me! If it interests you, I am in excellent
health.'

A faint smile touched Beaufort's lips. 'I'm sorry. I ought not to
have said that. But all this is so incredible. Try and see it from my
point of view. I arrive here, recognize my ship and make a bid to
win back my own with the help of a handful of men picked up on
the waterfront, whereupon I am fallen on by a gang of screaming
ruffians and hauled off to the so-called owner, only to find myself
face to face with the two of you —'

His eyes, as though drawn by a magnet, had returned to
Marianne, a white figure curled up amid a pile of silken cushions
in every shade of green. He stepped round the stove and came to
the divan, while she watched him in an agony of apprehension.
What was he going to do? He was smiling with what looked like
real joy, but his reactions were so unpredictable. Had he forgotten
all that had passed aboard his ship, or was the memory of that last,
terrible scene between them still with him, ready to stand between
them once again?

That had been on board the *Sea Witch*. Jason had been standing
on the quarter deck, watching while Caleb suffered punishment for
having tried to kill Dr Leighton and Marianne had turned on him,
wild with rage, and had snatched the bloody whip from the bosun's
hands. She saw again the figure of the pretended Ethiopian hanging
by the wrists from the mainmast, limp and unconscious. She heard
Jason's voice saying coldly: 'What is that woman doing? Take her
back to her cabin!'

They had faced one another before the whole ship's company.
She had hurled defiance at the man who stood there with a face of
stone and madness in his eyes, a man, she now knew, who was even
then in the power of a deadly drug. But what memories had the
drug left in his mind?

None, perhaps. For in the look that Jason bent on her face, she
saw all the old fire which she had thought never to see again. A
wave of happiness swept over her. Was it possible that the memory
of the horrible events off the island of Cythera could have faded
like a dream? If no trace of them remained in Jason's mind, how
gladly would Marianne erase them from her own.

Jason approached until he could rest one knee on the next divan
and, bending, offered her his hand as though in earnest of peace.

'Marianne,' he said softly. 'They told me you were here and that

I should find you but I never thought that it would be so soon. I think I must be dreaming. How is it possible?'

She raised herself from her cushions, her hands, her arms, her whole being reaching out to him with unthinking gladness.

'I'll tell you everything. But you are here! At last! That is what is so wonderful! Come and sit by me. Here, at my side.'

With an eagerness that she had not shown for many weeks, she tossed aside the cloth that covered the stove and made room for him among the cushions, her condition quite forgotten. She remembered it too late as she saw Jason draw away from her quickly, white-faced, when she revealed her shape all too clearly.

'So that at least was no dream?' he said bitterly. 'That was no nightmare brought about by Leighton's infernal drugs. You are with child —'

The light died out of Marianne's eyes and Jolival saw that once again all was about to be lost and that she was to be made to suffer yet again. He lost his temper.

'Oh no!' he said fiercely. 'Not again! Beaufort, I've had more than enough of your tantrums, your tragedy airs and your insufferable pride! You no sooner arrive than you begin to set yourself up as judge and jury! You come here out of the blue, in the unedifying character of one who has been caught trying to take what no longer belongs to him —'

'What gives you the idea that my ship no longer belongs to me?' Jason demanded haughtily.

'The law of the sea. Your ship, my good sir, was captured by the Turks and brought here as a prize by one Achmet Reis, the man who had taken her. She was bought from him by the Valideh Sultan, given a complete refit, which she badly needed after a spell in your friend Leighton's hands, and presented by her Highness to her kinswoman, Marianne. In other words, having permitted that damned doctor of yours to rob Marianne and do his best to murder her in the most hideous manner, you now come here to deprive her of everything she has and dare to get up on your high horse into the bargain when you find her in a condition which does not meet with your approval! Oh no, my friend, it won't do! It won't do at all!'

Jason shrugged. 'I don't understand a word you're saying. Leighton acted like a brigand by me but I had not thought that you had cause for complaint —'

Oh, hadn't you? You did not know that on the night after

Caleb's flogging, while you were snoring in your bed, sodden with rum and drugs, he stripped this poor child of all she possessed and set her adrift in an open boat, with nothing more than a nightshift and a pair of oars, and leaving her wretched maid, Agathe, to be raped by half the crew? If the boat had not been found by a man fishing out of Santorini, Marianne would be dead long ago of thirst, exposure and sunstroke. She was saved in the nick of time. And no thanks to you, as far as I am aware. So kindly moderate your transports and spare us your niceties of conscience. Yes, she is with child. In fact she will be brought to bed at any moment. But although you refused to listen to the facts on board your confounded ship, I swear to God that you shall hear them now, in full, if I have to ask Turhan Bey to have you put in chains!'

'Arcadius,' Marianne implored him, alarmed by her friend's fury, 'please! Calm yourself!'

'Calm myself! Not until I've forced this blockhead here to see the truth. Just you listen to me, Jason Beaufort. You'll not leave here until you have heard the truth, the whole truth about the night-mare Marianne has lived through this past year, and which you in your stupidity have only made worse. You had better sit down because it will take some time.'

Scarlet to the roots of his receding hair, Jolival faced up to Jason like a small fighting cock, his clenched fists itching to punch the stern face before him. He could not remember ever having been so angry, except perhaps once, when he was ten years old and a young cousin of his, out of pure spite, had killed his favourite dog before his eyes. The crucified look on Marianne's face as Jason uttered the words 'You are with child!' in a voice thick with contempt, had taken him back to that other horrible moment and had unleashed forces that had slumbered in him for years and Jolival found that, beneath the cynical, cultivated man of the world there was still the same small Arcadius who could be roused to a primitive and savage rage by an act of wanton cruelty and injustice. Then he had hurled himself on his big cousin and bitten him to the bone, like a small wild animal clinging so fiercely to the murderer's hand that they had had to haul him off bodily. Now Jolival was once more in the mood to bite.

Instinct told Jason he had gone too far and was near to making a deadly enemy of a man who, until now, had been a loyal friend. He gave in and sat down obediently, crossing one long, booted leg over the other.

'I'm listening,' he said with a sigh. 'Indeed, I am beginning to think there must be a great deal I don't know.'

He had deliberately refrained from looking at Marianne again, restrained by a kind of embarrassment, and she seized the opportunity to extricate herself from her nest of cushions.

'Jolival, will you call Dona Lavinia, please? I should like to go to bed now.'

Jason protested instantly. 'Why must you go? If I have wronged you, I ask only to acknowledge it freely for – for I too have suffered. Please. I'm asking you to stay.'

She shook her head, although she saw what this admission of his own unhappiness had cost his pride.

'No. What Jolival is going to tell you would only recall memories that are too painful for me. And I would rather not be here. You will feel less constrained and see things more clearly in my absence. I don't want to influence you.'

'You won't influence me. Stay, I implore you! I have so much to tell you also —'

'Then you may tell me another time – if you still want to. If not . . . you will be free to go away again this very evening and we will never meet again. After all, that is what would have happened, isn't it, if you had succeeded in taking the *Sea Witch* tonight? You knew that I was here in the city. You had been told – and a hard struggle I had to get here! Yet you would have set sail without even trying to see me —'

'No! I swear to you! I don't know what I meant to do really but I'd not have gone right away. You see, when I saw my ship tied up amid all that other riff-raff of vessels, I think I somehow lost my reason. I had only one idea, to get her back and take her out of there. I felt as if she were trapped in a dreadful swamp . . . So I got hold of some men I found idling on the waterfront who looked as though they might be useful and set out with them to make the attempt. I didn't think it would prove so very difficult. The watch looked casual enough. I was wrong. But I swear to you that I would never have left these shores without seeing you, without at least learning what had become of you. I could not have done it.'

'What would you have done?'

'The coast hereabouts is very rocky. It ought to have been possible to find some secret anchorage – but I tell you, I simply had not thought. I acted on an impulse stronger than myself, and a similar impulse would probably have brought me back to look for you.'

He was on his feet now, regarding her anxiously, alarmed by the dull resignation of her tone and the defeat it betrayed. He saw how frail and ill she looked. He saw little in this woman, heavy with child, of the proud, indomitable creature who had known so well how to drive him to distraction with passion or with fury. But he discovered, also, for all the revulsion her condition inspired in him, a new feeling, born of an instinctive urge to protect her and defend her against the burden of a fate too heavy for her fragile shoulders, to rescue her from the ridiculous pass to which ill luck and her own hotheadedness had brought her.

Watching her as she struggled with painful slowness to rise from her divan, clinging to the arm of Lavinia who had come at once to help her, he experienced a sudden wild desire to snatch her up in his arms and carry her away from this palace whose oriental splendours were as shocking to his austere taste as to his native puritanism. He even made a move towards her but she halted him with a look.

'No,' she said fiercely. 'What you feel now is pity. And I do not want your pity.'

'Don't be a fool! Pity? What gave you that idea? I swear to you —'

'Oh no! Do not swear! When you came in just now I was ready to forget all that passed on board your ship. I believe I had forgotten – but you reminded me! I won't listen to any more. You shall listen instead, to Jolival! Afterwards, as I said, you will be free to decide.'

'To decide what?'

'If you want us to remain – friends. When you know the facts, you will know whether you can still hold me in any esteem. Your feelings are matter for your own heart.'

'Stay,' Jason begged her. 'I know my own mind. '

'You are fortunate. I cannot say the same for myself. I was happy a moment ago, but now, I do not know . . . And so I would rather go.'

'Let her go,' Jolival said. 'She is tired and ill. She needs rest. What she does not need is the ordeal which the telling of this tale would be for her. There are things it does no good to recall. And I shall feel freer to say what is in my mind. Dona Lavinia,' he added in a much warmer tone, 'would you add to all your kindness by asking them to send us in some coffee. A great deal of coffee. I think we shall both be needing it.'

'You shall have all the coffee you want, Monsieur le Vicomte, and something more substantial to go with it. I daresay this gentleman could do with something to eat.'

Jason had opened his mouth as though to refuse when Marianne forestalled him.

'You may accept the bread and salt of this house for it belongs to the friend who has watched over you – and me also – for these past months. There is one thing more I wish to say before I go. Whatever you may have been thinking, you shall have your ship again. Jolival will give you her papers.'

'How's this? You told me she belonged to you. Yet she is flying a strange flag.'

'The colours are those of Turhan Bey,' Marianne responded wearily. 'He is the owner of this house. But they are only there to keep the *Witch* out of the English ambassador's hands. As Jolival has told you already, my kinswoman, the Sultana, purchased her as a gift to me but I have never thought of her as anything but a trust.'

With a strength surprising in her wasted body, she dragged Dona Lavinia from the room, striving to hold back her tears.

It cost her something to tear herself away from the man she had so longed to see, but it was more than she could bear to listen to Jolival recounting in detail those abominable nights in the Palazzo Soranzo and all that had followed. For although she had been simply a victim throughout, yet there were things it still shamed her bitterly to recall. And she was determined not to be put to the blush in front of the man she loved. Too often, in the past, he had been inclined to cast her in the undeserved role of the guilty party.

The American's nature was at the same time simple and highly complex. His love for Marianne was probably as great as ever and this was the one comfort she had been able to extract from the few, brief moments they had been together. On the other hand, Jason was the product of an almost puritanically protestant upbringing whose rigid moral principles did not, however, prevent him, in spite of a naturally generous and even chivalrous nature, from being an unquestioning supporter of slavery, which in his eyes was the natural condition of the Blacks, a thing with which Marianne could by no means agree.

It was this fundamental division which was at the root of all he said and did. A woman might look for every consideration and respect from him, but let her once err and his reaction would be harsh and complete. The unhappy female would be relegated in his mind to the common herd of creatures whom he must have met in every port on earth and who, in his eyes, deserved less even than the slaves at Faye Blanche, his family's plantation near Charleston. If once a member of this uncertain sex succeeded, as Marianne had done, in inspiring him with a real passion, then the exquisitely regulated machine which was Jason Beaufort was thrown wholly out of gear.

Back in her own room, Marianne eyed her enormous bed without enthusiasm. Tired as she was, she felt no urge to sleep. Her thoughts would keep straying anxiously to the warm *tandour* where Jason sat listening to Jolival telling the hateful story, without mincing his words, no doubt, because it had been clear that the Vicomte meant to spare his hearer nothing.

Marianne could not help smiling inwardly as she thought of her old friend's outburst of rage and she thanked heaven yet again for giving her one person in her turbulent life who would always spring to her defence. In her present state, she was in no condition to stand up to Jason's principles. Her cheeks still burned at the memory of the scene on board the *Sea Witch*.

Turning her back on the bed which a maidservant had turned down for her, she dropped on to the huge white satin cushion which was set before a low table covered with a vast assortment of pots and jars. Dona Lavinia came behind her and, settling a blue linen towel round her shoulders, began to take out the pins that held her heavy coil of hair in place. Marianne suffered her to finish and then, when her black locks fell freely about her shoulders, checked her as she was picking up the silver hairbrushes.

'Lavinia dear,' she said softly, 'I want you to go back to the *tandour*, or into the blue drawing-room, at least. Monsieur de Jolival might need you.'

The old lady smiled understandingly.

'I believe I sent for everything he should want. But perhaps you would wish me to deliver a message to him?'

'Yes. I'd like you to ask him – quite privately – if he will come here before he goes to bed. Tell him to be sure to come, however late it is. I shall not go to bed until —'

'But that is very wrong of you, my lady. The doctor said you were to go to bed early and get plenty of sleep.'

'That's easier said than done when I cannot sleep at all. Very well, come back and help me into bed but do not close the door or put the lights out. Then you may go to bed. There's no need for you to wait up for the Vicomte. The gentlemen may stay talking for a long time.'

'Should I give orders for a room to be made ready for your Highness's friend?'

Dona Lavinia's voice had stiffened slightly with the words. Her loving, faithful heart had made her sense in the tall and all too attractive stranger a danger and a threat to the master who had always been so dear to her. And Marianne was suddenly ashamed of the situation brought about by Jason's untimely arrival. She was a woman bringing her lover into her husband's house — a husband from whom she had had nothing but kindness. In vain she told herself that she was paying a high price for it. The unpleasant feeling remained. The part she had elected to play was certainly no easy one.

The look she gave Lavinia was unconsciously apologetic.

'I don't really know. He may go away at once, but on the other hand he may be glad to spend the night here. At all events, he won't be staying more than a few hours.'

The housekeeper nodded. She helped Marianne into her nightdress and put her into the big bed, arranging the pillows carefully at her back. Then she checked the lamps to make sure that oil and wicks were as they should be and went away, with a little curtsy, to carry out the task entrusted to her.

Marianne, left alone, lay still for a moment, savouring the scented warmth of the sheets and the soft light of the room. She tried to make her mind a blank, not to think at all, but it was more than she could manage. Her thoughts would keep returning to the *tandour*. She pictured the two men there: Jolival prowling round in the small space between the stove and the divans. Jason, sitting down, with his hands clasped between his knees in the way that she had seen him sit a hundred times, whenever he wanted to give someone his full attention. For all the coldness of her words to him, Marianne had never loved him more.

In an effort to distract her mind, she picked up at random one of the books that lay on her bedside table but, although she knew the text almost by heart, her brain seemed incapable of taking anything in, beyond the title. The book was *The Divine Comedy*, one of her favourites, but it might have been written in Hittite characters for all her eyes could make of it. She finished by tossing it aside impatiently, closed her eyes — and was asleep before she knew it.

She woke to a sudden pain. She could not have been asleep for long because the level of the oil in her bedside lamp had hardly dropped at all. Everything about her was in complete silence. The darkened palace seemed to be asleep, muffled in the soft cocoon of its curtains, its cushions and its hangings. Yet it was certain that not everyone could be asleep, for Jolival had not come.

Marianne lay for a moment with her eyes wide open, listening to the beating of her own heart and observing the progress of the pain which started in the lower part of her belly and spread slowly to invade her whole body. It was not a bad pain and already it was fading, but it was a warning, a foretaste, perhaps, of what was in store for her. Had the time come to lay down her burden at last?

She lay and wondered what she ought to do and decided to wait for another pain to come and confirm what might easily be a too-hasty assumption before sending for the doctor who, at this time of night, would certainly be fast asleep in his bed. She had just stretched out her hand to ring the bell for Dona Lavinia, to ask her what she thought, when there was a soft tap on the door. It opened, without waiting for an answer, and Arcadius looked in.

'May I come in?'

'Yes, of course. I've been expecting you.'

The pain had quite gone now. Marianne sat up in bed and settled herself among her pillows, refreshed by the smile on her friend's face, which bore no sign of the anger which had been there earlier. In the shadows of the big bed, Marianne's eyes were bright with the anticipation of happiness.

'Jason? Where is he?'

'At this moment I should think he must be getting into bed. He can do with some sleep. So can I, in fact, because, along with the coffee, Dona Lavinia sent in a bottle of first rate brandy. I don't like to think what she'd say if she knew we'd finished it.'

Marianne's jaw dropped. It was too much! While she had been picturing them engaged in serious, even tragic conference, there the two of them had been quite simply getting drunk together! There was no mistaking Jolival's beaming countenance, the flush mantling his nose and the glazed look in his eyes. He was in what was commonly called a state of mild inebriation and Marianne wondered whether this temporary euphoria was, after all, a cause for great rejoicing.

'You still have not told me where he is,' she said severely. 'Although I am glad to see that you appear to have passed an agreeable evening.'

'Most agreeable. We are in perfect agreement. But you were asking me where our friend is now? The answer is, he's in the room next to mine.'

'He has consented to spend the night here? In Prince Sant'Anna's house?'

'He had no reason to refuse. Besides, who said anything about Prince Sant'Anna? This house belongs to Turhan Bey. In other words, the man whom Beaufort knew as Caleb.'

'You were supposed to tell him everything,' Marianne burst out. 'Why didn't you say —'

'That, like the Deity, these were three persons in one? No, my child. You see —' Jolival dropped the bantering tone he had used so far and became oddly serious. 'It did not seem to me that I had the right to reveal a secret which is not my own – or yours either, if it comes to that. If the Prince wants Jason Beaufort to know that the man he treated as a slave and almost allowed to die under the lash was your husband, he will say so. But for my own part, I think that, considering Jason's attitude to coloured people, it is best that he should continue in ignorance. Since you mean to sever your connection with the Prince and resume your own life after the child is born, there is no reason why Beaufort should not go on believing he is dead. '

During this speech, Marianne's initial protest died away as she had time to think. Jolival's wisdom, even when drawn from a bottle, could be disconcerting, but it was sound. And very often, against all the odds, he had been right.

'But in that case, how did you manage to explain the fact that I was living in Caleb's house – and that I had suffered myself to remain in – in my present condition?'

Jolival, who seemed to be having some difficulty in retaining his balance on his feet, sat down cautiously on the very edge of the bed and, taking out his handkerchief, began to mop his brow with it. He was looking extremely warm and smelled strongly of tobacco, but for once Marianne did not even notice it.

'Come now,' she said again. 'How did you explain that?'

'Very easily – and without straying very far from the truth. You decided to have the child which was conceived in such frightful circumstances – and I may say it is well for Signor Damiani that he

114

has already departed this life because our friend's one idea at this moment would be to tear him limb from limb. Where was I? Oh, yes. You kept the child because it was no longer possible to be rid of it without putting your life at risk. Beaufort can scarcely object to that, especially since his moral code is so much stricter than yours – than ours, I mean.'

'What exactly *do* you mean?' Marianne asked crossly.

'Just this – that whoever the father and whatever the circumstances, Beaufort believes that any woman who procures herself an abortion is committing a crime. Well, he's a man of principle and that includes a respect for human life and what amounts to a reverence for babies carried to extremes.'

'In other words,' Marianne said, dazedly, 'he was furiously angry that I was expecting a child but by no means willing for me to get rid of it?'

'Precisely. What he actually said was that he had truly believed that this was simply one of the bad dreams which had haunted him for so long but that, since it was a fact, he was glad I had had sense enough to stop you doing anything so foolish. Women, he said, ought to realize that a child was much more their creation than the man's. Let the father be who he might, there was a bond between the child and its mother which some never realized until it was too late. So, you see, I had no need to look for many explanations. He found them for himself.'

'And my being here?'

'Just as simple. Caleb owed his life to you. It was natural that, once he had resumed his true identity, he should offer you a refuge from the animosity of the British ambassador in his house, where no one would ever think to look for you.'

'And Jason accepted that?'

'Without a moment's hesitation. He is filled with remorse at the thought of having treated as he did a man of his worth – and influence. He is determined to present his apologies tomorrow morning. Don't worry,' Jolival added quickly, seeing Marianne's start of anxiety, 'I mean to warn the Prince before I go to bed.'

'At this hour? He will be asleep.'

'No. He's a man who sleeps very little and does much of his work at night. He reads, writes, attends to his collections and his business interests, which are very extensive. You know nothing of him, Marianne, but I can tell you he is a very remarkable man.'

What had got into Jolival? Was he going to start singing the

Prince's praises? How could he let his mind wander so easily from the subject which was of such passionate interest to her?'

'Jolival,' she said, a little pettishly, 'can we, please, get back to Jason? What else did he say? What does he think? What is he going to do?'

But Arcadius, whose manners appeared to have deserted him, only yawned, rose and stretched himself like a scrawny cat.

'What did he say? Lord, I can't remember now! But I'll tell you what he thinks. He loves you more than ever and he's fuller of remorse than an overgrown garden is of weeds. And to what he's going to do – he'll tell you that himself in the morning. Because I dare say he'll come running to your door as soon as he's out of his bed. All the same . . . don't expect him too early.'

Marianne was too happy to reproach her old friend for a degree of frivolity which she put down largely to the brandy he had drunk.

'I see how it is,' she said, laughing at him. 'You think he'll still be suffering the effects of your potations.'

'Oh, he's a sound enough head on him. He's still young. But there, enough is enough. If it will stop you worrying yourself all night, I'd better tell you, I suppose, that Beaufort means to beg you very humbly to go to him in America as soon as your health permits.'

'Go to him? But why not go together? Why can he not wait for me?'

She had started up agitatedly and Jolival bent and pressed her shoulders gently down again on to the pillows.

'Now don't excite yourself again, Marianne. The situation in Washington is very grave, because relations between President Madison and the British Government are extremely strained. Beaufort told me that he met a friend of his in Athens, a cousin of that Captain Bainbridge who was obliged by the Dey of Algiers to carry a tribute to the Sultan aboard his vessel and so became the first American, before Beaufort, ever to penetrate this city. This man was making all speed back to the United States, for Bainbridge has been appointed admiral-in-chief of the American fleet and is mustering all the best ships and men. The war which is coming will be fought at sea at least as much as on land. Beaufort's friend wanted him to go with him, but he insisted on coming here to find you first —'

'And to find his ship, of course,' Marianne added gloomily. 'If America needs captains for her navy, she will need ships even more.

116

The brig is a well-found vessel, fast and well-armed – and she fits Jason like a second skin. It's nice of you to try and sugar the pill for me, Jolival, but it makes me wonder if the Prince wasn't right, that day when he slammed out of the house saying that if it hadn't been for the *Sea Witch* he doubted whether we should ever have set eyes on Jason Beaufort again. . . . In spite of all I've heard tonight, I still can't quite get that thought out of my head.'

'Then just you stop fidgetting yourself about it. Beaufort is not one to hide his feelings, you know that as well as I do. He has made a clean sweep of all his anger and resentment. What do you care for the international situation as long as you have found happiness again?'

'Happiness?' Marianne murmured. 'Aren't you forgetting that if there is a war, Jason will have to fight?'

'My dear girl, our country has been at war for ten years or more but that hasn't prevented a great many women from being happy. Forget the war. Rest and relax, give the Prince the son he wants so much and then, if you still want to, we will travel quietly back to Italy together so that you may settle the matter of your future. When that is done, there will be nothing to stop us setting sail for the Carolinas.'

Jolival's voice droned on soothingly, only a little thickened by alcohol, but Marianne did not miss the tell-tale phrase. She picked it up at once.

'If I still want to? Are you mad, Arcadius?'

He smiled rather vaguely and made an evasive gesture.

'Women change their minds,' was all he said, and made no attempt to explain himself further.

But how could you explain to a very young woman in her exhausted and exacerbated state, who had suddenly been given a fresh glimpse of life and happiness in the return of the man she loved, that she knew, as yet, nothing of the surprises of motherhood? She was looking forward to it as an ordeal and, at the same time, as a kind of formality. She did not know that putting out of her life and her mind the child she had never wanted might prove unexpectedly painful.

But it would be a waste of time even to try to bring her face to face with the truth. Not until she held in her arms the tiny, living bundle that had been born of her own flesh would Marianne begin to recognize her own reactions to that greatest miracle of all human life, the birth of a man or woman.

For the time being, her face was set stubbornly.

'I shall not change,' she declared, with the obstinacy of a child.

The last word ended abruptly in a little gasp. The pain had come again, striking without warning and expanding slowly. Jolival, who had been on the point of withdrawing, with a philosophic shrug, to seek his own bed, stopped suddenly.

'What is it?'

'I – I don't know. A pain – oh, not very bad, but it's the second time and I was wondering —'

She did not finish. Jolival was already out in the passage that separated Marianne's room from Dona Lavinia's, shouting loudly enough to wake the dead.

He'll rouse the whole house, Marianne thought, but she knew by now that she was going to need help and that the time had come for her to fulfil her great task as a woman.

CHAPTER SIX

'I come of a free people...'

'I come of a free people . . .'

Marianne had been in labour for more than thirty hours and still the child had not appeared. Dona Lavinia and the doctor stayed with her in her room while she endured the onslaughts of pain with ever-weakening resistance. As the contractions grew more violent, she had set herself not to cry out, making it a point of honour with herself to behave with the stoicism proper to a great lady. Scarcely a moan escaped from between her clenched teeth.

But the ordeal had gone on for so long that in the end the incessant torture of it had made her forget all her resolutions. Writhing like a captive animal, her sheets soaked with sweat, she was screaming now without restraint. She had been screaming for hours and her voice was growing fainter. All she wanted was to die, quickly, and get it over.

Her screams found an echo in the hearts of the two men who waited in the boudoir adjoining her bedchamber.

Jolival stood at the window, biting his nails and staring into space, as though fixed there until the end of time.

As for Jason Beaufort, his almost British phlegm had flown to the winds at Marianne's first moan. He was pale and hollow-eyed and smoked continuously, in a kind of frenzy, lighting one cigar after another and pressing his hands to his ears from time to time when her screams were more than he could bear. The heel of his boot had worn a large hole in the carpet.

Day was breaking. Neither Jason nor the Vicomte had slept since the previous night but neither seemed aware of it. Then, at the very moment when the distant gun proclaimed the dawn, a cry from the bedroom, ending in a despairing sob, made Jason start as if the cannon had been fired at Marianne herself.

'This is intolerable!' he cried. 'Can nothing be done? Must she endure this agony?'

Jolival shrugged. 'It is nature's way, it seems. The doctor tells me that the birth of a first child is often a lengthy business.'

'The doctor! Do you trust that pompous ass? Well, I do not!'

'Is that on account of his turban?' Jolival inquired. 'I suppose you

119

think no doctor can be any good unless he's dressed in a frock coat? This one seems competent enough, as far as I have been able to judge from talking to him. Not but what I'm beginning to share your opinion. When I looked in just now, he was sitting in the corner with his chin on his chest, playing with a string of amber beads and taking no notice whatsoever of poor Marianne, who was screaming her heart out.'

Jason strode towards the door as though intending to batter it down.

'I'm going to tell him what I think of him,' he said wildly.

'You will do no good. It makes no impression on him at all. I tried it. I asked him how much longer this agony would go on.'

'And what did he say?'

'Insh'Allah.'

Beaufort's bronzed face darkened to brick red.

'Oh, did he! Well, we'll see whether he'll dare to answer me in the same way!'

He was on the point of bursting into Marianne's room when a door which gave on to an external gallery was opened by a woman servant who stood aside to permit the entrance of an extraordinary apparition. The newcomer was a tall woman swathed in black muslin robes and wearing on her head a curious kind of pointed head-dress which gleamed with pure gold in the first rays of the morning sun. Gold, too, were the long earrings that dangled against either cheek.

The room was thick with the reek of Jason's and Jolival's cigars and Rebecca recoiled a little as she entered and waved her hand before her face in an effort to clear the smoke. She looked con-sideringly at the two men who were staring at her as though she had been the statue in *Don Giovanni* come to life to demand an account of their misdeeds. Then, going to the window, she flung it open, letting in the cold, damp air from the garden.

'One does not smoke near to the chamber of a woman in labour,' she said sternly. 'Moreover, men have no business in the women's quarters at such times. Go, now.'

The two men looked at one another, considerably taken aback by this quelling speech, but Rebecca was already opening the door by which she had just entered and pointing commandingly to the gallery.

'Go, I say! I will call you when it is over.'

'But – but who are you?' Jolival managed to ask.

'I am called Rebecca,' the strange woman deigned to answer. 'Judah ben Nathan, the physician of the Kassim Pasha quarter, is my father. The lord Turhan Bey sent for me an hour past to attend a friend of his who is suffering greatly in childbed.'

Satisfied with this information, Jolival turned meekly to the door but Jason stood eyeing this autocratic female, whose head-dress made her taller than himself, suspiciously.

'He sent for you, you say? I don't believe it. He has his own doctor in there.'

'I know that. Jelal Osman Bey is a good doctor but his ideas on childbirth are those of a true believer of Islam. The woman must fight her own battle and it is necessary to wait the outcome before interfering. But there are times when it does not do to wait too long and so, if you please, do not waste any more of my time with idle questions.'

'Come along,' Jolival said, drawing the reluctant American away. 'Leave it. Turhan Bey knows what he is about.'

Neither he nor Jason had set eyes on the master of Humayunabad since early the previous morning. He had appeared suddenly in the midst of the confusion caused by Jolival's cries for help and when Jason, who had also been awakened by the servants' clamour, had come to see what the matter was the two men had found themselves face to face.

The meeting had passed off quite smoothly, in spite of Jolival's fears and the fumes of old brandy. Jason Beaufort had thanked his preserver warmly and with perfect self-command. He had also contrived tactfully, and with unexpected delicacy for a man of his temper, to convey his regrets for the somewhat rough and ready treatment he had accorded to him when the true identity of the man was unknown to him and he had seen him only in the guise of an escaped slave. Turhan Bey, not to be outdone in courtesy, had assured his erstwhile captain that he bore him no malice for usage which he had brought on himself. Then he had begged the American to consider his house his own and to call freely on his wealth and influence.

He had listened without expression to Jason's halting words of thanks for having taken the Princess Sant'Anna into his house and, in some sort, making up for the grave wrongs which he, Jason, had unconsciously done her, replying merely that it was the least he could do. Then he had bowed politely and withdrawn and they had not seen him since.

121

When Jolival had presented himself at the door of the pavilion where he dwelt, he had been informed that the lord Turhan Bey was at his warehouse.

After being sent packing by Rebecca, the two men wandered down the long, covered passage which ran through the bare, wintry gardens to a brightly painted kiosk which rose up against the surrounding greyness like an outsized and improbable flower. Each was feeling awkward and out of place and neither could think of anything to say, although both of them were secretly relieved to have escaped from the smoke-filled atmosphere of the boudoir and the cries from the next room. The silence of the empty garden seemed to them delicious and each sought to prolong it as far as possible.

But their moment of respite was fated to be a brief one. Jason was just lighting a fresh cigar when the sound of running footsteps echoed along the gallery. An instant later, Gracchus appeared. He was out of breath and scarlet with exertion, while the carroty hair stood up straight on his head. Obviously the news he brought was far from good.

'The brig!' he called out as soon as he caught sight of the two men. 'She's not at her moorings!'

The colour drained from Jason's face and as the boy stumbled, exhausted, almost at his feet, he seized him by the shoulders and hauled him upright again.

'What's that you say? Has she been stolen?'

Gracchus shook his head, opened his mouth, gasping for breath like a fish out of water, gulped painfully two or three times and managed to say: 'Put . . . put her in quarantine, damn them! She's . . . riding at anchor . . . out in . . . the Bosphorus, near the Tower of the Maiden . . .'

'Quarantine!' Jolival exclaimed. 'But why?'

The one-time errand boy of the rue Montorgueil jerked his shoulders angrily.

'It seems one of the men on board her took ill and died suddenly of the cholera. They took the body ashore at once and burned it but the port authorities insist on the ship's being quarantined. When we got there, with Monsieur O'Flaherty, she'd just put out from her moorings with one of my lord Turhan's men made to pilot her. It's dreadful, isn't it, Monsieur Jason? What are we going to do?'

Gracchus, whose delight at seeing his favourite hero once again, aided by such explanations as Jolival thought proper to give him, had made the harsh memories of their last encounter melt like butter in the sun, had been despatched by Jason to find Craig O'Flaherty and instruct him to set about assembling a crew.

Unexpectedly enough, Jason's old lieutenant of the *Sea Witch* had not left Constantinople. Something in his Irish soul had responded to the colour and poetry of the triple city, and also to the possibilities, for a man with some small business sense, of the contraband trade in Russian vodka and the wines of the Crimea.

Left to himself, after Achmet Reis had taken the brig and some of those aboard her to the Ottoman capital, O'Flaherty had at first been at a loss what to do. It would have been possible, certainly, for him to have signed on with one or other of the British vessels which, like the frigate *Jason*, were frequent visitors to the Golden Horn, and so made his way back to Europe. But, once again, his Irish soul rebelled at the thought of treading an English deck, even with the object of returning to his native seas.

Furthermore, not only was he still a welcome visitor at the French Embassy, where he called frequently to see Jolival, but he was also drawn to the American brig by something stronger than himself. He loved the ship almost like a child and when he learned that the Haseki Sultan had bought her and given her to Marianne he, like Marianne herself, had settled down to wait for Beaufort, with the same complete faith and rather more patience.

The early days of waiting had not been easy. He had no very clear idea what to do with himself but divided his time and what little money he had between the various taverns in the city and the shadow play in the Seraskier Square, which delighted his boyish heart. He had gone on in this way until one day his thirst for alcohol had taken him into a certain tavern in Galata which was the haunt of the most fervent devotees of Bacchus of all the European shore.

There, he had made the acquaintance of one Mamoulian, a Georgian from the region of Batum, who was endeavouring, in the fumes of Greek and Italian wines, to forget the war which was slowly ruining him. For the hostilities between the Porte and Tsar Alexander had effectively put a stop to the profitable imports of vodka, since no seaman worthy of the name was willing any longer to run the risks of taking his ship into Russian waters.

A friendship, fostered by a few bottles of wine drunk in company, had sprung up between the two and they had agreed to form a temporary alliance. The end of the war was in sight and O'Flaherty, for his part, was unwilling to engage himself for any length of time, not wishing to outstay the brig in Constantinople.

As a result, leaving word for Jolival that he could be found at the bar known as the San Giorgio, which had become his favourite haunt, the Irishman had plunged happily into two smuggling expeditions both of which were crowned with success and, besides restoring his fortunes in a most agreeable way, had made the time hang much less heavily on his hands.

As luck would have it, he had just returned from the second of these voyages and was back in Galata when Gracchus came looking for him with the news of Jason's arrival and his initial instructions. Craig O'Flaherty had promptly celebrated the happy event by downing an enormous bumper of Irish whiskey, procured from heaven alone knew where, and had then set off, towing Gracchus after him, to cross the Golden Horn and hasten to the Phanar waterfront, to be greeted with the disconcerting sight which Gracchus had described.

The two of them had spent the whole day running up and down trying to find out where the brig was lying, so that sunset had caught them on the wrong side of the Golden Horn and they had been obliged to spend the night in a Greek taverna, at considerable risk of being taken up by the watch.

There they had drowned their sorrows in a resinated wine which had left them both with aching heads and, at daybreak, they had flung themselves into a boat to cross the water again and make their report.

Ignoring Gracchus's anguished query, Jason asked merely: 'Where have you left Mr O'Flaherty?'

'With the porter – the *kapiji*, I mean. He didn't like to come in – not knowing Turhan Bey. He's waiting there for your orders.'

'I'll go to him and fetch him in. We must decide what is to be done. And there's the child still not come —'

'*Mon Dieu*!' Gracchus exclaimed. 'What with everything else, I was forgetting the baby! Isn't it born yet?'

'No,' Jolival said. 'He – or she, because there's no saying it will be a boy, after all – is taking his time about it.'

'But – isn't it dangerous, taking so long?'

Jolival shrugged. 'I don't know. We must hope not.'

Their hopes were justified. For even as the Vicomte was speaking, Rebecca's long, supple and experienced hands, reaching right into

124

the body of her patient to turn the child, which was positioned badly, were delivering Marianne at last.

She, poor girl, had suffered so much that the actual birth drew from her no more than a plaintive cry, followed by merciful unconsciousness. She did not hear the baby's first, remarkably vigorous wail as Rebecca slapped it sharply. Or Dona Lavinia's delighted exclamation: 'It's a boy! Sweet Jesus, we have a son . . .'

'And a very fine boy, too,' the Jewess added. 'He must weigh nearly nine pounds. He'll be a splendid man. Go and tell those two fools who were smoking away in the next room. No doubt you'll find them in the gallery.'

But the faithful nurse of the Sant'Annas was no longer listening. She had fled from the chamber, picking up her starched petticoats to run the faster, and was making straight for the Prince's apartments. As she ran, she was laughing and crying and babbling aloud, possessed by a joy that must be shared.

'A son!' she was crying. 'He has a son! The curse is lifted. God has taken pity on him at last . . .'

In the meantime, while Rebecca attended to the new-born child, Marianne was recovering consciousness under the ministrations of Jelal Osman Bey. The doctor had roused himself at last from his fatalistic stillness and hurried to revive the young mother from her dangerous swoon. The life of a woman capable of bringing into the world such a boy as she had just given birth to was not to be lightly thrown away.

Marianne, opening her eyes, was vaguely aware of a dark face with a little pointed beard which she was able to identify after a moment.

'Doctor,' she breathed. 'Will it . . . will it be much longer now?'

'Are you still in pain?'

'N-no. No . . . that's right. The pains have stopped.'

'And so they should have done, for it is all over.'

'O-ver?'

Marianne drew the word out slowly, as though struggling to grasp its meaning. She was conscious of little beyond the blessed relief to her tortured body. Over! The frightful agony was over. The pain was not going to come again and she could go to sleep at last.

But the face was still hovering over her and she could smell the scent of ambergris that clung to his garments.

125

'You have a son,' the doctor said, still more gently but with a hint of respect in his voice. 'You should be proud and happy because he is a magnificent boy.'

One by one, the words were beginning to penetrate, to acquire a meaning. Marianne's hands moved slowly over her body, and as realization broke over her that the monstrous swelling had gone, that her stomach was almost flat once more, the tears welled from her eyes.

They were tears of joy, relief and gratitude towards a Providence that had taken pity on her. As the doctor had said, it was over. Never had the word delivery been charged with a deeper meaning.

It was as though the bars of an iron cage which had stood between her and a glorious landscape bathed in sunlight had fallen away all at once. She was free. Free at last! And the very word itself was as if she had newly rediscovered it.

Rebecca, returning with the child in her arms, mistook the reason for the tears that were rolling down her face in a melancholy stream.

'You must not cry,' she said gently. 'You made the right choice, for it would have been a shame to lose such a child as this. See, how beautiful he is.'

She was holding out her arms, with their soft burden but even as she did so the reaction came, harsh and sudden. Marianne set her jaw and turned her head away.

'Take it away! I don't want to look at it!'

The Jewess frowned. Accustomed as she was to the unpredictable ways of women, she was shocked by the violence in the girl's voice. Even where the child was not wanted, the most stubborn and determined woman would be softened with pride and pleasure after giving birth to a son. She persisted, as though she had not understood.

'Do you not want to see your son?'

But Marianne shut her eyes tightly, with a desperate obstinacy. It was almost as if she were afraid of what she might see. She rolled her head on the pillow and the damp mass of her hair clung like seaweed about her face.

'No! Send for Dona Lavinia. She must look after it. I only want to sleep . . . sleep, that's all I want.'

'You shall sleep later,' Rebecca said sharply. 'It is not finished yet. Another half hour or so.'

She was laying the child down in the big cradle of gilded wood which two women had brought into the room, when Dona Lavinia returned.

The housekeeper's eyes were like stars. Oblivious of everything else, she went straight to the bed and fell on her knees beside it, as though before an altar, and pressed her lips fervently to the hand which lay abandoned on the sheet.

'Thank you,' she murmured. 'Oh, thank you . . . our Princess!'

Embarrassed by a gratitude she could not feel was in any way deserved, Marianne tried to withdraw her hand. She could feel it wet with tears.

'Please! Don't thank me, Dona Lavinia! I – I don't deserve it. Only tell me – that you are happy. That is all I want —'

'Happy, oh, my lady —'

Unable to say any more, she rose and turned to Rebecca. Drawing herself up gravely, she held out her arms.

'Give me the Prince,' she ordered.

The sound of the title came as a shock to Marianne. She realized all at once that the tiny thing which, while it still lay within her body, she had refused even to think of as a child, this formless being had taken on a new identity on coming into the world. He was the Heir! The one hope of a man who, from the day of his own tragic birth, had been paying for someone else's sin, a man so wretched that he could be grateful for a son sired by another man – even such a man! On the little bundle of fine linen and lace which Dona Lavinia was cradling to her heart with all the love and worship she might have given to the infant Saviour himself, rested the weight of centuries of tradition, of a great name and vast estates and of fabulous riches . . .

A bitter, resentful voice muttered deep in her heart: 'It is Damiani's child! The monstrous issue of an evil man whose life was all wickedness.' And it was answered in Dona Lavinia's calm, grave tones: 'He is the Prince! The last of the Sant'Annas and nothing and no one can ever alter that now!' And it was the calm certainty of love and loyalty which carried the day, just as when light and darkness meet, the light always prevails.

Standing in a pool of sunlight that poured into the room, Dona Lavinia held up an antique flask which she had taken from a small box and it shone with a gleam of dull gold. She tipped a tiny drop from it on to a fine linen cloth and passed it over the baby's lips.

'This wheaten flour comes from your lands, my lord. It is the bread that nourishes all those who are your own, servants and peasants. They make it grow for you but you must watch all your life that it does not fail them.'

She repeated the action, with almost the same words, pouring out from another, similar flask the very life blood of the Tuscan soil: a wine, dark, red and thick as the vital fluid itself.

When it was done, the old woman turned again to the bed where Marianne sat watching, fascinated in spite of herself, the stages of this curious little ceremony which had the grave simplicity of a religious rite.

'My lady,' she said earnestly, 'the priest will be here in a moment from the church of St Mary Draperis to baptize the young Prince. What name is it your Highness's wish that he shall be given?'

Taken unawares, Marianne felt herself flushing. Why must Dona Lavinia force her into a maternal role she did not want? Surely the old lady must know that the birth was simply part of a bargain between her master and the woman she persisted in regarding as her mistress, a bargain that was only the prelude to a final separation? Or was she trying to ignore it? Probably that was it, because she was making no attempt to bring the child to his mother. Yet some answer had to be given.

'I don't know,' Marianne said faintly. 'I don't think it is for me to decide . . . Have you no suggestion to make?'

'Yes, indeed! ! If it is agreeable to your Highness, Prince Corrado would wish the child to be called by the family name of Sebastiano. But it is usual for him to bear that of his maternal grandfather also.'

'But surely Don Sebastiano was Prince Corrado's grandfather, not his father?'

'That is so. But he preferred that the name Ugolino should not be used again. Will you tell me your father's name, my lady?'

Marianne felt as if the jaws of a trap were closing around her. Dona Lavinia knew what she was doing. She was deliberately seeking to bind the child's mother, willy-nilly, to the family she was endeavouring to leave. Marianne had never felt so weak and exhausted. She was tired out. Why did they have to bother her with the baby? Why couldn't they leave her alone even now and let her rest? She had a sudden vision of the portrait that reigned over her salon in Paris. Surely the proud and splendid Marquis d'Asselnat, whose title of nobility went back to the Crusades, in whatever warrior heaven he was now, would be angry to see his name given to a child of the steward Damiani? But, even as the thought crossed her mind, she heard herself answering, in a dreamlike voice that did not seem to belong to her, as though driven to the capitulation, as it seemed to her, by some power stronger than herself.

'His name was Pierre . . . Pierre-Armand . . .'

Her whole subconscious being was in rebellion against what she felt to be her own weakness but, although she tried to fight it, the vast weariness overcame her. Her eyelids were like lead and her brain was sinking into a fog. She had fallen into a deep sleep even before Rebecca had finished her ministrations.

Dona Lavinia stood for a moment looking at the slender form, so slender and frail now that it seemed lost in the great bed. There were tears in her eyes. Was it possible for so much strength of will to endure in one so young and so exhausted. Even after all that she had been through, she still retained sufficient presence of mind to reject the child, refusing to allow herself to succumb to the powerful maternal instinct.

The old woman glanced down pitifully at the tiny face nestling with closed eyes in its lace cap, from which a single, saucy lock of black hair peeped.

'If she would only look at you, my little Prince . . . just once. Then she could never bear to send you away. But come along then. Let's go and see him . . . He'll love you with all the love he has to give. He will love you for two.'

Leaving Rebecca, aided by a waiting woman, to finish doing what was needful for the young mother and to set the room to rights, she wrapped the baby in a shawl of soft, white wool and tiptoed from the bedchamber. She was half-way through the boudoir when Jolival burst in, with Jason hard on his heels.

'The baby!' cried the Vicomte. 'He has arrived? We've only just heard. . . . Oh, God! You've got him there?'

Poor Jolival was beside himself with excitement. The anguish of the past hours had given way all at once to such a joy as he would never have believed possible. He wanted to laugh and sing, to dance and drink and do a thousand foolish things. Like the Prince himself, he had thrust the facts of the baby's conception behind him and, in his love for Marianne, he saw the baby only as her son, the son of one who was like a daughter to him. Suddenly, he was discovering the marvellous thrill of being a grandfather.

Dona Lavinia parted the shawl with a careful finger, to show them the little red face sleeping peacefully, the tiny fists clutching fast to the new life that had just been given to him. Jolival felt the tears prick at his eyelids.

'Oh my God, he is so like her! Or rather, so like his grandfather.'

He had gazed too often at the portrait of the Marquis d'Asselnat not to be struck instantly by the resemblance, even though the child was not yet two hours old. By a merciful dispensation of Providence, the baby had no trait of his real father. The imprint of his mother was too strong to leave room for any other influence and Jolival thought that it was as well that the little boy should be much more an Asselnat than a Sant'Anna. Nor did he think that Prince Corrado would be at all displeased by the resemblance.

'He's a beautiful boy!' Jason exclaimed, with a warmth in his smile that found its way straight to the housekeeper's reluctant heart. 'The most beautiful I ever saw, that I will swear. What does his mother say?'

'She could not help but think him beautiful, could she?' Arcadius said quickly, with a note of pleading in his voice.

Dona Lavinia clasped the baby tighter to her breast and looked at the American with the tears welling up again in her stricken eyes.

'Alas, Sir, she would not even look at the poor little angel. She told me to take him away, with as much loathing as if he were a monster.'

There was a brief silence. The two men looked at one another but it was Jolival's eyes that fell.

'I was afraid of that,' he said huskily. 'Ever since she first knew she was with child, Marianne has fiercely rejected the idea of the baby.'

Jason said nothing. He stood, lost in thought, a crease between his brows and another at the corner of his mouth. But when Dona Lavinia, after wrapping the baby again, made as if to go on her way, he checked her.

'Where are you taking the child?'

She hesitated, bowing her head in an effort to hide the colour which had flooded into her face.

'I thought – that is, it will be proper to show him to the master of the house.'

It may have been the unnatural stiffness in her voice, but Jolival was suddenly aware of an undercurrent he could not define. Neither of the actors in the little scene had stirred but Dona Lavinia seemed to be held, rooted to the spot, under Jason's searching glance, and her breath was coming in little short, quick gasps, like an animal scenting danger.

Then the American drew back a step to let her pass, bowing politely from the waist.

'Of course,' he said gravely. 'You are perfectly right, Dona Lavinia. It is a delicate attention that does credit to you and to the child.'

When Marianne awakened from the beneficent sleep which had engulfed body and mind, the curtains in her room were drawn and the lamps were shedding a warm, golden radiance, for it was already evening. The tiled stove was purring like a big cat and Dona Lavinia was coming towards the bed, carrying a tray with something steaming on it. It might have been some slight sound which had woken her, or hunger, stimulated by the savoury smell of supper, because she felt no wish to leave the quiet haven of sleep. The longing for it still pervaded every fibre of her body.

She opened her eyes, all the same, and stretched luxuriously, like a contented cat, with the sheer, physical enjoyment of rediscovered freedom of movement, after long months of hampering constraint. Goodness, what a joy it was to feel oneself again, after all this time when her body had seemed to belong, not to her, but to an increasingly alien burden! Even the memory of the hours of agony she had endured in this very bed was fading fast, swept away on the tide of time into the thick mists of oblivion.

She shook aside a heavy lock of hair which was tickling her cheek and smiled at the housekeeper.

'Dona Lavinia, I'm hungry. What time is it?'

'Nearly nine o'clock, my lady. You have slept for almost twelve hours. Are you feeling better?'

'Much better. A few more hours' sleep and I shall be quite myself again.'

Meanwhile, Lavinia had been busy helping her young mistress to sit up amid a nest of pillows and was bathing her face with a cloth moistened with a fragrant lotion of verbena. That done, she laid the black laquer tray on her knees.

'What have you brought me?' Marianne asked, finding her interest in food abruptly revived.

'Vegetable soup, roast chicken and fruit stewed in honey, with a glass of chianti. The doctor says a little wine can do you no harm.'

Everything disappeared very speedily, and the modest meal

131

seemed to Marianne the most delicious thing in the world. She was savouring each small, physical pleasure of recovery with such intensity that she had no time as yet for the moral dilemmas which would intrude themselves all too soon.

She swallowed the last drop of wine with a sigh of satisfaction and sank back amongst her pillows, ready to slip back into the sleep which at that moment seemed the most desirable state of being. But then something stirred beyond the curtain which hung over the door. A hand put it aside, revealing the tall figure of Prince Corrado, and all Marianne's sense of well-being was gone in an instant.

He was the last person she wanted to see just then. In spite of the white turban, set with a turquoise stone, which swathed his proud head, she thought he looked a sinister figure in his black caftan, unadorned save for the broad dagger thrust through the silken sash. He was the personification of the dark shadow on her life, the evil genius that dogged her steps. Or was it the symbol of a troubled conscience which would not leave its owner altogether at peace? Watching him as he came towards her, he struck her as more than ever like a black panther.

He crossed the big room silently, with his easy stride, until he reached the foot of the bed. Dona Lavinia had dropped a curtsy and vanished, taking with her the empty tray.

For a moment, the two partners in this unlikely marriage stared at one another without speaking and, once again, Marianne began to feel uneasy. This man had a strange capacity of making her always feel in some indefinable way in the wrong.

Not knowing what to say, she sought for something neither stupid nor clumsy and then, remembering that she had just presented him with what must surely give him pleasure, she decided to smile and make the effort.

'Are you pleased?'

He nodded but his dark face remained unsmiling. And when he spoke it was in the low, measured tones that she remembered hearing for the first time from the other side of a mirror, a voice that seemed burdened with all the sorrows of the world.

'I have come to bid you farewell, my lady. Farewell and thank you for performing so magnificently your part in the contract between us. I must not inflict on you any longer a presence which must revive unpleasant memories for you.'

'Never think that,' Marianne cried impulsively. 'You have been very good to me, and very kind. Why must you leave me so soon? There is no hurry.'

She meant it. For the life of her, she could not have said what made her say it. Why was she trying to keep her strange husband by her, when all her hopes were centred now on Jason and looking forward to a life of happiness with him?

The Prince smiled, the shy smile which sat with such curious charm on that face of a heathen god.

'It is kind of you to say so but there is no need to pretend, or try to make me believe the impossible. I came to tell you that you are free, now, to live your own life. Thanks to you, I have a son and heir. Now you may follow your own destiny wherever it may lead you. I will help you, for it is my greatest wish to see you happy . . . Whatever you decide to do, whether you continue to bear my name or whether you wish to be rid of it as soon as maybe, be sure that I shall still see to it that you want for nothing.'

'Sir!' Marianne protested, her pride stung.

'Do not be offended. I mean the mother of my son to continue to enjoy the position which is hers by right of birth and beauty. You may remain here until you are quite recovered and when you wish to leave one of my ships will take you wherever you wish to go.'

She smiled again, with an unintentional touch of coquetry.

'Why must we talk of this tonight? I am still very tired and my thoughts are a little confused. Tomorrow I shall be better and we can consider together —'

He seemed to be on the point of saying something but on a sudden thought better of it and instead bowed deeply in the eastern fashion and murmured quickly: 'Permit me to bid your Highness a good night.'

'But —' Marianne began in some bewilderment. Then she broke off, understanding the reason for his sudden change of attitude. Trembling with joy, she watched the door thrust open by a masterful hand and Jason stepped into the room.

She realized at once the reason for Corrado's withdrawal and made no attempt to detain him. It would not be fitting for Turhan Bey to pay more than a brief courtesy visit to his guest, the Princess Sant'Anna. In fact, she had ceased to be aware of his presence at all. Her eyes, her heart and her whole mind were focused on the man who had just entered.

The two men, however, greeted one another with the utmost

133

politeness and Jason's voice sounded unwontedly deferential for a slave owner as he said: 'I have to thank you, Turhan Bey, for your advice and counsel. If I may, I should like to come and discuss it with you shortly. I must see you before I leave.'

'Come whenever you like, Mr Beaufort. I shall be expecting you.'

He went away at once after that. But Marianne had grasped only one thing from this exchange of civilities. Jason had spoken of leaving! Almost before the door had closed behind the Prince, she had framed the question – and made up her mind.

'You are leaving? Then I am coming with you.'

Jason walked unhurriedly up to the bed and bending, took her hand and dropped a swift kiss on it. Then, still holding it between his own, he looked at her with a smile which did not reach his eyes or smooth out the anxious creases from his brow.

'We have always agreed that I was to go, and that it would be tonight,' he said bluntly, yet with as much gentleness as he could. 'As to coming with me, you know quite well that is impossible.'

'Why? Because of my condition? But that is all over! I am quite well, I assure you! To go with you, I have only to be carried to the landing stage and from there a boat will take us straight to the *Sea Witch*. Surely you can carry me that far?' she added, tenderly teasing him. 'I am not very heavy.'

But his face held no hint of a smile.

'Yes, that would be easy enough, but your health is not the only difficulty.'

'Then what is it?' she cried angrily. 'Your own feelings? You don't want to take me, is that it?'

Her face was very flushed and her eyes a little too bright, as though with a fever. Jason tightened his clasp on her hands which felt suddenly burning hot to his touch.

'I cannot take you,' he corrected her firmly but very gently. 'For one thing, you are not as strong as you think and it will be several days yet before you can leave your bed. You have been through a perilous ordeal and the doctor is adamant. But that is not the main reason. I cannot take you because it is quite simply impossible. Turhan Bey has been with you. Did he say nothing?'

'Should he have done? I have only just woken up and had my supper. He only came in to say good evening . . .'

'Then I'll explain what has happened.'

Sitting on the edge of the bed to be nearer to her, Jason gave

Marianne a rapid sketch of what Gracchus and O'Flaherty had discovered.

'Our host has had inquiries made in the city during the day,' he said, 'which was perfectly natural since the brig bore his colours and was supposed to belong to him. He didn't like that story of a man dying suddenly of the cholera, or the speed with which the body was burned.'

'Why not? So far as I can gather, cholera isn't exactly unusual here.'

'No, but it's more usual in summer. And if you have sufficient influence, there's nothing simpler than to get hold of a body and dress it up appropriately and then burn it in a hurry. Turhan Bey thinks it is a ploy invented by the English to keep the vessel under observation, and he knows what he's talking about. So far it's certainly succeeded brilliantly.'

'But then you can't go – you will have to wait! For forty days, at least.'

Her simple pleasure in the fact did nothing to lighten Jason's frown. Moving closer to her, he let go her hands and, taking her by the shoulders instead, spoke earnestly into her face.

'My darling, you don't understand. I must go and go now. Sanders is waiting for me at Messina so that we can try the Gibraltar passage together. If I want to join him, I will have to do what I failed to do the other night. I must steal my ship and escape that way.'

'But that is madness! How will you manage without a crew? She's not a fishing boat!'

'I know that just as well as you do. I managed to get together enough men to work the ship out of Constantinople the other night. I'm better off today. Craig O'Flaherty is waiting at Galata with a few men he's managed to round up from the taverns there. They're not first-rate seamen but they are seamen of a sort, Europeans, too, who are tired of the east. And, if you will entrust him to me, I'll take young Gracchus also. He wants to sail with me.'

'Gracchus?'

Marianne felt a bitter pang in her heart. So Gracchus, too, wanted to leave her? In the time since she had first begun to put down roots in French soil, the urchin from the rue Montorgueil, the grandson of the laundress of the rue de la Révolte, had become much more than a servant to her. He had been a faithful friend, one she could trust and rely on. His devotion to her had been absolute. But it had

135

not taken Jason long to win some of his heart and Gracchus loved him almost as much as he loved Marianne and admired him deeply. Then the voyage aboard the *Sea Witch* had finally shown the youthful coachman the path of his dreams. The sea, with all its beauty and its tricks, its splendours and its perils, had become a real vocation and, remembering the boy's eagerness in the skirmish with the English frigates off Corfu, Marianne thought that she had no right to stand in his way.

'Take him, then,' she said quickly. 'I give him to you because I know he will be much happier with you. But why must you go so soon, Jason? Why not wait a little while – only a few days, so that I can —'

'No, Marianne. It's impossible. I cannot wait. In any case, I shall have to go secretly. There will be risks, fighting, perhaps, for the English will not let me sail out of the harbour without giving chase. I don't want to expose you to those risks. When you are quite better, you can go quietly aboard a Greek ship with Jolival and sail peacefully back to Europe. Once there, you have enough friends among seafaring men to find a vessel willing to dare the English blockade and carry you across the Atlantic.'

'I'm not afraid of danger. Nothing can frighten me as long as I'm with you.'

'You alone, perhaps, but aren't you forgetting, Marianne? You are no longer alone. Have you forgotten the child? Do you want to expose him, when he's no more than a few hours old, to the perils of the sea, of gunfire and the risk of shipwreck? This is war, Marianne.'

She broke free of his tender clasp and fell back on her pillows. Her face had gone very pale and there was a painful tightness in her chest. The child! Did he have to remind her? And what need had Jason to trouble himself about the little bastard? Did he seriously imagine she was going to take it with her to that other life, which was to be all clean, and fresh and new? That she was going to bring up Damiani's child with his, the children that she longed to give him? In her uncertainty, she burst out angrily, to gain time: 'It is not war! Even here, at the ends of the earth, we know that there has been no formal declaration of war between Britain and the United States.'

'Certainly. War has not been declared but incidents are becoming more and more frequent and it will be only a matter of weeks. Mr Canning knows that. He'd not have hesitated to impound my brig if she hadn't been protected by Turhan Bey's colours. Would you rather it caught me here, and left me rotting in an English prison while my friends and fellow countrymen were fighting?'

'I want you to be free and happy . . . but I want to keep you with me.'

It was a cry of despair and in the same instant Marianne had cast herself on Jason's chest and was burying her face in his coat, while her thin arms – still so pitifully thin and the skin almost transparent – encircled his broad shoulders.

He held her to him, grieving for the hurt he had been forced to cause her once again, cradling her like a child while his hand caressed the soft curls at the nape of her neck.

'You can't keep me like that, my heart. I am a man, a seaman, and I must live according to my nature. Besides . . . would you truly love me if I were content to hide behind your skirts when danger threatened? Would you love a coward, without honour?'

'I should love you anyhow . . .'

'No, you wouldn't. You're deceiving yourself, Marianne. If I were to listen to you, my sweet, a day would come when you would blame me for my cowardice. You'd throw it in my face, with scorn and contempt. And you would be right. As God is my witness, I'd give anything to be able to stay with you, but I must choose America.'

'America!' she said bitterly. 'That endless country . . . with so many people in it. Does she really need you, just one among her countless children?'

'She needs them all. America only won her freedom because all those who wanted it joined together to make one people! I come of that free people . . . one grain of sand on the sea shore, yet that grain, carried away on the winds, is lost for ever.'

Marianne was weeping now, with little, hard, gasping sobs, and clinging with all her strength to the virile form that was a solid wall to her, a refuge that she was about to lose once more, and for how long? For she had lost, she knew that. She had always known it. From the first words he had uttered, she had known that she was fighting a losing battle, that she could never hold him.

As though he had divined her thought, he murmured into her hair: 'Be brave, my sweet. We shall be together again soon. Even if the chances of the war mean that I cannot be there to greet you

137

when you land at Charleston, everything will be ready to welcome you. To welcome you both, you and the baby. There will be a house, servants and an old friend of mine to look after you . . .'

Marianne had stiffened at the mention of the child and once again she avoided speaking of him, concentrating on her own misery instead.

'I know . . . but you will not be there,' she mourned. 'What will become of me without you?'

Gently but firmly, he loosened the clinging arms which held him and stood up.

'I'm going to tell you,' he said.

Before Marianne could recover from her surprise or make a move to stop him, he had walked quickly from the room, leaving the door open behind him. She heard him go swiftly across the bourdoir, calling: 'Jolival! Jolival! Come here!'

A moment later he was back with the Vicomte on his heels. But what made Marianne gasp was the realization that, in his arms, with infinite care, he held a small white woolly bundle from which emerged two tiny, moving pink blobs.

The blood drained from Marianne's face as it came to her that Jason was bringing her the child whose very presence filled her with loathing. She cast about her wildly, seeking childishly for a way of escape, for somewhere to hide from the peril advancing on her, wrapped in a snow-white shawl and carried in the arms of the man she loved.

Coming to the foot of the bed, he tossed back the lock of black hair which fell over his eyes with an automatic gesture and beamed triumphantly at the frightened girl.

'This is what is going to become of you, my sweet. An adorable little mother! Your son will keep you company and stop you thinking too much about the war. You can't imagine how quickly this little fellow will make the time pass for you.'

He was coming round the bed towards her . . . In another moment he would be laying the child down on the counterpane. . . . His blue eyes were alight with mischief and in that minute Marianne almost hated him. How could he?

'Take that child away,' she articulated, between gritted teeth. 'I have already said I don't want to see him.'

There was a sudden silence, a silence so vast and crushing that Marianne was frightened. Not daring to raise her eyes to Jason's face for fear of what she might see there, she went on, in a much milder tone: 'Try to understand what he means to me. I – I can't help it.'

She had been prepared for an outburst of anger but Jason's voice remained quiet and perfectly level.

'I don't know what he means to you – and I do not need to know. No, no, don't try to explain. Jolival has done so more than adequately and I am quite aware of the circumstances of the child's conception. But now I am going to tell you what he means to me. He's a fine, strong, healthy little man, something you have made very slowly and brought into the world with suffering that would have served to wipe out the worst of sins, if sin there was, and make it holy. And, most of all, he is your child – yours and only yours. He even looks like you.'

'That's true,' Jolival put in nervously. 'He looks like the portrait of your father.'

'Come, look at him at least,' Jason persisted. 'Have the courage to look, if only for a moment, or else you're not the woman —'

You're not the woman I thought you were. That was what he meant. Nor did his meaning escape Marianne. She knew his demanding private code of honour too well not to have scented danger. If she were to refuse to do as he asked, which he evidently regarded as a perfectly natural thing, a quite normal reflex, she would run the risk of seeing the place she held in his heart shrinking a little. Already she had some reason to think that place less than it had been. For too long life had conspired to show her to Jason in her least attractive light.

She surrendered unconditionally.

'Very well,' she sighed. 'Show him to me if you insist.'

'I do insist,' he agreed gravely.

Marianne had expected that he would show him to her in his arms, so that she could take a quick glance, but instead he bent swiftly and set down the trifling burden on one of her pillows, close by his mother's shoulder.

She shrank a little at the unexpected contact but managed to bite back the exclamation of annoyance that rose to her lips. Jason was looking at her, studying her reaction. So she sat up, cautiously, and turned a little on her side. But when her eyes rested for the first time on her son, the shock was not what she had expected.

Not only was there nothing in the baby to recall his horrible sire, but he was truly such a perfect little cherub that in spite of herself her heart missed a beat.

Swaddled in his absurdly complicated assortment of garments, the little prince was sleeping with total concentration. His tiny fingers lay spread like starfish against the woollen shawl. A cloud of fine black hair showed faintly under his cap of Valenciennes lace, curling lightly above a small, round face which had the downy softness of a peach. He seemed to be having pleasant dreams because the corners of his tiny mouth quivered slightly, as if he were already trying to smile.

Marianne stared at him, fascinated. The look of the Marquis d'Asselnat was unmistakable. It came chiefly from the shape of the mouth and the determination about the tiny chin and the promise of intelligence in the high, sculptured brow.

Looking at the small person she had feared so greatly, Marianne felt as if something inside her were struggling to spread its wings and be free. It was as though somewhere, in the secret depths of her being, there was another birth about to take place, unknown to her. A strange force, formed of a conspiracy between mind and heart, was welling up in her, whether she would or no.

Almost fearfully, she put out a cautious finger and touched one of the little hands as softly as a butterfly. The movement was too shy to be called a caress. But the tiny fist stirred suddenly. The miniature fingers uncurled and then closed firmly round their mother's with a tenacity unexpected in a new-born baby.

At that, something broke in Marianne. As though a window had been flung open, violently, by a gale of wind, the thing that had been struggling inside her took flight and soared heavenwards, flooding her with a joy that was almost painful in its intensity. Tears sprang to her eyes and poured down her cheeks in a refreshing stream, washing away the bitterness and disgust, all the mire which had clogged Marianne's soul for so long and stifled it. What did it matter now how the child had come into her life and, like a tiny, indomitable tyrant, had demanded her very flesh and blood. She discovered with a wondering amazement that he was hers, flesh of her flesh, breath of her breath, and that she acknowledged him for what he was.

The two men standing on either side of the bed held their breath and dared not move a muscle as they watched the miracle taking place before their eyes, the miracle of the awakening of mother-love. But when, still held prisoner by her son, she began to cry, Jason bent again and lifted the baby gently to place him in his mother's arms. This time they closed and held him.

The little silky head settled of its own accord against the warm breast in a gesture so instinctively caressing that it took Marianne's breath away. Then she looked up at Arcadius, who was weeping unashamedly, and at Jason, who was smiling, with eyes that sparkled through her tears like diamonds in the sun.

'You need not look like that,' she said softly. 'Your little plot has succeeded. You have won.'

'It was no plot,' Jason said. 'We merely wanted you to agree that your son is the most beautiful baby in the world.'

'Well, you've done it. I do agree.'

Meanwhile, Jolival, who had not shed so many tears since he could remember, was sniffing and fumbling in his pockets from which he extracted, first, a handkerchief, into which he blew with a noise like the last trump, and, secondly, his watch, which he consulted uneasily, then glanced with an anxious expression at Marianne. But Jason, who had observed this proceeding, spared him the role of spoil-sport.

'I know,' he said quietly. 'It is more than time and O'Flaherty must be at the beach already.'

The delicate veil of Marianne's brand new happiness was rent in an instant. Lost in her discovery, she had temporarily forgotten what loomed ahead.

'Oh no!' she cried out. 'Not so soon?'

Feverishly, as though feeling herself suddenly a prisoner, she thrust the baby at Jolival and threw back the covers as if to get up. But she had over-estimated her strength and almost before her feet had touched the ground she felt her head swimming and she fell forward with a little cry into Jason's arms, as he hurried round the bed to catch her.

He lifted her and held her briefly in his arms, alarmed to find her so light. He was suddenly torn by a parting he had not known would be so painful and covered her face with kisses before laying her back, with infinite gentleness, in her silky nest and drawing the covers tenderly over her trembling body.

'I love you, Marianne. . . . Never forget that I love you. But, for God's sake, be reasonable! We shall meet again soon, I know. . . . A few weeks, only a few weeks and we shall be together again, and you will have your strength and health again . . . and then nothing shall ever part us.'

He was so obviously overcome that Marianne smiled tremulously

141

at him, but still with a flicker of irony that showed a little of her old fighting spirit.

'Nothing? Not even the war?'

He kissed her again, her nose, her forehead, her lips and both her hands.

'You know very well that no power on earth can divide us for ever. Certainly no paltry war is going to do it.'

Then, almost as if he were afraid of a tenderness that might sap his courage, he tore himself from her arms and fled from the room, striding straight past Jolival who stood staring after him, the child in his arms.

Jolival's eyes turned uncertainly to Marianne. He wondered if he ought to give her back the baby. But all her new-found bravery had abandoned her and she was lying face down, with her head buried in her pillows, weeping as if her heart would break. At that moment, there was nothing the Vicomte could say to comfort her and besides, he wanted to go after Jason and see with his own eyes the success or failure of his rash enterprise.

He left the room on tiptoe and went to restore baby Sebastiano to Dona Lavinia.

The big bedchamber was quiet except for the soft purring of the stove and the sound of sobbing. But outside, in the cold night, the wind was rising.

CHAPTER SEVEN

A Night for the Devil

By the time that Jason, Gracchus and Jolival reached the rendezvous, which was that same unfrequented stretch of shore behind the mosque of Kilij Ali Pasha where the Klepht, Theodoros, had borne Marianne unconscious from the sea, it was so dark, in spite of the obligatory lanterns, that at first they did not see Craig O'Flaherty and his men at all.

A strong wind was sweeping along the beach, tossing up the sand and whipping the sea into heavy, grinding breakers that spattered the darkness with white foam.

The time was that moment, just before the dawn, when the night is at its darkest and thickest, as if all the forces of darkness were gathering to help it keep possession of the earth and fight off the onslaught of the light. The three were more than fifteen minutes late. Preparations for departure had taken longer than anticipated because Gracchus had been temporarily mislaid, having been locked in a cellar by an oversight of the butler's. In addition, the party had been stopped more than once in the two leagues between Bebek and Galata by patrols of Janissaries out hunting for a miscreant who had caused sacrilegious disturbances in no less than three separate mosques.

The beach was so dark and empty that for a moment the three men believed themselves alone. Jason swore furiously into the wind, regardless of who might overhear him.

'Perhaps they thought we'd never get aboard in this gale,' Jolival hazarded. 'Or else they decided we were not coming —'

'They had no business to think or decide,' Jason snarled. 'As to the gale, well, they're sailors, aren't they? In any case, I'm sure they can't be far off. I know O'Flaherty.'

His previous loud cursing might well have sufficed but to make doubly sure he whistled three times on a particular note and a moment later was answered in an identical fashion. Almost immediately, Craig O'Flaherty and his men appeared, dark, shadowy figures which the privateer's eyes, accustomed to peering through the blinding spray, were soon able to pick out from the surrounding blackness.

143

The crew the Irishman had assembled could scarcely have been said to constitute the cream of the world's seamen. There were two Genoese, a Maltese, a Greek, an Albanian and two Georgians whom Craig had ruthlessly bribed away from the service of his friend Mamoulian. But they looked capable enough and stood up to Jason's practised scrutiny.

'So here you are at last,' was Craig's welcome. 'We were beginning to give up hope.'

'I dare say,' retorted Jason dryly. 'Several hours without a drink is a long time. Where were you, O'Flaherty? Find a bar somewhere still open?'

'In a safe place, and on consecrated ground, what's more,' the Irishman retorted, indicating the vague outline of a small *tekke* of Whirling Dervishes which made a white blur against the dark bulk of the mosque. You may not have noticed, but it's blowing fit to skin a cat. It was all we could do to keep our feet on the beach.'

'You have a boat?'

'Yes. That, too, is in a safe place – in that fisherman's hut, down there on the shore. Do you see it? And now, if you want my opinion, we had better be moving, unless we want our boarding party to take place in broad daylight. Dawn is not far off.'

'Come, then. Run out the boat.'

While the men ran down to the hut, Jason turned quickly to Jolival and grasped both his hands in the warm, spontaneous fashion which won him so many friends.

'We part here, then. Goodbye, my friend. Take good care of her. This is not the first time I have entrusted her to you.'

'I spend my life taking care of her,' Jolival said gruffly, trying to shake off a nasty feeling of impending disaster. 'You take care of yourself, Beaufort. Wars are not precisely rest cures.'

'Don't worry. I'm indestructible. And look after the baby, also. His mother's love for him is very new and still very fragile, I think. It may be a long while before I am able to take care of him.'

The American's hands were warm and strong and firm. Returning their friendly pressure impulsively, Jolival was troubled by a slight feeling of remorse. Seeing the younger man so ready to be a father to another man's child, he was sorry he had not told him the whole truth. Prince Corrado, certainly, had approved his decision to conceal his true identity but at that moment Jolival wished he had not done it. Jason was obviously expecting Marianne to have little

Sebastiano with her when she landed in America, and might not be best pleased to find things otherwise.

The men, under Craig's directions, were running the boat down to the sea. It was a long caique, sound and well-built and looked capable of a pretty turn of speed.

Suddenly, the Vicomte made up his mind.

'There is something else I want to tell you – something about the child. I've not told you before because it did not seem to me that I had the right, but now —'

'What is there about now in particular to make you decide to reveal a secret which does not belong to you – and which I may very well know already?'

'Which you —?'

Jason laughed. His large hand came down heavily on Jolival's shoulder, warmly reassuring.

'Perhaps I'm not quite such a fool as you and Marianne like to think, my friend. So you may be at peace with yourself. You have given nothing away, because you had no need to. Nor, by the way, have I any intention of giving young Sant'Anna my name. And now, goodbye.'

He was about to turn away when he suddenly gripped Jolival with both hands.

'Kiss her for me – and tell her I love her.'

Then he ran to join his men. They were having some trouble in getting the boat into the water. It was as if the sea were trying to throw off the vessel that had the temerity to try to ride it. Jolival could see the dim figures of men moving about against the background of foaming breakers and his mind groped half-unconsciously for a snatch of forgotten prayer.

Then, suddenly, there came a triumphant shout and Jolival saw nothing more.

'Here we go, then!' a voice cried in Italian. Already it sounded some way off. 'But it's a real night for the devil!'

Left alone on the beach, Jolival shivered. A night for the devil? True enough, perhaps. The caique had vanished. The sea had swallowed it, like the dark, gaping jaws of some ravening monster. There was nothing to be heard but the frenzied pounding of the waves and the howling of the wind. Was the gallant little craft still afloat?

Unable to free himself from his sense of foreboding, Jolival turned up the collar of his coat mechanically and climbed back up the slope towards the three bare plane trees where they had tethered the horses. He had no wish to return to Bebek. What was the point? Marianne would only pester him with questions to which he had no answers. At that precise moment, he did not even know for certain that the caique had not gone straight to the bottom.

The wind dropped for a second and he heard a church clock in Pera strike five. It gave him an idea. The French Embassy was nearby and, having been built as a Franciscan monastery, it contained a belfry which, although in a somewhat dilapidated condition, commanded a view over the Bosphorus and the Golden Horn. From up there, as soon as it was light enough, it would at least be possible to see what became of the *Sea Witch* and perhaps even something of the gallant band of men attempting to gain posseession of her.

Leaving the horses tethered to the plane tree so that the noise of hooves should not wake the whole district, which at this hour of a winter's morning was still shuttered and empty, Jolival turned his steps in the direction of the embassy. He had no difficulty obtaining entrance, once he had succeeded in rousing the porter, in itself no easy task. The man stood in some awe of the gentleman who came to play chess with the ambassador and, although it was a considerable time since he had last been seen there, he was admitted without question. It was as much as he could do, however, to prevent them from waking Monsieur de Latour-Maubourg.

'I sat up late at the bedside of a sick friend who is not expected to live,' he explained. 'The churches are not open yet and I wish very much to pray for him. There is no need to disturb his Excellency. I will see him later. All I want at present is to be left alone in the chapel.'

This thundering lie went down beautifully. Jolival knew his man. Conan, the ambassador's doorkeeper, was a good Breton and of a rigid piety which found no joy in Islam. He was pleasantly surprised to encounter such lofty sentiments in his master's friend.

'Friendship is a fine thing,' he pronounced sententiously, 'and the fear of God a finer still. With Monsieur le Vicomte's permission, I will say a prayer or two for his friend myself. For the present, the chapel is not locked. Monsieur has only to enter. There are candles and a tinder box at the door. You will be quite undisturbed.'

Jolival asked nothing better. He thanked the doorkeeper warmly, feeling a trifle uncomfortable, for the man was looking at him as though a halo were already sprouting round his head. Then, having strengthened his good opinion by slipping a gold coin discreetly into his hand, he hurried away through the ancient cloister towards the chapel.

The door opened with hardly a creak and he found himself breathing in the familiar smells of melted wax, incense and well-polished wood. The worthy Conan, indeed, took touchingly good care of what he thought of as his chapel. It was his way of striking a blow at the Infidel.

To discover the candles and light one with the tinder box, so that the porter might see the light through the windows, was the work of a moment. Seconds later, Jolival was climbing the narrow spiral stair that led upwards from beside the doorway two steps at a time, with the vigour of a young man.

He knew where to find, in its niche beside the bell, an object of the greatest relevance to his present purpose. This was the telescope, used by the ambassador to survey the traffic of the harbour and also, from time to time, the movements of his diplomatic colleague and neighbour, his particular *bête noire*, the British ambassador.

The belfry was not very high but high enough, in daylight, for a person standing there to be able to see everything that was happening in the vicinity of the Tower of the Maiden. And by the time that Jolival arrived, somewhat breathlessly, at the top, the night was already beginning to pale.

A lighter strip was showing behind the hills of Scutari, as though the colour were being leached out of the sky. Very soon, the narrows would be visible but not yet. Jolival tucked the telescope under his arm and leaned against the wall, trying to master his impatience. The morning seemed unconscionably slow in coming.

Little by little, as if a curtain were rising very slowly on a new act in the theatre, the majestic sweep of the Bosphorus and the Golden Horn began to take shape out of the darkness, still clad in the grey light of early morning which made one colour of the sky, with its hurrying shoals of wind-driven cloud, and the sea, with its watery clouds of foam flecking the surface.

Suddenly, Jolival seized the telescope and clapped it to his eye with a joyful exclamation. Down below, near the little wooden fort that crowned the ruined tower, the *Sea Witch* was hoisting her sails. The foresail billowed out, followed by the jib. It was still blowing too hard for her to carry much sail.

'They've done it!' Jolival cried exultantly to himself. 'They're away!'

It was true. In the grey light that was clearing and brightening with every second, the brig was veering gracefully, like a huge, ghostly bird, setting her course for the open sea. But their bold stroke had not gone unnoticed, for Jolival heard the sound of a shot and saw the little puff of smoke break from the fort, so that it looked like a testy old man smoking a pipe. But the shot fell a long way short. The *Sea Witch* was already clear of the land and, scorning the efforts of her would-be keepers as contemptuously as the steep seas under her prow, was heading gloriously for the Sea of Marmara and freedom, with the stars of the United States climbing challengingly to her masthead.

Arcadius watched her for a little while with eyes that were full of tears and he was on the point of giving thanks for her escape when all of a sudden it happened. . . . In a moment, the sea was alive with sails.

Tall pyramids of white canvas sailing out from behind the Princes' Islands in line ahead. These were no xebecs or polaccas, or any of those antiquated vessels which, however seaworthy, remained somehow pathetic. These were big, modern warships, well-armed and formidable.

Jolival swore comprehensively and he recognized them. A ship of the line, two frigates and three corvettes: Admiral Maxwell's squadron, moving out slowly, with the serenity of conscious power, to bar the way. What could Jason do, alone against six, even the smallest better armed than he?

Jolival saw that the brig was cramming on all sail, regardless of the state of the wind and guessed the American meant to try and make a run for it. He had the wind with him and by making skilful use of it a seaman of his quality might still succeed in giving his more powerful, but less streamlined enemies the slip.

'He's mad,' a voice said calmly at Jolival's side. 'It takes a fine sailor to try a trick like that. It will be a pity if he runs her aground because she's a beautiful ship.'

It was almost without surprise that Jolival looked round and saw the Comte de Latour-Maubourg, clad in dressing gown and nightcap and provided with another telescope, of which he appeared to possess something of a collection.

'He is a fine sailor,' Jolival said. 'But I've a nasty fear —'

'Me too! Because there's another thing – look there! The wind's changing . . . Ha, damnation! By God, what wretched luck!'

The ambassador was right. The *Sea Witch*'s sail flapped suddenly and the vessel heeled over to the gale. Meanwhile, the English ships, which had been beating up-channel with the wind against them, now had the advantage of a following wind and were not slow to make use of it. Their tall black hulls seemed to leap over the troughs between the waves and they piled on more and more canvas as they prepared to run down the brig.

It looked as if Jason were bound to be captured. In a fight of one against six he was lost from the start and it was no longer possible for him to get up sufficient speed to out-distance his pursuers.

'But good God,' Jolival muttered through clenched teeth, 'what is the English squadron doing here at this of all moments? Have we been betrayed? Were they warned in advance?'

The ambassador's short-sighted eyes blinked at the Vicomte in real surprise.

'Warned about what? What is this talk of a betrayal, my friend? Admiral Maxwell is on his way to the Black Sea for an inspection of the north coast harbours. The two frigates are going as escort but the corvettes will stop short at the entrance to the Bosphorus.'

'A tour of inspection? By an Englishman?'

The French ambassador gave vent to a deep sigh which culminated in a violent bout of coughing. He went very red in the face and vanished behind a huge handkerchief which he fished out of his dressing gown pocket. When the coughing had died down, he reappeared, still looking very flushed.

'Forgive me. I have a dreadful cold . . . But you were saying?'

'That's it's queer to find an English squadron inspecting Ottoman defences.'

'My poor friend, can you tell me anything in these times that is not queer? Canning rules the Seraglio and has the Sultan in his pocket, because his Highness is relying on the English to help him bring about the great reforms he dreams of. He is also hoping for help from London in patching up some sort of decent peace with the Tsar. In all of which we are very much in the way. All the old friendship is quite dead. I may well find myself *persona non grata* before long. The Emperor has remembered us a little too late.'

Being reluctant to become involved in a discussion of the international situation, Jolival put his telescope to his eye once more and uttered a startled cry. The *Sea Witch* had extricated herself from her predicament by going about and was now fleeing before the English under full sail, making up the Bosphorus towards the Black

Sea. Her topsails grew larger and more clearly visible in Jolival's glass.

Latour-Maubourg had also returned to his observation of the vessel's movements.

'May I ask whither she was bound?' he inquired.

'Charleston – in North Carolina.'

'Hmm . . . she seems to be going the wrong way, then. I wonder what her captain hopes to find in the Euxine? I'll admit, though, you were quite right. He is a magnificent seaman.'

'I'm wondering, too. Yet he must know it's a dead end. But I suppose he has no choice. It's that or see his ship taken and himself made prisoner. But I think he's simply hoping to scatter Maxwell's pack and try the passage again later, with a following wind.'

'I agree. All the same, if I were he I'd haul down that American flag. It's asking for trouble. His only fear now is the guns of Rumeli Hissar.'

The *Sea Witch* was now running fast before the wind and it was clear that she was not only managing to maintain her lead over her adversaries but was actually lengthening it appreciably. Of course, she still had to run the gauntlet of the old fortress which guarded the narrows. . . .

'Bah!' said Latour-Maubourg, shutting up his telescope. 'I dare say he'll get away with it. But now, my friend, suppose you tell me where you've been all this time and how I come to have the pleasure of finding you at the top of my tower?'

But the poor ambassador's question was fated to go unanswered because Jolival, with a brief bow and a muttered: 'Forgive me, my dear sir,' was already clattering down the stairs at breakneck speed. Latour-Maubourg dashed to the stone balustrade and, leaning over so far that he all but overbalanced, called out: 'Hey, there! Where are you off to? Wait for me, can't you? I'm coming down!'

He might as well have held his peace, for Jolival did not hear him. He raced full tilt through the cloister, brushing past Conan, as that worthy was coming forward to express the hope that his prayers had been satisfactory, tore open the heavy door and shot out into the steeply sloping street and pelted downhill to the clump of planes. As he untied one of the tethered horses, he called out to a passing street-porter: 'These two horses! Take them to the French Embassy and say they belong to Monsieur de Jolival. Here's for you, and you'll get as much again for your trouble.'

A heavy silver coin spun through the air and landed in the man's grubby fist. He hurried to carry out the command, eager to double the unexpected windfall. Meanwhile, Jolival had set spurs to his mount and was riding as fast as the animal could carry him up the steep hill leading to the Buyukdere road. He was in a hurry now to get back to Humayunabad. He had to know how Jason fared with the guns of Rumeli Hissar and, above all, he had to warn Marianne. If she happened to catch sight of Jason's brig sailing up the Bosphorus instead of down, it might well be enough to throw her into a high fever.

When he reached Bebek, after a frantic ride, much of it across country because of the state of the roads, he was surprised to find the place unnaturally quiet. Ordinarily, the gatehouse of Turhan Bey's residence was a scene of bustling activity, with messengers arriving, bringing news from the harbour, and servants hurrying about their business, but this morning all was still.

The *kapiji* was smoking his pipe in the centre of a crowd of grooms and stable boys who looked as if they had been all talking at once. However, they all turned to greet Jolival and one of the grooms bestirred himself sufficiently to take the Vicomte's horse when he dismounted and flung the reins to him.

Within the palace, it was just the same. The servants stood about in little groups, chatting among themselves, and in the gardens the *bostanjis*, the gardeners, were also sitting on their barrows or leaning on their spades, apparently engaged in discussions of equal interest. Of Osman, the chief steward of Humayunabad, there was nothing to be seen at all.

'Perhaps they've gone on strike,' Jolival thought irritably. Yet it seemed unlikely that an institution infrequent even in the west should turn up in such an implacably feudal setting at the Ottoman Empire. But, if strike it was, it was Turhan Bey's concern and he, Jolival, had other fish to fry.

He went in search of Dona Lavinia, to find out if Marianne was awake and ready to receive visitors. But knocking on her door produced no answer.

The fact that Dona Lavinia was not in her room was not in itself particular cause for alarm. She was most probably with her mistress or busy caring for the baby. So it must have been some kind of premonition which prompted Jolival to open the door softly and risk a look inside.

What he saw brought a frown to his eyes. Not only did the room present that appearance of perfect, impersonal tidiness which is the mark of places that are unlived in, with not a single personal object left lying about, no sign of a human presence, but even the bed was not made up. Worst of all, the baby's cradle had gone.

Feeling increasingly worried, Jolival wasted no time going round by way of the covered gallery. Instead, he made directly for the passage linking Dona Lavinia's rooms with those belonging to her mistress, and burst unceremoniously in on Marianne.

She was standing in the middle of the room, barefoot and with her hair tumbling about her shoulders, dressed in a long, white nightgown that fell to her toes and gave her the look of a creature out of some Celtic legend. She was clutching what looked like a sheet of paper. Her eyes were wide open and set in a strange, fixed stare and tears were streaming down her cheeks on to her breast, but no sobs contracted her throat. She was weeping like a fountain, with a kind of desperation that wrung her old friend's heart. And on the floor beneath her bare toes lay something green and sparkling, like a slim, exotic snake.

She was so much the image of the *mater dolorosa* that Jolival knew at once that something catastrophic had occurred. Very softly, hardly daring to breathe, he went up to the trembling girl.

'Marianne,' he whispered gently, as if he feared that the sound of his voice might exacerbate her pain. 'My child, what is it?'

Without answering, she held out the paper she was clutching in her hand, stiffly, like the movement of an automaton.

'Read it,' she said simply, while the tears continued to flow uninterruptedly.

Jolival smoothed the paper mechanically and, glancing down, saw that it was a letter.

'Madam,' Prince Sant'Anna had written, 'as I was on the point of telling you this evening when we were interrupted, it is with the deepest gratitude that I acknowledge the magnificent way in which you have fulfilled your part in the contract between us. Never shall I be able adequately to express my indebtedness to you. Now it is my turn to keep my promise to you.

'As I have said already, you are free – perfectly free, and you will be altogether so whenever it may please you to travel to Florence where my legal representatives, Messrs Lombardi and Fosco Grazelli, will be provided with the necessary instructions for all to be settled in accordance with your wishes.

'I am removing my son this very evening, rather than continue to inflict upon you a presence which, as I have been told, is even more painful to you than I had feared. When he and I are far removed, you will recover more speedily and, I can only trust, will soon forget what, with the passing of time, will become no more than a disagreeable incident, the memory of which will gradually fade into insignificance.

'Should it be otherwise, however, and should you one day feel a wish to see the person to whom you have given birth, be sure that nothing can ever take away the fact that you are his mother, a mother whose memory he will be taught to cherish. Even when you bear another name, you will remain Princess Sant'Anna to your child, as you are to one who will ever remain your friend, your husband in the sight of God and your most faithful servant, Corrado Sant'Anna.'

Jolival finished reading and glanced up at Marianne. She was still standing where she had been, still with the same grief-stricken, somnambulistic air. Seeing her fixed in such stony misery, he had thought at first that Jason's departure was the cause of her grief, and now, behold, the thing he had hoped for and feared at once had come to pass and mother-love had woken in her and was demanding its rights. It was not her lover's absence which was the cause of those tears but the removal of the child whom only yesterday she had hated, yet who, in the space of a few seconds, had carved for himself the lion's share in his mother's heart.

As ill luck would have it, no one could have told the Prince of what had taken place in that room and in the heart of Marianne and, believing her still irrevocably set against the infant, he had done what he must always have intended and taken the child away to some unknown destination, unconscious of the despair he left behind him.

For Marianne's sake, however, Jolival forced himself to speak calmly.

'Well, what are you crying for, my dear?' he said, folding the letter and laying it aside. 'There is nothing here but what yourself have agreed to and desired.'

She turned her great green eyes on him, filled with an immense surprise.

'But Arcadius,' she said in a small voice, 'don't you understand? He has gone . . . they have all gone . . . and my son with them.'

She was trembling like a leaf in the wind. He went to her and took her gently by the arm to lead her back to bed. Her skin was icy cold.

'But my dear,' he reproached her tenderly, 'isn't that what you wanted? Think back. You wanted to go to Jason, to become his wife and begin a new life with him, have other children . . .'

She passed her hand across her forehead, as though waking from a dream.

'Perhaps . . . Yes, I think I did want that, and even nothing else. But that was before.'

He made no attempt to elicit a fuller explanation. Indeed, that was before. Before she had held a tiny body in her arms, a little thing that was soft and tender, with a tiny fist that had closed imperiously on her finger, as though to take possesssion.

'The Prince cannot have gone far,' he ventured, helpless in the face of such unhappiness. 'Would you like us to try and catch him? Osman —'

'Osman doesn't know where his master has gone. I sent for him when they gave me that dreadful letter, after I woke. He knows nothing of his intentions and never asks questions. Turhan Bey is absent frequently, and often for long periods. To please me, he promised to go to the harbour and see what he could discover but I have no great hopes. The Prince may be already far out to sea.'

'In this weather, with a new-born babe. Nothing of the sort!'

'Then he is hiding and it is a waste of time to look for him. He told me himself that after the birth he would vanish with the child. He has kept his word and I have no right to blame him.'

'Did no one tell him last night that you had taken to the child after all? I gather from this letter that you did not see him again after we left?'

'No. Oh, Arcadius, I was so wretched that I don't think I would see anyone, not even Dona Lavinia. I must have cried half the night.'

She was shivering more and more, from a combination of cold and nerves. Jolival went quickly to a chair and fetched her favourite big, red cashmere shawl and wrapped it round her. Then he hunted for slippers for her bare feet. Bending to put them on he saw that the thing which he had taken for a small, glittering snake lying, like the serpent's head beneath the foot of the Virgin, was in fact a magnificent emerald and diamond necklace. He took it up and let it hang for a moment between his fingers.

Guessing that it was the final princely gift from her husband, he would have forborne to question her about it, but Marianne moved suddenly and snatched it from him with a sudden blaze of anger and hurled it under a chest.

'Let it lie! It's my payment! I don't want it.'

'Are you mad? I'm very sure the Prince had no such idea.'

'What else? To him I am only a foolish woman to be bought. From there it is only a step to thinking that a handful of jewels will easily compensate me for the loss of my child. Oh I hate him, I hate him! I hate all men! All they know how to do is follow their own blind, senseless desires, and fight, and make idiotic wars which they all rush to join in as if they were glorious treats, without a thought for those they leave behind them! Why do they have to have sons only to bring them up the same way?'

'Marianne, calm yourself! You can't change the world and you will only make yourself ill . . .'

'What does it matter? What does it matter even if I die? Who would care – except you, perhaps? Jason is no better than the rest. He has bullied and misused me to make me forget my duty and my country, he has treated me worse than one of the slaves on his family's plantation and now he leaves me here, abandons me to go running off to a war that is not even declared yet and may never take place. Do you think he cares for my tears and my unhappiness, or even for the simple fact of how I am to accomplish the immense journey across half the world to join him? Who is to say that the ship that carries us won't fall into the hands of pirates like the Kouloughis? But all that is nothing to Jason Beaufort compared to his beloved battles! At this very minute he is sailing off to America without a care in his heart —'

Jolival seized on this as his opportunity to shake Marianne out of her despairing mood. He knew the ups and downs of her volatile temperament, in which the French and Italian elements predominated over the English, too well not to be sure that Jason's present danger would sweep away all her anger against him in an instant. For even if the privateer had taken second place in her memory just then to the newer attractions of the baby, Marianne's true feelings could not have undergone a change in that short time. She loved him still and even her immediate anger was only another proof of it.

'I'd not be too sure of that,' he said. 'Indeed, to be quite honest, he's not sailing towards America at all. Quite the opposite, in fact.'

As he had expected, Marianne's rage collapsed at once, like the sails of a ship in a dead calm. In its place, there came the old, anxious look which was certainly by far her most familiar sensation when she thought of her difficult love. But Jolival embarked at once on an account of what had taken place by the Tower of the Maiden, giving her no time to ask questions.

Almost before he had finished, Marianne had rushed from the room, forgetting her weak state and the fact that she was not supposed to be out of her bed yet, and was hurrying in the direction of the *tandour*, without even pausing to try her strength.

She did not get very far. Out in the covered way she was forcibly reminded of her weakness. She swayed and would have fallen but for Jolival, who had hastened after and was there to catch her.

'Don't be silly. Let me take you back to your room.'

Her eyes flashed dangerously.

'If you don't take me to the *tandour* this instant, Jolival, I will never set eyes on you again as long as I live.'

He was obliged to do as she asked. Half-supporting and half-carrying her, the wretched Arcadius succeeded in getting Marianne as far as her favourite look-out place, where they were just in time to see the *Sea Witch* driving, light as a seagull, under full sail, past the gilded lattices of the palace where they stood.

'Oh God,' Marianne groaned, 'if they open fire now it will be murder! Look at the towers of Rumeli Hissar! They are crowded with Janissaries!'

'If only —' Jolival began. But before he could finish, as if Jason had divined the thought in his mind, the impudent stars were descending swiftly from the masthead. A moment later, another flag was creeping up to take their place. With unspeakable relief, Marianne and Jolival recognized the lion and the flaming T which had protected the *Sea Witch* while she lay in harbour.

'Thank God!' Marianne breathed, sinking back on to the cushions. 'He had the sense to pocket his pride and do the one thing that could save him from the Turkish guns.'

The guns fired, none the less, but it was only a friendly salute to a vessel of Turhan Bey's. The tiny puffs of white smoke bloomed above the ancient ramparts of Mehmet the Conqueror like waving handkerchiefs held in friendly hands.

The *Sea Witch* passed on and dwindled. Soon she had vanished into the mist and Admiral Maxwell's squadron hove in sight. But the pursuit seemed to have lost its enthusiasm. With a sigh of relief, Jolival crossed to a small table on which stood coffee things and a pair of decanters. He poured himself a full glass of raki and swallowed it at a gulp.

'Well,' he said at last, 'that seaman of Jason's was right when he said that last night was a night fit for the devil. The morning has been exciting enough, I will say. What shall we do now? I hope you are going to consent to go to bed and rest at last? I'll call for your women to come and help you back to your room.'

But Marianne was already snuggling down among the cushions where she had spent so many hours. She drew the embroidered coverlet up over her legs.

'I can't possibly go back to that room where I can't see anything. I'm staying here, Jolival. As to what we are going to do now, I will tell you. We are going to wait. Sooner or later Jason will have to pass by here again to reach his own country, won't he?'

'He may pass by at night – in fact he almost certainly will. At night and with the ship in darkness.'

'It's possible. But one thing I am certain of, and that is that he won't pass by without stopping. There is no need for us to look for a ship, my friend. The *Sea Witch* herself shall take us to America! Jason will do as he said he would. He'll lie up somewhere and then come back and fetch us.'

There was a silence during which Jolival studied his young friend. She was becoming more herself again with every minute. Her eyes were shining, there was colour in her cheeks and she seemed to have forgotten all about the despair which had overwhelmed her at daybreak. He dared not tell her his own thoughts upon the likelihood of Jason's stopping but he privately resolved to ask Osman to see that a constant watch was kept on the narrows.

'Upon my word,' he said aloud, 'anyone would think you were not displeased at Jason's misadventure, eh?'

'And they would be right, my friend. I'm not only not displeased, I'm actually grateful to Admiral Maxwell. In blocking Jason's way he may have been only the instrument of fate, but he has done me a tremendous service.'

Part III

THE GOVERNOR OF ODESSA

CHAPTER EIGHT

The Woman with the Diamond

The woman who descended, on a morning in July, on to the wooden jetty at Odessa, bore only the very faintest resemblance to the one who, four months earlier, had settled down in a gilded cage suspended over the waters of the Bosphorus to an endless wait. Enforced rest, coupled with the admirable nourishment which Osman, Turhan Bey's steward, had provided for a guest concerning whom he had received the strictest orders, had worked wonders. In addition, as she grew stronger, there had been the beneficial effects of daily walks in the gardens of Humayunabad. The beauties of the Turkish spring, as they were unfolded to her day by day on Jolival's arm, had wrought their own soothing medicine on her overtried spirit, while motherhood had given a fresh bloom of perfection to her natural grace.

Marianne's figure had recovered its youthful slenderness but with none of the painful emaciation which had so alarmed Jolival and terrified Jason Beaufort. She had become a woman, sure of herself and armed to the teeth for the only war that fitted her, the war of love. Hence, the traveller's curiosity and interest in the motley crowd swarming about the harbour was fully reciprocated. The local inhabitants made no secret of their admiration for the lovely stranger, so exquisitely dressed in white sprigged muslin, flounced about the hem and with huge, emerald eyes sparkling from beneath the soft shade of an Italian straw bonnet with a high poke front lined with the same stuff.

After her came Arcadius de Jolival, clad in spotless white against the heat but spruce and fashionable as ever. An elegant straw hat and long, green sunshade tucked under his arm completed an outfit which was also not without its effect on the natives. They were followed by a number of porters carrying their baggage.

The two friends presented the serene and leisurely appearance of tourists enjoying the experience of a new country but this was all on the surface. Inwardly, both were wondering uneasily what awaited them in this, the chief Russian port on the Black Sea.

Odessa was a strange city, beautiful in its way but with a temporary look about it. The place was full of scaffolding and still too new to have acquired a distinct personality of its own. For it was less than twenty years since a decree signed by the Tsarina Catherine II had raised the village of Tartar fishermen, newly wrested from the Turks, to the status of a Russian port. The name of the village and its Turkish castle had been Khajibey. Catherine had rechristened it Odessa, in memory of the Greek colony of Odessos which had once stood on the site.

The village's elevation was no mere imperial whim. Situated in a rocky bay between the estuaries of the two great rivers, Dnieper and Dniester, it provided an outstanding strategic position and at the same time an outlet to the Mediterranean for the vast cornlands of the Ukraine.

It was corn, in fact, which seemed to hold a peaceful dominion over this naval port. As Marianne and Jolival walked up to the one respectable hotel in the town, preceded by an urchin who had graciously appointed himself their guide, in the hope of a tip, they saw dozens of wagons piled high with bursting sacks converging on the warehouses to be stored ready for loading in the holds of the waiting ships, some of which, as Marianne noted with a pang, were English. But she knew that she was in enemy territory now.

It was a full three weeks since Napoleon's Grand Army had crossed the Niemen to challenge Alexander on his own ground.

Marianne's eyes searched the huge harbour, big enough to shelter three hundred ships, hoping to catch sight of the familiar outline of the *Sea Witch*, but most of the vessels were European and the Russian fleet contained nothing like the antiquated Ottoman ships, so that there was little chance of distinguishing the brig's masts among that forest of spars.

The town, tumbling down a steep cliff to the sea in a froth of luxuriant vegetation, was like a link between two spaces of infinite blue but, mid-way between the busy harbour and the fashionable part at the top, the old Turkish citadel, now strengthened and restored, added a grimmer note. Marianne found her eyes drawn to it irresistibly. Was it there that Jason had been incarcerated all these months?

She had waited for so long, hope dwindling with every new day, that she could hardly believe he was so near to her now. News travelled slowly in the Black Sea, where no one saw the need for hurry, and anything was possible. Had the American privateer fallen victim to one of the sudden, fierce storms that could blow up in those waters? Or been taken by one of the pirate fleets of polyglot origin which still infested that inland sea? The Tsar's navy was powerless against these vermin who would descend without warning out of darkness or mist, attack like a swarm of wasps and vanish again as suddenly and completely as if the wind had carried them away.

And then, at the beginning of June, when the Ottoman Empire, weary of fighting, was making peace with Russia, Osman had come back from the harbour with news which, disquieting as it was, was nothing like as tragic as they had feared. The brig had been captured by the Russians and taken to Odessa where it was now in custody. Of the crew, there was no news at all.

The probability was that they were the prisoners of the formidable governor of the Crimea, that French emigré who, in spite of his name, had apparently made himself more Russian than the Russians and was now, by all accounts, devoting his considerable talents to developing the wealth of southern Russia and making Odessa into a real city: in a word, the Duc de Richelieu.

With the help of Princess Morousi who, by reason of the nearness of her estate at Arnavut Koy, was able to visit Marianne quietly without arousing the suspicions of the ever-watchful Mr Canning, the recluse at Humayunabad had been able to resume, at second hand, her friendship with Nakshidil. At her entreaty the Valideh had instituted discreet inquiries which had confirmed the supposition. The American was indeed the Governor of Odessa's prisoner and Nakshidil was compelled to own that she could do nothing to obtain his release. To disturb the fragile balance so recently established between the Porte and the Tsar's governor for the sake of one troublesome foreigner was out of the question.

Marianne had accepted it and had made her decision quickly. In any case, the news, however bad, was still better than she had feared and better, also, than the long uncertainty. Jason had lost his freedom once again but at least he was still alive.

Of her child, on the other hand, she had no news at all. The Prince, Dona Lavinia and the baby seemed to have vanished into thin air and when she tried to question Osman about where his master might have gone the steward had only bowed deeply and protested that he did not know at all. But his smile had been almost too guileless. That was another subject about which he must have had very strict instructions.

Marianne had confined herself, therefore, to asking him to

provide her with a vessel to carry her and Jolival with the greatest possible speed and comfort to Odessa. The Duc de Richelieu had been a friend and fellow-pupil of her father's at the Collège du Plessis and because of this she had asked for and obtained a passport in her maiden name. She had some faint hope that the Duke might be moved by recollections of his youth to gratify his old friend's daughter by releasing the *Sea Witch* and her crew. He would certainly do it more readily for her than for the intimate friends of Napoleon.

Even then, of course, they would still have to escape from the trap of the Black Sea and sail back through the Bosphorus, under the guns of Rumeli Hissar and under the noses of the English ships, but all these seemed to Marianne to be minor obstacles. The fact that she would be facing them with Jason at her side took away much of their power to scare her. The main thing, and the most difficult also, was to wrest the American away from his aristocratic captor, who was certain to be the mortal foe of liberalism in any form and, if he possessed even a fraction of the force of character of his illustrious ancestor, might well prove no easy nut to crack.

Marianne could picture him: lofty, arrogant, ruling his vast province with a rod of iron, a lover of luxury and of the arts, highly intelligent, almost certainly, but distinctly unapproachable.

Her fear of him was growing as she traversed the harbour, overflowing with life and activity. Even in the late afternoon, the heat was still tremendous but the crowd of tradesmen, clerks, peasants, seamen, porters and soldiers grew denser and busier the nearer they got to the long street which ran uphill to the administrative centre of the town. There, on the top of the cliff, above a handful of elegant pink and white houses built in the style of the preceding century, shone the gilded onion domes and rococo belfry of the brand new churches.

Buildings were going up on all sides and the sites were all alive with men at work. The biggest seemed to be the arsenal, which was nearing completion. Masons on long ladders were busy carving the Russian imperial eagle above the monumental gateway and their youthful guide began by leading the two travellers straight up to this, explaining engagingly, by means of a great many gestures, that before penetrating further into the city they must not neglect the opportunity to admire what was undoubtedly going to be one of the finest monuments anywhere to the glory of Alexander I, Tsar of all the Russias.

'Very well,' Jolival sighed. 'Let's go and admire it. It won't take long and we don't want to offend anyone.'

Standing on a block of stone a few yards away from the scaffolding was a man, apparently engaged in supervising the sculptors at their work. He was evidently a person of some importance because he turned from time to time and said a few words to a tall, dark young man carrying a writing block who at once made haste to copy it down.

The man's appearance was sufficiently remarkable. He was tall and thin and his rather aquiline features wore a slightly haunted expression. His hair, uncovered to the evening breeze, was short and wavy, still black in places but completely white in others. He was dressed all by guess in a frock coat that had seen better days, well-worn boots and black neckcloth knotted loosely round his throat. He was puffing away at a long meerschaum pipe which produced as much smoke as a small but active volcano.

He was turning to toss another word or two between puffs to the tall young man when Marianne, Jolival and their little procession entered his field of vision. A flicker of interest came into his eyes at the sight of a pretty woman but before he could do more than register her presence his attention was deflected by a frightful clamour of noise and shouting which broke out around him.

In another moment he had leaped down from his block of stone and rushed at them headlong, with outstretched arms, mowing the two of them down and collapsing on top of them on a pile of grain sacks awaiting loading.

Before either Marianne or Jolival had time to do as much as gasp, a cartload of stone had thundered past bare inches from their heaps of sacks and rumbled madly on to plunge into the harbour with a mighty splash. But for the stranger's prompt and courageous action, the two friends' journey would have ended there and then.

Blenching at the thought of what she had escaped, Marianne accepted her rescuer's hand to help her to her feet. Jolival was brushing dust from his elegant raiment, now irremediably crushed. Automatically straightening her bonnet which had tipped over one ear, Marianne turned on the stranger, now rather summarily slapping the dust off himself, a look swimming with gratitude.

'Monsieur,' she began brokenly, 'I don't know how to —'

The man paused in his work and cocked an eyebrow at her.

'Are you French? Have I had the happiness to oblige fellow-countrymen? If that is indeed so, Madame, then I am doubly glad to have preserved your beauty from harm.'

Marianne found herself blushing under his ardent gaze. But by now Jolival had recovered from his fright and decided to take a hand. Bowing with ineffable grace, despite his dented hat and crumpled clothes, he introduced himself.

'The Vicomte Arcadius de Jolival, entirely at your service, Monsieur. This lady is my ward, the daughter of the late Marquis d'Asselnat de Villeneuve.'

Again the man raised his left eyebrow in a way that might have indicated either surprise or irony, Jolival could not be sure which. Then, all at once, he started searching through his pockets so feverishly that the Vicomte could not help but ask him if he had lost something.

'My pipe,' was the answer. 'I can't think what I did with it.'

'You must have dropped it when you rushed so nobly to our aid,' Marianne said, bending down to look about her.

'I don't think so. I have a feeling it was gone before that.'

It was not far to seek. The necessary appurtenance was restored a moment later by the tall young man who now rejoined them unhurriedly and without losing one jot of his Olympian calm.

'Your pipe, Monsieur,' he said.

The stranger's harassed expression cleared.

'Ah, thank you, my boy. Just go along and see how the work on the guardhouse is coming along. I will be with you in a moment. And so,' he went on, sucking vigorously at his pipe in an effort to get it going again, 'and so . . . French, are you? Well, what the devil are you doing here, if I may ask?'

'Why of course you may!' Marianne smiled, finding herself liking him extremely. 'I am here to see the Duc de Richelieu. He is still governor of the city, I hope?'

'He is indeed – and of all New Russia. You know him?'

'Not yet. But you, sir, who speak French so well that you must surely be a fellow-countryman, are you, perhaps, acquainted with him?'

The man smiled. 'You would be surprised to find how many Russians speak French quite as well as I do, Madame. But you are correct on both counts. I am French and I do know the governor.'

'Is he here in Odessa at this moment?'

'Why – yes, I imagine so. I had not heard that he had gone away.'

'And what kind of a man is he? Forgive me if I seem to be presuming on your kindness, but I need to know. I heard it said in Constantinople that he is a very formidable man and somewhat difficult of access, that he rules here like a despot and is a hard man to cross. They said also that he hates the Emperor Napoleon and everything to do with him.'

The smile had faded from the man's face and he was regarding Marianne attentively, with a stern, almost menacing expression.

'The Turks,' he said slowly, 'have not so far had much cause to love his Excellency, who dealt them several sharp blows during the war. But do I understand, then, that you have come from the land of our erstwhile enemy? Have you no fear that the governor may require an explanation of what you were doing there? The ink is barely dry on the signatures to the treaty, you know. There is little mutual trust as yet and the smiles are still a trifle forced. I can only advise you to be very careful. Where the safety of his province is concerned, the governor is adamant.'

'Do you mean that he will take me for a spy?' Marianne said in a low voice, colouring with a rush. 'I do hope he won't because what I have to —' She was obliged to break off because the tall young man had come back at a run and was bending to whisper something in his master's ear with an appearance of unwonted agitation. Their new friend uttered an exclamation of annoyance and began to mutter angrily.

'Fools and half-wits! Nothing but fools and half-wits! Very well, I'm coming. Forgive me,' he turned back to Marianne, 'but I am obliged to leave you on urgent business. We shall meet again, I am sure.'

Cramming his pipe into his pocket without troubling to extinguish it, he bowed sketchily and was already hurrying away when Jolival called after him.

'Monsieur! Hi, Monsieur! Tell us at least whom we have to thank for saving our lives. Or how are we to find you again?'

The man paused for half a second in his stride and flung back over his shoulder: 'Septimanie! I am called Septimanie!'

Then he vanished through the gateway of the arsenal, leaving Jolival staring after him with a look of astonishment.

'Septimanie?' he growled. 'Why, that's my wife's name!'

Marianne burst out laughing and came to slip her arm through her old friend's.

'You are surely not going to take the poor man in dislike because of that? It's quite possible for a woman's christian name to be a perfectly respectable surname at the same time. All it means is that our friend must be a descendant of someone who once lived in the old Gallic province of Septimania.'

'I dare say,' Jolival retorted, 'but it's very disagreeable all the same. Upon my word, if I didn't know her so attached to England I'd be afraid of her turning up here . . . But there, come along now. I can see our guide is growing impatient. It's time for us to find out what a Russian hotel is like.'

A good deal to the travellers' surprise, the one to which the boy now led them bore a striking resemblance to one of the better Parisian hostelries of the end of the previous century. Jolival, who had been expecting a dirty, smoky isba, trod with relief across the clean, white doorstep of the Hotel Ducroux which, like the majority of Russian inns, was called by the name of its proprietor.

It was a fine, new building situated not far from the great barracks that were built into the side of the hill, pink-washed, with tall, white windows, their small panes gleaming in the last rays of the setting sun. The wide doorway with its shining brass fittings, flanked by a pair of orange trees in large, glazed pots, stood open at the top of the hill, at the beginning of the new town. It was clearly a very well-kept house.

Two maidservants in cap and apron and two men in red shirts, the only Russian note in this thoroughly European setting, rushed to take their baggage, while Maître Ducroux himself, magnificently attired in dark blue coat with gilt buttons which gave him the appearance of a naval officer, came forward with stately tread to greet the new arrivals. This haughty demeanour melted into an expression of real delight, however, as he took in the elegance of his potential guests and the fact that he had to do with French people.

Antoine Ducroux himself had once been a cook in the employ of the Duc de Richelieu. He had come, in answer to a summons, when the Duke had become Governor of Odessa in 1803 to provide the rapidly growing town with a fitting hostelry. Since then, the Hotel Ducroux had flourished. The food there was the best in all New Russia and a good part of the old, and it continued to prosper, thanks to the numbers of men of business who frequented the busy port, the newly rich settlers of what had formerly been an unculti-

vated desert region but was now in the process of rapid develop-
ment, and to the officers of the military garrison, which was main-
tained at considerable strength.

As Marianne and Jolival were bowed by their host into an
entrance hall charmingly decorated in panels of French grey picked
out with gold, they came face to face with a middle-aged woman of
striking appearance who was at that moment descending the stairs,
with a Russian colonel in attendance.

It was not so much her clothes that took the eye, although these
were remarkable enough, consisting as they did of a wide-skirted
dress of black silk of an extremely old-fashioned design, trimmed
at neck and elbow with falls of white muslin, and a very large hat
with a black feather set upon an edifice of powdered curls. Rather
it was the expression of her face, which bore a look of pride and
arrogance that almost amounted to a challenge. Her age appeared
to be about fifty and she was quite evidently an aristocrat. Judging
from the superb earrings of pearls and brilliants that dangled on
either side of her painted cheeks, she was also extremely rich.

The lady was by no means unhandsome, only there was a coldness
and calculation about her blue eyes and a hard line to her mouth that
rendered an otherwise harmonious set of features curiously devoid
of charm. Her glance, directed upon the world from behind a
delicately wrought lorgnette, left a disagreeable impression. This
weapon she now aimed at Marianne and she continued to stare at
her as the two ladies passed one another, even to the extent of turning her feathered head somewhat, until she was swallowed up in
the bustle of the street, the colonel still trotting meekly at her
heels.

Marianne and Jolival had halted instinctively at the foot of the
stairs, letting Ducroux get a few steps ahead of them.

'What an extraordinary woman,' Marianne said, when the two
were out of sight. 'Would it be rude of me to inquire who she is?'

'Not at all, madame. Indeed, I could see by the way she looked
at you that she will ask me the same question before long. It is
strange the way French people will recognize one another.'

'That lady is French?'

'Yes indeed. She is the Comtesse de Gachet. She came here from
St Petersburg two days ago, accompanied by Colonel Ivanoff, the
officer you saw with her. She is, as I have been told, a lady of quality
who has suffered much misfortune but who enjoys the special
interest of his Majesty the Tsar.'

'What is she doing here?'

The proprietor spread his hands in a comical gesture of ignorance.

'I am not precisely sure. I believe that she is considering settling here, on account of her health, which can support our mild climate better than the rigours of the capital. The financial loans and other advantages, quite apart from the allocations of land, which our governor makes available to those who are willing to come and colonize New Russia may also have something to do with it.'

'That woman a settler?' exclaimed Jolival, who had observed the behaviour of the woman in the black feathers with a quick frown in his eyes. 'I can scarcely believe it. I have a feeling I know her, although her name means nothing to me. But I am sure I've seen those eyes somewhere before . . . but where?'

'Well, you certainly look as if you'd seen a ghost,' Marianne said, laughing. 'Don't worry about it. It will come back to you. Now, shall we go and see our rooms? After so many days cooped up on board ship, I can't wait to find myself in a real bedchamber again.'

The room to which she was shown looked out over the sea and the confused bustle of the harbour, with its amazing variety of men and nations. There, in a dense huddle of huts, tents and houses, each of which bore something of the national characteristics belonging to its owners, dwelt Jews, Armenians, Greeks, Tartars, Turks, Moldavians, Bulgars and gipsies. Lights were springing up and fragments of song hung, with a strange scent of wormwood, on the salty air.

Marianne stood for some time leaning out of the window, forgetting to take off her hat, fascinated by the fantastic spectacle presented by the bay in the magic of a glorious sunset. The sea was on fire, reflecting the fading beams in great pools of purple and gold, shot with gleams of amethyst that turned to an incredible dark green in the shadow of the great mole. Drums and pipes sounded on board the ships. From every masthead, the colours were being hauled down slowly, as they were every night at this hour, all together, as though in a well-rehearsed ballet. But even from this point of vantage, Marianne was no more able to make out the vessel she sought than she had been from the harbour. Where could the *Sea Witch* be? And where was Jason? In the citadel, perhaps, or else in some other prison she could not see? This town was like no other she had ever seen. It was disturbing and yet strangely attractive in its intense vitality. Standing there at the window, she felt as if she were on the borders of an unknown world which drew her and yet troubled her at the same time.

'I've asked our good Monsieur Ducroux to have supper sent up to your room for us.' Jolival's familiar voice spoke behind her. 'I didn't think you'd want to go down to the dining-room, seeing that the hotel seems to be so full of men? I should say the best thing for us tonight would be to eat our supper and then get a good night's rest. The beds seem comfortable enough.'

She swung round to face him.

'I want to see the governor as soon as possible, Jolival. Can't we go to his house this evening and see if they will let us in?'

Jolival looked deeply shocked.

'My dear, you are a lady of quality. You cannot possibly go to the governor's palace yourself and demand admittance. Any more than I can. But don't be alarmed. One of the hotel servants is on his way there at this very moment, carrying a very proper note, composed entirely by your humble servant, expressing in the most formal terms your earnest wish to call on your father's old friend.'

Marianne sighed. 'You are quite right, as usual,' she said, warming his heart with a contrite little smile. 'Then there is nothing for us to do except, as you say, to have our supper and go to bed. I hope word will come from the Duke for us to visit him tomorrow.'

They spent a quiet, peaceful evening. Seated comfortably in the small sitting-room attached to Marianne's bedchamber, the two friends did ample justice to the Hotel Ducroux's admirable cooking. The cuisine throughout was French and recalled to Marianne the delicacies with which the great Carême had been wont to furnish Talleyrand's table.

As to Jolival, in his delight at this temporary respite from eastern cooking, he tackled carp à la Chambord, a salmis of duckling and tartelettes au fraises as though he had not seen food for weeks, breaking off only to savour, with the air of a connoisseur, the excellent champagne, produce of Epernay, which Ducroux was able to procure through the good offices of his former employer and a whole fleet of smugglers.

'You may say what you like,' he confided to Marianne as he finished his second bottle, 'but there is nothing like champagne for making you see things in a quite different light. I respect the Emperor's taste for Chambertin but, to my mind, he's a deal too exclusive. There is simply nothing like champagne.'

'I think he knows that,' she said, smiling at the candle flame seen through the airy bubbles rising in her glass. 'In fact it was he who introduced me to it.'

There was a flicker in her green eyes as she remembered that first night. Was it only yesterday, or hundreds of years ago, that Talleyrand, the old fox, had driven her out through the snow to the pavilion of le Butard, a young girl in a dress of rose-coloured satin, to charm away with her voice the melancholy humours of a certain Monsieur Denis who was said to be suffering from some unexplained misfortune? She saw again the charming, intimate little music room, Duroc's broad face, a trifle uneasy in the role of go-between, the fragrance of flowers everywhere, the bright fire blazing in the hearth, the frozen lake outside the windows. And then the little man in the black coat who had listened to her singing without a word, yet with such a look of kindness in his steel blue eyes. . . . She saw it all and even felt something of the emotion which had stirred her then as the heady fumes of the champagne had cast her, all too willingly, into the stranger's arms. And yet, at the same time, she found herself wondering if that pleasant interlude had really happened to her, or if it were not just a story she had heard, a fairy tale in the manner of Voltaire or la Fontaine.

She shut her eyes and took a sip of the cold wine, as though trying to recapture the taste of that night.

'France is a long way away,' she said. 'Who knows what awaits us here?'

Jolival cocked an eyebrow and smiled into his empty glass and then at the flower-decked table, still loaded with the remains of their meal.

'Just at this moment, it doesn't seem to me so very far. Besides, we are treading the same soil as his Majesty, the Emperor, you know.'

Marianne's eyes opened wide and she gave a little shiver.

'The same soil? What do you mean?'

'Only what Ducroux told me when I was talking to him before dinner. According to the latest information, the Emperor is at Wilna. That is why we have seen so much military activity here. The regiments of Tartars and Circassians are mustering to join the Tsar's army – and it's said the Duc de Richelieu thinks of marching at their head.'

'A Frenchman at their head? Jolival, you can't mean it?'

'Why not? Have you forgotten that the Marquis de Langeron fought under the Russian eagle at Austerlitz? Richelieu is like him, an irreconcilable enemy of France as she is today. All he wants is to see Bonaparte defeated, in the hope of putting those broken-winded Bourbons back on the throne.'

Jolival seized the slender crystal flûte from which he had been drinking and, in a sudden spurt of anger, sent it smashing violently against the white marble chimney piece.

'Then I wonder,' Marianne observed, 'what we are doing sitting here drinking champagne and philosophizing instead of trying to see this man and make him listen to reason.'

Jolival gave a shrug, then rose and, taking his young friend's hand in his, carried it to his lips with an affectionate gallantry.

'Sufficient unto the day, Marianne. The Duc de Richelieu won't be leaving tonight. And, may I remind you, we have a favour to ask and so are not precisely in the best position to start preaching him sermons. Forget what I have just told you, and my display of bad temper. I think I'm turning into an old fool, God forgive me.'

'No you're not. It's just that you see red as soon as anyone mentions the subject of emigrés or princes. Good night, old friend. And you too, try to forget . . .'

He was just leaving the room when she called him back. 'Arcadius,' she said, 'that woman we passed coming in, Madame de Gachet, have you remembered where you met her before? She looked like an emigrée. Perhaps she was a friend of your wife?'

He shook his head. 'No. She must have been very beautiful and Septimanie could never get on with pretty women. My impression is – yes, my impression is that she is connected with something unpleasant, with the memory of some horrible event buried deep in my memory which I can't quite recall. But I keep trying because when I saw her just now I had a kind of premonition, as if there were some kind of danger threatening —'

'Well, go and get some sleep. They say the night brings counsel. You may find you have remembered in the morning. Besides, we may be imagining things and giving a great deal too much importance to a poor woman who means no harm at all.'

'It may be so. But I didn't care for the way she looked at us and I shan't be happy until I've worked out who she is.'

Marianne slept soundly and forgot all about the woman in the black feathers. She was sitting up in bed the following morning, enjoying a real French breakfast of feather-light croissants, when there was a knock at her door. Thinking that the maid must have forgotten something, she bade her come in. But, instead of the chambermaid's white cap, what peeped in was the powdered head of Jolival's mysterious lady.

She had her finger to her lips, enjoining silence, and she glanced back to make sure that there was no one in the passage before closing the door noiselessly behind her.

Marianne had paused in the act of spreading butter on a croissant and was staring at her in astonishment, her knife suspended in mid-air.

'Madame,' she began, intending to request her uninvited visitor to let her breakfast in peace.

But once again the woman put her finger to her lips, accompanying the movement with a smile so charmingly girlish and confused that all Jolival's rather vague misgivings were forgotten in an instant. At last, when she had satisfied herself that all was quiet outside, the lady approached the bed and swept a curtsy that spoke Versailles in every line of it.

'I must beg you to pardon this unwarrantable intrusion when we have not even been introduced,' she said in a voice as smooth as velvet, 'but I do think that in a place where civilization is still in its infancy we may allow ourselves to dispense with some of the strict rules of polite society, while at the same time the natural ties which exist between people of the same nationality are strengthened to the point almost of brotherhood. But, please, do not let me interrupt your breakfast.'

This little speech had been rattled off with as much assurance as if the two of them were old acquaintances. Not to be outdone, Marianne assured her politely in return, though without any notable enthusiasm, that she was delighted to see her and begged she would be seated.

Her visitor pulled up a chair and sat down with a little sigh of satisfaction, spreading the shimmering skirts of her grey silk bed-gown about her. She smiled again.

'The proprietor of the hotel told me that you were Mademoiselle d'Asselnat de Villeneuve and I can see that you are indeed the daughter of my dear friend Pierre. I was struck when I passed you yesterday by your extraordinary likeness to him.'

'You knew my father?'

'Very well. I am the Comtesse de Gachet. My late husband was an officer in the same regiment. I knew your father when he was stationed at Douai in 1784.'

She had no need to say more. In mentioning the father whom

Marianne adored without ever having known him other than through his portrait, the woman had uttered the magic words. All Jolival's warnings and reservations were swept from her mind in an instant, and Marianne returned all her visitor's smiles and compliments in full. She even offered to share her breakfast with her but Madame de Gachet would not hear of allowing her to ring to the chambermaid to bring fresh coffee and another cup.

'No, no. I've already breakfasted. Besides, I would rather no one knew of this visit, so early and so unconventional as it is. People might start to wonder . . .'

Marianne laughed. 'My dear madame,' she said, 'I really think you are worrying yourself unnecessarily. As you said yourself, manners are not so strict here as they are in France, and I am delighted to meet someone who knew my father, since I never had the good fortune to do so myself.'

'I'm sure. You must have been very young when he died?'

'I was only a few months old. But do, please, tell me about him. You can't imagine how eager I am to listen.'

'He was, I believe, the most handsome, gallant and noble gentleman imaginable . . .'

For the next few moments, the Comtesse de Gachet held Marianne enthralled with an account of various occasions on which she had been in company with the Marquis d'Asselnat. But, deeply interested as she was in all her visitor could tell her, Marianne could not help noticing that she seemed peculiarly ill at ease and that she was continually casting quick, nervous glances at the door, as though she were afraid that someone might come in.

She broke off in the middle of her questions to say kindly: 'You seem anxious, Comtesse? You have been kind enough to come and visit me and here I am pestering you with questions when I am sure your time is precious. If there is anything I can do to help you, I beg you will tell me.'

Madame de Gachet smiled a trifle constrainedly, seemed to hesitate for a moment and then, as though reaching a rather difficult decision, she said in a low voice: 'You are right. I am in great trouble — so much so that I ventured to call on you, a fellow-countrywoman and the daughter of my old friend, in the hope that you might assist me. Yet now I hardly dare – I am so ashamed —'

'But why? Please, I beg of you, ask me anything —'

'You are so charming, and have made me so welcome that now I am afraid, in case I should turn you against me.'

'I assure you you will not. Speak, I implore you.'

The lady hesitated a moment longer and then, dropping her eyes to the lace handkerchief that she was kneading between her hands, she confessed at last: 'I have suffered a terrible disaster. It is my misfortune, you see, to be a gamester. It is a shocking vice, I know that, but I started at Versailles, in the circle of our unhappy Queen, and I can no longer help myself. Wherever I am, I have to play. Can you understand that?'

'I think so,' Marianne said, thinking of Jolival who was also an inveterate card player. 'Are you trying to tell me that you have been playing here and you have lost?'

The countess nodded, without raising her eyes.

'Here, as in every other port in the world, there is a district – far from respectable, I am afraid – where every kind of gaming is carried on. It is called the Moldavanka. There is a house there, run by a Greek and, I must say, by no means ill-run at that. Yesterday I had some heavy losses there.'

'How much?'

'Four thousand roubles. It is a great deal of money, I know,' she went on hastily, seeing Marianne's involuntary gesture of dismay, 'but I assure you that if you will lend it to me, with another thousand so that I may try to recoup my losses, it will not be money thrown away. I have something here which I should like you to accept as a pledge. Naturally, if I am not in a position to repay you by tonight, then you will keep it.'

'But —'

Marianne broke off with a gasp. From the folds of the handkerchief she had been clutching so tightly, Madame de Gachet had produced a magnificent jewel. It was a diamond drop so exquisitely pure and brilliant that the young woman's eyes widened in amazement. It was like a fiery tear, a miniature sun containing all the concentrated radiance of the morning.

The Countess let her gaze at it for a moment and then, with a swift movement, slipped it into her hand.

'Keep it,' she said hurriedly. 'I know it will be safe with you – and help me if you can!'

Marianne stared helplessly now at the diamond scintillating in her palm and now at the woman. The lines in her face and the bitter twist to her mouth showed clearly in the morning light.

'You embarrass me very much, madame,' she said at last. 'Although I know nothing of these things, I am sure this diamond must be worth a great deal more than five thousand roubles. Why not go to a jeweller in the town —?'

'And have him refuse to return it to me? You are new here. You do not know yet what these people are like. Many of them are nothing more than adventurers, drawn here by the loans to be had from the governor. If I were to show anyone this stone they would kill me before they would let me have it back.'

'Very well, then, there is the governor. Why not entrust this jewel to him?'

'Because he is a ruthless persecutor of gaming hells – and of all who frequent them. I wish to settle in these parts, where it is beautiful and mild and sunny. I should not be granted permission to do so if the Duc de Richelieu knew the nature of my troubles. I am not even sure that the Tsar, who has been good enough to take an interest in me and has even sent one of his officers to escort me, would look on it more kindly.'

'You surprise me. I thought the Russians were passionate gamesters?'

Madame de Gachet made a gesture of impatience and rose to her feet.

'My dear child, let us say no more about it. What I am asking of you is a small service, of a few hours, no more, or so I trust. If you are unable to accommodate me, please say no more. I will endeavour to make some other arrangement, although – Oh, good God! How came I to get myself into this dreadful fix? If my poor husband could see me —' And the Countess subsided abruptly on to her chair, shaking with sobs. Then, burying her face in her hands, she began to cry in good earnest.

Horrified to feel herself the cause of such misery, Marianne sprang out of bed and, pausing only to place the diamond carefully on the bedside table, scrambled hastily into a dressing gown and dropped to her knees beside her visitor, doing her best to comfort her.

'Oh please, please don't cry! Of course I'll help you, my dear Countess! Forgive me if I seemed suspicious and asked too many questions, but the sight of the diamond frightened me a little. It is so very beautiful that I am quite afraid to have it in my possession. . . . Only do, please, calm yourself. I will gladly lend you the money.'

Before leaving Humayunabad, Marianne had reluctantly accepted a large sum in gold and letters of credit pressed upon the

177

travellers by Turhan Bey's steward. She was unwilling, now, to accept money from the man who had taken away her child but Osman had made it clear that he dared not disobey what was an explicit order and in the end it was Jolival, with a much greater grasp of the practicalities of life, who had made her see reason. Thanks to his foresight, Osman had even been so obliging as to obtain Russian money for them, so sparing them the hazards and chicanery of the money market.

Rising quickly to her feet, Marianne now went to one of her boxes and, having extracted the required sum, returned to place it in her visitor's hands.

'There, take it! And never doubt my friendship. I cannot bear to leave a friend of my father's in difficulties.'

In a moment the Countess had dried her eyes and, tucking the notes away in her corsage, flung her arms round Marianne and kissed her effusively.

'What a darling you are!' she cried. 'How can I ever thank you?'

'Why – by drying your tears.'

'They are dried already. And now I am going to sign a receipt for you. I will redeem it tonight.'

'No, please. There is no need. Indeed, you will offend me. I am not a moneylender. In fact I should like you to take back this splendid stone also.'

But Madame de Gachet flung up her hand in a gesture of categorical refusal.

'Absolutely not! Or I shall be offended. Either I will return these five thousand roubles to you this evening, or you will keep that stone. It is a family heirloom which I could never bring myself to sell, but you may do so very readily, for I shall not be there to see it. I will leave you now and thank you again a thousand times.'

She went to the door but paused with her hand on the knob to look back at Marianne imploringly.

'Just one more favour. Will you be kind enough not to speak to anyone of our little transaction? By this evening I hope it will be settled and we need never mention it again. And so I beg you to keep my secret – even from the gentleman who is your travelling companion.'

'Have no fear. I shall say nothing to him.'

She had, in fact, no inclination to mention the matter to Jolival, in view of the suspicions he had voiced regarding the unfortunate creature, who was clearly more to be pitied than blamed. Arcadius clung tenaciously to his own ideas and once he had taken a notion into his head it was the devil's own job to get him to abandon it. He would have been furious to learn that Marianne had lent five thousand roubles to a fellow-countrywoman simply because she had turned out to be an old friend of her father's.

At the thought of Jolival, Marianne did admit to certain qualms. She had made short work of his advice and had undoubtedly been taking something of a risk in lending the money. She knew that gaming was a terrible passion and that she had been wrong to encourage it in the Countess, but she had been moved by the poor woman's tears and saw her above all as a victim. She could not, no, she really could not have left a friend of her family, a fellow-countrywoman and, especially, a woman of that age to the tender mercies of the owners of gaming houses or of the moneylenders of the town, who would have pounced only too readily on the improvident creature's remarkable jewel.

After watching her visitor's departure from the doorway, Marianne walked slowly back to her bed. Sitting down on the edge of it, she took the diamond drop in her fingers and watched the play of light upon it. It was certainly a very wonderful stone and she caught herself thinking that she would not be averse to keeping it if the Countess failed to recoup her losses.

If that happened, she might offer her a further sum to make up for her loss, but on no account would she ever sell such a treasure.

At the same time, staring at the diamond and remembering the magnificent earrings trembling in the Countess's ears the day before, she felt her curiosity awaken. Who were these Gachets who possessed such princely jewels and how had the woman managed to retain them after twenty years of exile, when so many other emigrés had been and still were reduced to dire extremities of need? Had gaming come to her rescue?

It was hard to credit, for those to whom whist, faro or any other game of hazard had brought lasting prosperity were few indeed. Besides, not even Madame de Gachet herself knew whether her winnings with the thousand roubles left over after her debt was paid would be enough to cover the initial loan.

The more Marianne thought about it, the more depressed it made her. She had not yet reached the point of regretting her generous impulse but she had to admit that she had been a trifle hasty. Perhaps, after all, she would have been wiser to send for Jolival and have discussed it with him. But then the Countess had been so insistent that the matter be kept a secret between her and her friend's daughter and that was surely natural enough. At all events, she had given her promise to say nothing.

Finding no satisfactory answer to any of these problems, Marianne stowed the diamond away safely in her reticule and turned her attention to getting dressed. For some reason she was suddenly in a hurry to find Jolival and discover whether he had learned any more about the widow of the late Comte de Gachet.

When she was dressed, she left her own room and went along the passage to her friend's, which was at the far end. At this point there were two doors side by side, both opening into the passage and since she had forgotten Jolival's number she knocked first on one and, receiving no reply, moved on to the next. When this too produced no answer, she returned again to the first.

Thinking that Jolival must still be asleep, she turned the handle. The door opened easily, revealing a disordered room. Since the feminine character of the belongings thus revealed was enough to inform her that she had made a mistake, Marianne withdrew her head and turned to find herself face to face with a chambermaid who was eyeing her suspiciously.

'Was madame looking for someone?'

'Yes. I thought this was the Vicomte de Jolival's room.'

'Madame is mistaken. This room belongs to the Comtesse de Gachet. Monsieur le Vicomte is next door – but I don't think he is there just now.'

'What do you know about it?' Marianne asked crossly, disliking the girl's tone. 'I hardly think he'd tell you where he was going?'

'Oh no, madame! It's only that I saw him go out at about eight o'clock. He asked for a horse to be saddled and rode off in the direction of the harbour. Does madame require anything further?'

'No . . . that will do, thank you.'

Marianne walked back to her own room, feeling puzzled and out of sorts. Where the devil had Jolival run off to at this hour of the morning? And why had he said nothing to her?

She had grown accustomed to the Vicomte's solitary expeditions, for he seemed to possess a peculiar faculty of making himself understood anywhere in the world, and of finding out whatever he wanted to know. But here, in this city where civilization was as yet only skin deep, a thin varnish on the surface of barbarism, it was uncomfortable to feel herself alone, even if only for an hour or two and in surroundings as typically French as the Hotel Ducroux.

The chambermaid had said that he had ridden towards the harbour. Why? Was he going to look for the *Sea Witch*, or to explore the neighbourhood of the old citadel in the hope of hearing some news of Jason? Or perhaps both?

She paced about her room for a while, uncertain what to do. She was longing to go out herself and begin inquiries on her own account but dared not for fear of missing Jolival if he should return with any news. As time passed she grew increasingly bored and discontented at being obliged to remain indoors when she wanted so badly to go out and start her own search for Jason. She unpacked her boxes and packed them again, did her hair afresh, put on a hat to go out after all, then took it off again and cast herself into an elbow chair, took up a book and threw it down, and finally donned her hat once more with the intention of going down at least as far as the front door and finding out from Ducroux whether any word had come for her from the governor's palace.

She was tying the wide, sea-green crape ribbons under her chin when all of a sudden an uproar exploded in the hotel. There were loud shouts and the sound of running feet in the passage, with a shrill voice shrieking in some foreign language, followed by the tramp of heavy, booted feet approaching, accompanied by a clash of arms.

Full of curiosity, Marianne was on her way to her door when it was flung open abruptly. In the opening, his shocked face whiter than his shirt, stood the hotel proprietor. He was accompanied by a law officer and two armed soldiers, and he looked like a man in the extreme stages of embarrassment.

Marianne stared indignantly at the intruders.

'May I ask, Maître Ducroux, what this means?' she asked icily. 'What kind of hotel do you call this? Who gave you permission to enter my room uninvited?'

'Indeed, Mademoiselle, it is not my fault,' the man stammered wretchedly. 'Believe me, I should never dream of . . . It is these gentlemen —' he finished, indicating the three Russians.

Meanwhile, disregarding both him and Marianne completely, the officer had stalked into the room and was flinging open trunks and boxes and tossing out the contents in such a cavalier fashion that Marianne lost her temper.

'This is your hotel is it not? Then get these men out of here this instant, unless you want me to complain to the governor!

181

Gentlemen, you call them! I don't want to know what they think they're doing. Get them out!'

'Indeed I can't help it. They insist on searching this room.'

'But whatever for? Will you tell me that?'

Racked by the glittering green eyes that seemed able to flay him alive, Ducroux tugged awkwardly at his shirt cuffs and kept his eyes fixed firmly on the ground at Marianne's feet, as though expecting the answer to come from there. A curt command from the officer seemed to force him to a decision at last and he lifted his unhappy gaze to hers.

'There has been a complaint,' he said, almost inaudibly. 'A lady, a guest in the hotel, has missed a valuable jewel. She insists on a search of the whole building and – unfortunately one of the maids saw you, mademoiselle, coming out of the lady's room this morning.'

Marianne's heart seemed to stop dead and the blood mounted to her cheeks.

'A valuable jewel, did you say? Who is this woman?'

'Madame de Gachet! She has been robbed of a very large, pear-shaped diamond – a teardrop, she calls it. It was an heirloom . . . she is making a great deal of fuss . . .'

Inevitably, the diamond was discovered a moment later in Marianne's reticule and, despite her furious protests as she realized, too late, the trap into which she had fallen out of pure innocence, she was dragged roughly from her room with a soldier on either side and hurried out of the hotel, watched by a large crowd which had been drawn to the Hotel Ducroux by the uproar.

Without further warning, she found herself hustled into a closed carriage which had been hurriedly fetched and driven away rapidly in the direction of the citadel which she had been so anxious to visit only a short while before. They had not given her time to utter so much as a single protest.

182

CHAPTER NINE

The General of the Shadows

The ancient Podolian stronghold of Khajibey, rebuilt by the Turks and won back by the Russians, had no doubt gained in strength and impregnability under its different owners but by no means in comfort. The cell into which Marianne was thrust unceremoniously, spitting with rage, was small and damp with grimy walls and a triple-barred window looking out at a grey wall and a line of stunted trees. Even the sight of these trees, however, was forbidden to the prisoners since the window glass had everywhere been white-washed over, so that a kind of fog seemed to hang over the prison even in bright sunshine.

The only furniture was a bed, consisting of nothing more than a plank and some straw, a heavy table and a stool, all three items bolted to the floor. An oil lamp stood in a recess but even this was behind bars, as though for fear the occupants of the cell might try to set fire to it.

After the massive door slammed shut behind her, Marianne remained for a moment sitting dazedly on the straw mattress where her guards had thrown her. It had all occurred so quickly that she could hardly take in where she was, or what had happened to her.

There had been that woman, the wretched creature who had used her father's name as an excuse to reach her, to melt her heart and so get money from her! But what was the purpose of this charade? To obtain the money and ensure that she was spared the necessity of paying it back? That seemed to be the only explanation, for it was impossible to think of any other motive for such a diabolical trick. Revenge or feminine jealousy were ruled out since she and Madame de Gachet had only set eyes on one another for the first time in the entrance hall of the hotel. Marianne could not remember ever having heard her name mentioned before and even Jolival, although thinking he had met that devil in female form somewhere, could not recall when or where, or even put a name to her.

As her initial bewilderment passed, Marianne was seized again by the anger which had swept over her as she found herself apprehended like a common thief. With a roaring in her head and a red light before her eyes, she saw again the officer's triumphant expression as he pulled the diamond from her bag, the anger and mortification on the hotel proprietor's face and the gaping wonder of those other inmates of the hotel who had been attracted by the fuss at the sight of the magnificent stone.

'Oh no!' Ducroux had cried out. 'It can't be true!'

It had been open to doubt whether this last remark was called forth by the splendour of the diamond or his own disappointment in his ravishing young guest. But with such evidence against her, how could she deny it? Especially since the devilish Countess had taken good care not to show herself. And now what was to become of her?

After a little while, however, she began to take some comfort in the thought that Jolival was still at liberty. He would be bound to learn of this catastrophe as soon as he returned to the hotel and he would hurry straight to the governor to put an end to the dreadful mistake before it could end in a miscarriage of justice. But would he manage to see Richelieu in time to rescue Marianne from her present predicament? It seemed not unlikely, even highly probable, in fact, for if the governor were anything like the gentleman his rank implied, he would never permit his old friend's name to be mixed up in such a fearful scandal.

She soon managed to convince herself that they would come for her before long and question her in some language she could understand. Then she would be able to make them listen to her, insist on being confronted with that dreadful woman, and then everything would be all right. They would even have to apologize to her, because after all she was the injured party, it was she who had been cheated out of five thousand roubles and with the most blatant effrontery. Well, they would see which rang clearer, the voice of truth or the voice of lies. How she looked forward to seeing the old harridan take her place in this cell . . .

Her spirits much restored, she was meditating along these lines when the brooding silence of the old prison was broken by a variety of sounds. There was the thud of heavy boots, the clatter of weapons and raised voices rising above the sounds of a struggle. To her horror, Marianne recognized that one of those voices was Jolival's.

'You have no right,' he was protesting furiously at the top of his voice. 'I tell you I'm a Frenchman, do you hear, a Frenchman! You have no right to lay hands on me! I demand to see the governor – I wish to see the Duc de Richelieu. Ri-che-lieu! For God's sake, why won't you listen to me, damn you?'

The last words ended in a kind of agonized grunt which told Marianne sickeningly that they must have struck the prisoner to quiet him.

Clearly, the unfortunate Vicomte had been apprehended on his return to the hotel, perhaps even without a word of explanation. He must be totally bewildered by what was happening to him.

She flung herself at the door and pressed her face against the grating, screaming out: 'Arcadius! I'm here . . . close by! They've arrested me too! It was that woman, Arcadius, that horrible Madame de Gachet!'

But there was no answer beyond another cry of pain, further away this time, followed by the noise of a door opened and shut again with a great crashing of bolts. Then a frenzy of rage seized Marianne. She hammered at the thick, oaken door with hands and feet, screaming insults and abuse in a variety of languages in the crazy hope that one of the dumb brutes who had arrested them might catch some fragments of what she was saying, and demanding that someone be sent at once to inform the Duc de Richelieu.

The effects of this clamour were not long in coming. The door of her prison was pulled open so suddenly that she almost tumbled into the passage. What prevented her was a hand belonging to a gigantic individual with a completely bald head, as though all his capacity for growing hair were concentrated in the enormous gingery moustache that dropped on either side of his mouth. With one thrust of his great hand he sent her reeling back on to the straw, at the same time shouting at her words she did not understand but which evidently contained a crude request to make less noise.

After which, the better to drive home his message, he took a long whip from his belt and laid about her back and shoulders with a force that made her scream aloud.

The thought that she was being treated like a vicious animal was the last straw to Marianne's temper. Writhing off the bed, she twisted like a snake and sprang, biting the man savagely on the wrist.

The gaoler roared like a slaughtered ox. He tore her off and hurled her bodily across the room, to lie half-dazed by a few more blows from his whip. Then he left her.

She lay for a long while on the floor, incapable of movement. Her back and shoulders hurt abominably and she had a struggle to

calm the frantic beating of her heart. Such was the fury and indignation that possessed her that, in spite of the pain of the blows, she
had not shed a single tear.

What kind of people were these who maltreated their prisoners
like this? Out of the depths of her memory she recalled things
Princess Morousi had told her while she had been staying in her
house. Justice, in Russia, was swift and summary. Often, those unfortunate enough to offend the Tsar or his representatives would
simply disappear. They would be sent in chains to the farthest
reaches of Siberia, to rot in the mines. They never came back because
cold, hunger and ill-treatment very soon opened for them the way
to what could only have been a better world.

Perhaps that was the horrid fate which awaited her and Jolival.
If the Duc de Richelieu, that dedicated enemy of Napoleon, were to
discover who she really was, then certainly nothing could save them
from that living death, unless the despot of New Russia should
prefer to follow the fashion of his Turkish neighbours and drop
them in the Black Sea with a stone around their necks.

At the thought of the governor, all her earlier anger revived.
What kind of a man must he be to permit such savage customs in
the land where he was master? Surely the most hateful and con-
temptible of beings? How dared he bear the name of the greatest
enemy of feudalism whom France had produced until Napoleon
and suffer himself to play the lackey to a Muscovite Tsar, the ruler
of a race of men more barbarous even than the rudest savages, at
least if her own galling recollections of the handsome Count
Chernychev were anything to go by!

Painfully, she dragged herself to her feet at last, but only to col-
lapse once more, helplessly, on her bed. Her back was hurting her
and she was beginning to shiver violently in her thin silk dress, now
rent and torn by the gaoler's whip. She was cold in her dank cell.
She was thirsty too, but the water in her pitcher, when she succeeded
in lifting it with an effort to her lips, tasted horribly brackish and
slimy, as if it had not been renewed for many days.

In an effort to obtain some meagre warmth, she huddled as best
she could into the straw, trying to avoid hurting her sore back more
than she could help. And to steady her fast waning courage, she
tried to pray. But the words did not come easily, for it was hard to
pray when she was full of anger, but at least that underlying rage
helped to stave off fear.

How long she lay like that, with eyes wide open and staring, as still as the dead in that oppressive silence, she did not know. The hours passed slowly and the grey light that filtered through into the prison became dusk, but the girl on the pallet did not seem to notice. All her thoughts were with her friends, with Jolival, who must be enduring similar treatment to herself, and with Jason, who would never now receive the help that he must need so sorely . . . To think that he might be only a few yards away from her, sick, perhaps, and in despair. No amount of whipping or ill-treatment would ever overcome his fury of resistance. God alone knew what these brutes might have done to him.

She did not hear the judas in her door open. Nor did she move when a thin pencil of light entered the cell by the same way and move across until it fell on her pale figure lying in the straw.

'Dear God, it is she!' murmured a voice. 'Open this door at once!'

The pencil beam grew until it became the bright light of a lantern carried by a gaoler. It filled the cell, banishing the shadows, and only then aroused the girl from her torpor. She sat up, blinking, just as a small man in a black soutane, with a halo of white hair, darted into the cell.

At the sight of that black robe, Marianne uttered a gasp of terror, for to a prisoner the arrival of a priest could scarcely be held a good augury. But it was only for a moment. A second later, the newcomer was hurrying across to her with outstretched arms.

'Marianne! My little one! What are you doing here?'

She gave a cry of recognition, feeling as if the heavens had opened for her.

'Godfather! You —?'

But the shock of joy breaking in on her wretchedness was too much for her. Her head swam and she had to cling to the old man who was hugging her in his arms, laughing and crying at once.

'Godfather! It can't be true . . . I must be dreaming . . .' She was stammering incoherently, still unable to believe that he was real.

By this time, Cardinal de Chazay had been able to appreciate his goddaughter's condition, her torn dress and pale face, with the imprint of fear still in her eyes, and the angry words burst out of him.

'What have these savages been doing to you?' He rounded on the gaoler and continued his tirade in Russian. The man had been standing by, watching in blank amazement a prince of the Roman

Church cradling a common thief in his arms as tenderly as a mother. Now he vanished in response to an authoritative command and Gauthier de Chazay turned his attention to calming his goddaughter's sobs. Her shattered nerves had given way and she was weeping like a fountain into his shoulder, gasping out apologies.

'I was so frightened, Godfather! I – I thought they would do away with me w-without even a hearing . . .'

'And not without reason. I shall never be sufficiently grateful for the providential chance that brought me to Odessa just at this time! When Richelieu told me a female traveller who arrived at Ducroux's yesterday had been arrested for theft and was claiming, on the strength of some slight resemblance, to be your father's daughter, I felt I had to make sure, and I hurried here at once. I'd no idea what could have brought you to this place but I knew of only one person who looked like your father, and that was you, yourself. Although the business of the theft still worried me —'

'I stole nothing, I swear to you! That woman —'

'I know, my child, I know. Or rather, I guessed as much. You see, I know the woman of old. But come, we must not remain here. The governor came with me and is waiting for us in the commandant's office.

The gaoler returned, bearing an army greatcoat and a steaming glass. The coat he handed nervously to the priest, the glass he set down by Marianne.

'Drink it,' the Cardinal told her. 'It will do you good.'

It was a glass of milkless tea, strong and very sweet, and it filled the void in her empty stomach and, with its warmth, restored some life to her. While she drank, the priest put the vast overcoat round her shoulders, hiding her tattered dress and bruised flesh. Then he helped her to her feet again.

'Can you walk? Would you like someone to carry you?'

'No, no, I can manage very well. The brute beat me horribly but he didn't kill me. But I should like someone to go and rescue my friend Jolival, Godfather. He was arrested not long after me. I heard them bring him here.'

'Don't worry. It shall be attended to. He'll join us upstairs.'

In point of fact, Marianne was still far from steady on her feet but the thought of seeing Richelieu so soon gave her wings. So much the better if it meant another battle to be fought. She felt strong enough to fight the whole world now and win. God had not deserted her. He had sent her one of His most distinguished representatives, and in the nick of time.

She had been too long familiar with the one-time Abbé de Chazay's mysterious comings and goings to feel much real surprise at finding him here, at the gateway to Russia and the east, dressed as a simple country priest. But a gasp of pure amazement was torn from her as she came face to face with the governor of whom she had been making such an ogre.

Still dressed in the same shabby boots and ill-fitting coat and still armed with the inevitable pipe, the man she had known as Septimanie was pacing irritably up and down the bare room which the commandant of the castle dignified by the title of his 'office', on account of the presence in it of a table bearing at that moment three sheets of paper and an inkwell. He turned at the sound of the door opening and stood with a frown between his eyes and head lowered like a bull about to charge while the Cardinal and the prisoner came in. He was evidently in an exceedingly bad temper and he spoke without preamble.

'So, it was your goddaughter, your Eminence? There can be no doubt of that?'

'None at all, my friend. None at all. This is Marianne d'Asselnat de Villeneuve the daughter of my unhappy cousin, Pierre-Armand and the Lady Anne Selton.'

'If that is so, I fail to understand how the sole descendant of such a man could so far have forgotten herself as to become a common thief.'

'I am not a thief,' Marianne protested furiously. 'That woman who accused me is the wickedest and most deceitful creature, and the most outrageous liar I have ever met. Only send for her, your grace, and we shall see then which of us is in the right.'

'That is precisely what I mean to do. The Comtesse de Gachet enjoys his Imperial Majesty's especial protection and I owe her my respectful consideration on that account. The same can hardly be said of you, mademoiselle. You have caused nothing but trouble ever since your arrival here. For all your name and your beauty, which I confess is striking, you seem to me the sort of young person who —'

'If you will allow me, my dear Duke,' the Cardinal cut in sharply, 'I had not finished my introduction. The lady you see before you is no mere young person. Nor should you address her as *mademoiselle*. Her full title, since her marriage, is her Serene Highness, Princess

189

Corrado Sant'Anna. Moreover I believe she has as much right to
your respectful consideration as this Madame de Gachet, of whom I
may, perhaps, know more than you.'

Inwardly, Marianne commended herself to heaven, cursing the
family pride which had led the Cardinal to impress his friend with
this blunt revelation of her real name. Richelieu's stern eyes had
widened and one eyebrow had lifted ominously. His rather high
voice went up a full three tones to a harsh squeak.

'Princess Sant'Anna, eh? I've heard that name. I can't remember
just what it was I was told about her, but I seem to think it was nothing very good. One thing, at least, is certain. She entered Odessa
under false pretences, taking good care to conceal her real rank and
travelling simply under her maiden name. There must have been a
reason for that —'

Gauthier de Chazay, Cardinal San Lorenzo, was not a patient
man. He had listened with clearly growing irritation to this speech
of the governor's and now he put an end to it by banging his fist
loudly on the table.

'We can consider her reasons later, if you please, my son! Are
you quite sure that your rather too obvious ill humour is not due to
the fact that you owe the Princess an apology, and that it galls you
to admit that Madame de Gachet is not the saint you had imagined?'

The Duke moistened his lips and hunched his shoulders, possibly
to hide the red that crept into his cheeks. He muttered something
half-inaudibly about the difficulties attendant on remaining a
faithful son of the Church when her princes were so unpleasantly
meddlesome.

'Well?' the little Cardinal insisted. 'We are waiting.'

'I shall apologize to – to the lady when the matter has been
cleared up. Let the Comtesse de Gachet be admitted.'

Watching the woman to whom she owed her recent unpleasant
experiences sweep into the room like a great actress taking the
stage, Marianne saw red and could have hurled herself at the
impudent creature. She came forward, more powdered and plumed
than ever and leaning on one of the tall, beribboned canes which
Marie-Antoinette had made the fashion for walking in the gardens
of the Trianon, the skirts of her purple gown brushing the ground,
and, after curtsying urbanely to the Duke, sat down, without waiting
to be asked, on a coarse wooden chair. The glance that rested briefly
on Marianne and on the unremarkable little priest standing beside
her showed precisely what she thought of them.

She arranged her silken skirts around her, as she had done in Marianne's bedchamber, and uttered a tiny laugh.

'Have you sealed the fate of this unhappy creature already, Duke? I see that you have fetched a priest to her, to prepare her, no doubt, for the proper punishment of her kind. I really think, however, that Siberia will do well enough for the girl and that you will not —'

'That will do, madame,' the Cardinal broke in curtly. 'You are here to answer questions, not to pass judgment in what does not concern you. Or to lay down the correct punishment for theft. That is a matter on which you have some experience, have you not? I believe it must be almost twenty-six years since —'

'My dear sir,' the governor began, but the Cardinal silenced him with a lift of his hand, although his eyes never left the Countess's.

She had paled visibly under her paint and Marianne saw to her surprise that there were beads of sweat along the line of the powdered hair, while the white fingers emerging from her black lace mittens had tightened on the cane.

Madame de Gachet turned her head, clearly unwilling to meet the calm, blue gaze fastened so steadily on her. She laughed again, lightly, and shrugged her shoulders with an assumption of indifference.

'Naturally I have experience, Monsieur l'Abbé. But indeed, I am at a loss to understand your meaning.'

'I think you understand me very well. The fact that you are here at all you owe to some of my own order, as well as to the unwitting kindness of the Tsar. Nevertheless, those few drops of royal blood that run in your veins do not authorize you to make fresh victims.'

Marianne had been following this strange and incomprehensible exchange eagerly. Now she saw the Countess's eyes start from her head. She put a shaking hand to her throat, as if she were choking, made an effort to rise and sank back heavily on to her chair, as though her legs refused to bear her.

'Who – who are you?' she whispered, almost inaudibly. 'How could you know that – unless you are the devil?'

Gauthier de Chazay smiled.

'Nothing so illustrious, and my dress should tell you I have not even the honour to represent him. But we are not here to play at riddles, or to uncover secrets. I have said what I have solely in order to persuade you to withdraw a charge which you know very well is false.'

The fear had not left her eyes but she said at once, with a kind of desperate haste, that she withdrew the charge, that it was all a dreadful misunderstanding.

But this Marianne would not have.

'That does not satisfy me,' she said. 'I mean this woman to confess the truth, the whole truth. Witnesses saw the officer who arrested me take the diamond drop from my reticule, so how can anyone say the woman was mistaken. She gave me the stone as surety for a loan of five thousand roubles which she needed to pay her gaming debts and was to pay back the same evening. I suppose she lost it all and made up this shameful story as a way of getting back her diamond without repaying the money.'

This time it was the Duc de Richelieu who interrupted.

'Is this true, madame?' he asked sternly, turning to the Countess, who was looking the picture of guilt.

She nodded, not daring to raise her eyes. A heavy silence fell on the room as they regarded her. The Duke tapped out his pipe mechanically on a corner of the table. His face was strangely blank and he was evidently torn between his sense of justice and the pressing instructions which had come to him from Petersburg. Justice prevailed.

'Then I have no choice but to place you under arrest . . .'

She looked up at that, but before she could speak the Cardinal had forestalled her.

'No,' he said, with unexpected authority. 'You will do nothing of the kind, Duke. You have had instructions from the imperial chancellory to assist the Comtesse de Gachet to settle in the Crimea – where she is to reside for the remainder of her natural life, with Colonel Ivanoff to – er, look after her. You will do just that.'

Now it was the Duke's turn to bang his fist on the table.

'Your Eminence,' he said forcibly, 'I yield to no one in respect for your cloth, but this is not a matter for the Church. It is a matter for the state. I shall inform the Tsar of what has occurred and I am sure his Majesty will agree with me. The woman must be tried and sentenced.'

The Cardinal did not answer at once. Instead, he took Richelieu by the arm and drew him aside into the embrasure of the single, narrow window which at this hour of night was in deep shadow. But Gauthier de Chazay was not after light. Marianne, watching him intently, saw him lift his hand, palm upwards, and display the ring he wore turned inwards on his finger, to the governor's eyes.

Richeliu whitened visibly and rewarded the little Cardinal with a glance of mingled awe and apprehension.

'The General —' he breathed.

'Well?' the priest said.

'I shall obey, monseigneur.'

'You will earn the Order's gratitude. And now, madame —' He turned back to the defeated Countess who had been watching this scene without understanding but with alternate hope and dread. 'You may return to your hotel where you will announce your departure for tomorrow morning. Colonel Ivanoff shall hear within the hour to which Crimean city he is to escort you and he will receive the appropriate papers. After that we must consider how best to establish the truth in the best interests of all.'

Madame de Gachet rose with an effort and stood leaning on her ridiculous cane like a wounded soldier on his musket. All her arrogance had left her. She looked now like a very old woman. And it was in a tone almost of humility that she murmured: 'I do not know who you are, monseigneur, but I should like to thank you – yet I do not know how.'

'Very easily. By honouring the bargain you made with Mademoiselle d'Asselnat. You agreed, did you not, that the diamond drop should be hers if you failed to return her five thousand roubles? Can you return them?'

'No – but if someone were to lend me the money I might —'

'You might do nothing of the sort. Your repentance is a fragile thing, madame, and deceit is second nature to you. On your return to the hotel, you will have the stone delivered to the governor's palace and he will see that it is handed to your victim. That will be safer —'

'But I don't want it,' Marianne protested.

'You will keep it, however. That is my order. You will keep it – in memory of your mother who died on the scaffold for having tried to save the Queen. Do not try to understand. I will explain later. But now you too should go back to the hotel and rest, for you stand in great need of it.'

'I won't go without my friend Jolival.'

Before she had finished speaking, the door opened and Jolival appeared. His eyes were closed and he was supported by a gaoler, for he seemed to have difficulty in walking. Marianne saw to her horror that there was a bandage round his head and that it was stained with blood.

'What have they done to him?' she cried, and ran to him.

But as she took his other arm to help guide him to a chair, he opened one eye and smiled at her.

'A tap on the head to keep me quiet . . . Nothing serious, but I feel a trifle dizzy. It's brought on one of my headaches . . . If you could manage to obtain a glass of brandy, my dear . . .'

The Duke opened a cupboard set in the wall and, after a glance inside, emerged with a bottle and a glass which he half-filled.

'There's only vodka here,' he said. 'Would that do as well?'

Jolival took the glass and gazed with some surprise at the man who proffered it.

'Well, well, if it isn't Monsieur Septimanie. What brings you here?'

'Jolival,' Marianne broke in, 'this gentleman is the governor, the Duc de Richelieu himself.'

'Well I never! And I was thinking —' He paused to swallow the contents of the glass, but showing no particular sign of surprise. Then he returned the empty glass with a sigh of satisfaction. A little colour had come back to his wan face.

'Not bad,' he said. 'I might even say it goes down like water.'

His eyes suddenly took in the presence of the Countess and Marianne saw them darken.

'That woman,' he muttered. 'I know now who she is! I know where I saw her last. My lord Duke, you are the governor here, then let me tell you that this woman is a thief, a creature publicly branded as such! The last time I saw her she was being held down while Sanson, the public executioner set his iron to her flesh. That was in 1786, on the steps of the Palais de Justice in Paris, and I can tell you —'

'Be quiet,' the cardinal interrupted him sharply. 'No one has asked you to say anything on that subject, or what you may think about it. I am Gauthier de Chazay, Cardinal San Lorenzo and Marianne's godfather. By the grace of God I was here when I was needed to set things right. That is now done and we need hear no more of the matter.' He turned to the Countess whose terrors had revived at the entrance of Jolival. 'Madame, you may go. Colonel Ivanoff awaits you. He will have his orders within the hour and you have only to pack your belongings. But if you wish to enjoy a quiet sojourn here, see to it that you do not indulge in any more such escapades. You will be provided with enough to live on.'

'You have my promise, your Eminence . . . Forgive me!'

194

She stepped forward timidly and, bending her knee with difficulty, bowed her head with a beseeching look. He made a quick sign of the cross above her purple feathered head-dress and then held out his hand for her to kiss. On that hand there now appeared only a plain gold band.

Madame de Gachet rose and left the room in silence, without looking back.

'She didn't even apologize,' Marianne said, when she had watched her go. 'I think she might have done that at least, after all I suffered on her account.'

'It is useless to expect it,' answered the Cardinal. 'Hers is the kind of mean spirit which never forgives its victims for the wrongs she has done them . . . and for the consequences.'

The governor came forward from behind the table where he had remained an observer of the preceding scene and spoke to Marianne.

'Then it is I, madame, who will offer you my apologies, for you have suffered at the hands of my subordinates. How can I make it up to you? When we met down by the harbour yesterday evening, you seemed most anxious to speak to the governor. Is there something you would ask him?'

Marianne's pale cheeks flushed with pleasure. Could it be that, after all, her unpleasant adventure was going to be rewarded, much sooner and more easily than she had imagined, with the release of Jason and his ship? It seemed not impossible, for the Duke was even then talking of compensation.

'My lord Duke,' she said softly, 'there is a boon, although I hardly dare to ask it, for I have not forgotten that I owe my life to the good Monsieur Septimanie. But it is true that I made the voyage from Constantinople with that object. My only fear is that it may have given you a distrust of me—'

Richelieu laughed and the sound was so warm and friendly that it lightened the tension left by the mystery of the Comtesse de Gachet.

'I know, but the Cardinal's warning cannot be lightly disregarded. As to Septimanie, it is merely one of the innumerable absurd names with which the children of certain families are apt to find themselves burdened. It amuses me to use it now and then. But do, please, make your request.'

'Very well. I believe that, at some time in March, an American brig called the *Sea Witch* was captured by the Russian fleet and brought into harbour here. I want to know what has become of her

and her crew and, if possible, to obtain their liberty. Captain Beaufort is a very dear friend of mine.'

'He must be indeed. . . . You took a very grave risk, madame, in
coming to this country to get news of him. This Beaufort is a lucky
man.'

There was a sudden melancholy in the eyes that dwelled on the
beautiful woman before him, so touchingly young and frail in a coat
many sizes too big for her which swamped the remembered grace of
her figure. Her face was pale with pain and weariness but her great,
luminous green eyes shone like emerald stars at the sound of the
American's name. She clasped both hands together in a pretty
gesture of entreaty.

'For pity's sake, your excellency, tell me what has happened to
them!'

The sparkle in the green eyes had grown brighter still and
Richelieu guessed that the tears were not far off. And yet, oddly
enough, his face seemed to harden.

'The ship and the men are here. But you must not ask me any
more for the present because I have no time to spare. Other less
pleasant but more demanding duties call me. But if you will give me
the pleasure of dining with me tomorrow night I may be able to tell
you something more.'

'My lord —'

'No, no!! Not another word. A carriage is waiting to drive you
back to Ducroux's, with an escort befitting your station. We will
speak of it again tomorrow evening. This is not the place.'

There was nothing more to say. Surprised and a little disappointed
by this sudden dismissal, which suggested a wish to avoid the subject, Marianne dropped a curtsy as deep as the wobbly condition of
her legs would permit. Her one wish now was for a hot bath and her
bed, where she could forget the horrors of the day she had just lived
through. Even Richelieu's announcement that he intended keeping
the Cardinal with him did not wring a protest from her. The
governor was clearly burning to question him about the strange
woman whom he had brought to heel in such a remarkable
fashion.

The same question was tormenting Marianne also but they were
no sooner in the carriage which was to take them back to the hotel
than Jolival fell so fast asleep that it took two men to get him out
and upstairs to bed in his own room, and even then he did not
wake. So she was compelled to master her very natural curiosity

regarding both Cardinal San Lorenzo and the mysterious Madame de Gachet.

She was forced to acknowledge that her godfather was a most remarkable person. He seemed to possess unusual powers and his path lay always in the darkest, most mysterious ways. Through all the years of her childhood and adolescence, she had built up a picture of him as a character out of a novel, the man of God who was also a secret agent, vowed to the twofold service of the Pope and the exiled royal family of France. She had seen him in Paris, at the time of Napoleon's marriage to the Austrian Emperor's daughter, decked in the scarlet of a prince of the Church, but a rebellious prince, in open revolt against the Emperor and compelled to fly by night to escape from Savary's police. Not that this had hindered him at all when it came to arranging her own marriage with a mysterious prince whom no one had ever set eyes on and of whom she herself had seen only a gloved hand during the wedding ceremony.

And now he was here, in Odessa, still engaged, no doubt, about some secret task, but clad it seemed in unusual and mysterious power which enabled the little blue-eyed priest to command even the highest in this strange land. What office did he hold now? What new, unsuspected dignity had he put on? Just now, looking at the gold ring on the cardinal's hand, Richelieu had used a strange, unlikely word to be applied to a priest. The General. Of what secret army was Cardinal de Chazay the head? It must be a powerful one, even if it operated in the shadows, thought Marianne, remembering the ease with which a sometime abbé, poor as a church mouse, had produced the vast sum in gold demanded by her first husband, Francis Cranmere.

Tired of wondering, Marianne let the answers to these questions wait. What she needed now was sleep, so that she would be fresh and wide-awake tomorrow evening to plead Jason's cause with the governor. That cause might not be easily won because Richelieu's manner had cooled noticeably when she had summoned up courage to put her request. But at least the brief exchange had told her that Jason was actually here, in the same town, and that she would see him soon.

With her mind thus far at rest, she was able to respond pleasantly to Maître Ducroux's effusive welcome and his reiterated apologies for his own unwilling part in what he referred to as 'the unfortunate incident'. But it was with real delight that she found herself once more in her own room. A chambermaid had been busy there and everything had been set to rights, presumably while the proprietor awaited the verdict in the case.

When she opened her eyes, late in the following morning, the first thing she saw was a bunch of enormous roses by her bed. They were a wonderful shell pink and the scent was so strong that she took them in both hands and buried her nose in them. It was then she saw that beside them was a small package accompanied by a note sealed with the cross and chevrons of Richelieu in red wax.

The contents of the package came as no surprise. It was, of course, the diamond, elegantly done up in a gilt comfit box, and once again Marianne fell under the spell of the magnificent stone. It seemed to glow within the curtains of her bed with a magical radiance. But the note gave her even more to think about.

It contained no more than a dozen words above the governor's signature:

'The most beautiful flowers, the most beautiful jewel, for the most beautiful . . .'

Yet the implication behind those dozen words was so agitating that she jumped out of bed and put on the first dress that came to hand, thrust her feet into a pair of slippers and, not even bothering to comb out the two thick plaits swinging at her back, rushed from the room, still clutching the gilt box and the note in one hand. She knew she had to talk to Jolival at once, even if it meant emptying a jug of water over him to wake him.

As she passed Madame de Gachet's room, she saw that the door was wide open and the room cleared of all her personal belongings. She must have quitted the town as soon as it was light. But Marianne did not stop. She opened the adjoining door and walked in, without pausing to knock.

The sight that met her eyes was a reassuring one. Seated at a table before the open window, wearing one of the loudly patterned dressing gowns that he affected, was the Vicomte, engaged in eating his way systematically through the contents of an enormous tray. These ranged from some of Maître Ducroux's airy croissants to victuals considerably more substantial and included, besides the tall silver coffee pot, a brace of promisingly dusty bottles.

The Vicomte appeared unperturbed by Marianne's tumultuous entrance. He beamed at her with his mouth full and pointed to a small elbow chair.

'You seem to be in rather a hurry,' he remarked when he could speak. 'I do hope nothing else disastrous has occurred?'

'No, no – at least, I don't think so. But tell me first how you are feeling.'

'As well as anyone can feel with a head like this,' he said, taking off his nightcap and revealing an empurpled lump the size of a small egg with a cut across the middle of it in the centre of his bald pate. 'I'd best be careful how I take my hat off for the next few days if I don't want to attract too much attention from the barbarians who inhabit these parts. Would you like some coffee? You look to me as if you'd got up in a hurry without waiting for any breakfast. And while we're on the subject, are you going to show me what it is you're clutching to your heart?'

'These,' Marianne said, laying them before him. 'I want to know what you think of this note.'

The aroma of coffee filled the room as Jolival went on calmly filling her cup. Then he read the note, drank a glass of wine, returned his nightcap to his head and settled back into his chair, waving the sheet of paper gently.

'What I think?' he said after a moment. 'Upon my word, what any fool would think! That his Excellency was very much taken with you.'

'And doesn't that worry you at all? Have you forgotten I am to dine with him tonight – and alone, because I don't recall hearing him invite you also?'

'Quite right, from which I deduce that he was not equally taken with me. But I don't think you need worry, because even if I am not there your godfather is sure to be present. In any case, you are bound to hear from him during the day and I believe that this is one occasion when he will be much better able to advise you than your uncle Arcadius because he knows the Duke. Your godfather is a very remarkable man – and one I'd very much like to know more of. You have often talked of him, my dear, but I had no idea he'd risen to such power.'

'Nor I! Oh Jolival, I can tell you – there are times when, for all his greatness to me, my godfather makes me uneasy. He almost frightens me. He is so mysterious. And it is his very power, as you say, that scares me. There seems no end to it. I thought I knew him, you see, and yet every time I see him there is something more that is new to me.'

'There's nothing odd in that. You knew someone who stood to

199

you in place of your father and mother, a little priest who gave you an unvarying affection. But you were a child and naturally you did not see the whole picture of the man.'

'It was natural when I was a child, yes. But not now. And yet the older I get, the deeper grow the shadows that surround him.'

She described, as best she could, all that had taken place in the commandant's office before Jolival's entrance, endeavouring to recall the exact words used and dwelling on the curious moment when Richelieu had capitulated instantly at the sight of the Cardinal's ring, and on the words *the General* which had escaped him.

Jolival stiffened as she uttered them.

'He said *the General*? You are quite sure?'

'Positive. And I must say I didn't understand it at all. What do you think he meant? I know it is a title sometimes given to the head of a monastic order but my godfather has never been a monk. He has always been in the world . . .'

She saw that Jolival was not listening to her. He said nothing but the look on his face was all at once so grave and so remote that she dared not break in on his thoughts. His breakfast forgotten, he took the little gilt box and opened it, holding the diamond between his fingers so that it blazed like a drop of fire in the sunshine. For a long moment he let the light play on it in blue flashes, as though seeking to hypnotize himself.

'So much suffering! So much pain and tragedy for the sake of this little bit of carbon and a few more like it. Of course,' he went on, 'that would explain it all – even the way the Cardinal seemed to be protecting that wretched woman, although neither you nor I could understand it at the time. But the ways of the Lord are very strange. And stranger still those of men such as these, to whom secrecy is second nature.'

However, Marianne had had enough of the atmosphere of mystery which had surrounded her for the past twenty-four hours.

'Arcadius,' she said firmly, 'I am wholly lost. Do, please, try to be a little more clear. Tell me in plain words what it is you think. Who is my godfather, and what is he General of?'

'Of shadows, Marianne . . . of shadows. Unless I am very much mistaken, he is at this moment the supreme head of the Company of Jesus, the leader of the most formidable army of Christ. He is the one who is called, fittingly enough, the Black Pope.'

Marianne shivered, despite the sunshine flooding the room.

'What a terrible name! But I thought the Pope, the one in Rome, that is, had disbanded the Jesuits in the last century?'

'Yes, in 1773, I think. But that was not the end of the Order. Frederick of Prussia and Catherine II gave it a home, while in Catholic countries it went underground and so became more formidable than ever. Your godfather, my dear, is probably the most powerful man in the world at this moment, because the Order has connections everywhere on earth.'

'But all this is only guesswork? You cannot be sure?' Marianne cried desperately.

Jolival returned the diamond to its box but did not shut the lid. Instead, he held it out to her.

'Look at that stone, my child. It is wonderfully pure and beautiful – yet this and a few others like it were enough to smash the throne of France.'

'I still don't understand.'

'You will. Have you ever heard of a fabulous necklace which Louis XV ordered from the royal jewellers Boehmer and Bassange, for Madame du Barry, but which was never delivered owing to the King's death and so afterwards became the property of Queen Marie-Antoinette? Have you ever heard of that dark and terrible episode known as the Affair of the Necklace? This drop is the central stone, the largest and most precious diamond of that necklace.'

'Of course! But, Jolival, you don't mean – that woman is not – she can't be —'

'The thief? The celebrated Comtesse de la Motte? Yes. I know she was said to have died in England but it was never proved and I have always been convinced that behind that woman there was another hand at work, a powerful, ambitious hand, pulling the strings of her greedy and unscrupulous little mind. I am sure now that I was right.'

'But . . . who?'

Jolival shut the box and put it into Marianne's hand, closing her fingers round it, one by one, as though to keep it safe. Then he rose and paced the room for a moment before coming to rest before her.

'There are state secrets which it is dangerous to touch and names whose very sound is death. Moreover, here, again, I have no proof. You can always try asking the Cardinal when you see him, but it would surprise me if he were to give you an answer. The Order keeps its secrets close and I am very sure that if I had uttered

Madame de Gachet's real name last night, I shouldn't be here talking to you this morning. Take my advice, my dear, and forget all this very quickly. It is a deep and dangerous business and full of pitfalls. We have enough to worry us without getting into such deep waters. And, if you'll be guided by me, you'll ask the Cardinal to give you back the five thousand roubles, which we might well have need of, and to take the stone in exchange. I have a feeling it will not bring us luck.'

Later in the day, however, as Marianne was considering her wardrobe, trying to decide which dress to wear to dinner with the governor, she was told that a Catholic priest was below, asking to see her.

Sure that it must be the Cardinal, she hastily gave the order for him to be shown up to the little sitting-room adjoining her bed-chamber. She was looking forward to a long talk with her god-father and had made up her mind to do what she could to confirm or deny Jolival's suspicions. But, to her disappointment, her visitor turned out to be the Cardinal's incorrigibly dismal secretary, the Abbé Bichette.

Even he, though, was an old acquaintance and for a moment she had some hope of learning something from him. But the abbé, looking more uncompromisingly gloomy than ever in a long, black soutane that made him look rather like a closed umbrella, merely informed her that his Eminence was deeply distressed to be obliged to leave Odessa without seeing her. He entreated his beloved daughter to put her trust in Our Lord Jesus Christ and to accept his blessing and the letter which his unworthy servant Bichette was charged to deliver to her, together with an accompanying packet.

Thereupon, he handed her a black leather wallet containing the sumof five thousand roubles. Marianne, a good deal surprised, was about to open the letter but then, seeing that the Abbé Bichette was about to retire, considering his mission accomplished, she detained him.

'Has his Eminence already left?' she asked.

'No, his Eminence is awaiting my return. Which means that I must hurry so as not to delay him.'

'I should very much like to go with you. How strange of the Cardinal to go so soon! Surely he knows how glad I was to see him again? And we have not exchanged a single word in private —'

'He is aware of that, but it would not be wise to go with me. His Eminence would be greatly displeased. Nor does he like to be kept waiting, so – with your permission . . .' He was almost running to the door.

'Where are you going?'

This time she thought he would have burst into tears.

'Indeed, I do not know. I only follow his Eminence and ask no questions. Perhaps that letter may tell you. And now I must beg you to let me go . . .'

He made a bolt for the door, as though seized with a sudden panic, and as he went he picked up a low-crowned, broad-brimmed black hat of such a characteristic shape that Marianne, who had failed to notice it when he came in, could no longer doubt that Jolival was right. Bichette was a Jesuit. Not one very high up in the secrets of the Order, but a Jesuit none the less. And seeing that he had, however unwittingly, provided her with the answer to one of her unframed questions, she did not prolong his torment but let him go. In any case, it was high time she read her letter.

It was very short. The abbé had already delivered the substance of it. Gauthier de Chazay only added that he hoped to see his dear goddaughter before too long and explained the five thousand roubles.

'The history of the stone is too dark,' he wrote, unconsciously repeating what Arcadius had said, 'for me to wish you to keep it, and that is why I am returning the money you gave for it. As to the stone itself, I ask you to take it back to France. It is worth a fortune and I cannot take it with me where I am going. In exactly six months from today, someone will come to your house in the rue de Lille. He will show you a disc with the four letters A M D G[1] engraved upon it and you will give him the stone. If you should happen to be away, I think you may safely ask Adelaide to do it for you, and you will have rendered a great service to your Church and to your King . . .'

This missive, which was, to say the least, extraordinary, coming from one whom she had always regarded as a second father, irritated Marianne profoundly. She screwed it up and threw it across the room. Really, she thought, the Cardinal was taking too much for granted. He had found her in dire straits and had rescued her, certainly, but then he charged her with a mission that was none of hers, without even stopping to ask what she was doing here, and what she might want or need. Take it back to Paris? But she was not going back to Paris! And what did he mean by that allusion to

[1] A M D G: *Ad Maiorem Dei Gloriam*, the motto of the Jesuits.

her Church and her King? She had no king, as the Cardinal very well knew. The only sovereign she acknowledged was the Emperor. So what did it all mean? And how long would people who claimed to love her go on thinking they had the right to use her and her time just as they liked?

Angry as she was, it still occurred to her that it might be unwise to leave lying about a letter from a man such as the Cardinal, and so she set about recovering it from under the heavy chest of drawers where it had rolled.

She was down on her hands and knees poking at it with a sunshade when Jolival came in. He stood watching her in some amusement and when she emerged at last, flushed and dishevelled, clutching the screwed-up paper in her hand, he helped her to her feet.

'What are you playing at?' he asked her with a smile.

'I'm not playing. I threw this letter away, but then I thought I'd better burn it. But read it. It should interest you.'

It was soon done. When he had finished, Jolival took out flint and steel and set light to a corner of the sheet . . . He carried the burning paper to the hearth and stood watching it until it was all consumed.

'Is that all you can say?' Marianne asked angrily.

'What should I say? You have been asked to do something. Do it and, as I have already told you, try and forget all about it. Whatever happens, we shall certainly be obliged to return to Paris.' He took out his watch. 'And now, it is time you were getting ready for dinner.'

'For dinner? Has it dawned on you that I shall have to go alone? And that I don't in the least want to? I'm going to write a note begging to be excused . . . until tomorrow, say. Tonight I – I don't feel well.'

'Oh no, you won't. Come here a moment.' Taking her by the wrist he drew her over to the window. The air outside was full of the sound of drums, trumpets and fifes and the earth resounded to the tread of some hundreds of horses. A huge crowd had gathered round the barracks and was watching a long ribbon of movement, like a steel snake, winding up from the harbour.

'Look,' said Jolival. 'That is Prince Tsitsanov's two regiments of Georgians disembarking. By what Ducroux tells me, the governor has been waiting for them with some impatience. In two days' time, he means to put himself at their head and ride to join the Tsar's army, which is even now retreating before Napoleon's forces in Lithuania. If you want to secure Beaufort's release, it is tonight or never.'

'Arcadius, think of that note! Are you quite sure that Richelieu won't attach certain — certain conditions to his release?'

'It's possible. But I trust you to play the game and not get burnt. If you refuse this invitation, not only will you not get what we came for, you may even make Richelieu angry enough to see to it that you never find your friend. The choice is yours, certainly. Only choose fast. As I said, he will be gone in two days. It's not easy, I know — but now is the moment for you to prove what you can do in the way of diplomacy.'

As she still hesitated he crossed to a chair on which lay a number of dresses and, picking one at random, came back and dumped it in her arms.

'Hurry up, Marianne — and make yourself look beautiful. You may have two battles to win tonight.'

'Two?'

'Jason's release for one. And after that who knows? You didn't succeed in keeping Kamenski's troops tied up on the Danube but you may yet keep the Circassians in Odessa. You've only to make him see the impropriety of a Frenchman taking arms against other Frenchmen.' Jolival smiled at her with disarming candour.

Marianne clutched the dress to her and scowled at him indignantly.

'My godfather may be the Black Pope, Jolival, but there are times when I wonder if you aren't the very devil!'

CHAPTER TEN

The Swedish Letter

The blue fragrance of tobacco smoke floated in the air of the room, at once cosy and elegant, where Marianne and the governor were finishing dinner. The almost over-poweringly heady scent of orange trees drifted in from the garden through the open windows and the noises of the town faded gradually and died away, as though the little yellow salon had broken some invisible moorings and sailed away into the sky, like a magic balloon.

Across the centrepiece of wilting roses, Marianne regarded her host. The Duke was leaning back in his chair, his eyes fixed absently on the tall white candles that were the room's only illumination, puffing slowly at the pipe which she had just given him permission to light. He looked happy and relaxed, a long way from the dramatic events of the previous day and from the cares of government. So much so, indeed, that she was beginning to wonder if they would ever get round to the subject she had come there to discuss.

She had not wanted to broach the matter herself because that meant putting herself in the position of a suppliant and so at a disadvantage. He had invited her here this evening: it was for him to make the first move and begin asking the questions. But he seemed in no hurry to do so.

From the moment when the carriage he had sent to the hotel to fetch her had deposited her at the steps of the small but palatial new building which was the governor's residence, Marianne had made up her mind to play the game through to the end, however it turned out. It would be gauche to do otherwise. And for the present it was simply a distinguished nobleman entertaining a very pretty woman to a little private dinner.

That much had been clear to her from the moment he bowed over her hand, where he stood at the top of the steps to greet her. Septimanie, the superintendent of the building works, in his tired old coat and dusty boots, had given place to a remarkably distinguished-looking man, arrayed in the most elegant of evening dress: black silk stockings and knee breeches, shining leather pumps, high shirt points and cravat of snowy white and the French order of the Saint-Esprit glittering on his black, long-tailed coat. And Marianne found to her surprise that there was something vastly romantic about the black hair streaked with silver and that smooth, yet curiously ravaged countenance. He was like one of the characters who haunted the imagination of that lame English poet of whom Hester Stanhope had talked so much, with a mixture of admiration and exasperation, in Constantinople, the young Lord Byron.

The Duke had shown himself the perfect host, a model of tact and considerateness. The meal had been light and delicate, such as might appeal to a woman, and was served to the distant accompaniment of a concerto by Vivaldi. Richelieu talked little while they ate, evidently preferring to leave the music to speak for itself and content, during its brief intervals, simply to contemplate the beauty of his guest. She was looking lovely indeed in a gown of pearly satin cut low on the shoulders and with no other ornament than a pale rose nestling in the hollow of her breasts.

One of the two footmen in powdered wigs and white stockings who had waited on them during the meal came in bearing with the greatest care a bottle of champagne, from which he filled two tall, translucent glasses before withdrawing again. When he had gone, the Duke rose to his feet and raised his glass. Without taking his eyes from Marianne, he said: 'I drink to you, my dear, and to your loveliness, which has made this one of those rare and memorable evenings when a man longs to be God and have the power to make time stand still.'

'And I,' she answered him, rising in her turn, 'I too drink to this evening, your Excellency. I shall remember it always as one of the pleasantest I have ever spent.'

They drank, still looking into one another's eyes. Then the Duke left his place and, grasping the bottle on the way, came round the table to refill his guest's glass himself, despite her laughing protests.

'Gently, my lord Duke! You must not make me drink too much – unless, that is, we have other toasts to drink to?'

'But we have.' He raised his glass again, but now there was no smile on his face and his voice was impressively serious as he declared: 'I drink to Cardinal de Chazay. May he return safely from the perilous mission he has undertaken for the peace of the world, and for Church and King!'

Startled, Marianne lifted her glass again, automatically, although this repeated reference to the King was by no means to her liking. Yet not for anything in the world would she have refused to drink her godfather's health. Besides, she had already gathered from

certain remarks dropped by her host during their meal, that he
believed himself in the company of a woman whose political beliefs
and aspirations coincided exactly with his own. He saw her only as
the Cardinal's goddaughter, the daughter of his own old friend, and
if he mentioned the name of Sant'Anna at all it was only to pay
tribute to that ancient, princely family with its wide connections,
and with no hint of distrust.

Prudence dictated that she should not disabuse him. On the contrary, she favoured the governor with her dewiest smile.

'To my dear godfather, whose vigilance and tenderness towards
me have never failed, and who gave me one more striking proof of
that last night when he cleared up that frightful mistake.'

'It is good of you to call it a mistake. Myself, I would rather
describe it as stupidity without precedent and unpardonable
brutality. When I think that those ruffians actually dared to strike
you — Does it still hurt?'

He let his gaze dwell on her shoulders in a lingering way that
suggested something rather more than simple Christian charity.
Marianne gave a light laugh and pirouetted, so that he could see her
back.

'It's nothing. You see, it is almost gone already.' Then, her voice
changing suddenly, she added on a note of real anxiety: 'But you
spoke of an important mission, your Excellency, and of . . . peril?'

She looked up at him with the beginnings of a tear in her eye and
he uttered a distressful exclamation, then bent and took her hand in
his and held it.

'What a fool I am! Why, you are really upset! I ought never to
have said that. Come, let us go out and sit on the terrace for a while.
It is a warm night and the fresh air will do you good. You look quite
pale.'

'Yes,' she admitted, letting him lead her out through the tall
french windows. 'I was frightened suddenly. My godfather —'

'Is one of the noblest, and bravest, and most generous-hearted
men I have ever met. He is worthy in every respect of the deep
affection I can see you have for him. But you also know him well
enough to know that he would not like you to fear for him when he
is serving the Cause.'

'I do know. He is too strong himself ever to understand such
fears, or that others may be a little over-sensitive —'

With something between a sigh and a tiny sob, she sat down on
a sofa upholstered in pale silk which, with a number of chairs, had

been placed out on the small terrace. It was a charming place, with a view extending out over the leafy gardens to the bay beyond, illumined faintly in the light of a crescent moon. It was also an ideal spot for the exchange of confidences and for the kind of private conversations in which the surroundings may be conducive to leading people on to say more than they mean . . .

Suddenly, Marianne wanted very much to know more about this mysterious mission of the Cardinal's. If he were endangering his life in the service of 'the Cause', then it was almost certainly Napoleon and his army who were going to suffer for it.

She leaned back on the sofa, drawing aside her skirt to let the Duke sit beside her, and sat for a moment letting the scented silence of the garden lap them round. Then, after a little while, she spoke, hesitantly, as though exerting a painful control over herself.

'Your Excellency,' she said, 'I know I ought not to ask you this, but it is so long since I have heard anything of my godfather. . . . And now I have found him again only to lose him almost at once. He has vanished, just like that, without seeing me again, without even a kiss . . . and I may never see him again – ever! Oh, tell me, at least, I implore you, that he is not going to – to the places where the fighting is, that he is not going to meet – the invaders?'

With a fine show of agitation, she had placed both hands in the governor's and was leaning towards him, enveloping him in the sweet, cool scent of her perfume.

He laughed gently, clasping her two slim hands in his, and moved a little closer, so close that his eyes were able to look down into the disturbing hollow between her breasts.

'Come, come, my child,' he said indulgently. 'You really must not worry. The Cardinal is a churchman. He is not going to attack Bonaparte, you know. I don't see that it can do any harm if I tell you that he is going to Moscow, where there is a great task awaiting him if, by any chance, the Corsican ogre should get that far. But you may be sure he will be stopped long before that . . . Dear me, what a nervous little thing you are. Wait here, I am going to find you a drop more champagne.'

But she clung to him firmly, having no desire to fall once more into the same sparkling snare as at Le Butard.

'No, please, don't go! You are very kind. You make me feel much better. See, I am quite all right now. Not nearly so frightened.' She smiled at him, hoping inwardly that her smile was as seductive as she meant it to be. At all events, he sat down again promptly.

'Really? You are not so worried now?'

'Not nearly. Forgive me. I am a little foolish about him, I know, but I owe him my life, you see. He was the one who found me in my parents' house after it had been sacked by the revolutionaries, who hid me under his cloak and carried me to England at the risk of his own life. He is all the family I have.'

'But – your husband?'

Marianne did not hesitate. 'The Prince died last year,' she declared boldly. 'He had property in Greece and also in Constantinople. That was the reason I made this long journey. You see, I am not the guilty creature you imagined.'

'I have already told you I was a fool. And so you are a widow? So young, so beautiful – and all alone!'

He moved a little closer and Marianne, who was already feeling slightly uneasy, thinking that she had perhaps led him on a little too much, made haste to change the subject.

'That is enough about me. It isn't really very interesting. Do you know, I never even found out what lucky chance it was that brought my dear Cardinal here? Was he expecting me? He must have second sight if that was so.'

'No. Your meeting was one of those accidents that come about God alone knows how. The Cardinal only reached here two days before yourself. He came from St Petersburg with important news for me.'

'From St Petersburg? News from the Tsar, then? Is it true what they say of him?'

'What do they say?'

'That he is as handsome as a Greek god! Altogether charming and attractive.'

'Quite true,' said the Duke, with a note in his voice that set Marianne's teeth on edge. 'He is the most remarkable man I have ever met. Men ought to kiss the ground he walks on. He is the crowned archangel who will save us all from Bonaparte . . .'

He had turned his head away and was gazing up to heaven, as though expecting this Muscovite archangel of his to descend with flapping wings. At the same time he embarked on a panegyric of Alexander I, who was clearly his great hero, which Marianne found tedious in the extreme. She was beginning to think it must be growing very late and she had found out very little. Jason's fate, in particular, had not even been mentioned.

She let him run on for a little longer and then, when he paused

210

for breath, she murmured quickly: 'A remarkable man, indeed! But I begin to fear I am trespassing on your Excellency's time. Surely it must be very late?'

'Late? Not in the least – besides, we've the whole night ahead of us. No, no, I'll not hear of it! Very soon now, tomorrow probably, I shall be leaving myself to take the Tsar some reinforcements in the shape of the regiments I've mustered here. This is the last evening of peace I shall have for a long time to come. Don't shorten it for me!'

'Very well. But aren't you forgetting, your Excellency, that I came here with a favour to ask you?'

He was so close that she could feel him stiffen and draw away. She guessed that that she had brought him back to earth a little too abruptly for his liking. But she made up her mind that if he had a mind to forget his promise, she would bring him to the point once and for all, even at the risk of putting him in an ill humour.

'A favour?' he said irritably. 'What then? Ah, yes – that American privateer. Almost certainly a spy, a spy in the pay of Bonaparte. Can't think what he could be doing here otherwise.'

'You don't often find spies going about with a brig of that size, your Excellency. It would be a rather obvious way of entering a country, surely? Up to now, Mr Beaufort's business has been chiefly in the wine trade. As to being in the service of Bonaparte' – Lord, this was going badly! – 'I can assure you he is nothing of the sort. It is not long since he saw the inside of a Paris prison – and the convict barracks at Brest as well!'

Richelieu said nothing. He had got to his feet and was pacing agitatedly up and down the little terrace, his arms folded across his chest and his fingers plucking at the folds of lace about his throat. Marianne watched him anxiously, thinking what a strange character he was. His reactions were wholly unpredictable and the least thing seemed to catch his nerves on the raw.

As abruptly as Napoleon himself could have done, he came to a sudden halt in front of her and shot out: 'This man? What is he to you? Your lover?'

Marianne took a deep breath and forced herself to keep calm. She could see that he was studying her face closely. He was evidently expecting her to lose her temper, to make one of those calculated outbursts of indignation that came so easily to women in love and deceived nobody. Easily, she sidestepped the trap and leaned back in her seat, laughing gently.

211

'That is not very imaginative of you, your Excellency. Do you think there is only one reason that a woman might wish to help a man when he's in trouble?'

'Of course not. But this Mr Beaufort is not your brother, is he? And you have undertaken a long and dangerous voyage to come and plead for him.'

'Long and dangerous? Crossing the Black Sea? Really, my lord Duke, let us be serious.' She stood up suddenly, her face growing very serious indeed, and said austerely: 'I have known Jason Beaufort a very long time. The first time I met him was at my aunt's house, Selton Hall, where he was a guest, received there as he was everywhere in England. He was acquainted there with the Prince of Wales. To me, he is a very dear friend, as I said, a childhood friend.'

'A childhood friend? You swear it?'

She heard the quiver of jealousy, bitter and desperate, in his voice and knew that if she wanted to save Jason it was necessary to convince him. With the faintest shrug of her lovely shoulders, she murmured in a tone of gentle raillery: 'Why, of course I swear. But, although I hesitate to say it, my lord Duke, surely you are behaving a little like a jealous husband – rather than a friend whom I have known only a short time, but to whom I had looked for more gentleness and understanding . . . for more affection, even, considering the old ties between us . . .'

He was staring at her intently, breathing rather hard, as though trying to read to the bottom of the green eyes, as deep and compelling as the sea. Gradually, Marianne felt something yield and relax in him.

'Come,' he said at last, taking her by the hand and hurrying her quickly inside.

She followed him through the little yellow salon, where the candles were already guttering, across a wide landing tiled in black marble and into a huge office, lit only by a nightlight on the desk. The long blue velvet curtains were tightly drawn and the room felt as close and dark as a tomb.

Still holding her hand, the Duke went straight to the writing table, which was littered with papers and a heap of green leatherbound despatch boxes. There he released her at last. Not even pausing to sit down, he opened a drawer and took out a large sheet of paper stamped with the double-headed eagle and already covered with writing. A space had been left blank. He filled it in, added a few more words and signed with a nervous scrawl.

Marianne had managed to read some of it over his shoulder and her heart beat faster as she realized that it was an order for the release of Jason and his men. But then, while Richelieu was hunting for sealing wax and melting it at the candle, her eyes wandered over the remainder of the desk and paused for a moment on a partially-folded document. She was not able to read more than a few words, but what she read struck her so forcibly that it was all she could do not to put out her hand and pick it up.

Meanwhile, the Duke had finished writing. He reread the order quickly and then handed it to Marianne.

'There. You have only to give that to the commander of the citadel and your childhood friend will be instantly restored to you, along with those who were captured with him.'

Flushed with happiness, Marianne took the precious paper and slipped it into a pocket cunningly hidden in a fold of her skirt.

'I am deeply grateful,' she said, much moved. 'But – may I ask if this includes the restitution of the ship?'

Richelieu stiffened and frowned.

'The ship? No. I am sorry but it is out of my power. By the law of the sea it belongs now to the Russian navy.'

'But surely, your Excellency, you have no right to deprive a harmless foreigner of his sole means of livelihood? What good is a seaman without a ship?'

'I don't know, my dear, but I have already gone as far as I dare in offering to release a man whose country is at this moment at war with our ally, England. I have given a fighting man back to America. Don't ask me to give her a ship of war as well. The brig is a fine vessel. Our navy will make good use of her.'

'*Your* navy? Indeed, my lord Duke, I begin to ask myself if there is anything French left in you. Your forbears must be turning in their graves if they can hear you.'

Unable to contain herself any longer, she had allowed her indignation to blaze forth and the governor blenched at the icy contempt that showed clearly in her tone.

'You have no right to say that!' he cried, his voice rising to the curiously shrill note it had in anger. 'Russia is a true friend. She took me in when France had cast me out and now she is mustering all her forces to fight against the usurper, against this man who, to satisfy his own insane ambition, has not shrunk from putting all Europe to fire and slaughter. Russia is prepared to shed her own blood to save France from this scourge.'

'To save France – but France has never asked to be saved. And if what they say in the town is true, you, the Duc de Richelieu, are going to march tomorrow at the head of the Georgian troops —'

'To crush Napoleon! Yes, I am! And gladly!'

There was a moment's silence, while both sides paused for breath. Marianne, breathless and blazing-eyed, could barely contain herself, but she meant to stop this man going to fight against his own people in the ranks of the Tsar if it was the last thing she did.

'So, you are going to fight him? Very well. But have you thought that in fighting him you will also be fighting men of your own blood, your fellow-countrymen, your brothers and your peers?'

'My brothers? The scum thrown up by the revolution and dressed up in fancy titles? Really, madame!'

'Your peers, I said! Not Ney and Augereau, Murat or Davout, but men with names like Ségur, Colbert, Montesquieu, Castellane, Fezensac and d'Aboville – to say nothing of Poniatowski and Radziwill! Because you will be raising your sword against them too, Monsieur de Richelieu, when you charge at the head of your half-savage Tartars!'

'Be quiet! I am bound to aid my friends.'

'Say your *new* friends, rather! Very well, then, my lord Duke, but take care that you do not serve the Tsar an ill turn.'

'An ill turn? What do you mean by that?'

Marianne smiled, pleased to have struck a spark of anxiety in the Duke's eyes. She had a feeling that her blows had struck home more truly than she had dared to hope. And a fiendish idea had just occurred to her, one whose destructive power she meant to put to the test.

'Nothing. Or nothing I can be sure of. But please, never mind. Forgive me if I spoke too sharply just now. You see – I like you very much. I cannot help myself, and not for anything in the world would I have you come to regret your – your truly generous heart. You have been so kind to me and to my friends. I would do anything to keep you from falling into a trap, even if it made you accuse me of Bonaparte sympathies, although of course it is not true.'

Richelieu softened immediately.

'My dear Princess, I know that. And I believe in your friendship. It is in the name of that friendship that I beg you to speak. If you have discovered anything that affects me, you must tell it to me.'

She gazed into his eyes and uttered a deep sigh. Then she shrugged.

'You are right. This is no time for scruples. Listen, then. You know that I came here from Constantinople. While there, I became friendly with Princess Morousi, the widow of the former Hospodar of Walachia and it was she who gave me what I can hardly call a warning, for at the time it seemed to me no more than a piece of gossip of no great importance.'

'Tell me. She is not a woman with the reputation of an idle gossip.'

'Very well. Then I will go straight to the point. Are you quite sure of the regiments that have just landed? It was Prince Tsitsanov who sent them, was it not?'

'Yes, but I fail to see —'

'You will. It is less than ten years, I believe, since Georgia came under Russian control? The majority of the people there are loyal, but not all. As to Prince Tsitsanov, according to what I was told, he seems to have been finding out that Tiflis is a long way from St Petersburg and that his governorship had something vice-regal about it. From vice-regal to regal is not so very far, my dear Duke, and by asking the Prince for troops you provided him with a convenient method of getting rid of unwanted troublemakers. He is not going to miss those two regiments, you may be quite sure of that. As to how they will behave under fire, shoulder to shoulder with the Muscovites whom they detest . . . But there, as I said, I am not sure of this. What I am telling you is idle drawing-room chatter, nothing more. I may very well be maligning Prince Tsitsanov —'

'But on the other hand, what you say may easily be true.'

The Duke had dropped into the chair behind the desk and was gnawing his thumb with a gloomy expression. Marianne stood for a moment, gauging the effect of her words. The man was certainly a genius when it came to organization. He was a great colonial administrator and possibly a great diplomat, but he was also a worried man, a man who lived on his nerves, and in these aspects of his character he was showing himself more vulnerable than she had dared to hope.

She hesitated, uncertain of her next move. Richelieu, staring into space, appeared to have forgotten her entirely. And then there was the order for Jason's release burning a hole in her pocket. She was impatient now to get away from the governor's palace and hurry to the citadel. And yet something drew her to that open letter on the desk which was stirring slightly in a faint breath of air, come

215

from nowhere in that close room, almost within her reach, as though to tease her.

The silence prolonged itself and at last Marianne gave a small cough.

'Your Excellency,' she said, 'I am sorry to disturb you when you are thinking, but if I might ask you to see me home . . .? It is very late and —'

Before the words were out of her mouth, he was on his feet and was stumbling towards her, like a man half out of his mind with worry, where she stood like a ghostly vision in the dimly lighted room.

'Don't leave me,' he said brokenly. 'Don't leave me alone – not now! I don't want to be alone here tonight.'

'But why ever not? What have I said to alarm you so? For you are afraid, aren't you?'

'Yes, I am afraid. But not for myself. I am afraid of what I was about to do. But for you – but for the advice you have just given me, I might have gone to Alexander bringing disaster, betrayal, even death. And that to the man to whom I owe everything, who has been good enough to call me his friend —'

'You mean – that you will not go?'

'Just that. I will stay here. The Georgian troops will be sent back again tomorrow. Only the Tartars whom I have trained myself and can trust will set out for Kiev. And I shall remain behind.'

A wave of joy swept over Marianne. Even now she could hardly believe that she had won, won all along the line. Within the hour Jason would be free and tomorrow Richelieu would remain in Odessa and two regiments of troops would never reach the battle-field. It was almost unbelievable. It was too much, and if she had only been able to recover the *Sea Witch* as well . . .

'Is it because of what I said to you?' she asked quietly.

'What did you say?'

'You will not fight against your own people?'

Marianne felt the Duke's hand tremble as they gripped her shoulders.

'I cannot fight my own brothers, however misguided, yes, there is that . . . But you have also made me see that by leaving New Russia I should be leaving the field open for others' ambitions. If I go, what is to stop Tsitsanov or anyone else from stepping in? The Crimea needs to be strongly defended. I must stay. Without me, God knows what might happen.'

Marianne was seized with a sudden and highly inappropriate desire to laugh. Politics was certainly a most peculiar game, and its practitioners the strangest people. You could rely on them to go one better and her pretended information had been a wild success. The Duke had built on it in a way she could never have expected.

However she managed to choke back the laughter that was bubbling up in her and merely smiled, although the eyes that met Richelieu's were twinkling so gaily that it was a wonder they did not betray her. Happily for her, the Duke mistook the real cause.

'You are wonderful,' he said softly. 'Truly, I think that Providence herself must have sent you to me. Are you really a woman, or are you an angel in disguise? The loveliest of all the angels. An angel with emerald eyes, unutterably sweet and beautiful, clad in the shape of an adorable woman . . .'

He was standing very close to her and all at once his hands slid down from her shoulders to encircle her waist. For a panic-stricken moment she saw the Duke's tormented face near to hers, his dark gaze thickened with desire, like a pool when the bottom was stirred up. She tried to push him away, startled to find him suddenly transformed into a different man.

'Your Excellency, please, let me go! I must go – I have to go home.'

'No. You shall not go. Not tonight, at least. I can recognize fortune when she appears, for she comes all too rarely. You are my chance, my once chance of happiness. I knew it the moment I saw you, the other day, down there on the crowded quayside. You were like a fairy hovering above a reeking bog. And you were beautiful, as beautiful as light itself. You have saved me tonight —'

'Nonsense. I have merely given you some good advice. Anyone would think, to hear you, that I had snatched you from the jaws of death.'

'You cannot understand. The thing you have saved me from was worse than death. It is a curse, a curse that has hung over me for years. God Himself has sent you. He has heard my prayers . . .'

His hold on her tightened and Marianne felt a moment's terror as she realized that she was powerless against him. That thin, almost fragile-looking body concealed a wholly unsuspected nervous strength. His arms closed about her like a vice and he was deaf to her entreaties, as though he had become, quite suddenly, another person. And he was talking so strangely. What had God to do with the fierce access of desire which had made him seize her like this?

'A curse?' she gasped, struggling to get her breath. 'Whatever do you mean? I don't understand.'

He had buried his face in the soft hollow of her shoulder and was covering it with kisses, his lips travelling by degrees up the slender neck.

'You can never understand, so do not try. Give me this night, only this one night, and I will let you go. I'll give you anything you want. . . . Only let me love you. . . . It is so long since I have known what it is to love. I thought I never should . . . never again. But you are so lovely, so desirable. . . . You have brought me to life again . . .'

Was he mad? What did he mean? He was squeezing her so tightly that she could almost hear her ribs cracking, and yet at the same time the softness of his lips upon her quivering flesh was almost unbearable. Marianne was conscious of a sudden lump in her throat and she knew, even in the midst of her anger and her shame, that she no longer had the will to fight. It was so long since she too had known the sweetness of love and of a man's touch caressing her body. Not since that unknown lover – some Greek fisherman, had he been? – had taken her in the recesses of a cave so dark that she had never even seen his face. He had been no more than a vague form in the night, a kind of phantom, yet he had given her the most exquisite pleasure.

The soft touch of his mouth was on her cheek, had found her lips which parted of themselves. Her heart was thudding like a hammer in her chest and when a hand crept up to her breast and imprisoned it, she felt as if her legs were giving way beneath her. It was a simple matter for the Duke to lower her gently on to the velvet covered sofa which stood close by the desk.

He took his lips from hers as he laid her down and turned briefly to extinguish the candles. The room was plunged into darkness. Her head swimming and her limbs on fire, Marianne thought for an instant that she was back again in that glorious cave in Corfu. She was at the heart of an impenetrable darkness in which there was nothing, only a warm, tobacco-scented breath and two hands that divested her skilfully of her dress and began a passionate exploration of her body.

He was quite silent now, and his only contact with her was through those roving hands, caressing her breasts, belly and thighs, lingering over each new revelation, before resuming their exquisitely titillating voyage of discovery, until it seemed to Marianne that she must go mad. Her whole body was on fire and crying out for the

218

satisfaction of its primitive desires. So that it was she, at last, who drew him down to her.

She reached up and linked her arms about the Duke's neck, seeking his lips, and they fell back together on to the cushions, she giving a little gasp of pleasure as she felt his weight upon her and sensed the pent-up passion in his body. In her eagerness to satisfy a hunger which had been too long denied and was now brutally awakened, she was already offering herself, but she waited in vain.

Silence fell, thick and frightening. The weight removed itself from her body and then, quite suddenly, out of the enveloping darkness, as thick and black as the tomb, there came the sound of a sob.

Marianne got up quickly and felt her way to the desk. Her trembling fingers found flint and tinder, and she struck a light and first one and then another candle came to life, revealing the room with its heavy furniture, its thick curtains and its oppressively businesslike atmosphere, as far removed as it was possible to be from the delirium of love.

The first thing to catch Marianne's eye was her dress, lying in a snowy heap of satin on the end of the sofa. She snatched at it in a kind of fury to cover her shivering nakedness, still striving to control her breathing and calm the frenzied beating of her heart. It was only then she saw the Duke.

He was sitting on the edge of a chair, his head in his hands and crying like a child whom Father Christmas had forgotten. His shoulders were shaking with sobs and he was shivering so wretchedly that all Marianne's feelings of bitter frustration were swallowed up in pity for him. At that moment, the powerful governor of New Russia looked more wretched and broken than the least of the Armenian beggars that crowded the port of Odessa.

Hurriedly, she slipped into her dress and did what she could to tidy her hair. She could not bring herself to break the silence, preferring rather to wait for his misery to subside, for she sensed in some confused fashion that it sprang from a deep and private hurt. But when, after a little while, his sobs showed no signs of abating, she went to him and laid one hand timidly on his shoulder.

'Please,' she said gently, 'don't cry. It is not worth it. You – you were unlucky. It happens sometimes. You must not upset yourself like this, over such a little thing.'

He lifted his head abruptly from his hands, revealing a face so ravaged with tears that Marianne's heart was touched.

'Not simply unlucky,' he said miserably. 'It is the curse I spoke of – earlier. I thought – oh, how I thought that you had banished it. That it was lifted from me at last! But it was not to be. I have it still. I shall always have it. It will be with me all my life and because of it my family will die with me.'

He had risen and was pacing the room agitatedly. To her horror, Marianne saw him pick up the heavy bronze inkstand from his desk and hurl it with the full force of his arm against one of the bookcases, the front of which shattered in a crash of broken glass.

'Cursed! I am cursed!' he raged. 'You can't know what it is to be unable to love, to love as other men love. I had forgotten it, but just now, when I touched you, I felt – oh, the wonder, the miracle of it – I felt that my power of feeling was not dead, that I could still desire a woman, that perhaps my life could begin again. But no, it could not! Ever since that dreadful day, it is all over – all over! For ever!'

He was shaken by a fresh bout of sobbing, so violent that Marianne was afraid. The poor man seemed so close to the depths of despair that she cast about in her mind for some way to help him. On a small table by a window, she saw a silver tray with a jug of water, some glasses and a decanter filled with a dark-coloured liquid that was evidently some kind of wine. Going quickly to the table, she filled a glass with water and then, just as she was about to take it to Richelieu, who had slumped down again on the end of the sofa, an idea came to her. She felt in the pocket of her dress and brought out a small sachet containing a greyish powder.

Earlier that evening, setting out to keep this dinner engagement which had filled her with such apprehensions, she had brought the sachet with her from her room. In it was a preparation with a base of opium which Turhan Bey's Persian physician had made up for her during the last weeks of her pregnancy, when she was finding it difficult to sleep. It had the power of inducing a swift and pleasant slumber and it had occurred to Marianne that it might prove a useful weapon if Richelieu's attentions should become too pressing.

Smiling a little ironically, she dropped a pinch of the powder into the glass, adding a little wine to take away the taste. The Duke's attentions could hardly have been more pressing, and yet she had quite forgotten what, only a little while before, had seemed such a vital weapon. Or had she simply refused to remember it, in her sudden, overmastering need for love? And now the helpful drug was to be used for a more charitable purpose, to obtain a little rest and forgetfulness for an unhappy man.

She bent and gently made him raise his head.

'Drink this. You will feel better. . . . Please, drink it and then lie down.'

He drank it all down like an obedient child and then stretched himself on the sofa where, not long before, he had laid Marianne. His eyes, reddened with tears, were full of a gratitude that went to her heart.

'You are very kind,' he murmured. 'You are looking after me as though I had not just made a fool of myself to you . . .'

'Please, we'll say no more about it.'

She smiled at him and slipped a cushion under his head. Then, so that he might breathe more easily, she unfastened the high cravat and opened the front of his shirt, so drenched with sweat that it stuck to his thin, dark chest. Then she went to draw back the curtains and open a window to let the cool night air in to the close atmosphere of the office.

'No,' Richelieu said, 'no, we must speak of it. You must know. . . . You have the right to know why the grandson of the Maréchal de Richelieu, the greatest womanizer in the whole of the last century, cannot even make love to one woman. Listen, I was sixteen in 1782 – sixteen when they married me to Mademoiselle de Rochechouart, and she was twelve! It was a great match, worthy of both our families and, like royal alliances, it was concluded by our parents without consulting either of us. And I married her by proxy. I was told that she was considered too young to consummate the marriage, although it was necessary for family reasons that it should take place.'

'Please,' Marianne said, 'do not tell me this. It will only rouse painful memories for you, I am sure, and —'

'Painful, yes,' he admitted with a bleak smile, 'but as to rousing them – even after all these years they will not sleep. Indeed, I believe it will do me good to tell someone, and for that person to be a woman – the one woman I might ever have loved. . . . Where was I? Oh yes, it was three years after that, when my wife had reached the age of fifteen, that our families decided to bring us together. And when I saw the person who henceforth bore my name, I knew why our parents had been so insistent on the wedding's taking place by proxy. It was so that I should not see my betrothed. . . . If I live to be a hundred I shall never forget the sight

221

which met my eyes as I ran – yes, in my eagerness to see her, I actually ran – up the great staircase of our house. A freak! Rosalie de Rochechouart, Duchesse de Richelieu, was a freak! A dwarf! Hunchbacked and pigeon-chested, with a wizened monkey face and a huge nose . . . a caricature of a human being, fit to be shown at a fair. Can you, who are so beautiful, even picture anything so ugly? I felt as if I had fallen into a nightmare. Whether I had a sudden vision of what life would be like with that creature by my side, I do not know now. All I know is that I gave a great cry and fell back unconscious, right to the bottom of the stone staircase.

'The next day I had myself put into a post chaise . . . I left a note behind me and I went to recover from my injuries on my estates in the country. I could no longer face Paris. From there, seeing no one, I went off to fight against the Turk, hoping that God would rid me of my life. By then I knew that, whether I wanted to or not, I had no choice but to remain faithful to my wife. . . . You see? It is as simple, and as senseless as that. A wasted life. It is laughable . . .'

But Marianne felt no wish to laugh. She knelt beside the sofa, once more cradling the hand of this man whom she had feared, admired, hated and even, for a moment, almost loved, and for whom she now felt a compassion that was something like tenderness. She felt to him as to a brother.

For her, too, the first taste of marriage had been a cruel disappointment, although it had come nowhere near in intensity to the tragic shock suffered by the young Duke. She stroked his hand with a timid gesture of affection, trying to convey to him how much she shared his bitterness and regret.

He turned his head and looked at her, his eyes already filming over with the effects of the drug, and made a sad attempt at a smile.

'It is – laughable, isn't it?'

'No. By no means. Anyone who could laugh must be singularly lacking in heart. The tale of your marriage is one of the saddest things I ever heard. You are greatly to be pitied – both you and she, for she must have suffered also. And – and you have never seen her since?'

'Yes. Once. When I – when I returned to France to aid the King, knowing his danger. I understood then . . . what you have just said, that she must have suffered also . . . poor, innocent child . . . poor, wretched soul, imprisoned in a monstrous form. We became friends, and are so still, I believe. She lives in France – at the Château de Crosilles. . . . She writes to me. . . . She writes beautiful letters, such beautiful . . .'

His words had been coming more and more slowly as his eyelids drooped more heavily and he had difficulty in keeping them open. Soon they closed altogether and all at once the only sound in the room was that of his calm, regular breathing.

For a moment, Marianne remained where she was, holding his hand relaxed in hers. Then she laid it gently on the cushion by his side and stood up slowly, wondering what she ought to do.

Silence had fallen on the house. The well-trained servants had evidently retired to bed or to their own quarters. Only the guards were presumably still on duty at the gates. Somewhere in the town a clock struck one, reminding her that the night was not yet over and that she had work still to do.

Through the satin of her dress, her hand touched the document which was to set Jason free and she began to tiptoe to the door. Her cloak was still across the landing, in the little yellow salon where they had dined. The duke had not allowed them to remove it when she arrived but had himself taken it from her shoulders and laid it over a chair, in case she might feel a chill from the open window. She decided to go and fetch it.

Then, just as she was about to leave the room, she thought that she would blow out the candles, so that the Duke might sleep on undisturbed. She went back to the desk and it was as she leaned across it to blow out the lights that she saw the letter.

In the varying emotions of the last half-hour, she had forgotten all about it, and now she reproached herself. Fate had put into her hand a document which might be vital to the Emperor. She had no right to pass it by.

She put out her hand quickly and, taking the letter, read it eagerly. It was from the Tsar in St Petersburg. What had attracted her attention was a name, that of the crown prince of Sweden, Charles-Jean. The Tsar sent his friend Richelieu confidential copies of letters written to him by the former Marshal Bernadotte.

'The Emperor Napoleon,' Charles-Jean had written, 'is accustomed to the management of great armies and this must inevitably give him confidence, but if your Majesty can use your forces sparingly and succeed in avoiding a pitched battle, so that you are able to reduce the war to a business of forced marches and minor engagements, then the Emperor Napoleon is certain in the end to make some mistake of which your Majesty can take advantage. The luck has so far been almost always on his side, for he owes his successes in the military, as in the political field, wholly to the novelty of his proceedings, but if intensely mobile units can be directed speedily against his weak or ill-supported positions, then there can be no doubt of a happy outcome for your Majesty and that Fortune, tired of serving Ambition, will join at last those ranks where Honour and Humanity command . . .'[1]

The letter went on to express the Prince's satisfaction at the conclusion of a peace with the Turks and his impatience for the arrival of 'subsidies from England' which would enable him, when the time was ripe, to 'take the Emperor Napoleon's armies in the rear and to attack the borders of his Empire. . . .'

In addition to this there was a note in which the future King of Sweden spoke of his great wish to annex Norway, then a Danish possession, and of the actions which the Tsar might take with regard to Denmark in order to assist his friend Charles-Jean in the achievement of his desires, in return for which he might count on the support, very far from negligible, of the Swedish army.

Marianne turned the dangerous paper round and round in hands that were suddenly icy cold, handling it as gingerly as if it had been dipped in gunpowder. She could not believe her eyes, and her brain simply refused to register at first what could only be read as the purest treachery. Bernadotte was a Swede by too recent adoption for such friendly letters to Napoleon's enemies to come well from him. But, well or otherwise, Marianne felt that Napoleon must be told of the danger threatening his rear.

With the idea of copying the letter, she had seated herself at the table and was looking for a pen when she changed her mind. A copy would not do without the Tsar's letter as well. She knew Napoleon well enough to be sure he would be unwilling to believe it. She looked at the sleeping man, her eyes full of trouble and remorse for what she was about to do. She did not like the idea of stealing his correspondence but it was the only way. She must take the Tsar's letter.

Without more ado, she thrust the letter into her pocket, snuffed out the candles and left the room, closing the door quietly behind her. To cross the landing to the yellow salon, recover her cloak and hurry downstairs, dragging it round her as she went, was the work of a moment.

[1] Taken from an actual letter.

A minute or two later she was scurrying past the drowsy sentries who barely opened an eye in time to glimpse a flash of white satin vanishing into the night, then drowsed again and troubled themselves no further in the matter.

Marianne was possessed now with a feverish haste. She had to wake Jolival, get Jason out of his prison and leave Odessa somehow before daylight. When Richelieu woke, he would know at once who had stolen his letter and would be bound to make a search for her. If she was to warn the Emperor, she must first make good her escape.

Marianne picked up her skirts and ran as fast as she could towards the Hotel Ducroux.

CHAPTER ELEVEN

Death of a Witch

From the moment when he was shaken awake by an excited Marianne from the chair where he had fallen asleep while waiting for her to return, Jolival knew that this was going to be a memorable night. Fortunately, he was not a man who ever found much difficulty in dragging himself out of the mists of sleep and it did not take long for Marianne to put him in possession of the facts.

He watched her dubiously for a moment as she waved the two letters under his nose, one the order of release, signed Richelieu, the other a letter from the Tsar which had come into her hands somewhat less honourably. Then he asked a question or two which very readily convinced him that there was no time to lose, if they did not wish to find their stay in Odessa uncomfortably prolonged. Complimenting Marianne briefly on her prompt action, he began to struggle into his coat.

'If I have it right,' he said, 'the first thing we have to do is to get Beaufort and his men out of the castle? But what then?'

Knowing Marianne, he had put this last question in a tone of perfect innocence, but she replied without a shadow of hesitation.

'Surely the Tsar's letter told you that? Wake up, Jolival! We must reach the Emperor on the march into Russia and see that he knows of the danger threatening him at home.'

Busy stuffing shirts into a big leather valise, Jolival only grunted.

'You talk as if this were Paris and we had only to travel as far as Fontainebleau or Compiègne. Have you any idea of the size of this country?'

'I think so. In any case, its size does not seem to have daunted the soldiers of the Grand Army, so there is no reason why I should let it frighten me. The Emperor is marching on Moscow. So to Moscow we will go.'

She had folded Alexander's letter again and now put it, apart from the other paper, into an inner pocket in the dress of smooth, dark woollen cloth which she had donned in place of the dress she had worn that evening.

Jolival went to the table and picked up the paper authorizing the release of Jason and the crew of the *Sea Witch*.

'And what of him?' he asked gently. 'Do you expect to persuade him to travel half-way across Russia with us? Have you forgotten his reaction in Venice when you asked him to sail with us to Constantinople? He has no more cause to love Napoleon now than he had then.'

Marianne's green eyes met her friend's squarely, with a determination in them that was new.

'He will have no choice,' she said crisply. 'Richelieu agreed to release him but he would not hear of letting the brig go. The harbour is too well guarded for him to repeat his exploit in February. And he can scarcely swim home.'

'No. But he might take a passage in any vessel sailing through the Bosphorus and the Dardanelles.'

Marianne made an impatient movement and Jolival saw that it would be useless to persist. Besides, they both had more important things to do than stand there arguing. They hurried on with their preparations for departure and, as two o'clock was striking from the nearby church, Marianne and her friend left the Hotel Ducroux. Each was carrying a single large valise containing their money, a few clothes and their most precious possessions. Everything else had been left behind as too cumbersome for fugitives to take with them. They had also left money, in the shape of a gold coin, on the table in Marianne's sitting-room, to pay for their lodging. The things they had left behind would have more than covered such charges as they had incurred but the affair of the 'stolen' diamond was still fresh in Marianne's mind and not for anything would she have left a dubious reputation behind her. It would be bad enough when the police came looking for her, as they surely would, on the grounds of tampering with the governor's private correspondence.

Almost running down the steep streets that skirted the barracks, the two of them reached the harbour in a very few minutes. At this time of night it was quiet and all but deserted. Only a gipsy violin wailed somewhere behind the closed shutters, making a weird background to the sounds of cats quarrelling over a pile of fish heads. Already, the dark walls of the castle were looming over the fugitives.

'I hope they'll agree to set them free at this hour of night,' Jolival ventured to say uneasily.

Marianne put out her hand peremptorily to silence him. Then she was hurrying towards the sentry who stood leaning, half-asleep, against his box, keeping his balance with the ease of long practice. She shook him fiercely and, when the man at last opened one sleepy eye, waved the paper under his nose so that he could make out the governor's signature by the light of the guttering lamp above his head.

It was unlikely that the man could read but the imperial arms on the paper were enough, together with the young lady's energetic pantomime, indicating clearly that she wished to enter the castle and be taken to the commandant.

Little as she cared to admit it, Marianne was at least as uneasy as Jolival. The commandant might easily refuse to release his prisoners in the middle of the night and if he were a difficult man, or a stickler for the rules, he could equally well insist on having the order confirmed. But it seemed that the gods were on Marianne's side that night.

The sentry made no difficulty about hurrying into the citadel, taking the paper with him. Not only that but he summoned no replacement and the two visitors were able to follow him into the courtyard which was as dark as the bottom of a well. No sound came from the guardroom and it seemed as though everyone were asleep. Now that the war with Turkey was over, everyone could relax.

Marianne and Jolival were left alone for a moment, standing close together at the foot of the stairs leading up to the commandant's quarters. Both their hearts were thudding and the same thought was in both their minds: were they going to see their friends appear, or a posse of soldiers to escort them to the commanding officer for further questioning.

But that night the commandant was delightfully if energetically engaged with a pair of pretty Tartar girls whose company he had not the smallest wish to abandon, even for a moment. He opened his door a crack at the sentry's knock, cast a glance over the paper which the man held out to him, while still standing rigidly to attention, cursed fluently but, recognizing the governor's signature and the fact that there seemed to be no fault to be found with the document, gave the order to release the men from the American ship at once. It did not occur to him that there was anything more he needed to know.

Only too glad to be rid of lodgers who had proved remarkably expensive and uncooperative, he hurried into his office, not even pausing to put on his clothes, and in that state of nature put his hand to the order without more ado. Then he barked some orders at the soldier, adding that he did not wish to be disturbed again that night and hastened back to his private paradise.

The soldier clattered down again to the courtyard and, making a sign to the two foreigners to follow him, trotted away towards the iron grille giving access to the prison courtyard which looked particularly grim in the flaring light of two torches. There he made them wait again while he summoned two men to work the winch to raise the grille.

Ten minutes later he was back with two figures behind him, and at the sight of the taller of the two Marianne's heart beat faster. A moment later, overcome by a joy she could not control, she had cast herself on Jason's chest, laughing and crying at once, and his arms had closed automatically around her.

'Marianne!' he exclaimed with stupefaction. 'You, here? It can't be! Am I dreaming?'

'No, you are not dreaming,' Jolival broke in, thinking that this was not the moment for mutual congratulations. 'Nor is there time for it. We must get out of here, and quickly. The governor has released you but the danger is not over yet, far from it.'

Nevertheless he himself was more moved than he cared to admit and he submitted to a warm embrace from Craig O'Flaherty, while the sentry looked on indulgently at a reunion of which he probably comprehended very little. Marianne and Jason, meanwhile, were locked in one another's arms, oblivious of all the world.

The two prisoners wore long beards and were filthy dirty but Marianne did not care. The body pressed to her belonged to Jason, the mouth crushing her own was Jason's mouth and she asked nothing better than to lose herself with him in a kiss which, if each had had their way, would have lasted for an eternity.

But Jolival decided that it had gone on long enough and parted them.

'Come,' he told them gruffly. 'That will do. You'll have time enough for kissing when we are on our way, but for the present let us be away from this place. I do not like it.'

Craig's cheerful laugh rang in his ears. 'Nor we, faith! Let's find a decent tavern! I'd give my right arm for a bumper of good old Irish whiskey.'

Marianne came back to earth and stared at the two men with some bewilderment.

'But – are there only the two of you? Where are the others?'

Where is Gracchus? The governor gave orders for the release of all the crew —'

'Precisely,' Jason answered her. 'And all the crew means us – all that's left of it, at least. This governor of yours doesn't seem to have much idea of the ways of soldiers, my pet. The commodore of the fleet that captured us saw no reason why the prison authorities should be at the charge of maintaining all the riff raff of the Mediterranean. He let the crew go as soon as we got ashore to go to the devil in their own way. Only Craig and I had the honour to be made prisoners of war.'

'But Gracchus? Where is he? Did they free him too?'

Seeing that she was really worried, Jason tightened the arm that he had slipped round her waist as they walked.

'Gracchus is French, my love, and, that being so, in more danger than either of us. These devils would have shot him without mercy. He played stupid while we were still at sea, but he's an enterprising lad and when we came into the bay, just before dawn, he jumped into the sea and swam ashore.'

'Good God! He may be dead!'

O'Flaherty gave a shout of laughter.

'You don't know him! Gracchus is quite the most astonishing broth of a boy it's ever been my luck to meet. Do you know where he is at this moment?'

As they talked they had crossed the ancient drawbridge with its rusty chains which had not been raised for more than a century and now, at the foot of the rocky outcrop on which the citadel was built, the cluttered maze of the harbour lay before them. O'Flaherty pointed to the squat shape of a little synagogue.

'Do you see that Greek tavern in between the synagogue and the big grain warehouse attached to the distillery? Gracchus got himself taken on as a waiter there. He talks a weird mixture of Greek and Turkish that he learned in Constantinople and doesn't manage too badly, especially as he's picked up a fair smattering of Russian since his arrival.'

'But how do you know where he is?'

'Because we've seen him. When he'd been there a few days he took to hanging round the citadel and whistling French sea songs. Our prison looked out over the rock that side and so we were able to communicate with him. Sometimes . . .' He paused and heaved a deep sigh that testified to the real depth of his gratitude. 'Sometimes the dear lad even managed to smuggle us in a bottle or so to comfort us. Unfortunately, we couldn't get out by the same way the bottles came in. The window was too narrow, and the walls too thick.'

The night was growing cooler and a light wind had sprung up off the sea. It caught at the four hurrying figures and the two seamen breathed in the smell of seaweed with delight.

'God, but it's good to be free!' Jason sighed. 'At last we can put to sea again. Do you hear how it's calling us, my sweet? Oh, for the feel of my own deck under my feet again!'

Marianne shivered a little, knowing that the difficult moment had come. She opened her mouth to tell Jason the truth but Jolival, guessing how hard it was for her, spoke first.

'You are free, Jason,' he said deliberately, 'but your ship is not. In spite of all that we could do, the Duc de Richelieu refuses to give her up.'

'What?'

'Try to understand, and above all do not lose your temper. It's wonderful enough that we were able to get you out of that rat hole. The brig is a prize of war and is now the property of the Russian navy. There is nothing that the governor can do about it.'

Marianne felt Jason's fingers harden against her side. His voice remained very nearly level but there was a disturbing note in it, as if he were very tense.

'I have stolen her once before. I can do it again. It's becoming something of a habit.'

'Have no illusions. That is not possible here. The brig is anchored out there, near the end of the long mole, and there are Russian vessels all round her. And besides, if it were daylight you could see that there are men at work making some alterations in her. What is more to the point, we have to leave this place without delay.'

'Why so? Have I or have I not been released on the governor's orders?'

'Yes. But you must be out of Odessa before sunrise. That is the order. If you are found here you will be imprisoned again and then neither we nor anyone else will be able to get you out. Not only that. Marianne is not precisely on the best of terms with the governor. He was inclined to be rather more – er – friendly than she cared for. So make up your mind. Stay and try to recover your ship and you will be running the risk of prison for yourself and the governor's bed for Marianne. I think our wisest course will be to leave as soon as possible.'

231

With Jason's arm about her, Marianne held her breath. At that moment she wanted to laugh and cry at once and she could have kissed her old friend for managing to put the matter in such a way as to avoid awkward questions. Jason was not an easy man to deceive and he knew how to cross-examine as skilfully as any experienced lawyer. She could feel his heart beating more quickly under her hand and a wave of pity, mingled with acute anxiety, swept over her. At that moment he was going to make his choice between her and the ship which she had often accused him of loving more than her, more indeed than anything in the world.

Jason took several deep breaths. Then his arm tightened spasmodically, almost fiercely round her and Marianne knew that she had won.

'You are right, Jolival. Indeed, you are always right. Let's go. But where to? It will be daylight in an hour.'

There was a brief silence and Marianne guessed that Jolival was picking his words, choosing those least likely to provoke a stormy reaction from the hot-tempered American. He made up his mind at last, and murmured reflectively, like a man thinking aloud: 'I think our best course . . . will be to travel further into Russia . . . to make for Moscow, for example. We heard on our arrival here that the Grand Army had crossed the Lithuanian frontier and was marching on the Russian holy city. Our best chance is to make contact with it and then —'

The reaction came, but it was less violent than Marianne had feared.

'Make contact with Napoleon! Have you gone mad, Jolival?'

'I don't think so. Isn't he responsible for the mess that you and Marianne have been in this past year? He owes you something. Even if only a ship out of Danzig or Hamburg to carry you to America.'

This time he had spoken the magic words. Jason's fierce grip on Marianne loosened gradually and his voice was almost cheerful as he said: 'That's not a bad idea. But I have a better.'

'What is it?' Marianne asked softly, sensing more trouble ahead.

'I've no truck with Napoleon but you're right, I do need a ship to get back home and play my part in the war. We'll go, not to Moscow, or only in passing, but to St Petersburg.'

'You want to cross the whole of Russia? Do you know that's something like two thousand miles?'

The American's broad shoulders, in the torn and much-abused coat he wore, lifted slightly.

'What of it? It's only a couple of hundred more, unless I'm much mistaken. Will you come with me, sweetheart?' he added, turning tenderly to address the girl at his side.

'I'd go with you to Siberia if you wanted me. But why St Petersburg?'

'Because my father, who was a great traveller in his youth, had a friend there, a rich shipowner to whom he once did a favour. We never asked for any repayment of the debt, indeed there was none in my father's eyes, nor would I claim any, but we have had news of the Krilovs from time to time and I know that they will help me. And I would rather ask help from a friend than from the man who condemned me to the convict chain.'

A brief glance only passed between Jolival and Marianne but they understood one another. They both knew Jason's stubborn nature of old and his near inability to forgive an injury. Better, they felt, to say nothing of the Tsar's letter and agree to Jason's plan. The road to St Petersburg passed by Moscow, after all, and so they lost nothing by it. And then luck might be on their side and once the letter was in Napoleon's hands there would be nothing to prevent Marianne from going with the man of her choice at last.

That he should have given in so easily was more than they had hoped. Knowing his almost physical love for his ship, Marianne had expected something of a fight. But she saw too, as they made their way down to the Greek tavern to seek out Gracchus, that Jason's eyes turned continually to the far end of the great mole. Gradually he began to walk more slowly. She urged him on affectionately.

'Come, we must hurry if we are to be out of the town in time. Dawn is not far off.'

'I know. But you don't need me to rout out Gracchus.'

He let go of her suddenly and she saw him run towards the site of the new arsenal. He came back holding an unlighted lantern.

'Have you got a light?' he asked Jolival.

'Of course. But do we need one?'

'No. I know. Only lend me flint and tinder and wait for me. I shouldn't be long but if I'm not back in, say half an hour, then go without me.'

'Jason!' Marianne cried, struggling to keep her voice down. 'Where are you going? I am coming with you.'

He turned and took her hand and squeezed it tightly before putting it in Jolival's.

'No. I forbid you. What I am going to do is my business. She is my ship.'

The Irishman already understood.

'But I am coming with you,' he said firmly. 'The rest of you, wait for us. Rouse Gracchus and try to find some kind of vehicle for the journey. We can't walk to St Petersburg.'

In another moment he was running after the dark figure of Beaufort who was making for the small beach where some boats lay drawn up out of the water.

'This is madness!' Jolival cried, no longer bothering to keep his voice down. 'We'll not find one, except at the post house by the Kiev gate, and for that we must climb the hill again to the other side of the town. And even then we may have trouble —'

Craig paused for a moment and they heard him laugh.

'Sure and you may have somewhat less trouble if we are successful. The folk hereabouts will have enough doing at the harbour to keep them busy awhile. They'll not be troubling themselves about the likes of us. Now hurry.'

A moment later Marianne and Jolival saw with a sudden chill a small boat put out from the shore and creep slowly and silently over the dark water.

'What are they going to do?' Marianne whispered fearfully. 'They surely wouldn't —'

'Yes. They are going to set fire to the *Sea Witch*. I was expecting something of the sort. A man like Beaufort could never have consented to leave his ship behind. . . . Come, we too have work to do. You can say your prayers later,' he added, not without a touch of irritation, as he became aware that Marianne was mumuring softly over her clasped hands.

The house of which the Greek tavern occupied the ground floor was small and square with only a single upper floor. There was one large window enclosed with a latticework balcony in the arab style and next to it another, much smaller one, closed by a simple wooden shutter. Feeling that there was a strong likelihood that this would be where young Gracchus slept, Jolival picked up a stone and threw it hard against the shutter.

He had guessed right, for after a moment a hand pushed the

shutter open with a faint creak and a tousled head looked out. Before he could say anything, Jolival called up softly: 'Gracchus! Is that you?'

'Yes, but who —'

'It's us, Gracchus,' Marianne said, 'Monsieur de Jolival and —'

'Mademoiselle Marianne! By all the saints! I'm coming down.'

The next instant Gracchus-Hannibal Pioche dropped quite literally into their arms and hugged them both with the utmost enthusiasm, seeing them in that moment not as his employers but as friends miraculously restored to him. They returned his greeting just as warmly but Jolival saw to it that their transports did not last too long.

'Listen here, my lad,' he said firmly, breaking in on the young man's exclamations of delight which, even in whispers, were still penetrating enough. 'We aren't here for a reunion. We need your help.'

Leaving Jolival to explain hurriedly what had been happening, Marianne made her way back to the waterfront. Already it was less dark. The forest of masts stood out more clearly, and so did the white crests on the small, choppy waves. A sudden gust of wind whirled round her, filling the wide cloak she was wearing and making it clap like a flag. She stood with every sense on the alert, straining her ears to catch the slightest sound of oars amid the rattle of small bits of wood blown by the wind and peering out into the shadows of the harbour.

It seemed to her that Jason and Craig had been gone for hours and his last words reechoed in her mind: 'If I am not back in half an hour . . .' It was too dark for her to see her watch but according to the pendulum of her heart that half hour must have been up weeks ago.

Suddenly, just when she could bear it no longer and was on the point of setting out along the mole whose long stone causeway lost itself in shadow, she saw a tongue of fire leap up in the darkness ahead, lighting up a thick cloud of smoke shot with a red glow along its underside. At the same moment, like rats fleeing a sinking ship, she saw two vagrants jump up from behind the pile of casks where they must have sought refuge for the night and run towards the houses, uttering some harsh cries she could not understand but which could no doubt have been translated as 'Fire! Fire!'

Immediately the harbour was wide awake. Lights sprang up and windows were thrown open. There were shouts and cries and dogs began to bark. Realizing that she was likely to be cut off from her friends, Marianne turned back to find Jolival and Gracchus. She met Jolival half way to the tavern and saw that he was alone.

'Where has Gracchus gone to now?'

'He's arranging our departure. I've given him money and we'll join him later in the upper town. He'll be waiting for us at the end of the main street, the Deribasovskaia, not far from the posting house. Let's hope Jason and Craig will not be much longer.'

'They've been gone so long already. You don't think —'

He took her arm and slipped it through his own, patting it reassuringly.

'No, I don't. It seem a long time to you, and that's quite natural. But it's barely a quarter of an hour since they left us and, if you ask me, they've not been wasting any time.'

The fire, in fact, seemed to be spreading. Tall flames licked up into the night and the wind was blowing thick waves of choking black smoke in towards the shore. Men with buckets were beginning to run towards the mole and the light of the fire showed more and more people crowding on to the waterfront. A bell somewhere began to toll wildly.

'It's a good thing the brig was anchored at the far end of the mole. Otherwise, with this wind, those two madmen would have stood a good chance of setting fire to half the town,' Jolival grunted.

His next words were swallowed up in a deafening roar, accompanied by a tremendous explosion of fire. Jolival scrambled quickly on to a stone block attached to a nearby house, dragging Marianne after him. They cried out at the sight that met their eyes.

Evidently the *Sea Witch* had blown up and now the fire was travelling to the other ships moored nearby. It seemed as if the sea itself were on fire and the screams of the crowd were drowned in the roaring of the flames, driven by the wind.

'Jason knew his ship,' Jolival muttered. 'He must have set fire to the magazine. That explosion was a ton of powder going up.'

In fact the after part of the stricken brig was still spitting fire like a volcano. The mizzen-mast flared like a torch and crashed in a shower of sparks on to the prow of a neighbouring frigate, which was already alight. Marianne swallowed suddenly and found that there were tears in her eyes. She had been jealous of the ship, seeing

her as a rival for Jason's love, but to see her perish thus, by her
master's own hand, was a shocking thing. It was as if she were
watching the death of a friend, or even her own death. She thought
of the figurehead, the figure of the green-eyed siren carved in
her own likeness, which in another moment would be burned to
ashes.

She heard Jolival at her side give a slight sniff and she knew that
he too was having difficulty with his feelings.

'She was a beautiful ship,' he said quietly.

Jason's voice, breathless and rasping, answered him.

'Yes, she was beautiful . . . and I loved her like my own child.
But I'd rather see her burn than know her in another's hands.'

Marianne saw by the light of the fire that both he and Craig were
white-faced and dripping with sea water. But neither seemed aware
of it. Both their eyes were on the *Sea Witch* and in both there was
the same fury of grief.

'Our boat capsized from the force of the explosion,' the Irishman
explained. 'We had to swim for it.'

All at once Marianne flung her arms round Jason's neck, shaking
with convulsive sobs. Tenderly, his arm went round her while with
the other he drew her head down on to his shoulder and gently
stroked her hair.

'Don't cry,' he said quietly. 'We'll have another ship, bigger and
still more beautiful. It was my own fault in a way. I ought never to
have called her *Sea Witch*. She was fated to be burned . . . like a real
witch.'

Marianne gulped miserably. 'Jason . . . are you superstitious?'

'No . . . not in the usual way. But it grieves me and maybe I am
not quite myself. Shall we go? The whole town seems to be converging on the harbour. No one will notice us.'

'But you're soaking wet and your clothes are in rags! You can't
travel like that.'

'Why not? I may be all you say but at least I'm free, thanks to
you, and that in itself is wonderful.'

With that, he swung her almost gaily off the stone bench on to
the ground and, still holding her hand, pulled her after him up the
street that led up the hill to the new town. Jolival and Craig hurried
after them, keeping close to the walls to avoid being swept away by
the ever increasing crowds of people flowing downhill to the
harbour.

Seen from above, the fire had assumed such proportions that the whole port area seemed to be alight. In fact, only three ships, those nearest to the brig, had been attacked by the flames. The four fugitives paused under the branches of a gigantic sycamore that overhung a garden wall to regain their breath after the climb and looked back for a moment.

The *Sea Witch* was dying. Her stern had gone and her bows, borne under by the weight of water, were lifting dramatically. For an instant the fine line of her prow reared up, still intact, holding up her figurehead like a last prayer to heaven before dragging it down beneath the waves. Then slowly, almost solemnly, she sank back and disappeared below the surface of the sea.

Marianne felt Jason's hand tighten on her. He was cursing hoarsely through clenched teeth. Then he raised his voice and, flinging the words out like a challenge, he cried out: 'I shall have another. I swear that before long I shall have another ship of my own to take the place of this one. Another ship just like her!'

Gently, timidly almost, Marianne began to stroke his cheek, feeling the muscles rigid under her hand as though turned to stone. 'But you will not give her my face, for it has not brought you luck.'

He turned to look at her, his eyes bright with unshed tears, and then, swiftly and suddenly, like a horseman gulping down a stirrup cup before a gruelling ride, he bent and kissed her hard upon the mouth.

'But I shall,' he answered her gravely, and then, with a tenderness that made her heart melt within her, he added: 'She shall have your face – and I shall call her *Bel-Espoir*!'

It was not long after that that they came up with Gracchus a short distance from the posting house. There had been a moment's panic for Marianne as they passed the governor's residence but it, like all the upper town, was quiet and silent as the tomb. Marianne spared a thought for the man within who must even then have been deep in the drugged sleep she had procured for him. Certainly no one would have succeeded in waking him. She knew the power of the drug she had given him and the sun would be high in the sky before the Duc de Richelieu opened his eyes. He would learn then of the conflagration in the harbour in the early morning and of the burned ships, but it might be some time yet before he discovered the theft of his letter, because he would first have to hurry down to the harbour to assess the damage and take such steps as might be necessary. That would give the fugitives a little more time if he decided to pursue them inland. But what was much more likely was that he would direct the search to sea, as the natural element of seamen – and their friends.

So that if he did eventually decide to pursue the thief she should, with luck remaining on her side, have acquired a very good start.

After they came upon Gracchus propped up tranquilly with folded arms against the side of an impressive vehicle drawn by three horses in the charge of a huge, bearded driver in a red hat with a square crown to it, Marianne was very nearly sure that luck was on her side, in the person of this resourceful Paris urchin who seemed to possess an uncanny knack of adapting himself instantly and imperturbably to any circumstances, however unlikely, and also of working miracles. The vehicle that he had acquired now was an example of this in its way.

It was a kibitka, one of the great four-wheeled covered wagons, not unlike those used by the American colonists, which the Russian merchants were accustomed to employ to transport themselves and their merchandize from town to town and from fair to fair.

Heavier, certainly, and also slower than the various other conveyances in use on Russian roads, the kibitka possessed a definite advantage in that it was more stoutly built, less conspicuous and able to carry more passengers, not to mention a great deal more baggage, than would have fitted into a telega or a troika. It would take all the fugitives, whereas in the normal way at least two carriages would have been needed to accommodate all the party. And finally, Richelieu would be less likely to look for the Princess Sant'Anna under the hood of a countrified wagon than amid the cushions of a more fashionable type of vehicle.

But Gracchus's genius did not stop short at the choice of transport. Poking her head inside, Marianne saw that it contained a number of rolled up mattresses, also designed to serve as seats, and a pile of new blankets, as well as cooking utensils and provisions. There were also spades and an assortment of weapons. Last of all, there were suits of clothes which, although they might not have been cut in London or Paris, were none the less respectable for that. These were evidently intended for Jason and Craig. It looked as though Graachus had laid out the money Jolival had given him to advantage, and with a speed that no one else could have hoped to rival.

239

'It's like magic,' Marianne said happily, emerging from the wagon to allow the two men to change their clothes. 'However did you manage it, Gracchus? There can't have been any shops open at this hour.'

Gracchus blushed crimson, as he always did when his mistress paid him a compliment, and chuckled.

'Well, it's not so wonderful, Mademoiselle Marianne. You can get hold of anything, at any hour of the day or night here, if you've got the money. You only have to know what doors to knock on.'

Craig O'Flaherty's coppery head peered out from inside the wagon. 'Well, you seem to know the right doors, me lad, and that's for sure! But I've a nasty notion there may yet be one thing we're lacking. You'll not have heard, maybe, but we poor prisoners were told by an Italian fellow back in the castle there, for his misfortune, that it seems that if you want to travel in these parts and, more important, if you want to be able to get fresh horses on the road, you need to have some kind of passport —'

'It's called a *podaroshna*,' Gracchus agreed placidly, and pulled from his pocket a paper bearing an official stamp freshly applied. He waved it at the Irishman. 'Like this. But to be exact, Monsieur Craig, the *podaroshna* is nothing more or less than a permit to use post horses. You can do without one if you've got the money, but it's a great saving and it ensures that the people at the posting houses treat you with some respect. Anything else you'd like to know, Monsieur Craig?'

'No, nothing else,' said the Irishman, gloomily extricating his large person from the cart, revealing himself clad in a pair of baggy trousers tucked into short boots and a grey shirt, buttoned at the neck and caught in at the waist with a leather belt. 'Except that I suppose I shall have to get used to these new fashions somehow, and that I could do with a shave.'

'And so could I,' added Jason, emerging also, dressed in a similar garb. 'We look just like our late keepers.'

Gracchus ran a critical eye over them, then nodded approvingly.

'Not bad at all. In any case, it's all that I could find. And if you'll take my advice, you'll stick to your beards. They make you both look like proper little sons of holy Mother Russia and that's the best thing we could ask.'

Gracchus, in fact, had shown himself a worthy general and, not liking to let his mistress travel deeper into enemy territory under her own name, had taken it upon himself to have the *podaroshna*

240

made out in the name of Lady Selton, an English traveller, and consequently eccentric, whose object was to see something of the Tsar's empire and to study the patriarchal customs of his people.

Gracchus, Jason and Craig were entered on this all-important document as the lady's servants, while to Jolival, rechristened Mr Smith, was allotted the role of secretary.

'Mr Smith!' the Vicomte grumbled. 'Was that the best you could think of? Where's your imagination?'

'Monsieur le Vicomte will pardon me,' Gracchus retorted with dignity, 'but Smith is the only English name I know, apart from Pitt and Nelson.'

'I've had a narrow escape, then. Well, Mr Smith, so be it. And now, I think it's time we were making a move.'

Dawn was already breaking in the glorious reds and purples of a blustery sunrise. From somewhere nearby came the chimes of a Russian orthodox monastery calling its monks to their morning prayers. The copper domes of a church gleamed like fire against a lurid sky suddenly filled with the gliding flight of gulls and the swift, darting black shapes of swallows.

The streets in the upper town were beginning to come to life. Those people who had run down to the harbour were drifting back again, talking noisily about what they had seen. Others, who had not thought it worth while to leave their beds, now opened their windows and threw back the shutters to shout their questions from house to house.

At the far end of the street, soldiers were taking down the heavy chain which was stretched between the two squat bastions of the Kiev gate to close it for the night. The first of the day's wagons of grain were visible on the other side.

The travellers climbed into the kibitka and settled themselves as comfortably as they could on the mattresses. Gracchus hopped up beside the driver who had apparently been continuing his interrupted night's sleep, because he found that it was necessary to shake him awake before he could take his place beside him on the wooden plank which served as a box.

Having cast a glance inside to assure himself that all was well with his companions, Gracchus addressed himself to the driver and declaimed majestically, and not without some consciousness of the effect he was producing: *'Fperiol!* Forward!'

The man chuckled to himself but he touched up his horses and the huge wagon lumbered away, lurching over the ruts, for such things as cobblestones were still unknown to the new town, and drew up to the gate.

Marianne slid her hand into Jason's and, leaning back against the side of the wagon, composed herself to sleep.

Not many moments later, the kibitka had left Odessa behind it and was beginning the long journey across the vast extent of Russia.